"BRING A TUB AND BATHWATER," RED HAWK ORDERED.

"Yes, sir," the clerk said.

The moment the door closed, Savannah whirled to face Red Hawk. "We can't share this room. Besides, you're going to bathe."

"We've been all but sharing a blanket for nine nights now. I'll stay on one side, but I haven't slept in a bed for eight long months. I haven't had a real bath in a tub for almost that long. You can leave the room, close your eyes, share the bath with me, or whatever you'd like, Savannah, but for months I've dreamed about a bed and a real bath."

He pulled his shirt off. The bandage around his arm was no longer blood soaked. She was relieved to see that he was finally mending, but her thoughts jumped back to all he had just told her.

"I'm not sharing any bath!" she snapped, glaring at him.

"Do what you want. I told you what I'm doing."

"I'm going down to the lobby." She strode across the room. "When you're through bathing—"

He caught her before she reached the door, his fingers closing on her upper arm and jerking her around. . . .

BOOK YOUR PLACE ON OUR WEBSITE AND MAKE THE READING CONNECTION!

We've created a customized website just for our very special readers, where you can get the inside scoop on everything that's going on with Zebra, Pinnacle and Kensington books.

When you come online, you'll have the exciting opportunity to:

- View covers of upcoming books
- Read sample chapters
- Learn about our future publishing schedule (listed by publication month *and author*)
- Find out when your favorite authors will be visiting a city near you
- Search for and order backlist books from our online catalog
- Check out author bios and background information
- Send e-mail to your favorite authors
- Meet the Kensington staff online
- Join us in weekly chats with authors, readers and other guests
- Get writing guidelines
- AND MUCH MORE!

**Visit our website at
http://www.zebrabooks.com**

COMANCHE PASSION

SARA ORWIG

Zebra Books
Kensington Publishing Corp.

http://www.zebrabooks.com

ZEBRA BOOKS are published by

Kensington Publishing Corp.
850 Third Avenue
New York, NY 10022

First Printing: August, 1999
10 9 8 7 6 5 4 3 2 1

Printed in the United States of America

To Dr. Clifton L. Warren:

What a propitious moment when Gracie said, "There's someone I want you to meet." Thanks for it all, from that first surprise party to this year. . . .

CHAPTER ONE

Steal the medicine and get back here. We're desperate!

Remembering those words on the battlefield at Mansfield, remembering his brother's pale face, Captain Quentin Red Hawk stood on the Vicksburg dock and watched steamboats arrive and depart. The hot June sun sparkled on the surface of the muddy Mississippi and drenched him in sweat. When he had reached the Union-occupied town yesterday, it had taken only a few minutes to get hired by one of the stevedore crews and fall into place unloading a ship. As an escaped prisoner, he wanted to blend into his surroundings and avoid catching notice of any of the Federals.

A steamboat coming down from a northern city should be well-supplied with morphine and laudanum, but by midafternoon, he was worried. There hadn't been any opportunity to get on board a likely ship. If he didn't find a chance by nightfall, he would go to the hospital and try to steal medications there. Wounded men, his own brother, were counting on him and waiting.

With sweat pouring off his body and his frayed chambray

shirt clinging to him, Red Hawk hoisted a crate and strode along the dock.

Churning up to the dock was the *General Thibodeaux*, a sternwheeler turned into a gunboat, flying the Stars and Stripes. The anchor dropped and the plank went down. As Red Hawk leaned back against the crates to watch the ship unload, a woman emerged on deck.

Feeling the breath rush from his lungs, Red Hawk forgot his surroundings. How long had it been since he had seen a beautiful woman in a dress that wasn't threadbare? He forgot his surroundings as he stared, looking at her fair skin and rosy cheeks. A green silk bonnet hid her face and the green silk dress clung to her tiny waist. Her voluminous skirts stood out, the hoops swaying gently with her steps. She turned her head, and he looked into her eyes. They were as green as her dress.

Her gaze locked with his, and he found it difficult to breathe. She looked delicate, lovely, a fantasy from another time and world, so far removed from guns and war and dying he felt as if he were seeing a mirage. Longing engulfed him, a yearning need that made his knees weak and caused him to shake. How long had it been since he had held a woman in his arms?

Standing near the rail, feeling only the slightest rocking of the ship beneath her feet, Savannah Ravenwood stared at the man who was studying her boldly. A hot flush swept up her cheeks, yet she could not tear her gaze away from his dark eyes. Despite the distance between them, she was caught in his direct stare and stood transfixed by the sheer audacity of his gaze.

She couldn't recall ever being looked at so openly, and her heart thudded. With an effort, she jerked her head, lifted her chin, and turned, bumping into the captain. His hands steadied her and then released her quickly as he swept his hat off his head and bowed.

"Good day, Miss Ravenwood. We'll miss you on the rest of our journey."

"Thank you, sir," Savannah replied, smiling at the Union officer. "It has indeed been a pleasant trip, thanks to you."

"I hope you travel with us again."

"Thank you, sir."

She turned to head for the gangplank and her heartbeat quickened again, but this time the swift beat was filled with trepidation. She walked along the polished deck, her parasol and reticule in hand. Muddy water lapped at the dock and the hull of the ship. Gulls circled noisily overhead, their shrill cries mixing with the sharp banging of crates being set down, sounds that she heard as much as she heard her drumming heart.

Lieutenant Goldsby stood beside the rail. As she passed him, his blue eyes were alert, yet his manner was relaxed and respectful.

"Good-bye, Miss Ravenwood."

"Good-bye, Lieutenant." She flashed him a smile, hoping she looked calm and cheerful.

At the top of the plank, she glanced over the busy dock and the buildings beyond the levee. Feeling compelled to turn, she looked over her left shoulder. The broad-shouldered man still stood beside the stack of crates. His shaggy black hair was tied behind his head, yet strands had come loose and hung on both sides of his face, giving him an air of wildness. His brown-eyed gaze swept boldly over her again, raising to look into her eyes. She lifted her chin, feeling hot from the arrogant, *indecent* look he had given her.

Only a few feet more down the plank to the dock and away toward town and she would be safe. She could leave the bottles of medicine with her friends and be on her way home to Mason, Texas. As she walked, she could feel the weight of the bottles and vials tucked into the pockets underneath her hoop skirt. They were carefully sewn into her crinoline and petticoats so they would not clink, yet she was aware of them with every step she took.

Her back prickled as she took the first step down the plank. She held her skirt, stepping carefully, wanting to run, but knowing she had to stay at ease.

Sunshine sparkled on the water that sloshed steadily against the dock. When she descended the plank, she felt eyes on her

again and, without thinking, glanced around to see the same
dark-eyed man looking at her. He was in a nondescript blue
cotton shirt and black pants, but there was nothing nondescript
about him. He stood out among the dock workers, looking out
of place—too powerful, too commanding for the menial task
he performed.

How had he escaped soldiering? His brazen glance embarrassed her. She drew her breath and looked away. Only a few
yards more, and she would be off the dock.

"Stop her!" The yell came from the boat, and her heart
lurched. "My morphine is gone!" Waving his arms, Dr. Wellborne ran across the deck. Lieutenant Goldsby turned toward
him.

Yielding to her first impulse, Savannah picked up her skirts
and dashed across the dock, racing through the crowd.

"Get her!"

"Miss Ravenwood! Wait!"

She glanced over her shoulder. Lieutenant Goldsby and three
other men charged after her, one going to the right up the next
street, the other two following her.

Cold with fear, she turned a corner and ran into the nearest
street, praying she would not lose her footing on the rough,
uneven stones. At the dark mouth of a narrow alley, a strong
arm reached out, wrapping around her waist.

"Let me go!" she cried, struggling uselessly in a grip like
iron shackles.

"This way!" snapped the man, drawing her into the shadowed alleyway. It was the black-haired man from the dock.
"They're right behind you."

Without stopping to reason what to do, she ran along the
alley with him. He climbed on a barrel, his strong hands closing
on her waist.

"Sir!"

"Quick!" he ordered, lifting her over a fence. He lowered
her to the ground. Swinging his long legs and booted feet over
the fence, he dropped down beside her. They were in an
enclosed courtyard surrounded by ironwork and pots of bloom-

ing plants. He took her hand and ran across the courtyard, stepping through a gate. He held her wrist as they hurried along a narrow street lined with shops.

She could hear shouts in the distance behind them and she ran faster. When they turned a corner, he flagged an approaching carriage.

Swiftly she climbed inside, her heart pounding. She peeped out the back window.

As they began to move, the stranger clung to the side, talking to the driver before he swung down, lowering himself into the carriage. He slammed the door and sat facing her. His broad-shouldered presence seemed to fill the carriage and overwhelm her. As she fell back against the seat, he lowered the leather flaps.

"My gracious!" She fanned herself with her handkerchief. "That was exciting. I don't know what made me lose my reason and run. They were mistaken in yelling at me, but it startled me so, I just didn't stop to think." She knew she was prattling on and on, but she was nervous, and the tall, quiet man looking at her with midnight eyes that seemed to draw her soul to him made her even more nervous.

"They may stop the carriage," she said, trying to catch her breath. It was hot, closed in, and his steady gaze was disturbing. She was shaken; the discovery of the theft and the chase had happened so fast.

Her gaze returned to the silent stranger and a current of heat flashed in her. There was an air of power, of masculinity about him that made her pulse race. His dark eyes were intense. She met his stare and it was like looking into a raging fire. Mesmerized, she was unable to tear her gaze away and the moment drew out until she was certain he could hear her heart beating.

"I don't think anyone will stop us. We'll be out of here in minutes." His voice was deep, husky, and filled with self-assurance.

She tore her glance from his. His sleeves were turned back, revealing smooth, dark skin on forearms that bulged with muscle. She wondered if she had left one danger for another. She wanted to escape from him, yet when his dark eyes met hers, she was caught, excitement stirring in her that she couldn't explain.

"*Ekahuutsu.*"

"I don't understand."

"It's my native language for redbird," he said, touching a braid of hair that was looped around her head.

He was Indian. Hatred, loathing, and fear coiled inside her, and she reminded herself she was in town with people all around her.

Her thoughts jumped to the letter she had received from President Lincoln that offered sympathy on the violent death of her father. Prescot Ravenwood had been a major in the U.S. Cavalry, on assignment from Fort Mason on the Texas frontier. One of the men who had been on the mission told Thomas the details of how her father had been murdered and scalped by savages.

Even though she knew it was unreasonable to despise the man seated facing her, she couldn't keep from feeling a rush of anger and resentment. His people had mercilessly killed her father.

She turned her head to stare straight ahead, yet she was too aware of the stranger beside her. She could feel the heat from his body, smell the odor of sweat and tobacco on him. He shifted his hand and she glanced down at strong brown fingers splayed over a muscled thigh, the worn denim pants pulling tautly across his leg. An old scar ran across the back of his right hand, reminding her that he was a warrior. No doubt this was the kind of man who had slain her father.

Anger burned like a low flame as she raised her gaze to stare ahead again.

Who was he? Why was he in Vicksburg? He belonged with his people on the frontier beyond the States. Why had he helped her? It didn't matter. In minutes she would be away from him and would never see him again in her life. She wondered how soon she could safely exit the carriage.

"Thank you for helping me. I appreciate it," she said stiffly, without looking at him, fearful if she glanced around, she would be ensnared by his gaze again.

"It seems they think you have their morphine," he said, and she wondered again why he had helped her. Chivalry? He didn't look the sort to know about chivalry.

"Mercy! I don't have their medications, but I didn't want to be detained." She glanced at him. His gaze was unwavering and she grew nervous, deciding she needed some explanation for her flight. "I must get to my poor father, who was wounded in the war. He's bedfast and expects me home today. I didn't think. I just ran." She couldn't tell whether the stranger believed the lie or not as she looked into his impassive black eyes.

"You're Miss Ravenwood?" he asked in his deep voice.

"Yes," she said, regretting he knew her name, although there wasn't any basis for her feelings.

"Where is your father?"

"He lives on First East Street," she lied, thinking she would get away from the stranger before she went to her friend's house. "As a matter of fact, if you'll stop the carriage now, I'll walk from here."

"Just a minute and I'll give the driver instructions. We can ride a little while longer. Won't they know where to find you if you go home?"

"I think Dr. Wellborne will find his morphine and forget about me," she answered readily, hoping that answer satisfied the stranger's curiosity. Though his long legs were turned away from her, her silk skirt half covered them.

"You've been up north?" he asked.

"Yes. We have relatives in Cairo, Illinois," she answered. "My family is divided by the war." That bit of the truth couldn't hurt.

Her thoughts shifted. Cynthia Jane would be waiting for her, and soon she would start to worry. If Cynthia Jane had come to meet her at the wharf, Savannah had missed her. All she had to do was leave the medications with her friends Cynthia Jane and Melvin Brandlett, part of the Confederate network of spies and smugglers that were moving goods to the soldiers. As soon as she deposited the medications with the Brandletts, she could be on her way west by stage to her sister in Nacogdoches, Texas. Melvin would take the medicine to Thomas in Tennessee. Confederate smuggling through Vicksburg was widespread, and Savannah was happy to think she could help her fiancé, Lieutenant Thomas Sievert, get the medicines he so desperately needed.

The stranger gave orders to stop the carriage, and he swung open the door, dropping easily to the ground. Momentarily, she had an urge to yank the door closed and yell to the driver to go, but she dismissed the notion as ridiculous. She was merely on the outskirts of town, and she would tell the stranger good-bye and never see him again. She moved to the door.

He reached up, his big hands closing on her waist as he lifted her out. Her heart missed a beat. She could feel the heat of his hands through her dress and underclothing. Her pulse raced and she placed her hands on his arms as he lifted her out of the carriage. Beneath her fingers was the hard flex of his powerful muscles. Brazenly watching her, he held her only inches from him. When his gaze lowered to her mouth, heat flared inside her and she was aware of a ridiculous fluttering in her stomach.

"I do thank you for coming to my aid. It was foolish of me to run like that."

Without answering, he set her on her feet and moved to the front of the carriage, where the two men talked a few moments before the stranger paid the driver. Then the carriage turned north on another dusty lane and disappeared. She looked around, startled to see they were beyond the edge of Vicksburg. No houses were in sight along the wide empty road. Tall oaks surrounded the crossroads, casting cool shadows, but her isolation and distance from town were frightening.

"We're out of town now," she said, her voice sounding loud in the silence. The stranger loomed tall, and in the solitary woods on the edge of town, he was menacing. His long silences added to her nervousness.

"It'll be safer to circle around this way and avoid the soldiers.

With your color hair and your green dress, it'll be easy to recognize you. I'll see you home.''

"That's all right," she said, anxious to be free of him. "My family will be waiting."

"I insist, Miss Ravenwood," he interrupted, and she was aware of a tug of wills between them. He held her arm lightly. "Where exactly is your house on First East?" he asked, falling into step beside her, and she realized that even though she was tall for a woman, she came only to his shoulder. With his height and strength, he made her feel smaller and more vulnerable.

"In the one hundred block."

She would get rid of him before she reached the home of her Confederate friends. Then she would be safe, because no one from the ship knew her connection with Cynthia Jane. In a sudden motion as Savannah stretched out her legs, a bottle clinked. Had he heard it?

As long as he didn't question her, she was scared to glance up. Twelve vials of morphine, four bottles of quinine, ten little bottles of laudanum, and a small jug of brandy were beneath her skirts. A treasure for the Confederacy, and all of it so badly needed now. She knew that Thomas was desperate for the medicine.

She refused to let this war destroy her. It had taken a large enough toll on her friends and on their way of life. By smuggling the medicine, she was doing what she could to help Thomas. As soon as this errand was complete, she had another equally urgent task to help her sister in Nacogdoches escape a loveless marriage.

While her skirts rustled with each step, their footfalls made a soft padding sound on the dusty road. Afraid the bottles might clink as she walked, she chattered steadily about the travel by boat to Vicksburg.

"When you're up north, you almost forget we're at war. It's different from here where everything is devastation—''

"Who is the morphine for?" he interrupted bluntly, and her heart missed a beat.

"I don't have any morphine," she replied, looking up into

the stranger's face and drawing her breath. As impassive as obsidian, his eyes looked as if he could see right into her thoughts and her heart and her soul. He couldn't do any such thing, she reminded herself, gazing at the road again. And she wanted to scream at him that his people had murdered her father.

"By night, you'll have all the Union soldiers in town searching for you. As soon as that lieutenant goes to Army headquarters here, they'll start searching the town."

The stranger's voice was low. His words frightened her, because he was right. She needed to leave the medicine with Cynthia Jane and get on a stage out of town right away.

"Dr. Wellborne will find his morphine and that will be the end of the matter," she said, hoping she sounded convincing. Tall oaks and thick underbrush lined both sides of the narrow road, and she worried about their isolation. "We're getting too far from town now," she said. "I think it's time we turn back."

"We're circling around the edge of town to avoid soldiers," the stranger persisted casually, holding her arm. "They'll be searching for you, so you need to use caution."

Her nervousness increased. Every moment it grew more dangerous for her to be in Vicksburg, and she didn't like being out on the edge of town with a stranger.

"Do you have someone fighting in the Confederacy?" he asked.

She debated only an instant before answering him. "My father fought for the Confederacy," she lied, guessing the stranger had no strong Union ties, else he would never have helped her escape from them. "My father's ill and injured now and expecting my arrival home. My fiancé is with the Confederacy," she added, telling the truth with the last statement, but lying about her father waiting at home for her. She wanted this forceful stranger to think a family would be concerned about her.

"Where is your fiancé now?"

"In Tennessee."

"And what was it you said your father suffers from?"

"I didn't," she replied coolly. "He was wounded at Gettysburg and can no longer fight." She saw the intersection of another road that should lead directly into town.

"Thank you again for your help. I'm indebted to you." She thought about the gold she carried. Should she give the stranger a generous gift? She would have been caught if it hadn't been for him. "We've gone far enough. We need to turn north."

"Just a little farther. You don't want to run unnecessary risks. Soldiers are everywhere."

"The sooner I get inside, the better I'll feel." She glanced around. The dense oaks held an ominous darkness; thick vines hung from the high branches. She guessed she had come at least half a mile from town with him. When she paused, silence enveloped them.

"We're getting farther from town. I'm heading west, back to town."

The man looked down at her, and she shivered with fear as she looked into his dispassionate gaze.

"Thank you for your help," she repeated, reluctant now to pull out gold and let him know what she was carrying. When she turned away, his hand tightened on her arm. His expression conveyed determination and danger. A premonition of disaster struck her. She looked down at his hand on her arm. It was the lightest of touches. Why did she feel immobilized by it?

"Sir—"

"Miss Ravenwood, you're coming with me," he said quietly.

"What are you talking about?" Savannah gasped, looking up at him. Backing away, she tried to pull free from his grasp. "I'm going home."

Before he could answer, they heard the jingle of harnesses and hoofbeats. Through the trees ahead, she glimpsed mounted soldiers approaching around the bend in the road.

As she swiftly debated whether to cast her lot with the stranger or with the soldiers, the stranger's hand clamped over her mouth.

CHAPTER TWO

Wrapping his arm around her, the stranger pulled her into the brush. They rushed through trees and down a slope. Her heart pounded in terror, and her struggles were useless. She scratched at his hand over her mouth. If only she could yell for help! His arm held her pinned against him. She tried to bite him, but his hand was tight against her mouth.

At the foot of a wooded ravine, he stopped behind some trees and held her close. Federal soldiers passed on the road. Blue uniforms showed through the branches, and she could hear the soldiers' deep voices and their horses. Common sense told her to stop struggling—Union soldiers were no longer her friends. Yet the swiftness with which the stranger had silenced her and held her captive frightened her, and she decided she would be safer struggling with Union soldiers than with her captor. In spite of the smuggling, she still had strong Union ties to her uncle. He could protect her, and her father's ties as a major in the U.S. Army had gone straight to President Lincoln himself.

As she struggled, trying to cry out, the stranger crushed her tightly against his chest. The scent of sweat and cotton in his shirt was strong, and she could feel the steady beat of his heart, the warmth of his body. She raised her foot and stomped on him.

Turning to face her, he jammed her against a tree, pinning her against it, spreading his legs to pin hers between them. She wiggled, struggling against him—and then she stopped. His body had responded to her twisting and turning. His manhood grew hard and pressed against her.

Shocked, she met his mocking gaze as he looked down at her. Flushing hotly, she closed her eyes and stood still in his arms. His strong, hard body pressed against her in a manner no other man's had. She burned with embarrassment and anger, held immobile until the soldiers had gone and the woods were silent. Every inch of his strong body was a burning brand against her; his maleness made her pulse race.

Then his mouth was at her ear. "I'm going to take my hand away," he said quietly. "If you scream, I'll tie a cloth over your mouth."

In defiance, she glared at him, angry and determined to get away from him. He shifted only slightly as he moved his hand away and reached into his pocket to withdraw a piece of rope.

"No!"

"Quiet!" he snapped, and she closed her mouth.

His body pinned hers tightly while he caught her wrists and tied them in front of her. He pressed against the length of her side, his chest against her shoulder, his groin against her hip, his legs holding hers between them with the hoop skirt flaring out on the opposite side of her. She flushed in anger and embarrassment that swiftly changed to terror as she watched him. She was his captive, completely at his mercy.

She wasn't experienced with men. She was unaccustomed to feeling one pressed tightly against her and had never been held captive by one. She strained to break free, but in seconds, her wrists were secure.

"Where are you taking me?"

"I'm getting this morphine to some men who need it desperately."

"I don't have morphine. Let me go. You're wrong." A new terror seized her as he bound her wrists. "You can't leave me out here alone. Wild animals—"

"I'm not abandoning you. Not yet." His arm circled her waist and he lifted her skirt.

Enraged, she struggled. "Stop that! You savage!"

He reached beneath her crinolines, his hand grazing her thigh. Even through her thin cotton undergarments, his touch was a brush of fire that made her heart leap. She gasped and his gaze flew to hers, mocking, curious. As he bent over her, holding her tightly, he yanked a vial of morphine from her crinoline and held it up.

"What's this?"

Furious with him, she raised her chin. "Very well. It's morphine and it's promised. I need to get it to wounded men. It's in short supply in the Confederacy."

"Yes, it is, but I have soldiers who're desperate, too. Where are you taking this? Answer me now!"

His fierce look made her heart pound wildly. "To a friend here in Vicksburg who will get it to a battlefield along the border in Tennessee. My fiancé is a doctor, and he expects the medications. He needs them desperately," she added, finally telling him the truth.

"And he sent you into Union territory to bring it back for him?"

"He doesn't know I'm the one who smuggled it past Union lines. The man who was supposed to go was caught by the Union. I know how badly Thomas needs this."

"He'll have to wait, because there are some men in Louisiana who need it just as desperately."

"No! I promised this," she exclaimed, panicked because she had risked so much and come so far only to have all her bounty taken from her.

"My brother and the men I've fought with are waiting, so you and your morphine are coming with me."

Savannah's heart pounded with fear. He was strong, implacable, and barbaric. He wasn't bargaining or asking, and she had no family to come searching for her, only Thomas, who was doctoring on a battlefield in Tennessee and had no idea where she was or what she was doing.

"Who are you?"

"Captain Quentin Red Hawk. I've been fighting with Confederates in the Trans-Mississippi under General Kirby Smith," he explained, looking tough and unyielding.

"You, fighting for the Confederates?" she asked in disbelief, remembering seeing him carrying cargo on the dock. A stevedore, a Confederate officer, an Indian—who was this man? Was he lying about being a soldier?

"I've fought four long years in this damnable war that shouldn't have been part of my life. We've had a recent battle at Mansfield. There were injuries, and we're out of morphine and laudanum."

"You're a long way from Mansfield."

"There wasn't any place between here and there to get the medicine we need. I was taken prisoner by Federals, but on the way here I escaped."

"So you're wanted by Union soldiers, too!"

"Yes," he replied solemnly. "We both need to be cautious. I need this medicine. My unit is out of supplies."

"There are few places anywhere in the South to get medicine," she said bitterly.

"The men in Tennessee may have other sources. My men don't."

"Thomas doesn't have sources now, except for people like me and my friends. He needs this supply and is counting on it. I don't want to let him down." She was frightened by this wild savage and didn't want to go with him. All her life men had treated her with respect; this man gave her none. From all indications, he did as he pleased and took what he wanted. She had no idea how to deal with him. She only knew she had to escape.

Before going home to Mason, she had to get a stage to Nacogdoches. She had written to her sister, Adela, that she would take the stage to Texas the first week in June. This stranger couldn't interfere with her plans.

"The first thing to do is get you out of that hoop skirt so we can travel. Take it off."

"No! I will do no such thing," she snapped, glaring at him with shock, her anger climbing another notch. "I absolutely refuse."

"You *refuse?*" A black brow arched and his gaze drifted down over her in a bold, amused glance that took her breath. As he stepped forward, she realized what he intended.

"Stop it!" she cried, pushing against him with her tied hands, her heart threatening to pound through her rib cage. Ignoring her protests, he circled her small waist with his arm, scooped her off her feet and held her up, reaching beneath her skirts, his hand brushing her from thigh to waist.

She burned with embarrassment, fright, and anger, yet beneath those emotions ran another she didn't understand. She tingled with that rush of excitement she had experienced in the carriage with him. He was powerful, unlike any man she had ever known. In spite of her fear and anger, she had to admire his audacity and forcefulness in coolly whisking them both away from the Union soldiers.

His fingers fumbled with her garments.

"You savage beast! You're a barbarian!" she cried, fury overpowering all else.

He held her against him, his gaze insolent as he looked down at her. Her heart pounded. He yanked free the crinoline and the hoop skirt and whisked them off her. The crinoline bounced on the ground and the hoop skirt stood on its own, bottles clinking.

Giving her a look that made her burn, he turned to the hoop skirt and began to divest it of all the bottles and vials. He glanced at her, one corner of his mouth lifting in a faint smile. "I didn't know a woman could get this much beneath her skirts. You're a walking trading post."

Her fear transformed to anger again, such deep fury that she shook. "I loathe and despise you and I'll scream the first time someone comes along. I won't cooperate with you one inch of the way!''

"Yes, you will," he said, giving another raking glance that made the next protest die in her throat. He picked up her reticule, and she remembered her gold.

"No!" When she tried to grab the bag, he turned his back. She hit his shoulder, losing her balance and tumbling against him. He caught her, a strong arm wrapping around her waist, hauling her up against his muscled body. They gazed into each other's eyes while she gasped for breath. His eyes were dark and harsh as he looked at her. Their black depths made her quiver. A melting softness responded deep within her. Her mouth went dry. She was caught in a tug of wills she didn't understand, yet she couldn't look away from his compelling gaze.

When his eyes lowered to her mouth, Savannah's pulse jumped. Her breath caught and the quiver changed to another feeling, as if something unfolded deep inside her. *What would it be like to be kissed by a man this powerful? A savage who takes what he wants?*

Her lips parted. Then she realized what she had done and clamped her mouth closed.

"I hate you for this," she said. Where had the force in her voice gone? She sounded as if she had run all the way from town.

"Hate?" In just one syllable, his voice was taunting.

Her cheeks flushed.

"When I look at your mouth," he said quietly in a voice that had become huskier, "Miss Ravenwood, you forget your fiancé in Tennessee." He lowered his gaze again slowly, looking at her mouth, and she tingled in response.

"No, I don't forget him," she said, wanting to fling the words at him. Instead, they came out breathlessly. How could this man by a mere look make her feel she was going to melt when she hated and feared him? "I don't forget Thomas for a second!" she snapped more firmly this time, looking at Red Hawk's broad forehead and straight midnight hair that flowed back from his head, shaggy and long on his neck. He had a fresh scar from ear to jaw. "You're Indian, aren't you?"

Mockery flashed in his dark eyes. "Yes," he replied in a cynical voice. "I'm a half-breed. Half white and half Comanche."

She gasped when he said the last, and his eyes narrowed as he continued. "And you're a southern belle who detests half-breeds." He swung her up and released her.

She was addled, uncertain what she was saying to him. "Actually, I've never known an Indian." He had stirred feelings and responses she didn't understand. Fright still tinged her anger as she watched him. *Comanche*. His people had slain her father out on the western plains.

Red Hawk pulled her closer to the trunk of a spreading oak and took off his belt. Looking at his slim waist, she drew a deep breath, feeling afraid again. He tossed the belt over a branch and looped it, drawing it tight. Then he yanked her hands up, looping the other end of the belt around her tied wrists and knotting it.

She stood on the ground, her wrists overhead, helpless, her heart pounding as he looked at her. Her dress pulled tautly over her breasts, and she was aware of his study. Vitality and power were as much a part of him as his shaggy black hair. She was overwhelmed by him.

Why had she trusted him in town? She could cope with the Federals better than with this ruthless man.

Now she was helpless, totally at the mercy of a primitive savage who cared nothing for the conventions of polite society. He stared at her boldly, making her pulse skitter.

"I'm leaving you here while I find us horses," he said, shaking her reticule and emptying it on the ground. As gold spilled out, catching glints of light, the coins clinking, he looked at her with satisfaction.

"Miss Ravenwood, what treasure have I found?" he asked, in a mocking tone. "A beautiful southern belle who in the fourth year of war still has gold."

"I have northern relatives who don't want me to starve,"

she replied in haughty tones, hating him for what he was doing, yet aware he had just called her beautiful.

"And you're probably spying as well as passing contraband goods." He scooped up the gold coins and pocketed them, then straightened to look at her, moving closer. She felt drawn to him in a way she didn't understand. When she raised her chin and glared at him, he looked amused.

"You'd cheerfully slit my throat if you had a knife, wouldn't you? If men pass on the road while I'm gone, don't scream and draw attention. They might want more than your gold." He moved away through the bushes and disappeared from sight.

She was amazed how quickly and how quietly he could move. She yanked on the belt to no avail. She tried to grasp the knot with her fingers to unfasten it, but it was impossible. As long as she didn't struggle, it wasn't too uncomfortable. She had to escape—what did he intend to do when he returned?

As time passed, her arms grew tired and she tried to think of some escape. For all she knew, he would take her medicines and abandon her, leaving her tied and at the mercy of animals and the elements.

Red Hawk, a half-breed Comanche, wanted to take her morphine to injured Confederates. If Thomas wasn't waiting and desperate, she wouldn't mind giving up the morphine to others, but Thomas needed the medicine. More worrisome, she didn't know if Red Hawk planned to let her return unharmed or if he would use her for his own purposes.

She heard the thud of hoofbeats first, and then Red Hawk appeared ahead through the trees. He strode toward her, silent, long-legged, leading a bay. He stopped to tie the reins to a bush.

"You frightened me!"

The corner of his mouth lifted slightly. "Why do I doubt that? Miss Ravenwood, I suspect your nerves have as much steel as the best cavalry saber."

Annoyed by his answer, she glared at him.

"I brought one horse. We'll share the animal so I can keep you close."

"So you intend to take me with you."

"If I have to."

She realized he was as eager to be rid of her as she was of him.

"You'll go with me," he said, "until you're no longer a threat to me."

"How can I possibly be a threat to you?"

"By turning me in to the soldiers searching for you."

He stepped forward and brushed against her as he reached up to unfasten the belt and lower her arms. As he replaced his belt around his waist, she moved away from him, watching him while he removed a gun belt and revolver from a saddlebag and fastened it around his narrow hips. Scuffed western boots showed beneath his denim pants.

Next he packed the morphine and other drugs. With a determined glint in his eyes, he faced her.

"Hold out your wrists." His warm fingers, his callused hands touched her as he loosened her bonds. He pocketed the rope, turning to the horse to remove folded material from a saddlebag. He shook out a blue poplin riding dress and tossed it to her.

"Soldiers will be watching for a woman in a green silk dress. Put this on."

She drew a deep breath and wanted to refuse, but Red Hawk frightened her. "Turn your back," she said.

Placing his hands on his hips, he shook his head and his eyes gave a wild challenge that made her pulse drum. "No, I won't turn my back and have you put a knife between my shoulder blades. Change and be quick, or I'll do it for you."

"Papa would call you out for this!" Her cheeks burned with embarrassment, yet she knew the man meant what he said.

Feeling mortified, her heart thudding and heat burning in her like a summer wildfire, she turned her back. Her fingers fumbled the green silk buttons as she twisted them free. She tried to think about the big gun on his hip and how she could get it from him. Fury and embarrassment warred in her. How she would like to turn him in to the authorities and see them haul him away in chains!

"You're a ruffian, a scoundrel of the highest magnitude, without a scruple or gentlemanly bone in your body!" She knew she was chattering, but she was nervous, burning with humiliation and anger over his cavalier treatment.

His silence made her all the more aware of his dark gaze on her. As she unfastened the buttons, her breath was ragged. How could she step out of her dress in front of him? She glanced over her shoulder and he looked as unyielding as the rocky ground.

"I can't undress before you," she said in little more than a whisper. "Turn your back."

"Take it off now—or I will." His voice was husky, his expression impassive, yet she was aware of him as a virile male.

The heat in her cheeks became flames. She turned around and gritted her teeth, pushing away the dress, knowing he watched everything she did. As the dress billowed around her feet, cool air brushed her bare shoulders.

His pulse drumming loudly, Red Hawk stood as still as a stone while he watched the green silk slide off her pale shoulders and over her slender hips to the ground. She wore a chemise and petticoats, but her shoulders were bare and her long legs were revealed. White cotton drawers covered her trim waist and the round curve of her bottom. After four long years of fighting and seeing damned few women, she was breathtakingly beautiful. He ached, longing swamping him to reach out and pull her to him.

Swift fantasies spun in him like leaves twisting in a summer breeze—images of her melting into his arms, pliant, feminine, eager. She was pale, golden skinned, and small waisted. While his pulse roared, his body responded swiftly. Watching her, he was on fire. She was as beautiful as she was brave.

He knew he could never be part of the life of a woman like her, never earn her admiration or love. He could imagine her contempt of his heritage. She was a belle, and they did not take to his kind. To her, he was a savage. In spite of his knowledge, he yearned just to reach out and see if her skin was as smooth as it appeared, to touch a lock of her hair and feel its silkiness run over his fingers. He remembered pressing against her when he held her to keep her quiet. Her body had been a flaming brand on his, her curves pushing his control to its limits.

His blood pounded hot and swift. He wanted to just touch her, to touch a woman again.

For too long now, his life had been mired in mud and blood and his only companions had been tough, angry men as lonely as he. Here, only a few feet away, stood a dream—she was real, but as unattainable as any dream he had ever had.

Silently, he watched while she stepped into the riding dress and yanked it up over her shoulders, struggling with the small buttons at the nape of her neck. He could see her hands shake, and he stepped forward to help her.

The instant his fingers brushed her skin, her hands stilled and dropped away. She stood without moving while he slowly buttoned her dress. Now *his* fingers shook, and he fought the urge to let them drift across her nape and down her back.

She glanced around angrily.

"I'm only buttoning this for you, so be still. If I wanted more, I wouldn't have waited until now."

He might not have wanted more, but his voice was tense and husky, making her acutely aware of each contact of his hands against her neck and back.

"You're a very beautiful woman, *Ekahuutsu*," he said softly.

She drew a deep breath. "Thank you," she said, not understanding the intense physical reaction she had to him. Another wave of heat unfolded inside her body, starting low in her, engulfing her.

Ekahuutsu. The name made her tingle as if a summer breeze had strummed across her burning nerves. His warm fingers brushed her skin and the tingles intensified.

No man had ever given her a second name. There was something disturbing and intimate about it—something she responded to.

Scooping up the green silk, he bunched it and thrust it beneath a bush. His actions jarred her out of her daze. "Give me my dress!" she cried. "With the shortage of war, I can't replace it."

"Our lives are more important, and we're going to have trouble getting away from Vicksburg. When I was in town, I heard two men describe you, including the green dress and green bonnet. I don't want you carrying it if we get stopped," he said, reaching out to undo the bonnet that had slipped behind her head and was tied beneath her chin.

When she looked at his solemn expression, her heart thudded. He slowly unfastened the ribbons, drawing the bonnet away. The cool silk slid across her skin like a caress while his gaze held her mesmerized.

The hat fell and he caught it, turning away.

"I brought you another bonnet," he said, rummaging in the saddlebag.

The blue shirt pulled across his broad shoulders. He withdrew a small straw bonnet trimmed in blue ribbons. It would give her little protection from the sun.

"Put this on."

"No!" she exclaimed, knowing she was unreasonably fighting him, but she was angry that he would take the morphine Thomas needed so badly and angry that he held her against her will, even more angry to have to obey all his commands.

He plopped the hat on her head and stepped close to tie it beneath her chin. His breath smelled faintly of tobacco. She looked down at the wide gun belt circling his slender hips. His pistol was worn in a holster on his hip and as he tied the ribbons, she attempted to grab his revolver. Her fingers closed around the cold grip.

His hand clamped on her wrist so tightly she cried out.

"Let go of the pistol now," he ordered, pulling her against him.

"I hate you for this, and the first chance I get, I'll gladly put a knife in your heart!"

"You're not going to get a chance," he said flatly, his breath warm against her temple. "We'll skirt around Vicksburg to the ferry."

"You have to let me get at least half of this morphine to Thomas!"

"Sorry," he said and shook his head. She knew he would never listen to her pleas or be moved by her tears.

Furious, she stared at him, angry, yet feeling a sizzling current that passed between them every time they fought each other or touched each other or gazed into each other's eyes.

Her gaze ran over his features. They were foreign and exotic to her—his imperious nose with a slight convex shape, his stark cheekbones, his dark skin. In her mind she could envision him riding toward her father, striking him with a lance, bending over him with a knife. She closed her mind to those thoughts.

Knowing she had no choice, she released his revolver, and he moved away. He stepped into a stirrup, swung his long leg across the horse and settled into the saddle, his black trousers pulling tautly over legs well defined with muscle. With an amazing ease, he leaned down to swing her up before him.

Squeezed brazenly against him, she felt the warmth of his body, his arm tight around her waist.

What was he going to do with her? When would he let her go? She looked down at his strong blunt fingers holding the reins. Her bottom touched his thighs; her legs brushed his. In the confines of sharing the saddle, she was jammed against him, the heat of his body permeating her clothing. The woodsy scent about him was stronger. She was caught by a force she couldn't combat and furious with him for taking the medications from her.

"There are Union soldiers everywhere. Vicksburg is held by the Union now, and the next Yankees we see, I'll scream for help."

"The first hint of a scream, you'll get a rag tied over your mouth and I'll leave it there. And remember, now we're both carrying contraband goods. They send women to prison for such."

"They would hang you!"

He ignored her, and she twisted to look up at him, her shoulder pushing against his broad chest. "Why are you taking me along? I can only be trouble to you. Leave me here."

He looked down at her and every time she had to gaze directly into his eyes, it was as jarring as physical contact.

"If I turn you free here, all you have to do is have a friend go to the authorities and give them my description and tell them I have the morphine and where I'm headed. No, you're coming with me."

CHAPTER THREE

"We'll cross the Mississippi and head west," he told her, mulling over how he could get rid of her without endangering himself. "I'll let you go either just before we board the ferry or right after we land. When I find my best chance to get away—when you can't turn me in to the soldiers—you may go."

Red Hawk watched as fires danced in the depths of her enormous green eyes, irises the color of early willow leaves, as clear as spring water. Eyes for a man's heart to drown in. Thick auburn lashes fringed them. Her hair would be impossible to hide, and the green dress would have been an instant giveaway to Bluebellies. Even if he had found a flour sack for her to wear, it wouldn't keep her from drawing attention. She was not only a beautiful woman, but she was also unusual.

"I saved you from being captured in town. They would have caught you and you would have gone to prison."

"I might not," she replied haughtily, "with my Northern connections."

"Perhaps, but your uncle is far away and these men are as desperate for this medicine as you and I. Also, you're a very beautiful woman. They would enjoy taking you to prison."

She wondered if he felt that way. Defiantly, she raised her chin. "You'll get us both captured and imprisoned."

"They'll be looking for you," he continued, "but they won't be looking for a couple," he said. Too bad he hadn't found some docile woman who was terrified enough of him to do what he asked without argument. He experienced a rush of cynical amusement; he should have known when he helped her that any woman who would smuggle contraband medicines to the Confederates would be plucky enough to fight his taking her captive.

"We're a highly unlikely looking couple! I am not a woman who gives in easily to fear."

Too bad she didn't give in easily to silence. From almost the first moments she could catch her breath in the stage, she had been talking.

"The world is filled with mismatched marriages. Or is it beyond your imagination to think of a lady married to a savage?" he asked, knowing full well it was beyond her imagination. "As it is," he added, noticing how tiny her waist was as he held her tightly, "no one knows I have the supplies."

She drew a deep breath. The dressed strained over her full breasts, and he had difficulty pulling his gaze away from her, imagining swiftly how it would feel to cup her breasts in his hands. He had been far too long without a woman, he thought again.

"If I promise not to go to the soldiers, would it matter?"

"What do you think?" he asked. Damn, he didn't want to take her with him! By fighting him every inch of the way, she would slow him down immeasurably, but he had gone over every possibility he could think of to leave her behind, and none of them were acceptable. Instead he had on his hands a feisty, talkative woman who was willing to take risks and make her own decisions.

With a sudden twist, she turned around, her bottom wriggling against him. He drew a deep breath. Did she have the slightest idea of the effect she was having on him? In spite of her travel and education, when it came to men, she seemed as innocent as spring flowers.

"I'll do my best to turn you over to the soldiers!" Her voice was low, intense. Instead of being angry, he admired her for her courage. His gaze lowered to her mouth. Her lips were overly full, curved and rosy, a sensual invitation to passion. How much had the fiancé kissed her? Had he seduced her? As Red Hawk gazed at her mouth, her lips parted and she drew another deep breath. Surprised, he looked into her eyes. For the first time he caught a glimmer of an expression that looked like uncertainty and something else, a yearning that made his heart miss a beat.

He stared into her green eyes, wondering about her, wanting to lean down and taste her mouth, her kisses. She turned away, but not before a pink flush suffused her cheeks.

So she was passionate as well as fiery. He laughed inwardly at himself. It didn't matter what she was—he knew southern belles who had family and influence and social standing. They viewed him as a savage, lower in society than their slaves. Under normal conditions, her men would haul him out and beat him near death for talking to her. For touching her and forcing her to undress before him, it would be death.

He stared at the back of her head. The bonnet perched on top of her head, and a mass of auburn braids were twisted and pinned high on the back of her head beneath it. He imagined those braids unfastened and tumbling down over her bare shoulders. Tiny tendrils escaped the braids, curling on the back of her neck. He was tempted to lean forward and brush the bare flesh of her nape with his lips, but he knew what a storm he would create.

Glancing around, he let his hand drift to his revolver. They were in danger, more than she realized. She didn't seem to realize how real the threat of prison was. He wondered how old she was—she looked seventeen. She touched her hair and he looked at her dainty wrist with its delicate bones. Again, he thought of her as *Ekahuutsu,* Redbird, but he knew she was thoroughly Miss Ravenwood, feisty and quick thinking. She was more elusive than any redbird he had ever encountered!

"You have a brother fighting for General Smith at Mansfield?" she asked.

"Yes. Caleb is wounded and he needs morphine desperately, as well as the other injured men. Five of us rode back to get medical supplies, but I'm the only one left."

"What happened to the others?"

"After being taken prisoner, we broke free of our captors. In the melee, one was killed. The rest of us escaped and we went our separate ways."

"I'm sorry your brother is hurt."

"Ahh, the ice thaws a fraction. Yet you would still put a shot through my heart if you could get my pistol."

"For taking the medicine and taking me captive, yes, I would. Are you married?"

"No." He wondered about her. Was her father the only relative at home? How long before he began a search for her?

She twisted to look up at him. "You don't have a woman. Is that why you're taking me with you?" she asked in a low voice as she faced the road again. He leaned forward slightly and saw her cheeks were pink again.

"No," he replied quietly. "My brother is suffering and needs that morphine desperately. I'm taking you for the reason I told you, to keep you from turning me in to the soldiers."

A jingle was faint, somewhere in the distance. He raised his head to listen, and the sound of horses and male voices was unmistakable. Instantly he jerked the reins and turned off into brush. Yards later, he halted and lifted her down, coming down beside her.

"What's wrong?"

He yanked her to him, her back against his chest, clamping his hand over her mouth and holding her tightly. Red Hawk glanced at his horse and prayed the animal didn't whinny or shake its head and jingle the harness, because he couldn't hold them both, and the woman was more dangerous. He leaned close to her ear. "Keep still!"

Struggling, she fought him, wriggling, swinging her foot as she tried to kick him. Annoyed, he shoved her down on the ground on her back and straddled her, keeping his hand over her mouth and holding her wrists with his other hand, pinning her to the ground where she couldn't kick or stomp him. She wriggled and a strangled protest rose in her throat.

He leaned over her. "Be quiet. Not a sound or word out of you or I'll squeeze you until you faint," he said. Her eyes widened and she became still, looking up at him.

He raised his head and stared at the road. The hoofbeats and voices grew louder, and then he saw blue uniforms. *Federals.* There had to be more than a dozen soldiers. As they neared, he looked down at her. Her eyes were wide, staring up at him. He held her wrists pinned to the ground over her head and he leaned over her. Her dress strained over her breasts, and he wondered what would happen if he placed his lips on hers.

Something clattered nearby. He released her wrists to yank out his pistol, and then he saw it was only an empty tin a soldier must have tossed aside.

She twisted suddenly, jerking free and grabbing his pistol, trying to wrench it from him. He didn't dare take his hand from her mouth. Fury welled up in him as they struggled.

He shifted, coming down on the length of her, stretching out so his body pressed her into the damp ground. Lying on top of her, he pinned one of her arms between them, and it was easy to wrest the weapon from her and hold it out of reach. He yanked his hand away and smothered her scream with his mouth.

She beat at his shoulders and tugged on his hair while he ran his tongue over her teeth and against her tongue. Her breath was hot and sweet and his body responded swiftly, his manhood throbbing into hardness.

All her resistance ended.

For an instant he forgot the war, the danger, the conflict between them. She was *woman,* desirable, soft, a fulfillment of his dreams.

She went still and her eyes flew wide. She looked shocked.

She was engaged, so surely she had been kissed, but she looked and acted as if she hadn't. Her mouth was unbearably sweet; his tongue stroked over hers. Lost in kisses, his awareness of danger vanished. Her eyes closed, the thick fringe of lashes coming down over her cheeks. The stiffness went out of her body.

He had no illusions. She still hated him and would betray him instantly if she had a chance, but she was passionate enough to momentarily forget their differences and stop resisting him.

He kissed her deeply, drawing it out. Sweet, searing, her kiss set him aflame.

Her body moving beneath his made his heart hammer in his chest and fires throb in his groin. He burned as if he had moved too close to the sun. If she were willing, he would swiftly possess her.

Her eyes were closed as she kissed him, and he longed to do more, to kiss her throat, to move down to her full breasts. His body was aroused at the wrong time, in the wrong place, and with the wrong woman.

Savannah had never been kissed in such a manner. Her senses whirled; heat was an agonizing flame low in her body. She wanted more kisses, more of him. Shocked at her own reaction, her eyes fluttered. His dark gaze watched her steadily.

She closed her eyes, her heart pounding as he kissed her hard. His tongue was an invasion of her body, an invasion of her soul. He was doing things to her no man had ever done, causing her to feel things she had never felt. He elicited responses from her that were beyond her control.

Never had she returned a man's kisses with wild abandon. Never had she been kissed with such ardor.

Thought stopped. She wound her fingers in his thick, coarse hair, aware of the strength of his body against hers. Why did what he was doing seem right? Was she a complete wanton? Had the savage in him awakened a wild, primitive streak in her?

She couldn't understand her reaction to him, yet, heaven help her, she liked what he was doing to her!

Red Hawk raised his head, listening, hearing no one. When he looked down, her cheeks flushed hotly, and she turned her head away.

He caught her up. Her hands flew against him, and she looked up, her eyes wide in what must have been alarm.

"You don't love your fiancé," he said, surprising himself. He didn't care whether she did or not. But she didn't, or she would have resisted his advances.

"I do love Thomas!" she protested hotly.

He stroked her cheek. "Not when you kiss me like you just did," he said in a husky voice that made her bite her lip and blush and look away.

He stood and pulled her up. "You did everything you could to make certain we were caught."

"To make certain *you* were caught!" she snapped.

He held her against him. Her hands rested on his chest, and he fought the urge to lean forward and kiss her again.

Instead, he lifted her into the saddle before him, wondering why she didn't scream now when she could. He was ready to grab her at the first hint of sound coming from her, but she rode quietly before him as he urged the horse back to the road.

He stared at the back of her head as they traveled, wondering what thoughts ran through her mind. He couldn't forget her response to him—a response that took his breath just thinking about it. Was she starved for love, starved for the fiancé caught up in war? Did she give much thought to the kisses they'd just shared?

"Do you have difficulty with your permit to travel?" he asked after a time.

"No. They don't know that my uncle is a captain for the Union."

"And your father fought for the South?"

"My father was—is a major." She corrected herself quickly, but he caught the first word.

"*Was?* Your father's no longer alive?"

"My father is ill and he's home from fighting. He expects

me to arrive today." She sounded convincing, but after her slip, he guessed her father was dead.

"Who else lives with you? Your father and—"

"My mother and my brother, and they expect me home. They'll go to the authorities when I don't show up. Probably that's where they are right now."

He wondered if he heard the truth from her. A woman who had stolen all the medicine she carried and smuggled it past soldiers had to be a master at deceit. If there was a brother at home, he would be a child, else he would be away fighting in the war.

"Did you take all of the medicines you carry from the physician on the boat?"

"No. I brought most of it from a hospital where I volunteered my help. I saw a chance to get some more on the boat and it was too tempting to resist, but I should have. Then none of this would have happened."

He wondered about her family, divided by war as too many families had been. "You have family on both sides."

"Yes. My uncle is a Union officer, and his son fights for the Union as well."

She did not mention her father and, once again, he suspected her father was no longer living. "And your fiancé is with the Confederacy."

"Yes. All of life is taken up by war. I hate this war!" she snapped, her voice filling with indignation.

Falling into silence, they crossed a meadow, riding toward tall, spreading live oaks with cool shade beckoning beneath their outstretched branches.

"How long since you last ate?" he asked.

"This morning."

He tugged on the reins and lifted her down, dropping down beside her. "We'll stop here and eat." He lifted a bundle tied in a cloth and unrolled the gray Army blanket kept behind the saddle, waving his hand for her to sit down. He caught the stubborn lift of her chin before she did, and he was amused.

She must be hungry to acquiesce without a protest, even in something she wanted to do.

"Your name again?" she asked, slanting him a curious look. She had an imperious note in her voice, as if she were accustomed to giving others commands and to having them obeyed. It was the same certainty he had heard from officers, but he rarely heard it in women.

"Captain Quentin Red Hawk."

"Captain Red Hawk, I have a sister who lives in Nacogdoches, Texas, and she needs my help. She isn't well, and I need to get to her as soon as possible. I expected to leave for Nacogdoches today."

He lifted down two tin cups and a bottle of brandy and sank down on the blanket facing her. As soon as he unwrapped the parcel of food and handed her a pickle, he poured the brandy.

"I don't drink spirits," she said quickly.

"I don't have water. A little brandy won't hurt you. Otherwise, you'll get uncomfortably thirsty."

Red Hawk handed her a slice of thick pink ham, knowing it was salty enough to drive her to the brandy. "What ails your sister?" he asked, watching her.

Her gaze flickered and she looked into the trees. "She is suffering, and I promised that when I left Vicksburg I'd go get her and take her home. There's a stage leaving Vicksburg for Texas this afternoon." She turned wide green eyes on him. "I need to be on it."

"You know soldiers will be watching to see if you get on it."

"I can cross the Mississippi by ferry and catch the stage in Louisiana instead of here."

"I have no intention of keeping you with me any longer than is necessary for my safety. Once I see a chance to get away without your turning me in, I will set you free."

"And if I promise—"

He gave a dry laugh. "To smuggle morphine across Union and Confederate lines, Miss Ravenwood, you are obviously quite good at deceit. I won't take your promise."

Without a flicker of expression, she stared at him, and he knew she was probably masterful at hiding her feelings. "You should learn to play faro and other games. You could bluff with the best of them."

"And I suspect you can as well," she remarked, studying him. She drank the brandy and coughed, blinking and wiping her eyes. "This burns!"

"You'll get accustomed to it swiftly, and it's all we have."

"I'll be foxed."

He smiled at her. "Not on a cupful, Miss Ravenwood. What's your Christian name?"

"Savannah," she answered, taking another cautious sip of brandy. She bit into the pink ham with dainty, white teeth. He couldn't stop watching her, as fascinated as if he had never seen a woman.

"This is good. I ate little breakfast and at noon I had to miss dinner."

He wanted to get enough brandy down her to get her tipsy. If she had never had any before, he suspected it would take little to have an effect.

"Savannah," he said, drawing out the name, watching her closely as he said it.

Her cheeks flushed and her lashes fluttered. She took another sip of brandy, coughing only slightly.

"Savannah is an interesting name. I haven't known any other woman with that name."

"I'm not altogether fond of my name, but I must live with it."

"Savannah. It's unforgettable." He refilled her cup with brandy, even though she shook her head.

"Please let me go. I have a ticket to catch the stage to Texas."

"I told you, you shall probably be free in time to catch the stage. If not, your family will have to get your sister without you."

"I'm the only one going!" she snapped. "So I must keep my promise to Adela."

"You'll travel across Louisiana alone?" he asked in surprise. She was brave to smuggle morphine past Union lines, but many southern women were involved in smuggling. To travel alone through territory still rife with fighting was unthinkable. Was there really a family waiting in Vicksburg? He began to question whether she had any family left. She was a lady, sounding educated, well-bred, yet the facts didn't fit that she smuggled contraband and traveled alone without concern.

"I think if I keep you from taking the stage, I'll be doing you and your family a favor. A woman alone in these perilous times could be in great danger."

"Sir, my whole family expects me to go get my sister and take her home to Texas."

"I thought your home was Vicksburg," he said quietly and received a cool stare.

"I have friends in Vicksburg," she replied smoothly. "Actually, we live in Mason, Texas."

"You're right on the frontier."

While he poured more brandy and she took another drink, he wondered why she had lied to him about her home. Was it simply an attempt to get him to let her go while they were in Vicksburg? Was it because she wanted him to think there would be a family and friends searching for her soon? He wondered about her and her life. Was there really a sister, or was that another mission she had to help the Confederate fiancé?

"So you see, I need to get home in time to get the stage. My ticket is in my reticule," Savannah argued. She fanned her face and tugged at the collar of her dress.

"I'll think about it," Red Hawk replied, not wanting to stir a storm yet and hoping he could leave her before he boarded the ferry. Then she could do as she pleased.

"I'm sorry you have an ailing sister. How did you meet your fiancé?"

"I've known him all my life. Our families were close friends and we played together as children. We've grown up knowing we would marry. Our fathers were very good friends, and they planned the marriage."

"Ahh, you don't love him."

"I like Thomas immeasurably," she said, aware she hadn't replied that she loved him. She had never questioned her feelings for him or the plans made by their fathers. Had Thomas questioned them? She suspected he had accepted them as readily as she had.

"So when is the wedding?"

"After the war, when he comes home."

"I should think he would have married you before he went to war."

"He thought I was too young when he left in 1862. I'm eighteen now. If this war doesn't end soon, I shall be considered a spinster by all who know me."

Amused, Red Hawk looked at her flaming hair and green eyes and full mouth and lush breasts. There would never be a moment when she would be considered a spinster. Nor would she go through life unwed.

"I'm amazed he is the only man who has proposed."

Her eyes widened as if she were startled by the thought. "Oh, no. I've never been courted by another man or even—" She bit the words off and blushed, looking down and taking a long drink of brandy.

"Even been kissed by another man until today," he finished, realizing every time she was flustered, she drank more brandy. Soon its effect should show. He caught her chin with his fingers. "Or was it simply kissed by a man? Has your fiancé kissed you?"

Her blush deepened. "It's ungentlemanly to ask something so intensely personal!"

"Being gentlemanly isn't part of my character. It's an unnecessary burden."

"Will you let me go?" She ran her fingers across her brow, which was beaded with perspiration, and her words slowed.

"I'll give it thought," he said.

Hot, she tugged at the high neck of the riding dress. She took another drink of the brandy and looked up, her head feeling light. "It's dreadfully hot."

"Take another drink. It'll cool you."

"I think the brandy is adding to the heat." She watched him peel an apple, the long red peel hanging down as he turned the apple in his hands. He twisted the apple in his brown fingers in a slow, deliberate manner, cutting carefully. He had dark brown, powerful-looking hands. He cut a slice of apple and handed it to her, his fingers brushing hers while he watched her.

She bit into it, relishing its juicy sweetness. She removed her bonnet.

"You've stayed with your uncle's family?"

"Yes, in Cairo, Illinois. They're not suffering the shortages the South is." She tilted her head and slanted him a look. "Let me go. I won't turn you in."

"You would turn me in to the Union officials before I reached the Mississippi River."

"I swear I won't!" she protested, sitting up straight and staring at him. "If I go to them, they'll arrest me for taking their morphine."

"Or you can get your friend to go to the Yankees about me. No, Miss Ravenwood, I won't let you go until I see a chance to get away from Vicksburg and the Union soldiers."

"I have to catch that stage."

"Your sister can wait," he said with clipped finality, and Savannah realized she had met a man who was completely unyielding.

The trees and grass were spinning. "No more brandy," she said, pushing his hand away as he started to pour more. "You will regret this if you take me with you, Captain. I promise you."

"I already regret it. But I'll regret it more if I don't. I need your help, whether it is given willingly or under force."

Savannah was hot and angry and desperate. She glanced around at the dappled shade, the leaves barely rustling in a slight breeze. Everything looked peaceful, belying her turmoil.

"Were you brought up to treat women this way?" she asked, hoping to appeal to gentler feelings in him.

"No, I wasn't. I was raised with my father's people and I respected women, but this is war and you're smuggling medicines. When you do that, you become part of war and vulnerable to anyone who wants to take the medicine from you."

"If you rode with a tribe, why did you become a soldier?"

His dark gaze slid away and focused in the distance as if looking into the past. "When I was a boy, soldiers came and captured us, taking my white mother, me, and my siblings back to civilization."

She stood up suddenly and he rose just as swiftly, towering over her. Light-headed, she reached out and grasped his arm to steady herself. "You have me foxed," she said, looking up at him.

He gazed at her, his dark eyes hard and unyielding. "Yes, because you're coming with me. I think you've had enough brandy. We're heading to the ferry, and I don't want to hear any protests from you if I take you on board."

"I can promise you that if you force me to board the ferry, I'll tell anyone I can that you're taking me against my will. I'll tell about the morphine, and I'll see you hang!"

Suddenly his features softened and the anger left his expression, amusement replacing it. "You want to watch me hang? I don't believe you, Savannah." The way he said her name sent a tingle through her, and she backed up a step as he looked down at her mouth. "You won't tell anyone about the morphine."

How could he feel so certain about what she would do or wouldn't do? Why did he seem so powerful?

"Yes, I will," she said, but her words were breathless. As she gazed into his eyes, her heart began to pound because of his knowing look, as if he knew what she would do better than she did.

Thoughts of his strong arms and wild kisses made her hot and uncertain. She was drawn to him even though every bit of logic in her cried out against it. He was a half-breed, born and raised his early years with wild Indians. His world was a world she did not know or understand. She had already seen the ruthlessness in him.

"You filled me with brandy so I would do what you want," she stammered, finding it difficult to talk.

"No," he said, shaking his head, studying her solemnly. "I've filled you with brandy so I can get you on the ferry without much protest."

"You're a . . . a—" She had difficulty coming up with an adequate word. "A ruffian!"

"Savannah, you need to learn how to put a man in his place. Calling me a ruffian doesn't do it," he said dryly, smoothing a tendril of hair away from her cheek. The touch of his fingers set her pulse racing. "We'll pack and go. I don't want to miss the ferry and have to go through this again."

"I hate you for this. My sister *needs* me."

Suddenly he caught her upper arms, holding her firmly. He tilted her face up with his forefinger. "Why? The truth now! Why are you going to Nacogdoches to see your sister?"

He startled her, and she was frightened again. How could he tell whether she was lying or telling him the truth? Most people could not. He went from kind and gentle to harsh and frightening in a breath's time and he kept her off-balance, not knowing what to expect from him.

"She needs me," she repeated, looking into fierce black eyes that made her heart jump in fright. Only seconds ago he was answering her questions in a pleasant voice. Now she felt as if her life were threatened. Suddenly she pulled herself up and tried to yank free. "Unhand me! You're a ruffian and you don't know anything about being a gentleman. If I get a chance, I shall plunge a knife right into your wicked heart!"

His fingers tightened. "The truth now!" His voice sent a chill down her spine. Suddenly she was uncertain what he might do.

"She needs to get away from her husband, and I intend to help her," she said, the words tumbling out in a rush. "He's cruel to her." *Forgive me, Adela.* Until this moment she had kept her promise and hadn't told anyone why she was going to Nacogdoches. Yet it wouldn't matter that she had told Captain Red Hawk, because he would have no part in Adela's life.

"If she has waited this long for your help, she can wait a while longer."

Angered, Savannah stared at him. His reaction was exactly what she had feared, and frustration welled up in her. She needed to get away from him, even if it meant leaving behind the morphine and laudanum.

"Let's go to the ferry." He rolled up the blanket and tied it behind the saddle, picked up the food, and finally mounted and lifted her up beside him.

"I'm dizzy, and I blame you for how I feel. If I get sick, it will be your fault."

"I'll take all the blame," he said cheerfully, and her anger grew. She held her head.

"Everything spins."

"Lean back against me and close your eyes."

"I've touched you quite enough for one day!" she snapped. "And when I close my eyes, it's worse."

"I'll tell them you're my wife. Try to cooperate."

"Your wife! They'll know I hate you."

"Is that so unusual for a husband and wife? I have seen some marriages where hate boils between the couple."

"Unfortunately, yes. My sister and her husband have such a loveless union. Although Adela fears her husband, I think my sister is incapable of hate. She's very gentle."

"So you're not alike."

Suddenly she laughed, wondering if he found her a complete vixen. She glanced over her shoulder at him and caught him watching her intently. He grasped her chin and ran his thumb along her cheek, creating fiery tingles.

"Ah, laughter, Savannah. I think men might kill to win a smile from you," he drawled in a voice like velvet.

Amazed, she looked into his dark eyes and was startled by his words. "I think not," she replied, but she wondered about his remark and how much he had meant it. *Men might kill to win a smile from you.* She could scarcely believe she had heard correctly. He did not seem the type of man to speak flowery phrases.

While she thought about what he had said, they rode in silence. Hot, her head spinning, she grew sleepy, yet she knew she must think or she would be crossing the Mississippi and on her way into Louisiana with a man who was ruthless and held no regard for gentlemanly ways.

"I will not get on that ferry with you!" she exclaimed suddenly, turning to look up at him.

"You have no choice. Remember, Yankees are hunting you as much as they're searching for me. If they find you, you'll go to a cold, confining prison for the duration of the war. That Bluebelly uncle of yours might not be able to keep you out."

Angry with Red Hawk, she shivered and was silent. Shadows were long when they topped a rise and looked down on the wide Mississippi. In the late afternoon, the river was a shimmering brown ribbon, its calm surface belying the strong currents that ran below. While wind blew against her, she gazed across the Mississippi to the west and was frightened, suspecting if she crossed the river with him, her life would change forever. Giving a shake, she tried to brush away the premonition as foolishness. She looked up to find him watching her with a curious look in his eyes.

"Don't do this," she said urgently. "Let me go home."

He stared at her, something shifting and changing in the depths of his dark eyes. What kind of complex man was he? Born of one culture, taken from it and thrown into another, now caught in a war, he wasn't like anyone she had ever known.

The men in her life had been like her father, who had always been kind and good to her. Thomas was always considerate; male servants were polite and respectful. Captain Red Hawk was something out of her experience, and she had no measure of what to expect.

She was half afraid of him, but the other half—she was afraid of herself and the inexplicable, tumultuous feelings he aroused. She didn't understand her own reactions to him. She liked his kisses. It went beyond *like,* and she knew it. She suspected no man's kisses would ever be the same as his, and that realization shook her badly.

As if he knew the train of her thoughts, his arm tightened around her waist while he urged the horse forward.

The dock teemed with people. Union soldiers boarded the large ferry. A sternwheeler passed, stirring waves that rolled in toward shore while the paddlewheel thrashed the water into foam.

Red Hawk rode down the slope and out toward the ferry, where he tugged on the reins and halted.

He dismounted to lift her down, leading the horse on board. Savannah tried to think. The world spun and nothing seemed to matter except to keep from losing her balance, but she wanted to escape. Once they were on the opposite shore, there would be no one to help her escape. Her gaze searched the crowd on the ferry. She spotted a man who wore a uniform and a cap and guessed he must be the ferry captain.

With Red Hawk's arm steadying her, they moved in a throng of people. She looked up at Red Hawk. He stared ahead, looking hard and dangerous, yet she had to risk getting help now.

With a twist Savannah broke away from him. She pushed through the crush of passengers, her gaze fixed on the captain.

She dared not look around and her heart pounded as she tried to get through the crowd. At any second, she expected a hand to clamp on her shoulder or an arm to band around her waist and lift her off her feet.

"Excuse me," she said, slipping past a couple herding three children aboard.

She rushed to the captain to tug on his arm. "Sir," she exclaimed, "that man is taking me from Vicksburg against my will. Please help me!" she cried.

The captain turned blue eyes on her as Red Hawk stepped to her side and slipped his arm around her waist. "Sir, please ignore my wife," Red Hawk said with a quiet note of patience she hadn't heard him use before. "She ran away with another man—"

"No!" she gasped. "I'm not—"

"While she may not be happy with me, she's wed to me and is the mother of our five children. I'm taking her home. Darling," he said, looking down at her, "please come back to us. All our little ones want you back so badly. My sister can't keep the babies much longer."

"No! We aren't husband and wife!" Savannah wailed, hating the slur in her words. "Please, he's lying."

"Five children? She looks young." The captain peered at her.

"I married her when she was thirteen. She's young, and maybe that's why—"

"We're not wed!" she exclaimed.

The captain tugged at his thick brown beard. His long face became longer as he scowled.

"She likes her brandy, but I'll get her sober before we reach home and the children. I had to take her away from him. He was a smooth-talking Rebel, and they had been at the brandy. I'm sorry for the disturbance. It's been a trying time and I know five children can be a task, but we need her," Red Hawk said. "When she left, I was fighting in the war and I had to leave my outfit and return to get her. Every night our children cry themselves to sleep for their mama."

"We don't have children! He's taking me against my will. Please help me. Please stop him."

"She's been at the brandy, all right. Some women just don't know when they're well off." The captain glared at her and shook a bony finger. "Young woman, you need to go with your husband and return to your family and be thankful if he doesn't beat you senseless for this!" He looked up at Red Hawk. "Maybe if you take a cane to her, sir, you won't have this trouble again."

"Perhaps, but she's their mother and I can't bear to lay a hand on her."

"Will you listen?" She tugged on the captain's arm. "I'm not his wife! Talk to—"

"Sir," he said, leaning closer to Red Hawk. "I'm telling you, some women need a firm hand. Five children need a mother. If I were you, I would give her a good beating. Then she wouldn't be as likely to do this again.''

"Yes, sir.''

"You may have my cabin while we cross the river,'' the captain said under his breath. "I'll be here. There's a stout whip in my cabin. You should use it, man.''

"I'll give it thought.''

"No! Please listen—'' Savannah cried, and received a stone-faced glare from the captain.

"Young woman, you need to mind your responsibilities to your husband and your children. Whiskey is never a good companion for a woman.'' He turned to Red Hawk. "Hitch your horse with the others and take her to my cabin. I'll see you're not disturbed.''

"Come along, love,'' Red Hawk said, propelling her away from the captain. People were staring. She would get no help. Two Union soldiers watched them, and she bit her lip, thinking of all the morphine and quinine in the saddlebags.

Red Hawk tied his horse with the others and then led her to a cabin and stepped inside, pulling her in and closing the door. He leaned against it, looking satisfied.

"How could that man think I have five children!'' Fury washed over her, and she turned away from him, her gaze sweeping the small cabin that held a desk, a bunk, and a washstand. Clothes hung on hooks on the bulkhead and a rawhide whip stood in a corner. Her gaze drifted back to the bunk. Hanging on a hook on the bulkhead over the bunk was a pistol. Savannah rushed to it, yanking it down, feeling the weight of it in her hand. Turning in the bunk, she aimed at Red Hawk.

CHAPTER FOUR

"We're getting off this ferry now, or I'll shoot you. Turn around and let's go. I'll be right behind you with this gun pointed at you."

Instead, he moved toward her, and Savannah drew a deep breath. Her head spun, and there was a double image of him. Her heart pounded because he was coming closer. She pulled back the hammer with a click.

He continued to advance, his dark gaze holding hers, taunting her. "If you shoot me in here, the captain will turn you over to the authorities for murder," he said softly. "And you're not going to shoot, Savannah. You won't kill me. You can't take my life from me."

"Yes, I can shoot you," she said, gazing into his eyes and feeling caught in another silent battle. He moved closer, and she raised the pistol to aim at his heart. "Stop where you are."

"You won't shoot, because you can't kill a man who hasn't harmed you."

As he moved closer, she licked her lips. She couldn't get her breath. She had to shoot or give up the pistol and let him take her to Louisiana. He was advancing, and she would lose her only chance if she let him frighten her. She could barely breathe.

"Savannah," he said softly, taking another step toward her.

"Stop!" Savannah's heart thudded as she scooted back on the bunk until she was pressed against a bulkhead. "Stay where you are," she ordered, knowing she had to shoot now. Her hands shook, and the pistol wavered. She didn't know how to aim and she couldn't bear to shoot her captor in the face.

While Red Hawk's gaze held hers, he moved closer. Shutting her eyes, she squeezed the trigger.

The blast was deafening in the small cabin. She felt as if a tree hit her as Red Hawk collapsed on top of her.

Her heart missed several beats. Had she killed him? Had she actually murdered a man? Horror numbed her while she stared at him and tried to wriggle away.

Then he moved, twisting, raising his head, his dark eyes causing her to flinch. To her horror, crimson blossomed over his shirt sleeve and across his shoulder and chest.

"You little witch!" He yanked the pistol from her hands, then ran to the door and opened it. She heard men's voices. "It's all right. An accident was all," he called to someone.

As he closed the door and turned around, she saw a dark stain on his upper arm. His eyes were filled with fire when she looked at him, and she shrank back against the bulkhead as he strode across the room.

"I warned you," she gasped, terrified of him, shocked by her own actions. She had *shot* him.

"You could have killed me!"

"I told you to get back!"

He leaned over her, his face inches from hers, his hands on the bunk on either side of her, his fingers splayed. A vein in his neck pulsed with each heartbeat.

She glanced at the wound, the scarlet soaking his left sleeve. *I shot him. He might die at my hand.* "You're bleeding."

"I should take that whip to you and beat you into submission!"

She raised her face, and they glared at each other.

"You're a little witch, Savannah Ravenwood, and in one more minute—"

He tilted her chin up, and her heart pounded. "One more minute until what?" she demanded, looking at him. He was too close, too angry. His eyes were thickly lashed. The look in them made her breath catch. His gaze burned, but it wasn't anger she saw. It was hot, blatant desire.

Her pulse raced. His gaze drifted to her lips, and her mouth tingled. On fire, she watched him, unable to get her breath. Her pulse skittered and awareness of everything else fell away. She stared into his midnight eyes until she was drowning in their darkness. Then he leaned closer, bending down, his gaze holding hers. He tossed away the pistol and his hands went into her hair, tilting her head.

His mouth slanted over hers, warm, demanding. Her heart thudded, and she struggled against him. His strong arms closing around her, he caught her up against him, sitting on the bunk and leaning over her, pressing her down as his tongue, wet and hot, stroked her mouth. Her lips parted, and his tongue went deep. She was possessed, united with his strength. Her muddled senses could not sort out thoughts, but it felt as if she belonged in his arms. Never had she known kisses like this man's.

An ache, warm and deep inside her, flowered and spread, making her hips shift as she returned his kiss. Her senses spun and reeled while sensations bombarded her. He had plied her with brandy and she was hot and dizzy and she wanted him with a painful urgency.

Stunned by her own feelings, she wanted his kisses in a manner she hadn't known was possible. He shifted her, pulling her down and moving over her, his long hard body stretching on top of her. His arousal pressed thickly against her as she kissed him. He raised his head to look into her eyes.

"You kiss like fire, yet you just tried to kill me."

"I wanted to kill you," she admitted breathlessly, her emotions swirling as much as the cabin was spinning. "You've filled me with brandy. It makes me want to kiss you," she whispered, wondering if that was the truth or not.

He shifted, raising slightly. "This damned dress is fastened to your chin," he said, moving away and pulling her up.

Her heart pounded at the need in his eyes. No man had looked at her in such a way before—as if he were desperate for her.

A blast from the whistle shattered the moment between them. While he swore softly, she pushed him away.

"I'm foxed on brandy, and you caused it. You have taken advantage of me," she said, barely aware of the words that spilled out of her. Her thoughts were on him, his kisses, the hungry look in his eyes.

"Not too much advantage, Savannah, when you shot me."

"I think you deserved it wholly," she answered solemnly as she straightened her clothing. "The cabin spins and it is far too hot. You're bleeding badly," she said, frightened at how quickly his shirt had become soaked in blood.

He turned away and yanked off his shirt. Muscles rippled across his chest, and her breath went out in a rush, as if someone had dealt her a blow. Mesmerized by the sight of him, she stared as he ripped off a piece of his shirt. At the sight of the ugly, bleeding gunshot wound, she felt faint. The wound looked dreadful, and guilt swamped her. Turning, he strode across the cabin, and she was startled at the sight of the scars and slashes across his back.

"Your back!"

He glanced at her and arched his brow. "I was taken prisoner and given a beating."

He picked up a pitcher and poured water over his arm, leaning over the washbowl. Now he looked more the wild savage than ever, with his bare skin and blood-drenched arm and long black hair. She was drawn and repulsed at the same time, fascinated and frightened.

She envisioned him again riding across the prairie, lance in hand, bearing down on her helpless father.

Red Hawk dried with his shirt and began to wrap his arm with the strip of cloth.

As he fumbled the binding, she crossed the cabin to take it

from him, wrapping the wound. She was intensely aware of his smooth brown skin and his bare chest directly in front of her. She had never been this close to a man who was bare to the waist, and her pulse drummed.

She glanced up to find him watching her.

"Your hands shake," he observed.

Unable to understand her reaction to him, she didn't answer. He was a danger in her life beyond any threat she had ever known.

She tied the strip and moved away, turning to watch as he retrieved a pack and unrolled it, removing another shirt. He carefully wrapped the bloody, torn one in the pack and then yanked on the fresh shirt.

As he sucked in his flat stomach to tuck the shirt into his pants, he looked at her. Embarrassed, she turned her back, admonishing herself for staring at him and telling herself to refrain from such activity in the future.

Someone knocked, and Red Hawk draped his shirt over his shoulder to hide his wound before he opened the door. "Sorry to disturb you, sir," the man said. "Land approaches."

"Thank you." Red Hawk closed the door and retrieved his pack, slinging it across his shoulder.

"How will you explain that I shot you?"

"I'll just say it was an accident. Some saw you and know you were tipsy."

"Thanks to you."

"Come, we'll get the horse and get ready to land. If Union soldiers are waiting to look at the passengers, I don't want to be standing around."

Red Hawk had already decided if they escaped unnoticed, he would release her when they were a mile from the ferry. By the time she walked back to the ferry, he would have enough of a start to escape from Vicksburg.

He would remember her for the rest of his life. He wanted one last kiss. It would be a long time before he got another chance to kiss a woman, maybe never again a woman like this one.

As his arm slipped around her waist, he drew her to him. Her eyes flew wide, her mouth opening in a protest that died when she met his gaze. She was silent, a lethargic, sensual look coming to her features. He leaned down, covering her mouth with his, capturing her sweetness.

When she melted against him, he could feel her heart pound with his. All woman, she liked to be kissed. His knees went weak and longing swamped him—longing for her body, but a deeper yearning that hit like a blow to his middle. All the loneliness of the war years crashed down on him, and he kissed her as if he could obliterate memories of the lonely nights, the constant death and despair.

This beautiful, responsive woman was life and hope and renewal. Holding her close, he tightened his arms, inhaling her sweetness and memorizing her softness.

Tomorrow and yesterday vanished. There was only now and a woman in his arms who was honey and fire. In that moment, he knew her kisses were branded into his soul.

As she returned his kiss, her eyes closed, and he might as well have been standing in a raging inferno. He wanted more, so much more from her.

When she pushed against his chest, he released her reluctantly, watching her eyes open slowly. Again he saw desire, longing, needs that fueled his own.

"I'm surprised you don't take what you want," she whispered.

"Never!" He shook his head. "My mother was raped," he answered in a breathless rasp, while he wondered whether he was a fool for not taking her. He suspected there would be little fight from her. It would be seduction, not rape. But it also went against the grain to take another man's betrothed while the man was on a battlefield risking his life.

As they stared at each other, they gasped for breath. Again the whistle shattered the moment. She jerked free and lost her balance, staggering against him. He steadied her, gazing at her calmly.

"I shall hate both you and brandy forever," she said.

"You will forget me all too soon, Savannah," he replied quietly, with regret.

He took her arm as the door opened and the captain faced them. When he saw Red Hawk's sleeve, his blue eyes widened. "Great heavens, man. You're injured!"

Red Hawk glanced down at his arm and saw a tiny spot of crimson that had bled through the bandage and his sleeve.

"It's minor, merely an accident. I'll be all right."

The captain looked back and forth between them. "Take one of my shirts—and here." He crossed to the corner of the room and handed the rawhide whip to Red Hawk. "Take this. I think you need to apply it often. A woman should obey her husband."

"I'm not his wife," she protested, though she knew her denial was futile.

"Missy." The Captain leaned forward to look her in the eye. "You go home and take care of those little tykes. You're taking advantage of a kindhearted man." He straightened and gazed at Red Hawk. "Shouldn't marry so young, but you've already done it. And you should've married a plainer woman. Just keep a firmer hand."

"She's promised to be obedient now," Red Hawk said, accepting the whip.

"Obedient!" the Captain snorted. "A few inches to the right and you'd be dead. You best take my advice and get control."

"I'll heed your advice, sir." Red Hawk had to hold back a smile at the look of consternation on Savannah's features. If she had the pistol in her hands, she might cheerfully shoot again. He suspected the captain would be none too safe.

They left the cabin, and Red Hawk led her to the horse. He kept his arm firmly around her waist, thankful she still suffered the effects of the brandy. As soon as he possibly could, he would let her go. If he thought she wouldn't turn him in, he would leave her here on the ferry, but he knew he couldn't trust her.

"Yankees are everywhere. You keep quiet. Remember, we're carrying the morphine, and you won't do your sister any good if you're in a Federal prison."

Savannah went along with him quietly. Her head was spinning, and she couldn't fight him until the brandy wore off. She was shocked she had shot him, equally shocked at how she had responded to his kisses. The gentle rise and fall of the ferry was churning her stomach. She wanted to stand on solid ground and feel cool air on her skin.

Red Hawk held the reins in one hand, keeping a grip on Savannah with the other. A mile from here, he could release her and be on his way. She slowed him incredibly.

His gaze scanned the crowd and met the blue-eyed stare of a tall, blond Union sergeant. Looking away, Red Hawk didn't glance back as they descended the plank.

"Thanks, Captain."

"You remember what I said, man."

Red Hawk knew he and the captain would never share the same views about dealing with women. He would never beat a woman, and he held only contempt for a man who would. He glanced at Savannah. She was not a woman to be treated with a whip. Far from it. Had she yielded her innocence to her betrothed? Red Hawk steadied her, holding her close. He suspected she had and was suffering longing and loneliness now that her fiancé was away in the war.

He drew a deep breath. His arm stung, but the wound was superficial. He shouldn't have run such a risk, walking up to a cornered woman who was filled with brandy and waving a loaded revolver, yet he could no more resist her challenges than he could resist breathing.

She moaned softly, and he was sympathetic. She was suffering from the brandy, the bobbing of the ferry, and the heat. He turned the reins, his gaze sweeping over the boat. The sergeant was talking to the captain and both were looking his way. Red Hawk knew he needed to move quickly. Bluebellies swarmed the dock. He kept the bay at a leisurely pace, because it wouldn't do to urge the horse faster. Nothing would draw attention more.

They left the dock behind and turned along a road west. His back tingled, and he wanted to look behind him, but he didn't dare. Savannah was too foxed to be subtle about it if he asked her to look, and she might try to signal for help. Lord help him, he had picked a feisty woman!

Finally they were alone on a narrow rutted road surrounded by brush and tall pines. As wind sighed softly through the trees, he turned to glance over his shoulder. The lane was empty, yet he couldn't shake the uneasy feeling that the Union sergeant was trailing them. Red Hawk tightened his arm around Savannah and urged the horse to a trot.

If the blond officer had followed them, Savannah might not be safe walking back alone to the ferry. Red Hawk glanced over his shoulder at the empty road. He needed to release her. He did not want to take her across Louisiana with him.

When he slowed, he glanced back again. The road was as empty as before, curving in a bend and disappearing. He turned off the road to wait beneath the trees in the shade. If it remained empty for another few minutes, he would bid Savannah farewell and let her walk back to the ferry. Then she could take a stage wherever she wanted.

Savannah twisted around to gaze up at him, and he knew he could look at her for hours and not get enough. Her mouth was full, tempting. He wanted to pull her off the horse and seduce her. He suspected she was no virgin and would be a willing partner. His blood heated at the thought, yet he would not take another man's woman while the man was away fighting or doctoring other soldiers.

Impatience tugged at Red Hawk. Caleb needed the morphine. Matthew needed him.

As soon as he got the morphine to Caleb, he would ride for San Antonio to get Matthew, his nephew. The thought of his sister's child with a cold, uncaring family was unbearable, and he wasn't going to wait until the war's end to go home to get him.

Red Hawk glanced at Savannah, who hiccuped softly. Instinct told him they had been followed, but he hoped he was wrong. He didn't want to take Savannah with him. He could make far better time without her, be in far less danger than he would be traveling with a beautiful woman wanted by the Federals. He glanced down at her dress and thought about the dresses worn by Comanche women, practical dresses that were made for ease of movement.

His gaze slowly traveled back up over Savannah's tiny waist and the thrust of her breasts. He had to admit there were some good arguments for the kind of dress she was wearing.

She tilted her head to study him. "Why are we leaving . . . the road?"

Her words were slow, and it seemed an effort for her to speak.

"I want to make certain we're not followed. We'll part here, Savannah." He drew her name out, saying it softly, aching to just touch her hair one more time. Yet he kept his hands to himself. "I'm letting you go back to your family in Vicksburg or Louisiana or wherever you want to go."

She stared at him as if stunned by his announcement. "Will you share part of my medicine? Thomas needs it desperately."

"No." Red Hawk knew men all over the south needed medicine. The damned war created the worst possible shortages, but she didn't have enough to share. "I'm taking the morphine. It is just as desperately needed in Louisiana. You can make another swift journey to your uncle's house and obtain more."

"It's mine!"

"I beg to differ. You stole it from someone."

"I bought some of it," she said drawing herself up.

"If you want to stay and argue the matter with me, mount up and come along across Louisiana. I'm not waiting here to discuss who gets the morphine." He lifted her down and released her.

She inhaled deeply, the dress drawing tight across her bosom, and he couldn't resist glancing down. She turned away. Her skirts held high, she stepped through the weeds, her chin lifted. If there were dangers in wandering alone on the road back to the ferry, they did not disturb her.

She never glanced back, yet he didn't want to stop watching her. She reached the road and walked with all the assurance and regal composure of a queen strolling her castle grounds.

Then Savannah reached a bend in the road and disappeared from his view. He remained immobile, images of her floating in his mind, her soft body under him, his hands spanning her narrow waist, green eyes blazing at him with anger and then, in their depths, that passion and longing that made his knees weak and took his breath.

Leaves fluttered in the breeze and the only sound was a bird's whistle, yet he couldn't turn away. He could still see her walking away, her back stiff and straight, her hips slightly swaying. He remembered exactly how she had stood before him and shed the green silk dress, leaving her pale shoulders bare and her long legs exposed to his view, the round curve of her bottom setting him aflame.

He could go after her. He could take her, possess her, and pleasure himself—and he suspected he could win her over and the fight would leave her. Although tempted beyond measure, he sat without moving, knowing she was not a woman to be taken by force, but a woman to be won by love.

Feeling a sudden desolation, he knew he was going to miss Savannah Ravenwood and have more than a few sleepless nights remembering her passionate kisses.

He barely noticed where he was going, his horse moving through the thick trees and brush as he turned once more to glance back. Dust motes danced in the sunlight that fell on the empty road. His heart was equally empty.

He turned, urging his horse forward. *Forget the woman.* His arm throbbed. Indeed, she had left him something to remember her by—a wound that would leave a scar he would carry the rest of his life.

In the distance, an unmistakable scream pierced the air, sending ice down his spine. He turned the horse and flicked the reins. Another scream ripped the afternoon quiet. It had to be Savannah.

CHAPTER FIVE

Savannah screamed again as she struggled with the Union officer. "Let me go!"

"You're a woman alone. No decent woman would be out here like you are. I think you're the woman the Army is searching Vicksburg for."

The sergeant shoved her to the ground, coming down over her. Her struggles were useless against him as he pushed her skirts high. "You stole the Army's morphine!"

"No!"

"You can't explain why you're here alone. I suspect you're headed for prison, but whether you're Miss Ravenwood or not, it doesn't matter," he said, pinning her to the ground, his body spread over hers as he caught her chin and held her head.

"The army is looking for five escaped Rebels. One was a redskin. The captain said that Indian you were with was your husband, but I don't think so."

Savannah struggled against him, fear and anger giving her strength, but she still was no match for the sergeant.

She opened her mouth to scream again and his mouth covered hers, just as Red Hawk's had done. Yet this time the kiss stirred only revulsion. Rage boiled in her while she pushed and fought him. Leaning forward, she caught his earlobe in her teeth, biting hard.

He let out a howl and raised up, his hand raising to hit her.

She lunged at his throat, but before she could grab him, he was flung away from her.

Red Hawk jerked the sergeant back, his countenance thunderous, the look in his eyes so filled with rage it momentarily stunned her.

He slammed his fist into the officer's jaw. Bone cracked against bone and the officer staggered back.

The sergeant drew his revolver, aiming at Red Hawk.

With a swiftness that was startling, Red Hawk kicked the weapon from the sergeant's hand and then leaped on him, both men going down and rolling over. She saw the revolver fly through the air and land with a dull thud in the weeds on the edge of the road.

Savannah rushed to pick it up, turning to aim at the sergeant as he hit Red Hawk. The sergeant gained his feet and she aimed at him again, but Red Hawk came up too swiftly for it to be safe for her to squeeze the trigger.

Red Hawk struck him again, and the sergeant sprawled on the road. She took aim.

"No!" Red Hawk thundered, suddenly in front of her and shoving her hand. When the shot fired harmlessly into the air, she stared at him in surprise.

"He drew on you and would have killed you. He attacked me."

"There's been enough killing in this damned war," Red Hawk said bitterly. "Are you hurt?"

She shook her head as he took the revolver from her and thrust it into his waistband.

"Not really, but he suspected who I was. He suspected who you are."

Red Hawk's head whipped around, his brows dancing together.

"He said five Rebels escaped recently—"

"Damn it," he swore and glanced over his shoulder. "The sound of the shot could carry to the ferry, and I doubt if the sergeant headed out here alone without telling anyone he was after you. You're coming with me."

"No!" She dug her heels in as he caught her wrist and pulled. "You promised."

"You'll meet a similar fate with more soldiers, and I can't risk leaving you. Besides, because of him"——Red Hawk glanced at the inert officer—"they'll be more determined than ever to get us both. Hurry!"

Even though she knew it was useless, Savannah tried to break free. She had come so close to freedom. To give it up now was bitter.

"I'm taking you if I have to throw you over my shoulder."

A distant shout galvanized her to action, and she ran with Red Hawk. Running swiftly, her wrist held fast by him, she plunged into the brush. Bushes tore at her, and she knew Union soldiers were coming. It would only be a matter of minutes before the sergeant regained consciousness and joined the chase.

Red Hawk reached his tethered horse and mounted swiftly, swinging her up in front of him.

She rode astride, trying to shift her skirt and petticoat to cover her legs as he turned the horse and they moved at a walk through the trees.

"Shouldn't you urge this horse faster?"

"No. The trees are too dense and we would make too much noise."

"Which direction will you head?"

"West and slightly south."

Savannah's mind raced. Mansfield was on the route to her sister in Nacogdoches. She could do worse than travel with Red Hawk. If he had intended to harm her, he would have done so when he first took her captive.

She looked down at his hands. They were strong, far larger than hers, dark-skinned and masculine. A shiver ran down her spine. Could she trust him? He was a savage. His people had murdered her father. Yet back there with the Union sergeant, it had been Red Hawk who had declared no more killing. She knew he was a warrior, familiar with battles and dying. What kind of complex man was this who had fought and killed, yet could still turn away from an enemy without killing him?

From the talk she had heard and from her brother's declarations, she had thought all Comanches were savages who would kill without conscience. But from what she had just seen, that was no more so than her own people would kill without conscience.

With a guilty twinge, she turned her head slightly and glanced at his arm. His shirtsleeve was crimson where she had shot him. She knew the wound was bleeding again and probably paining him badly.

He rode as if he knew exactly where he was headed. Would she be better off to go with him until they reached Mansfield, then leave him and travel west?

They were fighting at Mansfield, but rumors abounded in the North that the South was gasping its last breath. Yet how easily people far from the fighting might say that about the enemy!

She did not want to get caught in battle. They were heading into a part of the country where women traveling alone were almost unheard of and vulnerable to danger. He would surely let her go before they neared Mansfield.

Twice again he turned the horse and she wondered how he knew where he was going. The trees were dense, their shade leaving only glimpses of sunlight. She knew if she were alone, she would be hopelessly lost.

For the first mile she was tense, listening for any unfamiliar sound and expecting the soldiers to come charging after them. As time passed, she began to think they had eluded the Federals.

Hunger and exhaustion seeped through her, yet she did not want to complain. Making an effort to keep her questions to herself, she wondered about his arm. She was constantly tempted to break their silence, yet she was afraid their voices might carry to anyone following them.

More than anything, she was aware of her body pressed close against his—the woodsy scent of him, the feel of his thighs alongside hers. She rode as still as possible, remembering clearly how swiftly he was aroused if her bottom rubbed against him.

They stopped to water the horse, then were on their way again until dusk, when he called a halt. They were in the open, not far from a thick copse of pines to the west. All around them, and particularly back toward the east, the way they had come, was nothing but open space and knee-high grass.

"We'll be out in the open here," she observed, dismounting and looking around.

"It's a good place to be. From here, we can see if anyone approaches. I'll get out the supplies. We'll sleep here."

She watched as he began to unsaddle the horse. Once again, she looked around. "There's no water."

"There's water."

She frowned, annoyed by his cryptic reply.

Ignoring her, he busied himself taking care of the horse. Annoyed by his silence and grudging answers, she placed her hands on her hips and tapped her foot.

"How do you know there's water? And where is it? I'm hot. I'm tired and hungry and don't want to be here with you. The least you can do is cooperate."

He glanced at her and went back to removing the saddle. "We crossed a stream a while back. I figure it runs on around to the south where that line of trees is."

"What'll we eat?"

"I brought supplies." He took down a bedroll and saddlebags with provisions. He turned to hand the bags to her.

"What's this?" she asked, rummaging in one while he shook out a blanket. She removed packets of food: jerky, cold biscuits that now looked like a feast for a king, shiny red apples that made her mouth water and reminded her of her gnawing hunger.

"Did you buy all this with my gold?"

He gave her a cool look. "I'll share it all with you."

"You had no right to help yourself to my gold!"

"You probably stole it."

"I didn't. My uncle gave it to me, and I have a pension from my father which makes me independent."

He smiled. "Savannah, if you were penniless, you would be independent."

He turned his back to her, yanked off his shirt, and ripped a strip from the tail.

"You may need that shirt," she exclaimed, looking at his muscled back. "I can wash out the blood."

When he turned to face her, she drew a swift breath as her glance ran over his broad chest. He looked powerful, virile, and the sight of his bare chest stirred a mixture of reactions in her.

"The shirt isn't safe to wear anyway," he replied. "It's white and shows too clearly in the woods."

When he began to try to unloosen the binding on his arm, she set down the apples she had in her hands and crossed to him. "Let me do that."

"You will tend the wound you caused?" he remarked dryly.

She glanced up and was ensnared in his midnight eyes. She stood close to him, her hands on the bandage knotted around his upper arm, yet she forgot her purpose and was held immobile by his gaze. Feeling the crackling current that seemed to spring to life when she was close to him, she stared back at him.

"How many men have you shot, Savannah?" he asked softly.

Startled, she chilled. "None!" she exclaimed, her conscience plaguing her as she looked down at his bloody arm. "But none have given me such provocation until today!" she flung at him.

"You would have killed me if your aim had been good. You would have shot the sergeant."

Taken aback by his accusation, guilt swamped her. "I wanted to escape from you and from him. I fear I shall suffer for a long time to come, knowing what I almost did," she answered, glancing up to find his disconcerting stare on her again.

This time she tore her gaze away hastily and unwrapped his arm. "It looks as if the bleeding has stopped. Let me get one of the bottles of medicine. I want water first to wash the area around the wound."

"Take this." He bent to pick up a canteen that he handed to her.

"Should we use the drinking water for washing?" she asked, too aware how precious a commodity water could be.

"Yes. I'll get more drinking water. If you're thirsty, take a drink first."

She raised the canteen to her mouth and drank, the cool water going down her throat and refreshing her. When she lowered the canteen, she found him watching her and her pulse jumped beneath his unwavering study. She held it out to him and their fingers brushed as he wordlessly accepted the container and tilted it up to his mouth. She watched his Adam's apple as he swallowed. Then her gaze lowered to his chest again, to the flat nipples and powerful muscles that took her breath away every time she looked at him. She remembered his pulling her into his arms to kiss her, recalled clearly being pressed against his rock-hard body.

He lowered the canteen slowly and her gaze flew upward. Once again he had caught her studying him in a manner no polite lady would ever do.

He held out the canteen.

"No, thank you," she said breathlessly.

"For my arm."

Her blush deepened, burning her cheeks. She had completely forgotten. She grabbed the canteen from him and tried to concentrate on his arm, yet she was as intensely aware of him as ever.

She poured the water over the wound.

"Wait a minute." He moved away, flipped open a saddlebag and returned with a bottle he uncapped. He turned to pour the whiskey over his wound himself and stood without flinching or drawing a deep breath, yet she knew the whiskey must scald incredibly. "This will disinfect my wound as well as anything you're carrying, and we can save the medicines for those who have worse wounds."

His head was bent over his arm, his profile to her, the shaggy black hair falling forward. Once again she saw the Indian, the wild man of the plains. She could not feel safe with him even though he had not physically harmed her. There were other dangers with him—this wild response she was having to him was as dangerous to her heart as the most lethal knife.

You do not love your fiancé. She remembered his words. She cared for Thomas. She did! Perhaps not a wild, giddy love; they had known since childhood they would someday wed. She'd never had a passionate response to Thomas. His kisses had been chaste, proper, polite, not a searing possession filled with demands that she reacted to with abandon.

This burning attraction to Captain Red Hawk had to be fleshly longings and nothing more. Her world and her life were as unlike his world and his life as a wren's and a tiger's.

She watched as he capped the whiskey and turned to her. She began to clean the area around the wound.

"Bind it up and I will make a poultice tonight to put on it. It will heal."

"It has to hurt," she said, looking at him and suffering guilt again, torn between anger at his taking her prisoner and shame that she had shot him. "But, even so, I can't apologize," she admitted honestly.

"No, I don't imagine you can. If it gives you satisfaction, my arm hurts."

"Your pain gives me no satisfaction," she replied stiffly. "I merely was trying to get free." She wrapped and bound his arm with the strip of cloth. He picked up his rifle, gathered the reins, and swung up onto his horse's bare back.

He glanced down at her. "Don't run. You'll only get lost."

He turned the horse and rode toward the west, where the sun was a golden glow above the tops of the trees. She looked at his broad, bare back, his long black hair, the ends of the rifle lying across his thighs. He was a warrior, as strange to her as the land from whence he had come. She remembered childhood nights lying in bed with her sister, windows flung wide for the south breezes, and she could hear the voices of her father and his cronies who sat in the cool yard. Clearly, she could recall her father's deep voice describing the endless prairie with its high grasses and deep blue skies, flaming sunsets, the herds of massive animals called buffalo, how the train and the white man would conquer and drive out the savages.

One friend, Colonel Stanford, thought the army should put a bounty on each Indian killed.

"They will be killed without the army having to pay bounties," her father had replied. "We won't let them stop the railroad."

Her soldier father was hated by the Indians, and he hated them, always referring to them as savages.

She watched Red Hawk vanish into the trees. He couldn't have possibly been present when her father and the men with him had been massacred. From what Red Hawk had said, he had been fighting in the war at that time. Yet she couldn't stop feeling he was responsible. It could have been his cousins or uncles who had brutally slain her father. Her father and the men killed with him had been buried on the prairie by soldiers who had found the remains. He was buried somewhere on the vast western plains beyond the Texas frontier.

Silence descended. There was not so much as a birdcall, and she realized how completely alone she was. A chill ran down her spine, and she looked in the direction they had come. Across the open field to the east was another copse of trees. Staring into their dark shadows, she was aware of being alone, vulnerable, and exposed.

Why hadn't he chosen a place in the woods where they would not be so visible?

Was it foolish to wait because he had told her to stay? She studied the trees, wondering whether he was seated there, watching and waiting to see what she would do.

Uncertain where to go if she did run, she looked around. Red Hawk traveled as if he were on a road that led straight to his destination. If he stopped to study surroundings or gaze at the sky, she was unaware of it, yet he changed direction with uncanny sureness. She suspected he would get to his destination without mistake.

Cold with fear, she turned to stare at the way they had come. Could the soldiers track them? She had no weapon, no horse, no way to run or defend herself.

Were they being followed? She tried to think about food and unpacking supplies, but she glanced constantly over her shoulder. Finally she sank down with an apple and stared toward the east and waited.

Red Hawk rode back toward the camp. He had killed two rabbits for their supper. He half expected Savannah to be gone. If she was, he wondered whether he would try to find her or not. His arm still throbbed, but it was a clean wound and not a serious one. She was a strong woman with strong beliefs and he knew she did not like him or approve of him.

At the same time, he knew she suffered over having shot him. There were moments when guilt was in her eyes. As well as being strong, she was a desirable woman who continually earned his admiration. He remembered holding her in his arms. That moment before her lashes came down, he had looked into the depths of her green eyes and seen the questions, the flare of desire.

Responding to his memories, his body heated. She was fiery, determined, yet she could be soft and yielding. He groaned and tried to shift his thoughts. She did not like his lineage, and sometimes when he caught her looking at him he could see her distrust and revulsion. Other times when he caught her looking at him, it was with the eyes of a woman ready for passion.

Why didn't he take her? He could so easily. There would be no more than a fight of a few minutes. Yet she was a woman worthy of winning, and a few moments' satisfaction with a half-willing partner was not his dream. If they traveled together for several nights, how long before they would both succumb to the flames building between them?

Bracing for an onslaught of conversation, he dismounted and

held up the hares. Ignoring her stream of remarks about supper and hunger, he staked out his horse. Then, while he skinned the hares, he watched her move around him, getting things ready. He had brought sticks and a log and she built a fire with competence.

"My mother died when I was ten, so I learned early to keep the household running for my father. At night we often would have company to eat with us. Afterward, while the servants cleaned, I would play the piano for my father and his guests and my sister would sing."

He tried to keep his attention on his job of cleaning the hares, but his gaze constantly ran back to Savannah. He watched her pale hands move gracefully over utensils and food. Despite her constant chatter, he was more than starved for the companionship of an appealing woman.

Smoke curled into the sky as he set the hares on a spit. Soon juices dripping onto the flames spattered and sent a savory aroma into the air.

He was not surprised at how much help she was in getting their supper, and his admiration for her ran close behind his desire. As he ate the roasted hare, he continued to watch her. Her fingers were slender and dainty, and he remembered their softness. Too long away from beautiful women, he was as fascinated by her as the moths coming out of the night were captivated by the glowing red flames of the campfire.

His bare chest disturbed her, and that both aroused and amused him. Going shirtless was natural to him, particularly on a hot night. He was aware she had a constant struggle to look anywhere except at his chest.

She had unfastened the top buttons of the blue riding dress and rolled the sleeves high. He suspected she was burning in the heat of the night. There was no breeze and the grass stood still, the thick heat hanging over the earth.

Their fire died to glowing embers until he kicked dirt over it and the last gray curl of smoke wafted into the air.

The full moon rose over the treetops, round and silvery, bathing the landscape in its luminous glow.

She rose and moved around, cleaning and putting away their things. He stood and picked up his rifle.

"Come, and I'll take you to water. No talking, Savannah. It's best if I can hear what's around me."

"Of course," she answered, as if his request were ridiculous. He wondered how many minutes she could hold her endless chatter.

He moved ahead, certain she would follow. He heard the clatter of their tin dishes and knew she was bringing them to wash. While grass swished against his legs, he could hear her moving behind him. He kept watch constantly, both for the Union soldiers and wild animals, but he far more feared the soldiers. Never again did he want to be taken prisoner, and today they had compounded the reason for the Army to keep after them. He could not imagine the Union sergeant letting the incident pass without trying to ride after them and take them prisoner. If they did, Savannah's fate would be rape.

"Your scars," she said softly, and he glanced over his shoulder at her.

Without answering, he plunged ahead, knowing she was having to half run to keep up with his long stride, but he was vulnerable with his back turned to the east. If the soldiers had followed, that was the direction from which they would come.

They reached the trees and it was only yards to a swift, gurgling stream with splashing water sending up white bubbles.

"You said you were beaten when you were a prisoner of Union soldiers."

"Yes. I'll never be taken prisoner again." He turned to her and motioned upstream. "I'll leave you if you want to wash. Can you find your way back alone?"

She nodded and he moved away, satisfied she was certain of her answer. He heard her splashing, and images tormented him of her removing the riding habit and bathing in the creek. He could remember her standing before him, peeling off the green silk dress that revealed her alluring, womanly curves.

He ground his teeth and tried to shift his thoughts to the

Union sergeant. He should pay attention. The soldier could be following them right now.

He had to have been at least half an hour behind and Savannah kept up extremely well, so they may have made better time across country than the sergeant and his men could. If the sergeant and his men were good trackers, they should have caught up by now.

Reaching their campsite, Red Hawk sat down cross-legged, listening to night sounds, watching the east. They were far enough in the open to be out of range of rifle fire. No one could sneak up on them, but if the soldiers made a sudden charge, he knew it would be difficult to outdistance them and reach the cover of trees to the west. He had picked a place to hide during the daylight and was ready, but he wished Savannah would return. If the soldiers came now, he might have to leave her.

When half an hour passed and she hadn't returned, the glimmer of worry came. He glanced over his shoulder to the west, but there was no sign of her heading toward camp.

As he kept waiting, his glances over his shoulder came more often. Curiosity, annoyance, and nagging worry plagued him until he strode back to the woods, moving unerringly to where he had left her.

Not a twig crackled as he made his way through the woods. Had she run away? If someone had found her, she would have screamed—if she'd had the chance.

When he saw the glimmer of moonlight on cascading water through the trees ahead of him, his step quickened. He was almost to the water's edge, still in the copse of trees, when he stopped, held immobile.

CHAPTER SIX

Her back was to him as she stood in the stream. Moonlight spilled over her, catching the glitter of drops of water on her pale body. She was more than all the dreams and visions and fantasies he'd had on lonely nights on empty battlefields. His gaze raced over luscious curves, a firm round bottom, long, shapely legs. The woman was breathtakingly beautiful.

He might as well be on fire. With a primitive growl deep in his throat, he started forward, driven by an atavistic urge to claim her and discover all the secrets hidden in her soft body.

Then reason and memories halted him. Shaking, he had to fight the scalding desire.

She dropped into the water with a splash that startled him, a merry peal of laughter ringing in the night air. The laughter tore at his heart. How long since he had heard any woman's laughter? Savannah's was filled with sunshine. He wanted to watch her, but he knew if he stayed, he would be in the water with her and she would be in his arms. She began to sing softly, her lilting voice another torment in the night.

He turned, blindly heading back the way he had come. He was the one who needed to plunge into an icy creek. His heated body was torment and images floated in his mind—images he knew would be with him forever.

The first town they reached tomorrow, he would leave her behind. Let her get along the best she could.

But the Federals would be after her, and her Union relatives might not have enough power to keep her out of prison. They might not even hear she was in prison. No one would know if she was taken prisoner out here in the wilds.

He clamped his jaw closed and strode out of the trees. It wasn't until he was halfway to their small campsite that he remembered the danger he could be in. He swore softly, knowing his brain was befuddled by the woman. He had to stop thinking about her and keep watch until they were ready to travel again.

He had worried over wanting sleep. Now, plagued by images of her, he would have no need for sleep.

He reached the spot where he had spread a blanket, looking at her reticule, the blanket, and the saddlebags. His horse grazed only yards away. Red Hawk sank down, knowing his head would barely show above the tall prairie grass.

As time passed, he wondered if she was still splashing in the creek. He groaned, clenching his fists, fighting to tear his thoughts away from Savannah Ravenwood.

His throbbing arm pained him, and he was damned thankful it was only a superficial wound.

Finally he heard the swish and rustle of grass. He glanced around to see her walking toward him. His pulse jumped and he stood, watching her and forgetting danger once again.

"Bathing was marvelous! Except I hope I never know what kind of creatures were in the water with me."

He wanted to answer her, but his mouth was dry, his tongue thick. A clear image of her bathing in the swift, cold creek in the moonlight danced in his mind and stole his ability to speak.

When she sat down facing him and smiled, he felt another lurch in his pulse. Her soft lips parted, the corners of her mouth lifting. As he sat down facing her, he could not resist reaching out to touch her face, his fingertips lightly brushing her mouth.

"It is a good thing to see a beautiful woman smile. I have been too long at war."

"That creek would bring a smile to anyone," she answered, but now her voice had softened, and again he felt the current jump between them like fire springing from one twig to another.

He dropped his hand away and stared at her, torn between wanting to reach for her and knowing that he should all but ignore her. Reminding himself of their danger, he looked to the east.

"You're watching for soldiers," she said after a moment's quiet. "How likely do you think it is that they're after us?"

"If they were, I think they would have caught up with us by now and would have attacked. But there's a chance that they haven't picked up our trail and are still trying, so I don't want to stop watching."

"How many days' ride to Mansfield?"

"You won't have to ride as far as Mansfield. When we reach a town tomorrow, I'll let you go—unless you're afraid to go on your own."

"No! You know that's all I want. I'll be ahead of the soldiers and I'll find a way home." As she studied him with a slight frown, he knew whatever was bothering her, he would hear about it.

"You've told me before you would let me go and then you didn't."

He shrugged. "I planned to, but then circumstances changed. You could have turned me in, and I'm not going back to prison. Tomorrow you'll be free to go to your sister with only a small delay."

"A small delay and a loss of all I've worked for. I want my gold back."

"The gold is spent."

"All of it couldn't possibly be!"

Unwilling to argue with her over it, he shrugged.

"I should have settled for what I got in St. Louis and never taken the medicines from the boat, but I thought I could be gone before they were ever missed."

"I'm glad you did. They will do good for many."

When she didn't answer, he guessed she was still angry and probably trying to figure a way to steal them back, but without her hoop skirt and its pockets, she had no way to hide the medicine.

"So you'll go back to fighting." She reached up to touch her hair.

"No. As soon as I deliver the morphine, I'm through with this war."

Her brows arched as she lowered her hands and a braid of hair tumbled down, falling over her shoulder and hanging to her waist. She reached up to unfasten another braid that was wound on her head. "Where will you go? Where's your home?"

"My home was San Antonio, and that's where I'm headed now." He watched in fascination as another long braid fell over her shoulder.

"You're Comanche. How did you come to live in San Antonio?"

"Before I was born, my mother was with a wagon train headed west. It was attacked. Her parents were killed and she was captured by the Comanches. She was only fourteen at the time. My father wed her and I was born."

"Didn't she hate your father?"

"No, she loved him very much. The year after I was born, my brother Caleb was born, and then the following year she gave birth to Celia. When I was nine, my father was killed by soldiers. Two years later, more soldiers attacked our summer camp, and my mother and I were taken back to live with whites."

"You were nine years old when your father died? I was ten when I lost my mother."

"My mother married again—a San Antonio merchant, Bradford Porter. Thanks to him, Caleb and I were schooled. I went to Baylor. Before the war Celia married Dalton Ashman and had Matthew. Both my mother and stepfather are no longer living. I've lost every one of my family except Caleb and my nephew, Matthew. I'm not going to lose either of them," Red Hawk said, feeling the urgency to be up and traveling again. He had stopped to eat, let Savannah sleep, and rest the horse, but now he wanted to mount up and go, letting Savannah sleep in the saddle the way he would.

In the back of his mind a cynical voice nagged him. Was he so eager to travel, or did he want to have Savannah close against him again?

She picked up a plait and began to work free the tresses. "You said you were going to San Antonio. If your sister is no longer living—"

"I'm going for her son. Dalton was killed at Fredericksburg. Two years ago, Celia had scarlet fever. She recovered, but she wasn't ever well again. She was afraid she might not survive and she wrote to me, asking me to promise to come get her son and raise him as my own. She said even Dalton—her husband—said his parents should not raise Matt. They are cold, abusive people and Dalton was heartily glad to grow up and leave home."

"How dreadful! Your nephew may need you as much as my sister needs me."

"Matthew does need me." Red Hawk turned to stare at the dark trees on the eastern edge of the field while his mind went back to times at home with Caleb and Celia. "Celia died eleven months ago, almost a year now. She was sick for a couple of months before she died. It took a month for the letter about her death to reach me."

"I'm sorry," Savannah said quietly.

He barely heard her as old memories swirled like wood smoke. He had lost all he loved except Matthew and Caleb. Gone now were Tall Horse, his father; his mother, Martha; his stepfather, Bradford; his sister, Celia; and his brother-in-law, Dalton. Sometimes when he thought about them, pain came swiftly. He had loved each one of them. Celia had been safely married in San Antonio, not caught up in the frontline battles of war, yet she was gone now, too.

"I barely know my nephew, but I'm going to claim him and

take him to raise as my own. This is what I pledged to my sister that I would do.''

"Then you'll take him home with you?"

"I intend to."

"You say that as if you're going into battle," Savannah observed, wondering about this facet of him. She was surprised by the determination she heard in his voice, knowing it was over a child. She couldn't imagine him as a parent for a small boy.

"He's a six-year-old boy, defenseless against this pair. Yet the few letters I had from Celia indicate I'll have a fight when I try to get him. They want him because he has an inheritance—which they don't need," Red Hawk added angrily. "And Matthew's inheritance isn't theirs to spend. Celia described these people in her letters as cold, uncaring, and greedy.''

In the moonlight Savannah saw the muscle working in his jaw.

"I should have been there for Celia at the last," he said in a quiet voice, as if he had forgotten Savannah's presence and was talking to himself. "Celia should have had some of her family with her, and I should have been there to take Matthew with me. I was caught up in battle and hadn't received her letter. I didn't even know I failed her," Red Hawk said bitterly.

"If you didn't know and you were in battle, there's no way you could have been with her. You shouldn't torment yourself about something beyond your control. But you *should* understand why I need to go home. My sister is as vulnerable as your nephew. She's married to a cruel, ruthless husband.''

"She must have loved him at one time."

"No. She was promised to him by our father, the same way I have been to Thomas.''

"Ahh, another arranged marriage," he remarked quietly, and her defenses came up.

"That doesn't mean it won't be a good marriage for me."

While moonlight spilled over his bare shoulders, he sat with inscrutable dark eyes. Loosening her braids, she could feel him watching her every move. Her hair had been splashed with water, but as she unplaited a strand and ran her fingers through it, she knew it would dry swiftly.

"If your brother-in-law doesn't want to let your sister go, you'll be interfering where the law says you have no right," he remarked.

"The law isn't fair to women. I'm taking her home with me whether he wants it or not," Savannah replied, half of her thoughts on their conversation, half on him. He sat as still as a statue, his gun lazily resting on his crossed legs, yet she knew how fast he could move. "You'll break the law as much as I will if you try to take your sister's child from his grandparents."

"If they have his interests at heart, they will let me take him," he said, but his voice tightened, and she wondered if she had touched on a matter that worried him. "I have letters from Celia making me guardian," he continued. "She had an attorney draw up papers. What will matter most to the Ashmans is that I have Celia's notarized and certified will, witnessed by several upstanding citizens. She left all the money in my charge until Matthew comes of age."

"Then those people can't do anything."

"They can get an attorney and take the matter to court. If so, we would go to court in a town where they have many influential friends and I've been away for years."

"You're not married. It won't help your cause to be without a wife."

"I promised Celia I would take him, and I will."

"After all this time, they may be like parents to him."

"Both Celia and Dalton were convinced that his parents would never be good for Matthew," Red Hawk said quietly, with an implacable expression and a note of determination in his voice that made her wonder if anything short of death had ever thwarted him. "Dalton should have known. He was their son."

Red Hawk's gaze swept the field and the tall trees in the distance, but he couldn't detect anything amiss. He thought about what Savannah had said—that it would hurt his cause to be without a wife. For a few minutes while they sat in silence, he strained to hear any night sounds, but he detected nothing more than the whisper of wind in the grass.

"How long has your sister been married to this man?" he asked.

"Four years. Adela is older than I am. She was pledged to a boy when she was a child, the same as I have been to Thomas, but the boy died. Mr. Platt was an acquaintance of our father, a military man. When he saw Adela, he wanted to marry her. My father consented," Savannah said, her voice sounding pained. "With our mother dead, I don't think my father knew what to do with us, particularly Adela."

Red Hawk continued to scan the area, turning to look over his shoulder. He didn't want anyone coming up behind them.

While he searched the area around them, he listened to Savannah's soft voice and the thought ran through his mind that he could listen to her talk all night. He stared at her, wondering what kind of spell she had worked on him. When had he ever wanted to listen to someone talk all night? Never. Until now.

"I think my father shut all possibilities out of his mind that Adela might be in a bad marriage. Later, he knew it was bad, but he closed his mind to it and said Adela was too soft, overindulged at home. But we weren't overindulged, and Adela would never cause anyone trouble."

"Maybe she changed," Red Hawk suggested, but Savannah shook her head.

"Not Adela. She was only seventeen when she married Horace Platt. He's in the lumber business in Nacogdoches. Her letters sound the same to me as they did when she first went away."

Red Hawk turned to look at Savannah, and his breath caught. Before his eyes, she was undergoing a transformation. She freed the last braid and raked her fingers through long strands. Thick locks of hair cascaded over her shoulders, spilling to her waist. She ran her fingers through another braid and then another until a wild mane framed her face. Her hair was a dark, silky curtain streaked with moonlight. Gone was the fancy lady in her silk dress. Instead, only a few yards from him was a woman who looked ready for life and passion.

Again, he couldn't resist. It was as if his hand had a will of its own as he stretched out his arm and wound his fingers in a soft mass of her hair.

Incredibly silky, wavy from the tight braids, her hair spilled over his hand. He lifted the strands to inhale the faint scent of tea roses and to rub the soft locks over his cheek.

She watched him with wide eyes. All words vanished while tension arced between them. As his gaze lowered to her mouth and then to the vee of her dress where her pale skin was revealed, his pulse was thunder. Once again he was tempted to possess her, to relish all her softness and headstrong wildness.

Savannah's heart thudded. She knew he wanted her and he held himself in check. From the first moment with him, danger had swirled around her like hurricane winds.

Was he going to kiss her? *I want him to kiss me.* The realization shocked and frightened her. He was dangerous, a threat to her peace of mind and well-being. She jerked her head away, freeing her hair. His dark eyes were impossible to fathom, yet she could feel his desire, as tangible as the summer heat still rising from the earth.

Her heart pounded so violently she feared he could detect its beat. She knew the constraints of civilization were a thin veneer for him, that he was a man accustomed to taking what he wanted.

In a fluid movement, he rose to his feet. "We'll ride," he said flatly. His voice was husky, a mere rasp that made her tingle.

Before she could move, a wild howl rose in the night and chills went down her spine as she jumped to her feet. "A coyote?"

"Most likely."

"What else could it be? A wolf?"

"It could be a human signaling to other humans."

The idea was more chilling than that of wild animals. She

had bruises from the rough treatment by the sergeant earlier in the day. "Can we go?"

Without answering, as if there was no danger or reason for haste, Red Hawk stood and moved with deliberation. If he was alarmed, he didn't show it. He saddled the horse with the same careful movements as he had unsaddled it hours earlier. She looked at the black mass of trees to the east.

"We make a clear target," she said.

"Then get down in the grass," he replied dryly.

"Does anything frighten you?" she flung at him, annoyed with his cool poise.

"Yes," he replied. "Losing someone I love frightens me. Losing my freedom," he replied, with such force and determination that she was taken aback.

He gathered their things and she worked swiftly to help him. She paused to twist her hair into a long, thick roll and tie it behind her head, letting it tumble down her back. In minutes he swung into the saddle and lifted her before him. Another howl curled into the night, a high lonesome wail that made her shudder and lean against the warmth and solidity of Red Hawk's body.

"It has to be a coyote," she whispered.

"Perhaps. If it were soldiers, they would have attacked by now. We're outnumbered and defenseless."

"Not completely defenseless," she said, thinking of the rifle that was almost an extension of his arm. She remembered the murderous look in his eyes when he had grabbed the sergeant and suspected the soldier would think twice before tangling with him again.

"You may have broken the man's jaw today."

"I hope I did," Red Hawk replied with a quietness that frightened her.

"You don't know him."

"I know men like him."

She remembered his remark about his mother. "You were angry because of your mother. You said a man attacked her."

"Three white soldiers attacked her," he said, his voice a

deep rumble. "They were her own people, but when they took her back from my father, they treated her like dirt. She might as well have been a full-blooded Indian as a white woman for all the respect they gave her. We had a two-day ride back to Fort Belknap. The second night, three of the men raped her."

"When you were eleven?"

"Yes. I tried to stop them. They beat me into unconsciousness," he replied, remembering the blows, the terror in his heart, his mother's screams when they began clubbing him. Blows reined over him and he knew he couldn't fight them, couldn't save her. The knowledge made him wild and gave him strength beyond his years, but it wasn't enough against three grown men.

All that night, he had drifted in and out of consciousness, his mother tending him, though she was as battered and bloody as he. Caleb had stormed into them as well, but one blow had sent him sprawling in unconsciousness. The men never beat him as they had Red Hawk, who was large enough to fight them. Celia was carried away, tied to a tree, and mercifully wasn't present.

The next day he couldn't take more than a few steps without collapsing. They devised a travois and hauled him back to the fort, where he was put into the army hospital with a broken arm, broken nose, broken ankle, and broken collarbone. Red Hawk stared into the night and closed his mind to a time that was long ago and well over, but today had stirred memories when he had seen the sergeant crawling over Savannah.

"He deserved worse than he received," he said, not realizing he had spoken aloud until she answered him.

"Yet you are the one who stopped me from shooting." She twisted slightly to glance over her shoulder at him. "You said your mother married again. It must have been after she was attacked."

"Yes. She had three months at Fort Belknap that were pure hell for all of us, and then she met Bradford Porter, who was traveling through. He was a banker, related to the major who ran the fort. He met my mother and fell in love. For three months I hated whites with every ounce of strength I had.''

''I can understand,'' she said in a strange voice and he caught her chin, leaning forward to look at her.

''Who's caused you to hate, Savannah? You have relatives on both sides of this war. You can't be filled with hatred for Federal or Rebel. So who do you hate?''

She stared up at him in the darkness and didn't answer. Suddenly, with instinct he knew it was his own people. ''You hate Indians,'' he said, his breath coming out swiftly. Her lips firmed, and she pulled away from him to turn her face away.

''You're a southern lady.'' He knew her soft southern accent. ''How could my people have stirred such hatred? Or is it stories you have heard of the wild savages of the plains beyond civilization?''

''My father was a major in the United States Army and he was killed by Indians,'' she answered stiffly.

Coldness ran down his spine as he heard the bitterness in her voice. He could easily guess that her father had been a soldier sent to fight Indians. He realized she had lied to him earlier, confirming his suspicions about her deviousness.

''Only hours ago you tried to convince me that your father would be wildly searching for you. You told me how he was wounded in the war.''

''I wanted you to think he would be after you. I wanted you to let me go!'' she blazed at him, her voice filling with fury. ''He was slain out west. I don't even know where he's buried.''

''He was killed by Indians?''

''Yes,'' she said, in a hiss. ''He was killed by Comanches.''

''My people. So you blame me,'' Red Hawk said, understanding her hatred and anger, yet feeling his own because her father was killed fighting the Comanche and trying to kill them, like the soldiers who had killed his father.

''I know you didn't hold the knife that killed him,'' she said.

''But his blood is on my hands because I'm Comanche.''

She kept her face averted, staring ahead. ''My anger may

be unreasonable. I know you haven't lived the life of a Comanche in years.''

"I intend to return to it.''

She turned to look up at him. "Why?" she asked, sounding as horrified as if he had just announced he would return to cannibalism.

"With this war, I have seen the white man's determination and power. In years to come, the frontier will vanish. My people will be driven from their land and their way of life will change forever. I want to experience it one more time.''

"You don't know that they'll be driven out.''

"It had already started before the war. When this war ends, the politicians and military men will turn their attention west. I want to go home before that happens.''

"Your native way of life seems barbaric.''

"No more so than the white man's,'' he said quietly, thinking of the battles he had fought in. "The war is a good example.''

Forgetting war, Red Hawk looked at the thick mass of hair gathered behind her head. He wanted to reach up and untie the silk ribbon that bound it and let it fall over her shoulders freely as it had earlier. He leaned forward, inhaling the sweet flowery scent of it while he caught up the ends in his fingers, knowing she could not feel the touch.

Silky strands slid over his fingers, making him think of holding her in his arms and of her kisses. He shook his hand free and rode in silence, knowing that she must hate him simply because he was Comanche.

He thought about getting Matthew and about Savannah's earlier arguments. *You're not married. It won't help your cause to be without a wife.* She was right. If he had a wife, how much easier it would be.

She was talking about the war and her father, but Red Hawk didn't listen. He was thinking about her and about getting Matthew. If he were married, it would be easier to get the boy. Or even if he had a fiancée like Savannah. Sophisticated, what Matthew's grandparents would call well bred, a lady, Savannah was a woman Celia's in-laws would respect. With her, he would have an additional way to bargain.

Only half listening to her talk about her sister, he rode in silence, thinking about taking her with him. He waited to discuss it until they halted at sunrise.

He dropped to the ground and lifted her down, feeling the narrowness of her waist and watching her. Her face tilted up to his, her green eyes wide, looking guileless, yet he knew better.

She didn't look as if she had ridden most of the night or had a harrowing day. She looked refreshed, as tempting as ever. Her hands rested lightly on his arms and he reluctantly released her and stepped away, letting his horse drink from a stream while he unsaddled it.

She studied him. "How's your arm?"

"It's healing. Fortunately, it wasn't serious."

Guilt brought a flush to her cheeks and shadowed her eyes. Even so, he knew full well she was capable of doing the same thing again. "We'll stop a while, eat and rest."

"There hasn't been a sign of anyone behind us. Maybe no one followed us."

He shrugged. "I don't think that sergeant would let it go. He could have gone back to Vicksburg, but I think he'll come after us. You have the medicines, I'm an escaped prisoner, and you're wanted by the Army. They'll come."

She frowned and caught her lower lip with even white teeth. Her gaze swept the woods around them. A stream ran through the trees and it was shaded, cool in the early morning. Birds sang. Here one could forget war and tempest and heartbreak.

He unsaddled and watered his horse while Savannah shed her shoes and blithely waded into the shallow stream, splashing and laughing as if she had no cares.

He watched her openly, struggling to keep his control while she splashed and held her skirts above her knees to reveal her shapely legs. He turned and led his horse away, starting tasks that he did without thinking, his mind still on Savannah, his ears straining for every sound from her.

Later, as they sat eating jerky and cold biscuits beneath dappled shade, he tried to sort out all she had told him. "Your father wasn't even Confederate, was he?"

"No, he wasn't," she admitted with a cool stare. "Our home is Mason, Texas. Our county voted against secession and it's divided in its sentiments. My own loyalties are divided. My father was a major in the U.S. Army. He'd been in the military all his life. Thomas Sievert is a lieutenant in the Army of the Confederacy."

"Yet your father was willing to pledge you to a Rebel officer?"

"He and Thomas's fathers have been best friends for years. Many families are divided. Thomas is a medical doctor. He isn't fighting. He's trying to save lives."

"You live in Mason and you're going to Nacogdoches first to get your sister?"

"Yes. It will be on the way. If we reach a major town, I can still get a stage to Nacogdoches."

He picked up a shiny red apple to peel. As he handed a slice to her, he watched her. "Savannah, I have a proposal to put to you."

"Yes?" she responded, barely giving him a glance. She was seated on the blanket after wading in the stream. Her feet were bare, her skirts pulled up to reveal pale, trim ankles and slender feet that held him fascinated.

"I think we can help each other."

She had started to bite into the slice of apple, but she stopped and gave him a quizzical, wary look. "I don't see how you can be of any help to me, unless you escort me straight to Nacogdoches."

"Actually, that's what I had in mind."

Her brows rose and curiosity filled her green eyes. "Why? It's on your way to San Antonio, I suppose, but why would you accompany me to Nacogdoches? It's even more beyond my imagination how I can be of aid to you. Far from it. You have told me constantly how much you would like to be rid of me."

He shrugged. "I've been thinking about something you said. I've been thinking, too, about Matthew's grandparents. You want to get your sister. I want to get Matthew."

Scowling, Savannah lowered the slice of apple. "There's no way I can help you," she said.

"If you go with me to San Antonio as my fiancée, help me get Matthew—"

"That's ridiculous," she said.

"Not if you think about it."

"You're not taking me to San Antonio with you," she said, suddenly coming to her feet as if she would break into flight.

He rose swiftly, closing the distance between them. His hands dropped lightly onto her shoulders.

"Hear me out," he stated. "And listen to what I'll do in exchange."

She stared at him, feeling disaster looming like storm clouds.

CHAPTER SEVEN

Aware of his hands on her shoulders, Savannah gazed up at Red Hawk. She knew if he wanted to take her with him to San Antonio, she wouldn't be able to stop him.

"When we leave Mansfield, we can go to Nacogdoches. It's not out of the way to San Antonio or Mason. I'll help you get your sister away from her husband."

Savannah's pulse jumped. She would welcome help in getting Adela away from Horace Platt, a brute of a man who would be in a rage the first moment he discovered Adela gone. Yet what did Red Hawk want in exchange? "And the help you want from me?" she asked.

"Go with me to San Antonio. Let me tell them you're my fiancée. You're the kind of woman they will listen to and respect."

"It's a deception."

He gave a dry laugh. "My lady, that's a strange charge to hear from one who has stolen the Federals' medicines, lied to who knows how many, including me—"

She flushed a deep scarlet and lifted her chin. "It was for a good cause."

"This is for a damned good cause," he said, sobering. He rubbed her shoulders lightly with his hands, feeling the delicate bones, wanting to pull her closer.

"We'll have your sister, so we can say you are my fiancée. With your sister as chaperon, no one would question your traveling to San Antonio with me. They will think you've come to San Antonio from Mason, which is not far."

"I don't see how I can be of any help. Besides, I suspect if they don't let you have him willingly, you'll simply take him and disappear."

He shook his head. "That's what I'd like to do, but I won't. I want him to have his inheritance, so I want it done right—legally and with their consent or a decree of the court. Matthew will have a nice inheritance and when he's grown, I want it to be there for him."

"If you take him to live with your people, he won't need a penny!"

"That way of life won't last, and he may not like living with them. I want it to be his choice."

"It's still a deception of the highest magnitude. They will think you want to provide a home with me for him. Instead, he will be a warrior and at risk every day of his life."

"Look how at risk your fiancé is and your father was, yet they were civilized. Matthew has no guarantees in life. You know that."

She couldn't think with his hands moving lightly on her shoulders and his dark eyes boring into her. Ride with him all across Louisiana and Texas? Each hour was a strain. They had spent only one night, less than twenty-four hours, together. To spend days, even with Adela at her side, took her breath away.

She moved away, winding her fingers together as she turned back to face him. "They would know all is not loving between us."

"No, they wouldn't. You know the social graces a woman needs. You are intelligent, educated. They'll be more willing to listen to you and perhaps more willing to give him up."

"It's still a deception," she argued.

"So instead of deception, would you keep a child in a family where there is no love for him? His father bore scars because of their brutality—"

She drew a swift breath, her breasts thrusting against the blue poplin. "Is that the truth?"

"Yes," he said, holding up a hand. "I swear. I can show you Celia's last letter. In case I have to produce her letters someday for a judge, I have always carried a few of them. I have mailed other copies to my attorney at home." Red Hawk pulled off his boot and removed wrinkled, yellowed pieces of paper. He searched through them, selected one, and held it out to her. Her fingers brushed his as she took the letter.

She unfolded the paper and sat down to read. He sat cross-legged in front of her and watched in silence. Sunlight spilled between the leaves and highlighted her hair with glints of deep red and gold. Wispy tendrils escaped, and he longed to reach out and unfasten the ribbon that held her tresses.

Her lashes were thick, dark shadows above her cheeks as she bent over the paper.

Savannah smoothed the faded, wrinkled paper. The penmanship was fine, with great loops and scrawls, yet still plain to read. She read avidly, curious about his life and his sister and their relationship.

Tosa Nakaai.

Savannah paused and tried to read aloud the strange words. She glanced at him.

"*Tosa Nakaai,*" he said carefully for her. "It is Comanche for hawk, which she called me instead of Red Hawk."

"*Tosa Nakaai,*" Savannah said, rolling the name off her tongue, listening to the strangeness of it and wondering about his life as a Comanche. She remembered the letter in her hands and looked down, smoothing it out again to read:

Tosa Nakaai,
    I pray each day that you and Caleb are all right. Will this terrible war never end? It is not your war or Caleb's,

and I wish you would leave it and come home. Matthew and I need you.

"I have not been well and I want your promise that if something happens to me you will come get Matthew and raise him as your own. I know this is a burden to place on you, although there will be money to care for him. You already know that.

"Promise me, please, that you will do this and I can sleep easily. He is like you, as you will see. He must not be given to the Ashmans. You know Dalton bore scars from Casper's beatings.

"Dalton has told me dreadful tales about his father and his cruelties. His mother was no better. They are cold and uncaring. If they take Matthew at all, it will be because of his inheritance. They have no interest, much less love, for my child.

"Before he left for war, Dalton made me swear that I would never let them have him. I tremble at night when I think about them taking my precious Matthew. Please, my brother, do this one more thing for me. I have loved you always and will always love you and know in my heart what your answer will be. Thank you and bless you. I pray for you and Caleb constantly.

I shall write Caleb about this matter. How fortunate I am to have my two brothers. Please come home safely. I have lost Dalton to war. I don't want to lose anyone else I love. Take my baby and raise him to be the man you are. I am not well, brother, but I try to be strong for Matthew's sake."

    Your loving sister,
    Sutaitu.

Savannah thought of Adela and how close they were. If Adela had a child in a similar situation . . . She folded the letter and held it out to him.

"I'll go with you to get your nephew."

He inhaled deeply, his broad chest expanding as he took the

letter. His fingers closed over hers and held her hand with the letter between them. "Good. It is best for the boy. My sister tells the truth. Their own son felt that way."

"I'm willing, but I don't think my presence will make that much difference."

"I think a wife will make a lot of difference."

"Fiancée," she corrected. She was aware of his fingers over hers as she gazed into his dark eyes, and tension jumped between them. Silence stretched, becoming a heavy weight until she thought she could hear each beat of her heart.

He released her hand and tucked the letter away in his boot, then stood. "We should travel now. I'm certain soldiers come behind us. Or have telegraphed ahead."

Startled, she looked up at him. "There's still fighting in this part of Louisiana."

"We'll circle north to try to avoid the fighting."

"So you think we'll be in danger if we go into any towns?"

He shrugged. "Perhaps. If anyone is watching for us, we won't be able to fade into the crowd. I'm clearly a half-breed and you have that flaming hair."

She frowned and touched her hair. "I can hide my hair under a bonnet. We can cut yours quite short. It would make your appearance different and the first town you could ride in alone and buy a bonnet for me."

"I think the ride in alone part is wise," he said, hoisting saddlebags and gathering their things.

In minutes she was in the saddle with him, more aware than ever of his body pressed close against hers. Each minute of travel was becoming more disturbing to her and she suspected he was as physically aware of her as she was of him. She should be exhausted, falling asleep in the saddle. Instead, she was buoyed up and excited, unable to close her eyes. Now she would travel across Louisiana and Texas with him!

The notion made her pulse flutter. His hand rested lightly on his thigh, and she remembered his hands stroking her shoulders.

"Tell me how you plan to get your sister away from her husband. Are there any children involved?"

"No. Adela has been married to Horace Platt for four years and, blessedly, there are no children. He owns a lumberyard in Nacogdoches and does quite well. He's more than twice Adela's age."

"If she wants to leave him, why does she need you?"

Savannah twisted slightly in the saddle to look up at him. "Adela is very gentle and she's—" She paused, searching for the right word and hating things that unkind people had called Adela through the years. Their aunt always referred to Adela as slow-witted, while their father called her his timid daughter.

"Adela is shy and quiet and gentle. Sometimes things are a little difficult for her, but she has a simple way of looking at life and she's the most kindhearted person I've ever known, which is all the more reason she shouldn't have to live her entire life with a man who is arrogant and cruel."

"Do you really know he is arrogant and cruel, Savannah?" Red Hawk asked quietly.

"Yes, he is. I begged Father not to promise Adela to him. I don't have letters from my sister—not with me—but she has written how terrified she is of him and, when she displeases him, how he strikes her." Anger filled Savannah each time she thought of her gentle sister married to such a monster. "Adela should never be treated in such a manner. I long to get her away from him."

"We do have a similar situation. I fear for Matthew's well-being. At least your sister is an adult, even if she is shy."

"She's too timid to run away from him on her own, and too timid to ever oppose him."

"Good thing your father didn't give you to this Platt in marriage," Red Hawk remarked dryly, suspecting the marriage would have ended within the first month through mutual choice.

To his surprise, she shuddered. "I loathed the man, and Adela did, too."

"You have much feeling in your voice. Has he done anything to you?"

Savannah rubbed her arms as if she were cold. "He tried to kiss me," she said in such a low voice he barely heard her. "I loathe him," she repeated. "Before her betrothal, I don't know which of us shed the most tears. But I know which one of us has shed the most tears since. I have to get her away from him!"

"That we'll do, Savannah," Red Hawk stated quietly.

Winding her fingers in the bay's coarse, black mane, Savannah wished Adela knew she was on her way.

At the first town they reached, they stopped on a rise almost a mile from the outskirts. Red Hawk dismounted and pulled out his knife and began to cut his long black strands of hair.

She watched a few moments and then, in exasperation, moved to his side and held out her hand. "Give me the knife and find a place to sit. You will draw attention with a haircut that resembles something gnawed off by rats."

With a shrug he handed her his knife and watched her intently. She realized he didn't like placing a weapon in her hands, and guilt stabbed her again over his wound.

They spotted a tree stump, and he sat while she moved around behind him and cut thick strands of hair. Aware of standing close and touching him, she became prickly and nervous. As she cut his hair shorter, she had to rest her hand on his head to steady herself. She cut the back as short as possible, looking at the thick, strong column of his neck, his smooth brown skin. His shoulders were incredibly broad. How much easier it was to stand here behind him, brush her hands against him, cut his hair, *look at him* all she wanted.

Finally the back was cut and she began moving first to one side and then the other until she had no choice if she wanted to finish but to step in front of him.

Instantly she was aware of his unsettling gaze boring through her.

"Close your eyes," she said.

He did so and sat as still as the trees surrounding him. "Why do I need to close my eyes?" he asked quietly.

He made her nervous even with his eyes closed. His forehead

was wide, his brows thick, black, and straight. His lashes were thick and straight and his nose had an imperious crook. His skin was taut over his prominent cheekbones. He had a recent scar from ear to jaw and an older scar on his temple. She wondered again about his life.

She frowned and paused. "You make me nervous when you watch me," she answered truthfully.

She tried to avoid touching his knees and had to lean forward to continue cutting. Strands of black hair fell on his cheeks and he opened his eyes, brushing away the snipped hair at the same time she tried to. Their hands collided, and she might as well have brushed her fingers against a flame. Why did she always have this intense reaction to him?

Once again his dark eyes watched her.

"Here," he said, as she leaned forward to cut more strands of his hair.

His hands closed on her waist and he shifted, spreading his legs and moving her between them, so she stood closer. Her heart thudded. Now his face was almost touching her bosom. She stood between his thighs, his leg touching hers.

She knew he was watching her steadily and she stood too close to him to get her breath. He disturbed her as no man ever had. Beneath her drumming pulse and tingling skin was an urge to touch him and a desire for him to touch her.

She tried to hurry and cut his hair. Taking a deep breath, she slowed. "Close your eyes."

"Why? Do I disturb you, Savannah?" he asked. His voice had thickened and was husky. She wondered what ran through his thoughts. She knew she had an effect on him and she knew he wanted her.

"I'm unaccustomed to doing this, and it plagues me to have you stare."

"I like to watch you," he said quietly.

Her hands were on his head, holding strands of hair, combing it out with her fingers, but all she could think of was his watching her and how close she stood.

"Thank goodness your hair will grow back out," she said,

knowing she was chattering and probably not making good sense, but she was nervous. "It is a dreadful cut and still may look as if rats have gnawed on it. I've never cut a man's hair before."

"Have you ever stood between a man's legs before?" he asked.

She drew a deep breath and looked down at him. His dark gaze devoured her, slowly drifting down to her mouth, making her lips tingle.

Her pulse drumming, she stepped back. "Your hair is cut," she said, tossing down the knife and dropping the strands of black hair she held in her hand. She whirled to rush to the stream to get away from him. Her heart raced, and she could barely get her breath. His question rang in her ears in that husky voice, like a caress skimming over raw nerves.

Her hands shook and she was on fire, an inner burning no creek water could cool. She wanted him. Wanted him to pull her down to him, wanted to feel his mouth on hers, wanted more of his wild, breath-stopping kisses. *What is wrong with me?* "How can he do this to me?" she whispered to herself.

When she went back to join him, he was ready to swing into the saddle. She watched him mount up, looking at him with his hat pulled low, his black hair all but gone.

"There's no way to hide your heritage."

"True, but it isn't quite as plain. Also, no fiery-headed woman will be with me."

She studied him. "You will never escape notice," she finally decided.

"Perhaps. If I'm not back by nightfall, Savannah, you're on your own. I shall never forget you."

Flustered by his words, she bit her lip. "Nor I you," she whispered. She cocked her head to look at the bulging saddle-bags. "Are you riding into town with all the medicine? Shouldn't you leave it here? If they catch you with it, things will be worse for you."

He gave her a mocking smile and his eyebrow arched.

"Leave it with you and find you and the medicine gone when I return?"

"I can't get far on foot," she said, remembering midmorning. They had heard shooting and had to circle around a skirmish that could have been Federals against Confederates or could have been renegades attacking.

"I suspect, Savannah, you would find a way," he remarked dryly.

Over a year ago, Port Hudson had fallen to the Federals, splitting the Confederacy in two, weakening their hold in the west. Now Union forces were gaining all through Arkansas and Louisiana, fighting along the Missouri and Kansas borders.

Scoundrels raided, burning and looting. Bands of outlaw Rebels still fought their own way, and she knew it wasn't safe in any part of the south or southwest.

"You're making a mistake, taking all the medicines with you," she said darkly, knowing she would take everything and try to get away. She guessed she would have two hours' head start on him. Even on foot, she might elude him.

"You have enough of my gold left, I'm sure, to get me a bonnet and possibly a dress that's cooler to wear."

"If this town has been under siege, there won't be any dresses or bonnets. I'll do what I can. Wait for me."

He grinned and turned the horse, riding away along the beaten trail. She watched him ride out of sight and then, on impulse, followed him cautiously, trailing after him, hanging back so he wouldn't see her. She could hear the hoofbeats of the horse ahead and knew if he discovered her, he might tie her to a tree again. She had little to discover, but she was tired of being out in the wilds, away from towns and people. She could follow close to the edge of town, where she could see what was happening.

Over a mile later, she was tiring. The midday heat was muggy and stifling; trees and thick undergrowth crowded the path. It narrowed and twisted, and she listened carefully to his horse's steady hoofbeats, afraid Red Hawk would realize he was being followed and circle back.

Then the hoofbeats stopped. Pausing, she listened. Only the faint breeze and the whistle of birds disturbed the heavy silence.

Afraid he realized she was behind him, she moved deeper into the woods lining the road. Twigs cracked, and she stopped instantly and waited. Still nothing. Curious, she stepped back to the road and tiptoed forward.

With every nerve tingling, she crept along the road. At any moment she expected him to step out of the dark shadows. Ahead, something rustled.

She rushed along the road until she glimpsed him. He mounted up and rode on without a backward glance.

She waited until he was out of sight. Why had he stopped? To relieve himself? She moved to the road and hurried after him, looking at the place where he had stopped, seeing nothing except the usual brambles, brush, pines, and oaks. She turned to trail after him.

In minutes trees and brush thinned, and she saw she would have to stop following him or he would see her. He rode into the open, where there were no trees to hide her.

She looked at his straight back. Doing nothing but riding quietly into town, he would draw attention. There was something fierce and commanding about him that couldn't escape notice. Her gaze traveled down his back to his slim hips, the big pistol on his hip. Her gaze ran over his long legs, and then flew back up to the saddle.

Where were the saddlebags?

She remembered them bulging when he mounted up. If she was remembering correctly, they were gone. When he had stopped, had he hidden the saddlebags until he came back from town?

Eagerly, she rushed back the way she had come. Could she find where he had stopped? When she scanned the trees, every spot looked like the one next to it.

She should have paid more attention! If he had left the medicine, she could take it and have a head start on him. She was on foot and she no longer had her hoop skirt. Could she carry the heavy bags? Could she get to a town and get the medicine back to Vicksburg? She would have to try.

Searching the woods, she picked up her pace. She could take most of the bottles, enough to get some smuggled to Thomas. She could go to the nearest town where there were Confederates and find someone going to Vicksburg, someone to take the medicine back to the Brandletts and get it passed on to Thomas.

She knew Red Hawk had come out of the trees on the north side of the road. Trying to remember, she searched for any sign where he had walked. In a few more minutes she decided she had gone too far, so she turned around and went back.

In half an hour, she had gone back and forth several times. Now she was searching off the side of the road, pushing her way through thick brush. Discouraged, she slumped down, rubbing her temples in frustration. She picked up a stick and threw it and watched it hit a tree trunk and fall. Where it fell, she noticed something beneath some brush at the base of the tree. She stared at it, wondering if she was seeing merely part of the tree trunk or a log, but it looked like brown leather.

As excitement gripped her, she moved quickly, her discouragement vanishing. Shoving aside bushes, she let out a cry of joy. Instantly she clamped her hand over her mouth. There at her feet were the saddlebags, propped against the tree trunk.

The medicine! Triumph leapt in her and she knelt, her heart pounding. The bottles of medicine were hers again. She had to get away!

She still wore one petticoat and she ripped a large section from the skirt and laid it out, placing bottles on it and finally tying the corners together so she would have a knapsack. She rushed around, gathering any stones she could find to replace the bottles in the saddlebags, so they would still feel heavy when he picked them up. She shouldered her pack, knowing she couldn't possibly carry all of it and expect to escape from him on foot. As it was, it would take a miracle for her to do so with even part of the medicine.

As she hurried away from the place where he had hidden the medications, she decided to go on to Nacogdoches and try to find someone to take the medicine to Vicksburg. The sun was high overhead. They had been heading directly west from Vicksburg. She turned south and pushed through the trees, hurrying and wondering how soon he would return.

At every turn for the first hour, she expected to see Red Hawk loom up before her. She prayed she was heading south and every chance clear of trees, she tried to use the sun as a guide, heading southwest. She worried about encountering soldiers from either side or meeting one of the bands of renegades that roamed the countryside.

When she found a trail where grasses were worn and beaten down and wagon ruts showed clearly, she followed it south until another wider one crossed it, and she turned west.

The latter course seemed the wisest choice. For an instant as she looked at her surroundings, she paused. She was throwing away the safety of his company, his promise to help her whisk Adela from Horace Platt. Savannah squared her shoulders and hefted her burden.

By late afternoon, she paused beside a stream to wash. She had neared only one town, but, watching from a distance, she had seen the Federal uniforms, so she skirted the town and went on. She was famished, thirsty, and hot. The bottles of medicine had become a tiresome weight, and she feared she would have to abandon some, wishing she had left more behind for him to take to wounded men. Better that than simply leaving them in the wilderness.

Her feet ached and her head pounded. She slipped off her shoes and stepped into a creek. Mud oozed between her toes and swirled in the opaque brown stream, yet the cool water and mud felt so good, she didn't care.

She took a step deeper, pulling her foot from mud and feeling the suction tug on it. Brown water swirled around her and she knew she shouldn't go farther, yet it was mercifully cool.

Her stomach rumbled with hunger and she thought of the beef jerky and apples and crackers that Red Hawk had carried. Why hadn't she grabbed some provisions instead of taking only the medicine?

She waded out and walked toward a log. Her steps snapped twigs. Only feet away something moved swiftly, dislodging leaves and brush. A snake with a patterned back coiled in front of her.

Savannah's heart thudded, and she realized how defenseless she was, her feet and ankles bare. There was not so much as a rock to throw at it. She couldn't get her breath, but could only look into the flat black eyes. She gasped, trying to move, to run, to do something, but she was immobilized.

A knife sliced into the snake, pinning it to the ground.

CHAPTER EIGHT

Red Hawk jumped to the ground and finished the task, clubbing the snake and then slicing its head from its writhing body.

Instinct galvanized Savannah to action, and she ran toward the bay. Desperate to avoid Red Hawk's anger, she grasped the saddle, stepping up to place her foot into a stirrup. He yanked her back. When she struggled wildly, his arms tightened around her waist.

"I should have known not to trust you," he snarled, his breath warm on her temple as she fought him blindly. "And I should have been more careful." He grasped her shoulders and held her tightly. "Where are the bottles of medicine?"

Gasping for breath, she glanced at the knapsack.

His gaze followed hers. "I'll know better than to trust you again, Savannah Ravenwood."

She glared at him, her heart still pounding over the scare from the snake. "I should thank you for killing that snake."

He released her. "Fortunately you haven't been spotted by any soldiers. I encountered some when I was trailing you. What were you going to do with the medicine? You're going the wrong direction to get it to Tennessee."

"I can find someone in Nacogdoches to take it back to Vicksburg. People go back and forth."

"You might find someone and you might not. You know it'll get to wounded men with me."

"I swore I would do everything I could to see that Thomas got medicine. Let me go."

"No. I can use your help, and you need my help with your sister. If I let you go, I promise you, I'll keep the medications. Next time you're on your own. Don't wade in muddy creeks without a weapon." He nodded, his gaze fixed on something behind her.

She looked at the creek and saw another snake swimming toward the bank, ripples flowing out behind it in a long vee. Shivering, she turned back, glancing at the dead snake he was picking up. She shuddered. "What are you doing?"

"We can eat supper now."

"Snake? No, thank you!" She looked at the two horses standing nearby. "You have another horse."

"Yes. And more provisions and a bonnet and dress for you."

"A dress? You bought a dress for me?"

Her green eyes sparkled, and Red Hawk had to smile at her eagerness. He turned to get the dress out of a saddlebag. "I don't know how well it will fit—"

"It'll fit." She took it from his hands and shook it out. "It's beautiful! Thank you!" she cried, holding it up and smoothing it down over her waist. "Oh, thank you!" she exclaimed again and hugged him.

Instantly, his arm went around her waist. Her smile vanished as she looked up at him, and her cheeks flushed, her eyes darkening. She stepped away quickly, sounding subdued, but he always felt a swift, scalding tension when they touched or stood too close.

"Thank you for the present. I'm so glad to have something to change into." She glanced around, looking at the creek and frowning. "I'll wear it later," she said. "I couldn't bear to bathe and encounter another snake."

"I'll start skinning this one."

With a shudder, she turned away as he began to cut the snake. In minutes he had a fire going and chunks of snake roasting over it. The aroma was tempting. She was starving, and the thought of anything cooked made her stomach rumble and her mouth water in anticipation.

When she took a bite of snake, she closed her eyes and tried to forget what she was eating. He had brought a long loaf of bread with him and the food tasted delicious.

"The town was held by Federals. They have descriptions of us and have had a telegram about us."

"How did you learn all that?"

"I listen to people talking when I bought the other horse."

"Weren't you in danger?"

"They're looking for a couple. There were a lot of men in town who probably are drifting through because of the war."

"You must have spent all my gold."

"Not quite, Savannah. I had some of my own to spend."

She was frustrated that he had found her and, for once, she did not want to talk. After eating, they mounted up to ride, and he led the way. Twice during the day they had to hide because of soldiers passing them. The first group were Federals, the second Confederates. She wondered who held this part of Louisiana.

They halted at nightfall and ate. When they finished, he reached out to catch her wrist.

He held her firmly while he tied her wrist and then secured the other end of the rope to a nearby tree.

"Now, I can sleep without wondering whether I'll wake to find you gone, along with the horses and the medications. This way I won't have to worry about a knife in my heart."

She glared at him, but exhaustion had overtaken her. She hadn't really slept since she was on board the *General Thibodeaux.*

"We shall both sleep for a time," he said. He unrolled another blanket and spread it near her, then stretched out upon it. He placed his gun belt and pistol beside him, away from her, and pulled off his boots.

Moonlight spilled over them and he watched her untie the ribbon that held her hair. Fiery tresses cascaded over her shoulders. He rolled on his side to watch her, propping his head on his hand. She was only a few feet away. When she stretched out, she turned to look at him. Her eyes were wide, impossible to fathom in the dark shadows. He fought an impulse and lost, reaching out to pick up a lock of her hair.

"To take you as a wife, this Confederate lieutenant must be very strong-willed."

"Thomas? He's quiet and gentle—"

Red Hawk gave a disbelieving chuckle. "Then you will terrify him, Savannah. Will you tell him you shot a man who opposed you?"

"Yes, and I don't terrify Thomas. We are friends and have always been friends. We like the same things, the same music, the same books. We're of the same world."

"While I am an uncivilized savage and deserve to be shot."

"I didn't accuse you of that."

"Oh, yes, you have," he said. "You have beautiful hair, Savannah."

"Thank you," she whispered. He saw her eyes were closed, and studied her, suspecting she was asleep.

"Savannah?" he asked and received no answer. He reached out to stroke her cheek, feeling her smooth skin. When she didn't move, he guessed that she was in the deep sleep of exhaustion. He had been surprised she could go as long as she had. He had caught snatches of sleep in the saddle. Each time he had dozed, she had been talking. When he awakened, she had been still talking.

Her lashes were thick, feathery shadows on cheeks silky smooth. Longing engulfed him to move the few feet between them and pull her into his arms. How many times today had he had to fight that impulse? Now she rode on another horse, no longer pressed close against him.

She was a beautiful woman with spunk and grit. He had

been careless beyond measure today. She had followed him, and he hadn't noticed. He had underestimated her, thinking she would docilely wait while he rode into town. He should have known better.

She was easy to track. She had crushed plants as she moved through the brush; threads from her dress had caught on sharp twigs.

He envied Lieutenant Thomas Sievert. He was getting not only a beautiful, desirable, passionate woman, but a woman who was also brave and intelligent. This was no spoiled southern belle who expected the men around her to care for her and protect her. He had known such women, but Savannah was not one of them.

And even when he had found her today, she had still tried to escape, flinging herself at the horse. He sighed, remembering the snake and his own fear for her safety. When she stopped at the creek, he had been following her over an hour.

He had almost yelled to her when she waded into the muddy water to warn her that snakes were likely to be there. As she waded out, he had spotted the rattler and hadn't needed to hear the warning rattle to know her danger.

She still wore her blue poplin, but it was unbuttoned into a deep vee and now was pushed open, showing the beginning of the curve of her breasts.

He ached to reach out and push away the poplin and slide his hands over her full breasts.

Her breathing was even and deep. He let his hand drift over her shoulder lightly, then trailed his hand down her side to the narrow indentation of her waist. Red Hawk could remember exactly how slender she was when he had wrapped both his hands around her tiny waist.

He let his hand move slowly, lightly over her hip. She didn't shift or change in any manner. Her deep sleep made him bold and he continued his exploration, letting his hand trail down her leg. He was aroused, his body hot and aching. He rolled away and stood. Snakes be damned. He had to cool down.

He moved upstream and stripped, making noise to scare

away any snakes and splashing into the creek. In minutes he waded out, letting the night breezes dry his skin, still aroused, still wanting her.

He had been befuddled with her, thinking about her all the earlier ride into Bellefontaine, the small town on the banks of the winding Grayson River.

Looking at material in the general store, he asked about a dressmaker. The shop owner told him about a woman who sold dresses she acquired from others. Red Hawk had bought a green cotton with pink roses in the material. It was not new, and it had belonged to someone else, but he suspected Savannah would be glad to have a change from the blue dress. He'd found a bonnet for her and stood in the general store, listening to men around him talk. He went to a saloon to join in a card game, winning enough to make up for his purchases in town.

The Federals occupied the town and were making gains in Louisiana, Missouri, and farther west. Little Rock had fallen to them the year before. Red Hawk could see the end coming for the South, and he wanted out of the war.

In Bellefontaine, a few men looked at him with curiosity in their eyes, but most paid him no heed. He kept his hat on, suspecting his haircut would draw a lot of attention, since it was the first haircut Savannah had ever given a man. He thought about her standing between his legs, so close to him he could have leaned forward two more inches and buried his face in her full breasts.

He groaned. It was driving him beyond sanity to travel with her, and he would have been better off to let her go and keep part of the medicine. He swept his fingers through his short hair. It was already drying. He wouldn't have let her go alone. She wasn't safe, and it was fortunate she hadn't met with more mishaps than the rattler, although that could have been a disastrous one.

He had a suspicion she would have managed even the rattle-snake had he not been around.

He strode back to the blanket, knowing he should be as exhausted as Savannah. Yet every time he looked at her, all possibility of sleep fled, replaced by erotic images that taunted him and pulled him closer to a brink that would be disastrous for both of them.

He stretched out, looking up at the branches overhead, twinkling stars showing when limbs moved in the wind. He could catch a glimpse of the sky beyond. He tried to think about Matthew, about going back to the Comanche, about Caleb, about anything except the woman lying so near.

He slept, stirring only when the first graying of day came. He thought of Savannah immediately and turned on his side. His breath caught, desire flashing white hot in him. She lay dishevelled, her hair across her cheek and over her shoulders and arm and breasts. She was turned on her side facing him, and her skirts were pulled high.

White drawers should have come to her knees, but were pushed a few inches above them. Her legs and feet were bare.

He rolled to his feet and strode away to the creek again to try to wash and cool and forget her. When he returned, he called to wake her, instead of yielding to the impulse to haul her into his arms.

Barely listening to her morning chatter, he unfastened her wrist. She gathered her things and disappeared upstream. When she returned, she looked refreshed, and she wore the dress he had bought for her in Bellefontaine. She strode into view and he forgot everything else, staring at her. The green cotton was far lighter material than the poplin and clung to her, outlining clearly the curve of her hip and the length of her long legs.

The top was cut low, revealing the gentle rise of her breasts. Short puffed sleeves bared her long arms. She had braided her hair and looped and pinned it on her head. The blue poplin was folded in her hands.

She smiled. "I do thank you for this dress. It's much cooler. It's a nice fit for a dress that was not made for me. A little loose in the waist."

She turned in a circle so he could see, then smiled at him again.

"It's a very nice fit, Savannah," he said in a husky voice.

Something flickered in the depths of her green eyes and her cheeks flushed.

She stood as immobile as he, staring up at him, wide-eyed and solemn. He felt as if those green pools were pulling him down into places he shouldn't go.

She's pledged to another, he reminded himself. He turned abruptly and moved to the bay to mount up.

While they traveled, days were a constant watch for soldiers from either side. Nights were a torment for Red Hawk, who felt his control pushed to the limit.

Days later, when they reached Mansfield, they found the wounded had been moved farther south.

It was another night before they approached tents and the campsite for the injured men. Red Hawk braced himself for what he might find when he got there.

The tall blond doctor, Williamson, came striding toward him. His filthy coat, once white, now blood-drenched and stained, hung loosely from his thin shoulders and gaunt frame. "Quent, thank goodness!"

"I got medicine," Red Hawk said, dismounting and shaking the physician's hand. "This is Miss Ravenwood, who was instrumental in helping me get all this. Savannah, this is Doctor Abraham Williamson."

"How do you do," Savannah said, in a manner as gracious as if she had been meeting a guest at a drawing room tea.

Red Hawk unfastened the heavy saddlebags and handed them over. "Caleb?"

"You two are tough hombres. Go see for yourself." The physician pointed to a tent. Red Hawk was gone, and Savannah turned to trail behind him.

He reached the tent and saw Caleb on a chair outside. For a moment he held his breath as his gaze raked over his brother. When Red Hawk saw his brother still had two legs, he exhaled in relief and started running.

Caleb saw him coming and picked up crutches, trying to stand.

Savannah watched Red Hawk spring to a man who struggled to stand. The man's crutches fell as the two men hugged each other. The man with crutches was shorter and thinner than Red Hawk, but he had the same dark skin, the same dark eyes, the same slightly crooked nose, the same arrogant look, as if the world would do what he wanted. His long braid fell over his shoulder and hung halfway to his waist.

The two men moved apart and Red Hawk bent swiftly to pick up the crutches and hand them to his brother.

Embarrassment made her uncomfortable. A single woman shouldn't be traveling across country unchaperoned with a man, and she wondered if every man would decide she was a soiled dove picked up along the way.

"Savannah, meet my brother, Lieutenant Caleb Red Hawk. Caleb, this is Miss Ravenwood, who managed to whisk bottles of morphine and laudanum and other medicines away from the Bluebellies."

"Thank you, ma'am," Caleb said politely, grinning at her with fine white teeth that made him irresistible. She had to smile in return. "I can't tell you how much I thank you and how much every man here thanks you. Never did the South have anyone to smuggle medicine who looks half as pretty as you do."

"Thank you, Lieutenant. I have to admit, I had other purposes in mind for it, but I know it will go to good use here."

Caleb looked back and forth between the two and curiosity lit his brown eyes. "Get chairs, Quent, and come sit down. Or are the two of you hungry? Get some food and come back here."

"You're better," Red Hawk said, studying his brother.

"I began to mend. It wasn't my time to go. Doc can't explain it, but I've been using our grandmother's old remedy as a poultice. Thank the saints I didn't lose my leg. I wouldn't let him take it and he expected gangrene to set in. Instead"—he waved his hand—"here I am."

"Thank heavens. We'll get something to eat and come back."

Savannah went with Red Hawk, meeting soldiers, names swirling in her mind. They ate a meal that wasn't much better fare than Red Hawk had provided while they were crossing Louisiana. They had potatoes, cold biscuits, cold beef. Afterward, she sat in the night listening to the two brothers talk, Red Hawk's voice a deep rumble.

"I'm going to San Antonio, Caleb. I'm leaving and going to get Matthew."

"Don't blame you. If Celia had asked me and I'd said I would, I'd go now to get him. The Ashmans have had him almost a year now. That's too long."

"I plan to change that soon."

The longer the two men talked, Savannah knew Caleb grew more curious about her. His glances became more numerous and lingering. Finally a tent was offered to her. With relief she excused herself and left them.

That night she stretched on a cot and, for the first time since she had left the *General Thibodeaux*, she was alone.

In minutes she was asleep.

She woke to someone shaking her. "Savannah, wake up."

She opened her eyes to look at Red Hawk, who was bent close over her, speaking softly.

"Federals are headed this way. The men received word to break camp and retreat south. I'll go with them to help move the badly wounded, and then we'll turn west for Texas."

She sat up. "I'll be ready right away."

"There's a creek behind the camp. I'll accompany you and see that you're undisturbed by any of these soldiers, but you'll have to hurry."

She rose and they left, moving swiftly. As she walked through the camp, men were dark shadows outlined against a graying sky while they readied for travel. At the creek, Red Hawk turned back toward camp.

"No one will disturb you here. Join us when you can."

In less than an hour, they were on the move and Red Hawk

had mounted to ride beside her. "We'll go with them until they set up another camp. They can use my help."

She nodded, suspecting she could help as well.

They made slow progress, and her heart ached for the injured men, who had to be transported over rough terrain. The sun was high in the sky when they finally stopped to set up another camp.

While Red Hawk worked with other soldiers setting up tents and moving the wounded inside, she tried to get water and talk to the injured.

A blond boy, his chest swathed in bandages, watched her move among the beds. When she came close to him, his wide blue eyes were steadfastly on her.

"Ma'am, are you real or part of my imagination?"

"I'm very real," she said, taking her hand in his.

"Oh, ma'am. I ain't seen a pretty lady in so long, I can't remember. You're the prettiest lady I've ever seen."

She smiled. "Thank you. Want me to bring you water?"

"Yes'm."

She retrieved a cup of cold water and bent down to hold it to his mouth, waiting patiently while he sipped. "Thank you, ma'am. Aren't you far from home?"

"Very far."

"So am I. What's your name?"

"Savannah Ravenwood."

"Miss Ravenwood, I'm Theodore."

She was aware of someone moving near her and glanced around to find Red Hawk watching her.

"Theodore, I'm glad to meet you. You get well now and get home, you hear?"

"Yes, ma'am."

She turned away and replaced the cup by the metal bucket.

"We can ride now. Your things are packed and ready. I told Caleb good-bye," Red Hawk said.

She nodded and followed him to their horses. They mounted up. As they rode away, she glanced over her shoulder at the encampment. "I hate this war!" she said, hurting for all the injured men she had just talked to.

"I don't think the South can hold out much longer. They're losing everywhere now, and they don't have the men or the supplies to keep fighting. From what I've seen, I don't know how they'll make it through the winter."

"That's what I heard when I was up north."

"We're not in safe territory here. When we cross into Texas, it'll be safer."

The sun was hot on her shoulders and they rode hard the rest of the day, crossing into Texas, but they wouldn't reach Nacogdoches until the middle of the following day. The setting sun sent pink rays shooting high through white clouds when they slowed to look at a town less than a mile away.

"Get out that bonnet and cover your hair. We should be out of Union-held towns now, and we can stay in a hotel tonight if there is one. If there isn't, we can at least find somewhere to get a hot meal."

"I won't argue with that—unless we ride into town and it is held by the Union."

"We'll watch," he said, halting on a slight rise and studying the town in the distance. She saw people on the main street, but no uniforms, blue or gray. The thought of a cooked meal made her mouth water. "I'm so hungry I could eat most anything. That horrible snake even sounds delicious right now."

He laughed softly and glanced down at her with a sparkle in his eyes. "I'll remember that if we don't go into town."

She gazed up at him, thinking even the hint of amusement in his expression softened his harsh features.

After another quarter hour of watching, during which she had dismounted and stretched out beneath a tree, he straightened in the saddle. "Get that bonnet. I don't see any soldiers."

She came to her feet, brushing twigs and grass off her dress. She looped her long braid of hair, winding it around her head and pinning it. Then she put the bonnet on and looked up at him.

"If we had a veil to hide your face, it would help."

"No one will have that good a description of me."

"Savannah, no man who looks at you can forget you," he said. Before she could thank him for the compliment, he continued, "But we can't put a veil over your face. Just be the timid wife and keep your eyes down and let me do the talking. Do you think that's possible, Savannah?"

"Of course!" she snapped, wondering if he must think she prattled on endlessly.

He dismounted and opened a bag, withdrawing a large, worn rag doll. He handed it to her.

"What in heaven's name are you doing with a doll?"

He pulled out small blankets and gave them to her. "We're spending this night in a hotel, if there is one, and not out on the ground. They're looking for a half-breed and a redheaded woman. Your hair doesn't show. They won't be looking for a family. Wrap that doll up and carry it like a sleeping baby and no one will know the difference."

He removed his hat, uncapped the canteen to take a long drink, and then poured water over his head. Carefully, he combed his hair with his fingers so it was slicked down, then placed his hat on again.

"Do I look white?"

She laughed and he smiled in return, touching the corner of her mouth. "You don't laugh enough, Savannah."

"I can't recall seeing you laugh once," she replied, wondering if he ever did and what it took to really amuse him. She couldn't imagine him doing anything frivolous.

"War doesn't engender laughter. Shall we go? Anything happens, we'll split up and you ride for Nacogdoches. I'll try to lead anyone after us away from you."

She nodded as she wrapped the doll in the blankets, thinking it was ridiculous, but there was little more she could offer. A wooden sign proclaimed they were entering Cheraw, Texas.

They rode into town, Savannah holding the doll in her arms and occasionally casting a glimpse at her surroundings.

"A hotel," Red Hawk said with satisfaction, and they stopped at a hitching rail, where he tethered the horses. He carefully helped her from her horse while she clutched the doll. His arm circled her waist protectively as they stepped onto the boardwalk and crossed to the single-story wooden hotel.

"Evening," Red Hawk greeted men seated on a bench. One whittled on a stick. Savannah merely nodded at them and then looked at the doll's face, twiddling the blankets as if she were checking on a baby.

Red Hawk led her to the desk. "Solano," he said in a commanding voice, and she shot a quizzical look at him. "Johnny Solano is my name. I want a room for me and my family. One on the south."

"Yes, sir," the clerk said.

Shocked, Savannah stared at Red Hawk, who stood with his hands on his hips, an arrogant look about him as if he owned the hotel. The clerk must have had the same impression, because he scurried around to get them a key.

"The same room?" she whispered, leaning close to Red Hawk and standing on tiptoe.

He gave her a sardonic look with an arch of his brow and a pointed glance at the doll in her arms. "I would hardly put my wife and child in another room."

"And you look as much Italian as I look Spanish!"

"We wouldn't be allowed to stay here if he knew I had a drop of Indian blood."

"We can't stay in one room!"

"We can't stay in two. It would cause too much speculation and cost twice as much. Calm down, Savannah. I won't ravish you. If I intended that, I would have done so long before now."

Then the clerk was back to place the register in front of Red Hawk for his signature.

He scrawled *Mr. and Mrs. Johnny Solano* on the register in bold writing and paid the clerk in gold.

She looked at the fictitious name and her pulse drummed. She had been sleeping each night on a blanket only yards from Red Hawk, but to share a hotel room with him was another matter. It put them back into an ordinary setting, a place where she would never share a room with him. She looked up at him to find him watching her. The clerk handed him a key.

"Where can I find a place to eat?"

"There are two places. Mrs. Johnson's boardinghouse will take people from the hotel, and there's the Sunshine Cafe just next door." The clerk came around the counter. "Do you have bags for me to carry? I'll show you to your room."

"We'll get our things later," Red Hawk said.

The clerk nodded and led the way to a large room in the southeast corner of the hotel. He opened the south windows and let in the evening breeze. Savannah moved around the four-poster bed that seemed to overwhelm her.

How could they share a room? He had said he was sleeping in the bed. She looked at the bed again. It was covered in a red and blue quilt. The puffed pillows were an invitation. Her bunk on the *General Thibodeaux* had been none too comfortable, and she had gone all across Louisiana without sleeping in comfort. But it would never be easy to sleep with Red Hawk only inches from her in the same bed. At the thought, she could feel her face flush. She looked at the straight-backed chairs in the room and clamped her jaw closed. She couldn't sleep in one of those.

"Bring a tub and bathwater," Red Hawk ordered, dropping more coins into the clerk's hand.

"Yes, sir," he said.

The moment the door closed, Savannah whirled to face Red Hawk. "We can't share this room. Besides, you're going to bathe."

"We've been all but sharing a blanket for nine nights now. I'll stay on one side, but I haven't slept in a bed for eight long months. I haven't had a real bath in a tub for almost that long. You can leave the room, close your eyes, share the bath with me, or whatever you'd like, Savannah, but for months I've dreamed about a bed and a real bath."

He pulled his shirt off. The bandage around his arm was no longer blood soaked. She was relieved to see that he was finally mending, but her thoughts jumped back to all he had just told her.

"I'm not sharing any bath!" she snapped, glaring at him.

"Do what you want. I told you what I'm doing."

"I'm going down to the lobby." She strode across the room. "When you're through bathing—"

He caught her before she reached the door, his fingers closing on her upper arm and jerking her around.

CHAPTER NINE

"No, you'll not go sit in the lobby where someone might spot you. They've telegraphed our descriptions to lawmen all over this part of the country."

"I'm not watching you strip naked and bathe!" She thought amusement flickered in the depths of his dark eyes, only adding to her fury.

"You can turn your back while I bathe."

"It's indecent!"

"Savannah, you tossed aside all the rules when you stole medicine from the Federals. Now you can watch me strip naked and bathe or you can turn your back, but you aren't leaving this room." As they glared at each other, there was a soft rap on the door.

"Get your baby, my dear," he ordered dryly.

Furious with his high-handed manner, she jerked free and crossed the room to pick up the doll. It was simple and had seen use. Its face was smudged, the collar of its pink dress was ripped, its yellow yarn hair tangled. She tucked the blanket around it and wondered what little girl had to give it up and why. She thought of her own doll and the one Adela had

with their fine bisque heads and fancy lace dresses. When she
married, Adela had taken her doll with her.

Holding the doll in her arms, Savannah moved away to the
window to look outside on a yard filled with spring flowers.
A tall mock orange bush bloomed beside one window, a shower
of white petals strewn on the ground, its sweet scent filling the
air. She glanced around as two men brought a tub into the
room.

Red Hawk stood bare-chested, his back to her, his hands on
his hips as he gave directions where to set the tub. Most of the
cuts and welts from the beating he'd had as a prisoner had
healed and were fading.

As her gaze raked over his muscled back, her pulse raced.
He reached out to move a small table out of their way, and she
watched the ripple of muscles across his shoulders. Her mouth
had gone dry and she knew she should stop staring, but she
was mesmerized by him.

He glanced over his shoulder and caught her looking at him.
She whirled around, aware that he had seen the flush that rose
in her cheeks and burned like hot sunshine. The men were
talking and, after a few minutes, she glanced back at them.

The tin tub was large, and suddenly she wanted a bath desperately. All the grime from travel grated against her skin. She
longed for a real bath instead of a dip in a creek or, worse, a
muddy stream.

She watched as the clerks poured four buckets of water into
the tub in a silvery arc. Water splashed and made her even
more aware of the heat, the dust she was coated with, her dress
clinging to her.

Telling Red Hawk they would return with more water, the
clerks left. Towels were on the chair.

He looked around at her. "Would you like to bathe first,
Savannah?"

She wanted to fling a *no* at him and keep an invisible wall
of anger between them, but her gaze went again to the tub that
held clean, clear water. She looked at the soap and the thick
towels and licked her lips.

He laughed. "Give in. You're almost green with longing. I'll give you the privacy you need. I'll stay as far away from you as the room allows, and I'll keep my back turned."

"Yes, I want to bathe," she said.

After knocking, the men entered with more buckets, this time filled with steaming water. They poured the water into the tub and turned to go. Red Hawk followed them to the door and talked to them at length while she waited impatiently, longing to get into the water.

Finally he closed the door and locked it, turning to her. "I ordered supper from the cafe next door and they'll bring it here in an hour. That should give us long enough to enjoy our leisurely bath."

"If you think—"

He grinned and her heart missed a beat. He had teeth as white as the morning clouds. Against his dark skin, they were a startling contrast. When he smiled, his features changed, transforming into a heart-stopping handsomeness.

"I'll turn my back." He made a swooping bow. "It's all yours, Savannah. Do you need help with buttons?"

"No!" she snapped, seeing his dancing eyes and knowing he was teasing her. He moved past her to the window and stood with his back to the tub while he gazed outside.

"You promise to keep your back to me?"

"I promise."

She tossed the doll on the bed and rushed to the tub, her fingers already fumbling with her buttons. In minutes, she stepped out of her dress, glanced over her shoulder at him, then shed the rest of her clothing and sank into the tub. While she unfastened her braids, she sat with her knees bent.

"Want me to wash your back?"

She twisted around to see him seated on the edge of the bed, his back to her while he gazed out the window. "No, I do not want you to wash my back!"

She knew he was teasing, but his question still disturbed her and made her pulse skip erratically. She sank down beneath the water, got her hair wet, and then rubbed in soap, luxuriating in the cool water and the soap lathering her hair.

Red Hawk sat staring out the window, but saw nothing except Savannah. He remembered her naked in the creek; he imagined her now, seated in the tub only half a room away from him. He could hear her humming and splashing. He glanced over his shoulder. She sat with her back to him. The tub was at a slight angle, but for her to see him, she would have to look over her shoulder. He was willing to risk her anger if he was caught watching her. It wasn't a promise he had intended to keep.

Her pale shoulders were wet and glistening. She had unbraided her hair and it was dark, wet, clinging to her head. She had one leg in the air as she soaped her foot, and his body tightened and grew heavy. Heat flashed through him. He wished now he had never ordered the damned bath. The walls of the room seemed to close in, and he was no longer on a creek bank where he could stride away and get far from her and temptation or where danger was a distraction. They were safe, locked together in a small space, and every sound she made was a siren song, every glimpse of her a torment.

She raised her arms to wash her leg and he could see the slight curve of her breast. Water came high and white soapy bubbles covered the surface, making it impossible to see beneath the water.

He turned to the window without seeing anything outside. The world had vanished. The only sound he heard was Savannah's soft humming. His only vision was mental, the image indelibly etched in his mind of a slender white leg extended in the air, her dainty foot and trim ankle splashed with soapy water.

He groaned softly, clenching his fists, feeling as if he should climb through the window and move around outside to get his thoughts on something else. Sweat beaded his brow, and he felt as if the temperature in the small room had soared.

When he heard loud splashes, he turned to look at her. She stood up, reaching for a towel, and glanced at him. With a shriek, she dropped back down into the tub. "You promised me!"

His pulse roared and her words were dim in his ears. He didn't give a damn about them as his gaze roamed over her.

With deliberation, he crossed the room to her and her green eyes widened endlessly, great pools that drew him and challenged him and questioned him.

He couldn't speak. His tongue thickened, his throat closed. Breathing was difficult, and his roaring pulse shut out all other sounds. He moved as if he no longer had control of himself.

The space between them closed down, and all he could see were her great, luminous eyes. Her body was a pale blur, but he knew too well she was wet, naked, and sweet-smelling.

Rosy flesh. Pink nipples. Thick red curls at the juncture of her thighs. Curves. Desirable woman. *Savannah.*

He didn't stop when he reached the tub, but bent down, sliding his hands beneath her arms and lifting her out of the water.

"No!" she whispered, a faint protest, her hands going in front of her to cover herself as he finally tore his gaze from her eyes. One hand spread ineffectively in front of lush, upthrusting breasts, the other hand lower. His gaze went to her mouth. Her lips parted and there were no more protests. He pulled her against him.

She was wet, warm, soft. *Naked.* He lowered his head, his mouth covering hers.

Savannah thought she would faint with pleasure as his arms tightened around her and his mouth took hers. His tongue thrust over hers and then stroked hers in a shocking, repetitious motion that reminded her of intimacy. His denim pants were coarse against her thighs, his belt buckle cold metal against her middle, but his chest was warm, solid. His arousal pressed against her belly.

Savannah knew she had to stop him now, but she was melting in his arms, aware of his hard length, his thick shaft, his arms like iron bands holding her, this strong, warm male whose desire for her was consuming.

Never had a man looked at her as he had. Never had a man kissed her as he was kissing her. Never had a man made her heart race and her knees turn to butter.

His hand slid down her back and over her buttocks, and reason and reality returned with the shock of his touch.

"No! You promised me!" she gasped, twisting her face from him and struggling. She broke free and yanked up a towel, but not before his scalding gaze raked over her naked body again.

"If I had a pistol I would put another shot in you right now!" She shook with fury, angry with herself for succumbing; worse, more than succumbing—for shamelessly responding and returning his kisses. "You promised me you wouldn't even look!"

He turned away and went to the door and then looked back at her. Glaring at him, wrapped in the towel, she was shaking, aware of him, of every touch, of their kisses that seared and melted and bound part of her heart to him.

"I'll be back when you're dressed," he said in a rough, husky voice. He was still fully aroused; his clothes were soaked from her wet body. He unlocked the door and left, locking it from the other side.

She closed her eyes. Her mouth still tingled, her body ached, and she had longings she had never known. Her breasts were tight, an aching in them. Memories were a stormy torment, and she would always remember the desire in his eyes as he crossed the room to her. She could never imagine being looked at in such a manner again, as if his very life depended on reaching her. As if he wanted to devour her.

And she wanted him to. That's what frightened and shamed her and made her conscience ache. She was betrothed to Thomas, who was on a battlefield in Tennessee while she was naked in another man's arms. A man to whom she meant nothing.

Why did she all but melt into a puddle when Red Hawk touched her? Worse, when he kissed her, she returned it eagerly, in a manner that plainly told him what she wanted.

She did want him. Desperately, shockingly.

Stunned by the intensity of her reaction to him, she couldn't move. *Am I falling in love with him, with all his strength and wildness?* She trembled, wanting him, knowing she shouldn't. Closing her eyes, she relived every second of the past moments in his arms.

With shaking hands, she dressed hurriedly. She looked at the bed. How could they share this room tonight? How could she continue saying no? How could she do anything except say no?

If anyone knew that she had traveled with him, her reputation would be shattered forever. Never could she explain her actions to Thomas—Thomas, who was every inch a gentleman and believed in all the conventions of polite society. He would never understand such a breach of propriety.

She tried to think about Thomas, but it was becoming more difficult to conjure up anything except dim memories.

She brushed her hair and then washed the green and pink dress and wrung it out. She washed one of the doll blankets. Gathering them up, she heard the key turn in the lock.

Red Hawk stepped inside, his dark brows drawn together in a frown.

"I'll wait in the yard while you bathe," she said, her pulse jumping at the sight of him, in spite of all her self-lecturing and resolutions.

He merely nodded, and she noticed a muscle working in his jaw. His gaze dropped to the wet dress and blanket in her hand. "The doll blanket?"

"I thought it would seem more like a real baby. They always have things to wash." Too conscious of his unsettling gaze on her, she hurried past him and went outside.

The sun had dropped below the horizon and dusk was deepening. She hung the clothes on a line strung between two thick oaks, then sat on a wooden bench. The breeze was cool, but her thoughts were hot and stormy, still on the incident between them.

It was dark when the door opened and he stepped outside. He crossed the yard to her. "Our supper is here."

She stood and he slipped his arm across her shoulders.

Startled she looked up at him.

"We're Mr. and Mrs. Solano, remember? The clerk was in the hallway when I came outside. I told him the baby was sleeping."

The moment he touched her, every nerve came alive. He smelled of soap, and he wore a fresh black cotton shirt.

When they went inside, the hall was empty and she hurried to their room. Red Hawk locked the door behind him. Savannah barely noticed. Her attention was on the food spread on a small table. Steam rose from pieces of golden fried chicken. A blue crystal bowl held collard greens. On a plate beside it were pieces of golden cornbread. Another glass bowl held thick hominy grits. He had drawn two straight-backed chairs up to the table, and she hurried to sit down.

"Fried chicken! This is a feast."

"It looks that way after days of cold biscuits and jerky and snake."

She smiled and then was caught in his dark gaze. For a moment food was forgotten. With his black shirt and pants, he looked darker, more dangerous than ever.

He waved his hand, but his eyes never left hers. "Shall we, Savannah?"

She drew a deep breath and looked away, clenching her fingers and telling herself to stop reacting to him, but his eyes were mesmerizing. When they locked gazes, the sparks dancing in the air between them were magic. Black magic, she thought darkly. She was engaged to Thomas Sievert, and if she lost her heart to the wild man seated across from her, he would take it as his people took scalps.

The tempting smell of the fried chicken made her mouth water and she served herself. "I'm starved."

"No more than I am. I haven't seen food like this in more than eight months."

She wondered what kind of hardships he had been through in the past year. She placed some grits on her plate and returned the serving spoon to the bowl.

"We've been fortunate to not have suffered so badly from the war in Texas. Not like people in Vicksburg," she commented. "There hasn't been flour, though, so there have been no biscuits. I heard conditions were dreadful in Vicksburg."

She bit into thick, golden chicken covered in a crisp crust and closed her eyes to chew. Red Hawk lowered his glass of water and watched her, remembering her kisses, her wet, warm body in his arms, and her response that set him aflame.

For breathtaking moments she had responded to him, kissed him in return and stood in his arms, her naked body pressing tightly against him.

He watched as her tongue came out to catch a tiny speck of chicken on her full lower lip. He drew a deep breath, all food forgotten.

"Damn," he said quietly.

"What on earth is wrong?" she asked. "This is the best food I've ever eaten, I'm sure."

"It's good, Savannah," he said evenly, avoiding looking at her. He stood and retrieved the bottle of brandy he had purchased and started to pour her some. She waved her hand.

"Good heavens, no! The last time you did that, I got quite foxed and shot you. Never ever again."

"You won't shoot me, and it'll be good with your dinner."

"I don't think I dare. I need my wits about me."

He sat facing her and took a long sip of brandy, lowering the glass while he studied her. "Why do you need your wits about you?" he asked, his curiosity rampant.

She looked at him with wide, guileless green eyes. Then they changed, and he could swear there were golden pools in their depths. The change was the seductive look she got when he kissed her.

"You're a challenge, Captain Quentin Red Hawk, and I need to keep my wits around you. You don't keep promises and I can't trust you one bit."

"I'm a challenge?" His pulse raced. "And *trust?* You shot me, Savannah. You stole the medicine and ran away the first chance you had. You lied to me about your father and your family living in Vicksburg.''

She raised her chin, taking a dainty bite of cornbread. Then she closed her eyes and made a sound deep in her throat that made him think of passion.

''Ummm. I'm not going to argue with you right now. I'm going to enjoy this supper to the last scrumptious bite. This has to be the most delicious food ever cooked.''

He buttered yellow cornbread, spread thick red strawberry jam on it, and held it to her mouth. ''Here, try this, Savannah.''

She leaned forward, taking the bite. His fingers brushed her lips only the slightest, but he was aroused and wanting to shove aside the food and take her in his arms again.

He knew he should resist touching her. She was as forbidden to him as a married woman. She was engaged to a man away at war and he would not take another man's woman. And she would never love him. Every breath she spoke about Indians was with either fear or contempt, yet he could hardly eat for watching her. She was enjoying every bite in the most sensual manner, taking her time and savoring each morsel.

He tried to concentrate on his food, to forget her, but she kept a conversation going that made it impossible to ignore her.

''How did you expect to get your sister away from her husband?'' he asked bluntly, interrupting her chatter about her favorite foods.

''Adela? I'll go visit her and when Horace is at work, we'll leave on a stage for San Antonio.''

''Don't you think her husband will know what you did and go after the stage and bring her right back home?''

Savannah frowned. ''I've worried about that and am counting on the stage leaving in the morning and Mr. Platt not realizing she's gone until the evening when he returns from work.''

''I think it would be better, Savannah, to get one more horse and go our own route and forget the stage.''

''That will be good.'' She thought it over as she took another bite of chicken. ''He doesn't know about you. I can stay with them as their guest. You stay elsewhere. When we get an opportunity, we'll all leave town.''

"I'll purchase another horse in Nacogdoches. We can stop at the nearest town this side of Nacogdoches and put you on a stage there. This Platt will think you have come from Vicksburg by stage.''

"That's much better for my reputation anyway.''

He gave a dry laugh. "Savannah, if it mattered, your reputation would be in shambles, but it's wartime and nothing is the same. Standards don't apply that did before. You've traveled all over the countryside smuggling stolen goods, either alone or with me. I don't think you need to concern yourself with reputation. And who really knows what you're doing? Not that fiancé doctoring the wounded in Tennessee. Is he a jealous man?''

"Thomas? Heavens, no! My goodness, whole years have gone by without us seeing each other. Or even writing.''

"This doesn't sound like a great love,'' Red Hawk said quietly, leaning forward to reach behind her head and untie the ribbon that held her hair. It swung free behind her shoulders. "I like your hair better this way.''

"It's not an acceptable way for a woman to look in society.''

"Right now, there's no one to see except me, and I prefer it.''

She drank her glass of water and ate more chicken. "This is the best meal I've ever eaten. I didn't think food could be so good. We've had cooks, but they've seldom been great cooks.''

He wondered if Savannah herself had ever had to cook or do any type of work. Most women in her station in life did not, but the daughter of a military man who lived on military posts might not have servants on all occasions.

"Was it a dreadful change for you to leave your father's people?''

"Yes. We were treated worse than beggars at Fort Belknap, almost as if we weren't humans. Then my mother married and life became easy.''

"How can you possibly want to leave that life for one of hardship and danger?"

"I don't see the Comanche way as hardship and danger. It's freedom at its best—the best of life and nature."

He sipped the golden brandy, the crystal looking fragile in his big hand, and she wondered about him. He was commanding, tough, and fearless. "Have you ever been in love?"

His brown eyes settled on her. "I think the war eliminated chances for that."

"Your Matthew should have a mother."

"He'll have a lot of mothers when I get him back with the Comanche. They're good to children."

"I don't see how you can turn your back on the life you know the best."

He pushed back his chair and stretched out his long legs, leaning back and looking relaxed, yet she was always aware of how quickly he could move and his great strength.

"I'll have to go back to it someday. I don't expect the frontier to last, but it has years yet. Maybe my lifetime. I hope so."

"You sound so certain."

He stood and took her hand, his fingers warm around hers. "We'll sit by the window where there's a breeze." He carried the chairs to the window and put out the lamps, leaving the room washed in moonlight.

"I am certain, Savannah. Why was your father out west?"

"To protect settlers."

"Right, and settlers will keep expanding west. I've seen the weapons the white man has. They're powerful. My people don't have those weapons. They don't have the factories or the steel. No, they won't be able to stop the white man when he turns his full attention west."

"How can you go back when you've become civilized?"

He gripped her shoulders, leaning close to look at her, and her pulse jumped. "My people are civilized. As much as yours. I've seen more killing by the white man than I ever saw by the Comanche."

"Whatever life you've had, you're no gentleman," she said, giving her shoulders a little shake, but his fingers only tightened.

"No, I'm not a gentleman and I don't have to observe foolish rules, but you're not much of a lady at times yourself, Savannah."

She was glad he couldn't see her blush.

"It'll be easier to get Adela if you're with me, although I'm not certain I can help you get your nephew."

"I think they'll listen to you and respect you. You're one of them. I'm not," he said, releasing her and leaning back in his chair. He propped his booted feet on the window ledge, resting his hands on his thighs. "Have you thought about what happens when you get your sister home to Mason? Won't her husband come get her and take her back home?"

Savannah ran her fingers across her brow. "I've been worrying about it. For a time, I think Adela may have to stay in San Antonio where Mr. Platt can't find her. Adela has never lived alone, and I'm not certain she can take care of herself."

"Then you're not alike at all. I can't imagine circumstances where you can't take care of yourself."

"I don't know whether I should say thank you or not. I don't think that's a very good description of a lady."

His white teeth flashed in a grin. "It isn't, by your great southern standards of what a lady is."

"Now I know I shouldn't thank you," she said, annoyed by his remarks.

"Don't you think Platt will look for her in San Antonio if he can't find her in Mason? It's the logical place and the closest large town."

"If he comes to Mason, I'll tell him Adela has gone up north to our relative in Cairo."

"Then he'll go see them."

"And that will take him quite a bit of time. His business is all important. I don't think he'll leave it that long." She raised her chin and determination filled her. "Whatever happens, I won't let him take her back home with him again. Adela is the sweetest, most gentle person on this earth and to think of that monster beating her—'' She broke off as tears threatened. She hated to cry and knew Red Hawk would see it as womanly weakness, but the thought of her sister being treated so cruelly was overwhelming. She wished she had been able to get to Adela sooner.

Red Hawk reached out and wiped away a tear on her cheek with his thumb. His skin was rough and warm. She was embarrassed, but unable to stop the emotion.

"We'll get her away from him. A man should never beat his wife."

"I'm surprised you feel that way," she said, remembering the ferry captain.

"Because I'm a savage," he remarked sharply, and she was remorseful.

"You're a forceful man and one who is determined to have your own way."

"We're a match there, Savannah. You've just described yourself, except for the male reference."

"If I have seemed willful, it is simply a desperate attempt to keep what was mine and what soldiers needed so badly."

He chuckled. "What was *yours,* Savannah, was actually medicine belonging to the United States Army. The description fits you no matter how you try to excuse it."

"Why did you get into this war? Your parents weren't living, from what you said."

"My stepfather felt strongly about the South. He was from Georgia. And I despised the Federals for taking Caleb, Celia, and me from our people. I was young and brash and didn't know what it would really be like, this killing and hurting of so many people, both soldiers and civilians."

Savannah listened to him talk about his first battle. His voice was quiet and deep and she was transported to the Shiloh battlefield.

"We're fortunate Texas hasn't been torn apart by the war."

"Texas will have another war when this one is over. A war on the frontier with my people."

"And you'll go on fighting and fighting. You could settle

in San Antonio and go into the business your stepfather was in. You have an education.''

He shook his head. ''I'll never be a merchant. He had a large store which we sold after his death. I have to go back to my people, to live that life at least for a time. And I want Matthew to know it. The white man's way can never be as good.'' He studied her, touching her collar. ''How will you and Adela survive, Savannah—at least until you marry your doctor?''

''My father was military, so there is a pension that Adela and I can live on quite easily. And Thomas will let Adela live with us, I'm certain. He is very kindhearted and generous.''

''He sounds like a paragon of virtue.''

''Thomas is. He is tall and blond and quite handsome.''

''Savannah, I'd as soon hear about something else than the wonderful Thomas.''

''Now why in the world would you tire of hearing about Thomas?''

''I suppose few men are fascinated with descriptions of other men,'' he answered dryly. They were silent for a few moments and then he glanced at her. ''We should make plans. If possible tomorrow, you'll go by stage to Nacogdoches. Then tomorrow night, after they've had time to go to sleep, I'll come to the Platt house about midnight. Can you give me some sign so I'll know which room is yours?''

''Yes,'' she said, mulling over the possibilities. ''I can place my hat in the window. I'll watch for you. I'm certain they'll retire early, because Adela wrote that Mr. Platt goes to the lumber yard before dawn most mornings.

''Fine. If anything happens and you can't signal, I shall still come to the house each night. If you can't signal the first night, surely you can the second.''

She nodded, thinking about trying to whisk Adela away from Horace Platt. With Red Hawk to help them, it seemed a simple task.

''I must warn you,'' she said, ''Horace Platt is a giant of a man. He is as tall as you, thicker through the middle, and Adela says he is incredibly strong. I have to get her away from him, but he will be formidable if he catches us."

"I'm not worried about that," Red Hawk answered quietly, and she was certain he meant what he said.

"My sister is the most beautiful woman in the entire country."

"She would have to be very pretty if she's prettier than you, Savannah."

"Thank you," she said, suddenly intensely aware of him and the compliment that shocked her. Few men told her she was pretty. Every man in Mason had known she was betrothed to Thomas, so perhaps that had kept them all at a distance and from saying such a thing. She had thought she looked attractive enough, but she knew she was no beauty like her sister.

Red Hawk's compliment, spoken in his deep voice, stirred her deeply. *He thinks I'm pretty.* Pleasure was sweet, yet she wondered how easily such words came from him. But then, he was not talkative, and she couldn't imagine glib words falling from his tongue.

"Adela has beautiful pale skin that is perfect. Her hair is golden blond and her eyes are wide and blue. You'll see for yourself. Men are always noticing her and are taken with her—or they were until she wed Horace Platt. Now I'm certain none dare look more than a second at her. She is taller than I am and has a soft, sweet voice. Almost from the first Horace Platt wanted her for a wife."

"I'm surprised he didn't want you."

"Oh, no! He thought I was dreadfully forceful for a woman. I suppose I must admit that the steamboat captain has not been the only man who thought I should be physically reprimanded. Yet I think those men are monsters. Horace Platt urged my father to teach me submission and a woman's place in order to marry me off. He told Papa that I needed a very strong-willed man who would teach me how to behave. I found him most loathsome."

"I'm sure you did," Red Hawk replied. "And I'm thankful that your father didn't decide you would wed this Platt fellow."

"Mr. Platt would not have had me, thank heavens."

"Yet your Thomas Sievert is gentle and kind. So he can put up with a forceful woman?"

"I don't think Thomas sees me as a forceful woman."

"Then he doesn't really know you," Red Hawk replied, annoying her.

"I have repeatedly said I needed to be that way with you because of the circumstances."

"Perhaps," he said lightly. "Tell me about you and Adela. Did you grow up in Mason?"

"Oh, no! My father was in the military, so I have lived all over the States. I was born in Georgia, and then we were up north when I was a small child." As she talked, she was aware of Red Hawk seated so close to her. Once he reached out to touch her collar; later he picked up locks of her hair, and while she talked about her grandmother, she was aware of tugs against her scalp as he turned the locks in his hands. Every little touch was fiery and made her want him to keep touching her.

The moon moved across the sky and shadows shifted as they talked. She found him fascinating. His early life was exotic and beyond her imagination. He told her about Comanche ways, how they were nomadic people who preferred to camp near streams.

"Before breaking camp, a crier rides through the camp to pass the word that the next day we will move. The women pack and get ready. The first ones to go get the choice spots at the next site. The women set up camp and the tipis. The tipis have twenty-two poles when completely set up. Buffalo skins are the covering and thongs of buffalo hide are used to lash the poles together."

"What do the men do?" she asked, aware of him in the darkness, filled with memories of this afternoon when she had bathed. Her nerves were raw, her body clamoring for his touch. She had her fingers laced together in her lap to keep from reaching for him, though she desperately wanted to touch him.

"Hunt. Provide food. Practice horsemanship. They have their own kind of warfare. They discuss matters important to the camp and make decisions about where and when to move, when to hunt, when to fight,'' he said, tilted back in his chair, his long legs bent, booted feet propped on the window sill.

All she could think about was his strong, hard body pressed against her, his hands roaming over her naked body. *I want him.*

''After a meal, water is offered to all who have eaten, then often a pipe is passed among the men. When the pipe is passed, the women withdraw. A person's wealth is counted in horses and warfare is an important part of life.''

She listened as he explained that counting coup was any exploit against an enemy. She was fascinated by his life as well as by him, listening while he talked far into the night.

''Savannah, if we keep talking longer, this night is going to pass without either of us touching that bed.'' He stood up and her pulse drummed and her mouth went dry, all words failing her.

Could he ignore their earlier moments, their kisses? Did he take them lightly? She felt on fire, unable to answer him.

He pulled off his shirt, tossed it aside, his muscles rippling. Her pulse roared, drowning out all else. She watched as he pulled back the covers.

CHAPTER TEN

"I broke a promise to you today, but I'll keep my promises tonight. I will stay on the far side of the bed. You may have this side by the window. I'll turn my back and keep it turned."

He moved past her and walked around the bed. Her pulse drummed and she stood in uncertainty, staring at his broad shoulders and dark shape. He bent to pull off a boot and dropped it on the floor. Her pulse skittered even more as she watched him remove another boot.

"It's hot in here. If you want, take off your dress, Savannah. I won't watch or disturb you."

A voice deep inside her screamed that he already disturbed her beyond measure. Yet she was hot and the bed looked inviting. She glanced at the straight-back chair and then at the floor, her only other choices. With a determined set of her jaw, she unbuttoned her dress and shoved it away, sliding beneath the sheet swiftly and burning with flames of embarrassment and awareness. She turned on her side, her ears picking up every rustle and sound. Was he *completely* undressing? The thought killed every notion of sleep, and she almost came back up out of the bed, but there was nowhere else to go. Sleep in one of the chairs was impossible. Sleeping on the floor—ridiculous! And it would make how she reacted to him even more of an issue.

The bed shifted and she knew he stretched out on his side. A breeze blew through the window, but it couldn't cool her heated skin or burning imagination.

Time slowly passed while she remembered being in his arms, his kisses, his teasing, his moments of anger. Finally she realized he hadn't moved since he lay down in the bed, while she was a constant fidget, trying to keep her back turned to him, but shifting her arms and her legs and her head, pushing her hair away from her face and neck.

Was he asleep so easily?

She turned carefully on her back and then looked at him.

Her eyes had adjusted fully to the darkness and she saw the outline of the bulk of his body, his broad shoulder, his narrow waist and slim hips covered by his black denim trousers. She turned even more carefully on her side and studied him. Moonlight highlighted his muscled back, the scars not visible in the semi-darkness.

All possibility of sleep was gone. She could reach out and touch him easily. Every inch of her tingled. With an effort, she turned away and faced the window, watching the leaves shift and flutter outside and trying to get her thoughts calmed.

They should reach Nacogdoches tomorrow and she would stay with Adela. With Red Hawk's help, it would be so much easier to get Adela away from Horace Platt.

Finally her eyes closed and dreams of being in Red Hawk's arms filled her sleep.

It was barely dawn when Red Hawk opened his eyes and stepped out of bed. He turned to look at Savannah and drew a sharp breath, turning his back to her swiftly. He washed and pulled on his shirt and boots and in minutes left the room, quietly closing the door behind him.

He returned long after sunrise and found Savannah in the yard, seated on the bench in the shade, the doll snugly wrapped and tucked into the crook of her arm. At a glance, she looked like a young mother cradling her baby. He felt a strange twist of longing, thinking this would be the way she looked when she was married to the Confederate lieutenant. For a few minutes, he stood just inside without moving, watching her through the screen door and feeling a sad yearning, wanting a future with her.

Savannah saw Red Hawk emerge from the hotel and stride leisurely toward her. Her pulse jumped the moment he came into sight. As soon as he was close, he held out his hand. She remembered his gestures were for the sake of anyone watching.

"We need to go now."

Suspecting something was wrong in spite of his bland tone, she stood and walked toward the hotel with him.

"There are Union soldiers in town and they're asking about us," he said quietly.

A chill ran down her spine. If she were caught now, it would come out that she had traveled across country with Red Hawk. Thomas would believe whatever she told him, but he would be deeply shocked and he would never approve. Her aunt and uncle would be far more critical.

They reached their room. As soon as Red Hawk closed the door behind them, he looked around. "We'll gather the few things we have. I have the horses saddled and ready at the side of the hotel. If we can get around the corner, then we can stay off the main street. Keep your head down and let me do the talking."

At the door to the room, she glanced back, knowing she would always remember this room and the moments she had spent in it—the four-poster bed with its corn-shuck mattress that rustled with every move, the worn braided rugs made of faded green and brown cotton, the chipped furniture, the tin tub where Red Hawk had pulled her up and kissed her so wildly.

He closed the door behind them and they walked down the hall without hurrying. "It's a grand morning to travel. No sign of rain, and no danger from the fighting as long as we keep to the road west from here."

In the lobby he spoke in a cheerful tone. "I hope the baby sleeps as long as possible."

Red Hawk's dark eyes scanned the room and then he looked down at her with an impassive gaze. She looked at the doll in her arms and let Red Hawk steer her across the lobby. At the door, he leaned down.

"Soldiers are across the street. Hold the doll so they can see you appear to be holding a baby, and take your time."

He held her arm, moving around her. She tucked the blanket tightly around the doll and glanced across the street. Three soldiers glanced at them and then looked away.

They turned the corner and Red Hawk took the doll from her arms. "Mount up and I'll give this back to you."

As he held up the bundled doll, she took it from him, her fingers brushing his. "Careful with our little Esmerelda."

"Esmerelda?" He shook his head. "Then I'm not the father."

She couldn't laugh at his comment while she knew soldiers were right around the corner.

She followed Red Hawk and they rode to the back of the lot to head down the alley. At the street, they turned away from town. The next block held simple houses constructed of pine logs. At the end of the block the town ended. They rode across an open field.

"If anyone sees us riding away like this—we're not on a road—won't that bring them after us?"

"It might, but don't turn around and look until we reach the cover of trees," he said.

Her back tingled, this time with fear that a Union soldier would be behind them, watching them ride away and growing suspicious about it. It looked like three miles to the next stand of trees, yet she knew it had to be only three hundred yards.

They rode in a tense silence while she wondered where he had gone during the early morning hours.

The moment he reached the shadows of a stand of pines, he reined in and turned. She did the same and looked at the field they had just crossed.

To her relief, it stood empty.

"We're in the clear," he stated. "Let's go before they begin to give much thought to the couple who rode into town yesterday. I'll put the doll in my saddlebag to keep in case we need it again. You can throw it away before you get on a stage to Nacogdoches."

"I won't get rid of it anywhere!"

He glanced at her and his dark eyebrow arched quizzically.

"Adela loves dolls and I shall take it to her. Besides, some little girl probably loved this doll. It would be a shame to simply toss it aside." And she didn't want to tell him that the doll would be a remembrance of this time with him.

At midafternoon, she waited on the edge of a small town while Red Hawk rode into Squire, Texas. The town was along a stagecoach route from Louisiana. An hour later, Red Hawk returned and dismounted.

"Here's a ticket for the stage. We need to go, because it's already in town and leaves shortly. They've had time to change horses and are still waiting for passengers who are eating."

She placed the ticket in her reticule, which he took from her hands. She saw him remove gold pieces from his pocket and drop them into her reticule.

"You're returning my gold?" she asked incredulously.

"Just some of it so you'll have something should you need it."

She started to mount up and he caught her arm. When she looked up, her pulse drummed and she wondered if he was going to pull her into his arms and kiss her again.

Instead he gazed down solemnly at her. "We have a bargain, Savannah, and you haven't been good at keeping bargains. I want your help in getting Matthew away from the Ashmans."

"I'll keep my promise," she said, flushing. She hadn't kept any promise to him yet. "And you're to help me get Adela out of town and back home."

He nodded. She looked into his brown eyes and experienced that scalding attraction that made her pulse race. With an effort, she turned away and placed her foot into a stirrup to mount up. His hands closed on her waist and he lifted her into the saddle. He mounted his horse, and his bay pranced close to her black horse. To her surprise, he reached beneath his shirt and produced a small derringer.

Startled because she had not seen it before, she looked up when he held it out.

"I don't know that I should offer this to you. I can only hope you won't use it on me."

"Of course not! Will I never hear the end of that?"

"Not as long as I bear the scar," he drawled, and her face grew hot with embarrassment.

"I have apologized and have suffered for my impetuousness."

"And well you should," he said. "Take this and put it in that little bag you carry. You might need it, Savannah. You seem to have good enough aim to stop a man."

"I really know little about pistols."

"Take it and pull the trigger if he threatens you, just the way you did with me."

"You will never let me forget!"

"Soon we'll part, and then you'll go through the rest of your life without hearing about the man you shot."

She looked into his unfathomable dark eyes that didn't reveal whether he was teasing or not. He sounded solemn. What really ran through his mind?

"I telegraphed your brother-in-law that you would be arriving on this stage."

"I detest that man," she said, remembering the time before he had wed Adela when he had called on them. During the evening, Savannah had been alone in the hall with him and he had grabbed her and tried to kiss her. He had held too tightly, hurting her, his hands roaming freely over her. If she had only had the gumption to tell her father, it might have turned him against Horace Platt.

As it was, she was too shamed to try to broach the subject with her father, and then it was too late. The memory was foul

and made her stomach churn and the thought of poor Adela
being married to such a monster tore at Savannah.

"The town is filled with Confederates. Fighting was west
of here, and some have fallen back."

She saw he was correct the moment they reached the edge
of the tiny town. It held only a few stores, a saloon, a bank, a
livery stable, and little else except the way station for the stage
line.

They rode silently into town, the doll safely secured in a
saddlebag, out of sight. Dressed in the blue poplin and sedately
sidesaddle, Savannah rode beside Red Hawk.

At the stage he held her hand as she started to climb inside.
"You'll let me know where you're staying?" she asked him.

"Tonight I'll come to the Platt house around midnight."

She nodded and he assisted her into the coach. She climbed
inside the hot, stuffy interior and sat next to a long-legged man
in a rumpled black suit. She sat down in the corner of the coach
and looked through the open window at Red Hawk, who was
already striding away. He mounted up, leading her horse, turning to go out of town without glancing back. She felt a sense
of loss that was ridiculous. It should mean nothing to tell him
good-bye, and she would see him again by midnight tonight.

A woman climbed in and sat facing her, their skirts taking
up most of the interior. When they started moving, a cloud of
dust rose around the window as they pulled into the street.
Savannah looked outside, but knew she wouldn't glimpse Red
Hawk again until their midnight rendezvous.

Hours later in Nacogdoches, as she emerged from the dusty,
stifling stagecoach, she saw Adela standing beside Horace Platt.
Shock riveted her, and a pang tore at Savannah at the sight of
her sister. She loved Adela and, though Adela was older, Savannah had always taken care of her as if she were the younger
sister.

Now, her sister, who had always been so beautiful that people
turned to stare at her anywhere she went, looked like a tall,
pale ghost. Her dress hung on her slender frame, and she was
little more than bones covered with taut flesh. Her face still

held its beauty, more ethereal than ever with skin as pale as snow, her cheekbones standing out starkly, her large blue eyes circled with black shadows. Her cheek was bruised; the dark blue tinge to her skin made Savannah's stomach clench. Anger replaced her shock and worry.

She smiled tentatively at Savannah, who waved in return.

Her attention shifted to Horace Platt and revulsion was all she could feel. He loomed over Adela and the rest of the crowd, a scowl on his face. Above his thick black beard, his blue eyes blazed as if fires burned deep within them.

While Adela looked pitiful in a drab black dress that had sleeves to her wrist even on such a warm summer day, her husband was a contrast in a well-cut black suit and beaver hat. To Savannah he looked strong, prosperous, and evil. She couldn't wait to get Adela away from him.

She waved. Adela returned the wave and they moved forward to meet her.

"Savannah," Adela said, her voice choking as she hugged Savannah long and hard, yet Savannah returned the hug lightly, afraid that beneath the coarse black cotton, there might be more bruises. When she moved away, Adela's eyes were tear-filled.

She looked up at Horace Platt and revulsion surged in her again. He wrapped his arms around her, hugging her and trying to place a kiss on her mouth. She turned her head and the wet, hard kiss fell on her cheek, making her want to reach up with her handkerchief and scrub her face.

"Sister," he said. "Welcome to Nacogdoches."

As soon as she wriggled out of his grasp, he took the small bundle she carried and raised his eyebrows. "You travel lightly, Savannah."

"I thought it best if I didn't try to bring too much."

He nodded and took Adela's arm. Savannah saw Adela wince, and it took all her control to keep from yanking his hand away from her sister. *By tomorrow night,* she thought, *I will have her away from him. Only a little more than twenty-four hours from now.*

She looked at him out of the corner of her eye. He was much

heavier than Red Hawk and just as tall. She realized she might have a dreadful time hiding Adela from him once they went home. If he got the chance, he wouldn't hesitate to try to beat any information out of her about Adela. For the first time, fear coiled in Savannah at the thought of crossing him.

She squared her shoulders. If they had to leave Mason and move to San Antonio to escape Horace Platt, then they would do so. With the pension from her father, they could live in San Antonio. She could tutor little children. Adela did beautiful handiwork. Savannah thought of some of the boardinghouses she had stayed in and wondered if running a boardinghouse would be a better thing for both of them to try to do.

"We worried about you coming across Louisiana," Horace said. "There's still fighting."

"It was safe enough. I was delayed in Vicksburg briefly."

"You shouldn't travel alone, Savannah. Your father always let you have your own way far too much. More than any woman should. It exposes you to danger," Horace said.

The only danger she felt exposed to now was him. She listened in silence, refusing to argue with him and seeing no need to anger him. He might take his fury out on Adela.

They crossed a wide street filled with busy people and carriages, men on horseback, and women who were shopping. Most people spoke to Horace Platt, who acknowledged them with a tip of his hat and a hello.

Across the street, leaning against the bank in the shadow of the doorway, Red Hawk watched the three. His hat was pulled low over his head, and he took his measure of the man who might be a foe before many hours had passed.

The man looked like trouble, with his scowl and thick brawny shoulders, the swagger to his walk. Red Hawk's gaze shifted to the woman at his side who had to be Adela, Savannah's sister.

She was incredibly beautiful in a pale, fragile way, looking like a tall china doll. Her skin was perfection, except it was too pale. Her lips were full, her blue eyes wide and thickly lashed. Her features were symmetrical; golden blond hair was

piled on her head. She was too pale, too thin, but her beauty
still shone through. Men turned to look at her. Most of them
spoke to Platt, but their gaze went straight to his wife.

She was tall enough to draw attention, with a lush, full bosom
and a waist as tiny as Savannah's. She would draw men's
attention anywhere. He saw the bruise on her cheek, another
dark bruise on her throat.

Anger filled him that any man would treat a woman in such
a manner. He inhaled swiftly, feeling hot and wanting to stride
across the street and strike Platt now and take both women
away from him. Small wonder Savannah was determined to
get her sister from the man.

Platt's blue eyes were narrow and close set, adding to his
unappealing appearance. Red Hawk clenched his fists. Savannah might be in far more danger than she realized, and he
wished she had more than the tiny derringer for protection. His
gaze ran over Platt's bulk again. Unless it was a direct shot to
the heart or brain, the derringer would be a small deterrent to
a man of his size.

Savannah would be under his roof, a guest in his house. No
one would know what he was doing. Red Hawk wanted to go
get her and keep her from staying with them. Instinct told him
she was in danger. If Platt wanted to force himself on her, no
one would be there to stop him. No one would hear Savannah's
cries for help except Adela, who looked as if she couldn't help
anyone.

Red Hawk was tempted to throw all caution and wisdom
aside and go get her, but he knew she would never forgive
him. He would reveal himself to Platt, and Savannah probably
wouldn't go with him. He watched Platt take Adela's arm and
saw her blanch and bite her lip.

The man was deliberately hurting his wife, who was doing
nothing to warrant it. Platt helped Savannah into the sleek,
black buggy and his hand ran down from her waist over her
backside. Red Hawk made a low growling noise in his throat,
wanting to tear into Platt and now worried deeply about Savan-

nah when nightfall came. She should not stay in Platt's house as his guest even one night.

Yet how could he get her away?

Red Hawk watched the carriage pull from the curb and start down the street while all three of them conversed. He felt helpless and frustrated and frightened for Savannah. She was a capable, feisty woman, but she would be no match for a man the size and temperament of Platt.

Red Hawk moved leisurely around the corner to the bar next door to see what information he could pick up.

"Tell us about Cairo," Horace said when they started down the shady street. Like the town of Squire, Nacogdoches was filled with Confederate soldiers.

"It was bustling. Uncle Timothy sends his regards," she told Adela. "His mill is busy night and day."

"Yankee enterprise," Horace said. "I've thought of moving us farther north to Kansas City, but my business is booming, too. War helps some things," he stated with a smile.

In minutes, they turned up the lane to the Platts' house. It was a two-story Victorian of dark granite, large, imposing, and grim, just like its owner. It sat in the center of the block, flanked by graceful Victorian homes that were painted white and looked cheerful and welcoming.

A woman in the yard of a neighboring house waved, and Adela returned the wave. "That's Hortense. Mrs. Rufus Nardin. I'm sure you'll meet her," Adela said quietly.

"Adela, you leave the Nardins alone. That woman is a busybody," Horace snapped.

"Yes, Horace," Adela answered, with a quaver in her voice that Savannah hated.

The driver halted the buggy and Savannah reluctantly let Horace help her step down. His hand closed on hers in a tight grip, his thumb running over her wrist.

"I will leave you two ladies while I return to work. I will be home for supper at six, Adela."

"Yes, Horace," she answered meekly.

He climbed into the buggy and turned to go.

"Come inside," Adela said. "Thank heavens, you're here! I have been waiting and praying each day you would come."

Guilt tugged at Savannah for taking so long. "Adela, if only you had let me know long ago what kind of life you live with him, I would have done this sooner."

Adela's lip quivered and she ran her fingers across her brow. "I dare not displease him, but he's getting more demanding. He's angry with me for not having a son." Her eyes brimmed with tears again, and she wiped at them quickly. "I mustn't let him see me cry. It sends him into a rage."

"The man is inhuman. By tomorrow night, I hope we are on our way home."

"Oh, Savannah, I'm so eager! I have dreamed—though I knew I dare not dream—about escape."

"We can talk inside, Adela."

"Not in front of Miss Prewitt. She's a cousin of Horace's, a spinster who fell on hard times. He's provided for her and she's our housekeeper, only I think she spends half her time spying on me and reporting to him, which I'm certain is exactly what he intended and why he puts up with her. So we must be careful what we say in front of her."

"How can we avoid her hearing?"

"After you freshen up, I'll show you the garden in the back. She can't follow us and eavesdrop outside. She does eavesdrop inside."

"Oh, Adela. I can't wait for tomorrow to come. I have so much to tell you."

"We'd best go in. She'll tell him how long we stood out here talking."

They entered the house. It was filled with dark, heavy furniture, depressing Savannah even more. To spend one night in this house seemed like a dreadful burden.

When she discovered that her room would be on the second

floor, where Red Hawk couldn't signal to her or come close enough for them to talk, she was frightened and worried.

"You will be upstairs, across the hall from our room," Adela said. "Let's put your things there. Then I will introduce you to Miss Prewitt and we can go outside.

As they walked through the wide front hall with its bare plank floor, Savannah looked through an open doorway into a front parlor filled with more dark furniture.

They climbed the stairs, and Adela showed her their bedroom with a four-poster made of mahogany, ornately carved, with a dark brown coverlet. "This is our room," Adela said in a dead voice. She turned to grip Savannah's arm. "You must get me away from him!"

"I will. I promise, Adela."

"I'll show you your room. It's across the hall."

"Adela, you've written there's a bedroom downstairs. I need to be downstairs," Savannah said.

Adela shook her head. "Horace made that into his library. Why do you care?"

Savannah remembered what Adela had warned about Miss Prewitt eavesdropping and glanced at the door. "We should talk in the garden," she whispered, and Adela's eyes grew round as she nodded.

"I'm sorry. You have to be upstairs."

Savannah's mind raced. That meant she would have to slip downstairs to signal to Red Hawk. If Horace Platt caught her walking around downstairs, there would be all kinds of questions and trouble. She was chilled, wondering if their plans were going to be thwarted right here.

"Come, let me show you your room," Adela said, leading the way across the hall to another room filled with heavy mahogany furniture. The room held a bed, a small chest with a washbowl and pitcher, and little else. It was within yards of Horace Platt's room, and Savannah chilled at the thought of spending one night under the same roof with him.

She placed her few things on the bed and removed her blue hat. "Now we can see that garden."

Linking her arm with Adela, shocked at the thinness of her sister and how frail she was, Savannah walked beside her downstairs.

"This way to the kitchen."

They entered a large kitchen with an iron stove along one wall. Glass-fronted cabinets lined the walls and it seemed the cheeriest room in the house, even with the dark oak table and heavy chairs at one end of the room.

Then Savannah forgot her surroundings as she looked at the woman who turned to face them. Dressed in a white uniform with a white apron, she was as grim and forbidding as Horace Platt, and almost as tall. Large, raw-boned, with a ruddy complexion and a square jaw fully as large as her cousin's, she looked Savannah over with a cold stare. Her thin lips were compressed; her hair was pulled on top of her head and fastened in a knot.

She folded her hands across her ample middle and stared at Savannah.

"Savannah, this is Miss Prewitt. Miss Prewitt, this is my sister, Miss Ravenwood."

"How'd you do," Miss Prewitt said abruptly.

"How do you do," Savannah replied.

"We'll be in the garden," Adela announced and motioned toward the back door. Relieved to escape the house, Savannah stepped outside, where the yard was immaculate, with low hedges trimmed to perfection and clipped bushes lining the sides of the yard. Beside a magnolia were several wooden chairs, and they sat down.

Savannah glanced at the house and saw Miss Prewitt at the window watching them, but they were far enough to be out of her hearing.

"Adela, how early in the morning will Horace leave for work so we can get away?"

Adela frowned. "He has taken to coming home mid-morning lately. I don't know why, because I do the same thing most every day, but he's getting so he lets me go out less and less, unless I'm accompanied by him. I checked and there's no stage to San Antonio until ten days from now."

Savannah said a swift silent prayer of thanks that she wouldn't have to stay at the Platt house for ten days. "That's what I want to tell you, Adela. We won't have to wait for the stage, but we want to leave at a time when your husband won't come home unexpectedly."

"How can we go if we don't leave by stage?"

Savannah took a deep breath. "When I left Cairo, I brought medicine to Vicksburg to send to Thomas. I shouldn't have, but it seemed so simple at the time to help myself to some of the medicine from the doctor on board the *General Thibodeaux*."

"Savannah!" Adela's eyes widened. "You took them?"

"The North has more than they need, while all across the South men are dying and suffering for lack of medicine. It was to help Thomas."

"But Savannah, the medicine didn't belong to you! How could you do that?"

"Adela, think about men suffering without any morphine or having a limb sawed off—"

"Do stop! I don't want to imagine that. And I suppose the cause was right. Go ahead. I interrupted you."

"As I was going down the gangplank, the doctor missed them and guessed who had taken them. I didn't stop to think. I ran. A man on the docks saw me and he helped me get away. He is Captain Quentin Red Hawk, with the Confederate forces in Louisiana, and he was on the same mission I was—trying to get medical supplies to take back to his men. He took the medicine from me, but he couldn't let me go because he was afraid I would turn him in. He took me with him to Louisiana."

"You traveled with this strange man? Your reputation is ruined. Thomas Sievert will be horrified. He may not marry you."

Savannah experienced a twinge of impatience. "Great saints, Adela! I had no choice. He forced me to travel with him, and Thomas will never even know unless you tell."

Suddenly tears filled Adela's eyes, and she grasped Savannah's hand. "Dear sister, I'm sorry! Here I am scolding you when I should be thanking you for coming to save me. I'll never tell Thomas and of course it was against your will, so it's not wrong on your part."

"Don't cry, Adela. Miss Prewitt is watching us, so laugh. You don't want her to tell Horace you were crying." Adela and Savannah both smiled and Savannah nodded with satisfaction. "Good. Anyway, Captain Red Hawk and I left Vicksburg with soldiers after us. The captain is an escaped Union prisoner and I had stolen their medicine. As we traveled together, we decided we could help each other. He's going to get his six-year-old nephew in San Antonio, who's with cruel grandparents, much like your own situation. I had already told him about my plans to get you away from your husband. So he'll help us and we won't have to take the stage. This way, it'll be far more difficult, most likely impossible, for Mr. Platt to find us."

"Can you trust this man?"

"Yes. If he had intended harm to me, it would have come long before now."

Adela clapped her hands. "Savannah, you're an angel! I was so fearful that Horace would set off at once after the stage and overtake it. This way he will never find us. I'm glad for Captain Red Hawk. Red Hawk is an unusual name."

"He's Comanche."

Adela's hand flew to her mouth and her eyes widened again. "The Comanche killed Papa. How can you travel with a savage?"

"Adela, his mother was taken back to the whites when he was eleven. He was raised much the same as you and I. He has an education. Now let's make some plans."

"Where is this Captain Red Hawk staying?" Adela asked, glancing around the yard as if he were hiding in the bushes.

"He's here in Nacogdoches. He's coming to meet me late tonight after everyone is asleep, and I will tell him our plans."

"You mustn't let Horace catch you! He would kill the man

for trespassing, and he will beat me dreadfully if he has any inkling what I plan.''

"Don't worry," Savannah said, hating the distraught note in her sister's voice. "I shall take great caution to keep Mr. Platt from discovering what I'm doing. You can see why I wanted a bedroom downstairs, but that's not possible, so I'll manage.''

"If Horace discovers you, Savannah, it'll be dreadful," Adela said, shivering and rubbing her arms.

"Stop worrying, Adela. I shall be very careful. Now let's plan what to do. You said Mr. Platt comes home in the mornings. Does he come home in the afternoon?''

"No—at least he hasn't lately. Also, he'll be gone tomorrow night. There is a city board meeting, and he's on the council.''

"Tomorrow night? That seems the best time. If not then, we'll try the next afternoon, but I will talk to Captain Red Hawk about tomorrow night.''

The thought of spending one moment longer than necessary in the Platt house was chilling. Savannah stared at the house as if it were a prison. She had been in it only minutes and already found it oppressive.

That night dinner was agonizing. Horace Platt seated her, his hands lingering on her shoulders and giving her chills. He talked steadily to her, quizzing her again about Cairo.

"Who waits for you to get home to Mason?" he asked suddenly, abruptly changing the topic.

"No one since Papa is gone," she answered. The instant the words were out of her mouth, she wanted to take them back. The gleam in his eyes frightened her, and she was deeply thankful for Red Hawk and the knowledge they would be away from Nacogdoches and Horace Platt in another twenty-four hours.

Throughout the meal, Adela sat in silence, ignored by her husband. When Savannah tried to draw her into the conversation, she saw it made Adela uneasy, so she ceased attempting to do so.

After supper, Savannah and Adela adjourned to the parlor,

where both took up their sewing. Adela had given Savannah one of her dresses, and Savannah was changing it to fit herself. The moment Horace finished his cigar and brandy, he joined them, sitting as close as he could get to Savannah. She had chosen a brown leather chair near a matching one where Adela sat quietly sewing.

Platt's portrait hung above the mantelpiece, and mounted heads of deer and mountain lion and a stuffed eagle adorned the walls, their glass eyes staring fixedly. The moment the tall clock chimed half-past nine, Savannah excused herself and went to her bedroom, wishing she could lock the door. She was thankful for the tiny derringer that Red Hawk had given her. Yet she knew if she tried to threaten Horace Platt with it, he would beat her for her actions.

The minutes seemed to drag, and she sat near a window, staring at the darkened yard until midnight came. Eager to see Red Hawk, she stared at the yard, also terrified of having to go downstairs and prowl alone through the house.

She changed to the green dress because it was a softer material that would rustle less. She pulled off her shoes and opened the door slowly, her heart pounding with fear that she might encounter Horace.

Their bedroom door was closed; the house was silent. Savannah stepped into the hall and moved as quietly as possible toward the stairs. Her eyes had adjusted to the night, but it was still impossible to see into dark corners.

She could scarcely breathe, and her heartbeat seemed loud enough to alert Platt. As a step creaked, she froze, her gaze flying back to his closed door.

Inching her way downstairs, she took another step and then another, her gaze going over the empty hallway and her heart pounding fiercely. Hurrying to the southwest corner, she entered and crossed the library.

To her relief, all the windows were open. She tugged a window higher, placed her hat in it, and then sat down beside it to wait, constantly glancing back and forth between the window and the hall door to watch for Horace.

If only Red Hawk would arrive. *Please hurry! Please come soon!* she thought, nervous and anxious to see Red Hawk.

"Savannah!"

Her pulse racing, she jumped to her feet and peered into the darkness.

CHAPTER ELEVEN

Red Hawk's broad shoulders were silhouetted outside the window. She longed to throw herself into his arms and knew she couldn't.

"This isn't my room." She cast a nervous glance over her shoulder at the closed door. "My bedroom is upstairs, so I need to be quick. If Mr. Platt discovers I'm down here, it might be terrible."

"How soon can you leave?"

"Adela said Mr. Platt will be away from home tomorrow night and in the afternoons. He comes home during the mornings, so that won't be a good time to leave."

"I'll come tomorrow night about half-past eight. Can both of you be ready to go?"

"Yes. I can't wait to get out of here."

She heard a scrape in the hall behind her. "You leave! I heard someone."

"Are you safe?"

"Yes," she said, fearful Platt was prowling around downstairs. "Please go. I'll see you here tomorrow night."

She looked around the room frantically and then impulsively

stepped behind a drape. If Horace found her and trapped her in this room, she would be at his mercy. In his house this late at night with only Adela, who would be no help, Savannah knew she wouldn't be able to compete with his brute strength.

The tiny derringer was upstairs beneath her pillow, and she felt foolish for coming downstairs without it. It was stifling and dusty behind the drape, yet she knew it might be her own fear that made the room seem stifling. She heard the rattle of the doorknob, the floorboards creaked, and she saw golden light around the edges of the drape. Horace Platt was in the room with her.

Her heart thudded. If he found her, she had to try to get out the door, her only possible escape. She didn't dare breathe or move the slightest as she heard heavy footsteps and the creak of boards.

"Savannah? Where the devil—"

Platt was searching for her! That could only mean he knew she was not in her room. Terror filled her. The man had gone to her bedroom looking for her. She wouldn't be safe going back there, either. How long would he search?

She heard him moving around the room, and her heart's pounding sounded incredibly loud in her ears. *If he finds me, I'll run,* she thought, her nerves tense. A board creaked nearby.

The next creak was farther away and then she heard his footsteps receding in the hall. The light at the edge of the drapery was gone. She was too frightened to move, afraid she would discover Horace standing in the darkness, waiting and watching for her.

At the same time, she was frightened to stay where she was. If he searched the house without finding her, he would come back and search again.

Unable to get her breath, with shaking knees she moved the drape and peeped out.

The room was empty. Yet where could she go that she would be safe? She looked at the open window. With trembling hands she left the safety of the drapes and tried to unlatch the window hooks.

Terrified that he would return and catch her, she looked over her shoulder. One hook snapped free, but the other wouldn't give. She tugged and prayed and was about to give up when it came free. She pushed open the screen, slipped through the window, dropped to the ground, thankful she had worn the dark green dress that didn't show easily in the night.

She pushed the screen back in place carefully. Light shone through the parlor windows. She raced across the yard to a clump of lilac bushes and moved through them.

With a thudding heart, she stopped, terrified that he might have seen her. She looked back at the house. As she stood quietly, a hand clamped on her shoulder and spun her around. When she gasped, a hand went over her mouth.

"Savannah, shh!"

Red Hawk! Relief made her sag. Her arms went around him. Instantly, his arms circled her waist to hold her tightly. His deep voice was reassuring; his strong arms were a haven.

"Did he hurt you?"

"No. He hasn't found me, but he's searching for me and he knows I'm not in my room."

"That bastard. Do you have the derringer?"

"I left it in the bedroom."

"Savannah, the point of having a pistol is to defend yourself. You can't do it if you leave the pistol behind and are caught empty-handed."

"I realized that too late."

"You'll stay with me."

"Surely he won't look out here," she said, thankful to be with Red Hawk. "Tomorrow, if he asks, I'll just say I was hot and went outside." Her fear had vanished, and she was aware of standing in Red Hawk's strong arms, being held close against him. His hand stroked her head. Why did this feel incredibly right? Why was it exciting beyond measure, while standing like this with Thomas never once evoked the same sensations? At the recollection of Thomas, guilt stabbed her and she pulled away reluctantly. "I'm all right. I don't want him to find you."

"If you think I'll leave you now, you couldn't be more

mistaken. If he's been in your bedroom, Savannah, there's only one reason, and you're in his house where no one can help you. To make it worse, he's strong.''

"How do you know that?"

"You told me. Also, I saw him today when he met your stage."

Startled, she looked up at him. "I didn't see you."

"I didn't want you to see me, but I was near enough to see him and your sister. I'll get you tomorrow. You mustn't spend another night under the same roof with him."

"We can't stand out here in the lilac bushes all night."

He took her hand. "Come with me." He led her to the back of the lot and spread a blanket on the ground, then sat down and pulled her down beside him.

"I'm afraid he'll come out here searching for me."

"If he does, we'll go over the fence into the alley. My horse is there. Let him search, Savannah."

"It's dreadful in that house. I can't wait to get Adela out of it. She's so thin and gaunt, and he treats her abominably."

"I hope I cross paths with him."

"No, you mustn't. We have to slip out and go, but at least we'll have you with us to ride across country, so we won't have to worry about Mr. Platt finding us."

"Don't you think he'll go to Mason after her?"

"Probably. We may have to live in San Antonio, but we can do that. Adela's best friend from Mason, Bertrice Gaston, has married and lives in San Antonio. That might be a place she can hide. He knows little about her friends from home."

While she talked, Red Hawk reached out to touch her braids. "Your hair is back in braids on top of your head, which is probably a good thing around Platt."

"It's not fashionable for me to wear it down," she said, aware of Red Hawk's hands in her hair.

"I bought another horse today so we'll have three horses."

"Good. We should get hours ahead of him. Even then, he won't know where to start. He knows I have close friends in Vicksburg and Adela and I have an aunt and uncle in Cairo."

"Would you be better off going back to them for a time?"

"No. My uncle would see only that Adela is Mr. Platt's wife and she belongs back with him no matter how cruel he is to her. There are many men who see a woman only as a man's possession, having no rights of her own no matter how the man treats her."

"Unfortunately, that's true in more cultures than the white man's," Red Hawk said dryly. "Shhh," he cautioned, and she looked over her shoulder to see a light bobbing near the house.

Her pulse skittered again, and she stared through the darkness. "He's searching the grounds."

"Come on," Red Hawk said, standing to pull her up. "Go over the fence." It was a stone wall the height of her shoulders and Red Hawk hoisted her up easily. She sat on the top and then dropped down on the other side. With the blanket across his shoulders, he followed and leaned back against the wall. "We can wait here. He won't come over the fence."

"How can you be sure?"

"It's unlikely that he'll think you're out of the yard. He'll give up his search because you're supposed to be there for several weeks. He'll think he has all the time he wants."

She looked at the top of the stone wall as if she expected to see Horace Platt looming over it.

Red Hawk placed his hands on her shoulders, pulling her close to him. Her pulse jumped again, this time not from fear, but excitement.

Leaning down, he whispered in her ear. His breath was warm and ticklish. "We can't talk because he might come out this way and hear us."

She was aware of his breath on her ear, aware of how close she stood to him and his hands on her shoulders. She couldn't move.

They stood in silence, but her heart was beating wildly. Excitement strummed in her, along with desire. She wanted his kisses. Then he tilted her face up to his and his dark eyes held hers.

All sense of danger was transformed into blinding desire.

Their surroundings vanished and the world narrowed to only the tall man looking down at her. He stood so close she could feel the heat of his body, feel the warmth of his hands on her shoulders, smell the clean scent of him.

Silence stretched raw and thick between them. He bent his head, leaning down to take her mouth.

"We shouldn't," she whispered.

"In two more weeks or so, we'll part ways and never again see each other. What does this hurt?" He trailed kisses along her throat.

How could she resist? She closed her eyes. With each kiss, was she losing part of her heart to him forever? Her breath went out in a long sigh, and he brushed her lips lightly with a kiss. An aching need burst in her, and she leaned closer to him.

When his lips touched hers again, he kissed her hard, his tongue going into her mouth, and she felt giddy and aflame. His arm slipped around her waist and he pulled her tightly against him. He was solid, hard against her softness. His wildness burned away her conventionality.

Her thoughts spiraled away like night breezes. She yielded to his kisses, winding her arms around his neck, standing on tiptoe to return them. Her tongue slid into his mouth; sensations rocked her. She moaned softly, her hips thrusting against him. His shaft pressed against her and his breathing was as ragged as hers. When his fingers wound in her hair, pulling against the pins until they came undone and her braids fell over her shoulders, she barely noticed what he was doing. While he kissed her, his hand stroked her nape. He spread his legs farther apart, and his hand pulled her up against him, cupping her bottom and then caressing her.

She moaned again, her fingers tangling in his short, coarse hair, stroking the strong column of his neck, running across his broad powerful shoulders. She never dreamed kisses could be like this. Even his slightest touches were exhilarating and magical. He was forbidden to her, yet how could she stop?

His fingers brushed her neck and back, and then he peeled her dress down to her waist. Cool air touched her bare shoulders as Red Hawk pulled the straps of her chemise down, freeing her breasts.

She gasped, clinging to him, unable to stop him, unable to do anything except relish every touch. His big hands cupped her breasts, his thumbs circling her nipples. The sensations ignited fires deep within her. Her body came alive. Moaning, she clung to him. The look in his dark eyes melted her into liquid heat. Their brown was too dark to distinguish from his pupils, yet desire flamed in their depths.

Red Hawk trembled. He wanted to pull her down in the grass and take her, all consequences be damned. If he got her with babe, it would ruin her life. No matter what the consequences were, he knew she would never wed him.

Never would she be part of his life. Yet he couldn't stop kissing and caressing her. She was soft, *so soft,* full of curves, with silky skin and magnificent hair. He wanted to drive himself into her heat, hear her cries of passion, feel her beneath him, moving in complete abandon.

He groaned, his hungry kisses taking her mouth, his tongue going deep while he stroked her breasts. And then he bent his head to take her breast in his mouth. His tongue circled her nipple as his pulse became thunder in his ears. He had to stop, or in a few more moments he wouldn't be able to.

As if she could read his mind, she raised her head and pushed away. Moonlight fell over her and he looked at her beautiful body. It took his breath and made him feel weak-kneed and giddy. Her breasts were high, firm and full, with pink nipples. "Savannah," he whispered, reaching out to trail his fingers over her breast and nipple.

"I have to stop!" she exclaimed in little more than a whisper.

He couldn't speak or move. If he did move, he was afraid he would reach for her again, and this time there would be no stopping.

She tugged her dress in place. "This is wrong!" she whispered as she fastened it at the neck.

"I'd better get away from you, Savannah," he declared

hoarsely. He turned and walked down the alley. She watched him fade into dark shadows and disappear.

She trembled—and she had felt him shake, which meant he was as disturbed as she. While she struggled with her buttons, she heard a noise.

Jumping back against the wall, she whirled around and stared into the darkness. A dog moved down the alley and went on past her. Her heartbeat raced and she peered into the night, but didn't see any sign of Red Hawk.

She spread the blanket and sat down on it. In minutes he reappeared and hoisted himself to the top of the wall.

"Come on, Savannah. You never know who or what will roam down an alley. Let's go back into his yard. He's gone now."

She stood and let him help her over the wall again. She sat on the blanket, and he sat down facing her.

"I don't see a light in the house."

"He probably went back to bed."

She shivered, thinking what might have happened if she had gone to bed and fallen asleep as Horace had expected her to do. She was aware of Red Hawk seated so close; she wanted him to reach out and pull her into his arms again, but she knew he should not.

"We'll go to San Antonio, and I'll get Matthew. Then I can escort both of you to Mason if you want to go."

"I don't know whether it will be safe for us to go home right away."

"If you stay in Mason, be careful, Savannah. I don't think it'll go easy with you, either, if he finds her staying with you."

She shivered. "I'll be glad when tomorrow night is here."

They talked quietly about Adela and their plans. Finally Red Hawk tugged lightly on her shoulder.

"Lean against me or stretch out and sleep while you can. I can catch some sleep during the day tomorrow. When tomorrow night comes, we may need the rest badly."

Red Hawk pulled her back against his shoulder and she let him, knowing she wasn't doing it because it would be the most comfortable way to sleep. Far from it. Leaning against his shoulder and chest meant that she probably wouldn't sleep at all. While her pulse raced, her body pressed against his length. She was conscious of his scent, his warm body, and his solid chest.

Her eyes grew heavy and she closed them, listening to him talk about going to San Antonio.

When her weight sagged against him, he looked down. Gently, he eased her down with her head in his lap. He drew a deep breath. Just the slightest touch from her and he was aroused again. He wound his hand through her hair and caressed her cheek lightly, drawing his fingers over her smooth skin. He looked at the steady rise and fall of her breasts as she breathed deeply in sleep. In his imagination, her green dress was gone.

"Damnation," he whispered, aroused, not wanting to move her off his lap. His gaze swept the yard and he thought about Platt, hating the man and wishing he had a few moments with him. Thank heavens Savannah had left her room. She wasn't going to spend another night in the house, and Platt would not find them as long as Red Hawk was with them.

Red Hawk shifted, studying the house and watching for any sign of Platt, but he didn't see any. His gaze went back to Savannah and he stroked her head. The doctor would come home from the war and marry her and she would go back to the kind of life she had always known.

Without thought, he lifted locks of Savannah's hair and rubbed his cheek with silky strands, catching her rose scent, feeling the softness against his rough skin. The moments he'd spent holding and kissing her were paradise. Sleep was lost to him because of troubled and erotic dreams about her. He wanted her as he had never wanted a woman, but she would never freely give herself to him—never under any conditions love him.

He wanted more than to hold her and kiss her. Images of her full pale breasts, remembrance of their softness and weight in his hands, made him clench his fists. He was aroused, aching, filled with desire that was white hot. She lay innocently sleeping in his lap, trusting him.

He groaned and shifted her carefully, knowing he had to move away or he was going to haul her up into his arms and finish what he had started earlier.

It was almost dawn when Savannah felt someone shaking her shoulder. She opened her eyes sleepily and then came fully awake as she looked up at Red Hawk. Sitting up, she looked at the blanket spread on the grass, the lilac bushes in front of her, their dark green leaves sparkling with dew.

Through the bushes, she could see the stone house and she remembered the night and her flight from Platt.

"So once again, I spent a night with you," she said, and then was immediately embarrassed that she had spoken her thoughts.

"Your reputation is still quite intact, Savannah. The kind of nights we have spent together count as nothing."

He made the remarks in a sharp voice and his words stung. To him it had been nothing, while she would never be the same again and would remember those nights for years to come.

She smoothed her dress, busying herself so she wouldn't have to look at him. She didn't want him to know how his words hurt her or that what he said mattered so much to her. The last twinkling stars disappeared in the morning light. The earth was quiet, with pink rays streaking the sky overhead and a fresh dewy smell in the air.

"I saw the cook go into the house. I thought you might want to go inside now," Red Hawk said.

She nodded and stood. He shook out the blanket and stood beside her. "I'll be here at eight tonight. I won't be far away. If he bothers you, scream. And use the derringer. It would stop him. If he tries to do anything to harm you, get out of the house. Just get out. I'm in the Nacogdoches Hotel."

She nodded, straightening her wrinkled dress, touching her hair. She caught it and twisted it to loop it around her head. "Tonight," she said, reluctant to leave him.

She turned to hurry to the house. She went through the library window and when she looked back at the yard, Red Hawk was gone.

Hurrying across the library, she opened the door cautiously. Horace Platt stood only yards away in the hall, and his eyes narrowed as he looked at her. He looked larger and more forbidding than ever. Dressed in a black suit with a white shirt, he took in her dishevelled appearance.

"Miss Ravenwood, where the devil have you been?"

Her pulse jumped, and she raised her chin. "I couldn't sleep, so I came downstairs and fell asleep in the library."

"In the library? I was downstairs early this morning and I didn't see you," he said, disbelief in his voice. "No one was in the library." His gaze raked over her boldly and made her skin crawl with aversion.

"I was there," she said calmly. "Where else would I have gone?"

"I don't know how I could have missed you," he said, coming toward her. Her pulse raced, and her revulsion grew.

"Your hair is down," he said in a voice that made the hairs on the nape of her neck stand on end. He reached out to touch her.

Ducking, she rushed past him, circling him enough that he couldn't reach out easily and stop her. "I must freshen up. I'm quite a wrinkle."

Rushing up the stairs, she didn't look back until she reached her door. As far as she could see down the stairs, he was not in sight. Relieved, she rushed into her room and ran straight to the bed to retrieve the derringer. Never again under the Platt roof would she be without it.

She combed and braided her hair, pinning it on her head. Her dress was wrinkled, but she wore it anyway. Placing the derringer in a pocket, she stayed in her room until she heard a knock at the door. She opened it to face Adela, who looked paler than ever this morning. She wore a dark blue dress that did nothing for her pale skin, and her eyes had dark circles beneath them.

"Would you like to come downstairs for breakfast?"

Savannah glanced across the hall at the open door of Adela's and Horace's bedroom and wondered whether he had left the house yet.

"Horace has gone," Adela said quietly.

Savannah nodded and went downstairs with Adela.

"He said you didn't sleep in your room last night," Adela said.

"I didn't."

"I shouldn't worry about you. You can always take care of yourself."

"I slept outside, Adela."

Her sister looked at her with worry-filled eyes. "Because of Horace," she said.

Savannah nodded, suspecting Adela could guess exactly why she had not been in the house. "I told him I was in the library, but I was actually out in the yard."

"Savannah, he's dreadful! You're not safe here."

"We'll leave tonight. Be—"

She stopped because Miss Prewitt appeared only a few feet away, coming out of the library. She carried a feather duster. "Will you be ready for breakfast now, ma'am?" she asked Adela.

"Yes, thank you."

The woman bustled ahead of them and disappeared into the kitchen. Adela gave Savannah another worried look and leaned close. "She could have heard us talking."

Savannah shrugged. "I'm sure she didn't," she said lightly, feeling no such certainty, but wanting to keep Adela from worrying about it. "Even so, there's nothing she can do. She knows nothing, and she won't be able to stop us." Savannah placed her hand on Adela's arm. "Adela," she whispered solemnly, "if we shouldn't get away from here tonight, can you possibly slip away from him while he sleeps?"

Adela bit her lip and frowned. "I don't know. I can try."

"Put your valise with your things in my room today. We have to take very little."

Adela nodded. "I don't have much here I want to take with me."

"If anything happens to thwart our plans for leaving early in the evening while your husband is gone, then let's try and go in the night. If I'm not in my bed, I'll be in the back of the yard behind the lilac bushes. You come out there."

"Savannah," Adela said, looking more frightened than ever, "if this fails and he learns about it, he will beat us both senseless. You will have no one to defend you. That captain you traveled with isn't here, and he won't be able to help you. Horace can be a demon if he's crossed."

Savannah couldn't imagine her gentle sister crossing anyone, and her anger boiled at the thought of the treatment that Adela had been given.

"Don't you worry. We'll get away. Just get yourself outside even if he's chasing after you."

Adela closed her eyes and for a moment Savannah feared she was going to faint. "Adela!"

"Savannah, I can't imagine running away with Horace after me. He's terrifying. He's strong and he's very quick."

"I'm sure he is. I promise you, by this time tomorrow, you won't be living in this house."

Miss Prewitt stepped out of the dining room. "Your breakfast is served, ma'am."

"Thank you," Adela said perfunctorily.

Savannah knew that once again, Adela was worrying whether or not Miss Prewitt had overheard them. Savannah worried about it, too, and knew they had to stop discussing their plans until a better time.

They entered the dining room. Even though sunshine streamed in through the tall narrow windows, the house still was forbidding to Savannah. The mantelpiece and the woodwork were dark oak, and Horace Platt's invisible presence hung over every room. The sight of her sister, so thin and pitiful and cowed, tore at Savannah every moment they were together.

They ate thick, hard biscuits and steaming grits. Part of Adela's thinness was from Miss Prewitt's dreadful cooking.

After breakfast, Adela paused in the hall. "I have tasks I must take care of. I have Horace's mending and I keep the upstairs clean. Miss Prewitt just cooks and cleans the downstairs."

"Good. Let's start with the upstairs," Savannah said cheerfully, and took Adela's arm to lead her to her bedroom and close the door. "Now we can talk."

"No, we can't," Adela said, looking miserable. "Miss Prewitt will come listen," Adela whispered.

"I thought she cleaned downstairs, so why would she be up here?"

"She puts away the laundry. She watches me all day long. Horace has given me a list of tasks to complete. There are certain rooms I'm to clean each day and things I'm supposed to have done. I have to have my chores finished when he gets home or he gets very angry."

Savannah bit back a retort. Adela could not change her husband's demanding ways. "What are today's tasks? I'll help, and we'll be through sooner. Then we can go into the yard to talk where Miss Prewitt can't hear us."

"Oh, Savannah, it is so good to have you here!" Adela burst into tears and Savannah ran to hug her, hating how frail her sister felt, almost nothing but skin and bones.

"Don't cry. It's over. You'll be gone this time tomorrow. I promise."

"I can't believe I can really get away from him. He gets more demanding all the time, more cruel. I think he enjoys being cruel. She's like him. Occasionally she'll give me a pinch. When I complained to him, he told me he didn't want to hear about my difficulty managing the hired help."

"That's dreadful," Savannah said, patting Adela's shoulders. "Well, dry your eyes and pack a valise and bring it in here and let me help with your chores."

"I mustn't let her see the valise."

"We won't," Savannah said. "Put it in my room. If you get caught, you can say you are giving me a dress to wear while I'm here."

When she smiled at her sister, Adela hugged her tightly. "I can't believe you are really here and you'll take me away from him."

"I am and I will. Now let's pack while Miss Prewitt is busy with the breakfast things."

It gave a painful twist to Savannah's heart to watch her sister scurry fearfully from bedroom to bedroom, bringing a few meager possessions to pack for their journey. At last, Savannah had the two bags ready and pushed beneath the high bed.

The day seemed doubly long, and dinner was another solemn time. Everyone ate in silence. Platt's gaze was constantly on her, and he occasionally broke the silence to ask her more questions about Cairo and Vicksburg.

When they were finished, they adjourned to the parlor. Horace left the house to go to a town meeting. Miss Prewitt cleaned after supper and Savannah and Adela sat in the parlor to wait until Miss Prewitt finished her tasks and left.

For the next hour they sat with Adela's head bent over mending while Savannah held a book. She couldn't read a page; instead, she kept glancing at the clock.

"Won't she ever leave?" she whispered to Adela. She could hear Miss Prewitt in the kitchen, still banging pots as she cleaned.

Adela frowned and looked again at the clock. "She's usually gone by this time. I don't know what's keeping her tonight. I'll go get something from the kitchen. A lamp to sew by," she said and stood, placing the white shirt she was mending in the chair. Savannah's nerves were stretched tight. Platt had been gone an hour now. Adela was uncertain when he would return, and they needed to get away from the house. At half-past eight, Red Hawk would be here, and Miss Prewitt might still be working. Then what would they do?

The clock chimed eight times, a steady sonorous ding that reverberated in Savannah and increased her nervousness.

Adela returned, looking worried. "She is slower than any time I can remember. I don't know what she's doing. She said she would be finished in another ten minutes."

It was twenty minutes later, almost half-past eight and almost time to meet Red Hawk, when Miss Prewitt said good night sourly and left. The instant she closed the door, Adela and Savannah raced upstairs to get their things.

"Be quick! We're so late," Savannah said.

"He could come home at any time. He said it would be nine, but with Horace I never know," said Adela, fastening a bonnet on her head.

Savannah handed a valise to Adela and picked up hers and her reticule and they started to leave. Adela leaned down to put out the lamp.

"Leave the lamps," Savannah said, urgency prodding her. They were taking a huge risk trying to escape the house. Now that the time had come, Savannah wanted to be out and gone as swiftly as possible.

They reached the front hall when a key scraped in the lock.

Adela froze, staring at the door. As the knob turned, Savannah reached out to grasp Adela's arm. The door swung open and Horace Platt faced them.

CHAPTER TWELVE

Frowning, he stepped into the hallway. Savannah wanted to pick up her skirts and run like she had when she'd fled the *General Thibodeaux*. But she couldn't leave Adela, who had gone white as a sheet. Adela dropped her valise and began to back away from him, wrapping her arms around herself.

"What in damnation are you doing?" he stormed, slamming the door with enough force to rattle the panes.

Adela backed up. "Nothing," she said, barely able to get out the words.

"Miss Prewitt told me you were up to something. What's that you're carrying? Where the devil are the two of you going at this hour?" He stomped toward Adela, his face turning scarlet and his fists doubling.

She backed away, bumping the wall.

"Horace—"

"You thought you were going to run away?" he shouted, waving a thick fist at her.

Savannah's wits returned in a rush as anger replaced her first shock and fear. In horror she watched as he swung his hand

and slapped Adela with such force that the sound was a loud crack.

Screaming, she flew backwards and he charged after her, and the two of them disappeared into the parlor.

"You would run away, you ungrateful—"

Savannah heard another blow and Adela screamed again. She was sobbing now. Savannah burst into the room and saw Adela cowering over a chair and Platt hitting her.

Rage enveloped Savannah and without thinking, she looked for the nearest object, anything to get his attention and make him stop beating poor Adela. Rushing to the closest marble-topped table, she grabbed a vase and threw it at him. "Leave her alone!" she screamed.

The vase hit him squarely between the shoulder blades, fell to the floor, and smashed to pieces. As he turned, Savannah pulled out the derringer and raised it.

He laughed and his eyes glittered. "You witch. I told your father he would never be able to marry you off until he beat the impudence out of you. Well, now someone is finally going to do that."

"Leave my sister alone. Adela, get your things."

"You can't go, and she won't. The law is on my side where Adela is concerned, and they'll never know about you. You're in my house now. There's no father to protect you here."

Platt's blue eyes glittered wildly, and saliva ran down his chin as he came toward Savannah. "That little pistol is nothing."

"It is enough to stop you, and I'll fire it. Adela, get over here."

"Stay where you are, Adela," he snarled. He whirled around and raised his hand to hit Adela again.

"No!" Savannah screamed, moving closer.

With lightning swiftness he spun and struck Savannah, sending her stumbling. Too late, she realized she had done exactly what he wanted her to do.

He was down on top of her in a second, his heavy weight pinning her to the floor, his breath foul with tobacco and alcohol.

He slapped her and pain exploded. Stars danced in front of her eyes.

He grabbed her wrist to take the pistol. That would be the end, she knew. He twisted her wrist.

Crying out with pain that shot up her arm and struggling against his strong grasp, knowing he would break her wrist in another second, she twisted the derringer to aim at his head. As they struggled, the muzzle of the little gun was only inches from his forehead. He laughed at her as she cried out in pain.

She squeezed the trigger.

The blast was loud, and a look of surprise crossed his face. As blood spurted from a wound in his forehead, he plunged forward, falling heavily atop her.

While Adela screamed, Savannah shoved at his heavy body, trying desperately to push him away.

"Savannah!" The deep masculine cry from another part of the house was Red Hawk.

"We're here in the parlor," she shouted in answer and heard him run down the hall. Scooting away from Platt's body, Savannah rushed to Adela, who was sobbing wildly. Blood streamed from her mouth and a cut on her cheek. Her flesh was red from the blows, her face already swelling.

Red Hawk charged into the room with his pistol drawn. "What the hell—"

"I shot him," Savannah said woodenly, dropping the derringer. She was shaking from head to toe, horrified by what had happened, stunned by the swiftness of it all. "He hurt me and he kept on and I had to shoot."

"That bastard," Red Hawk said, looking at Adela and then at Savannah. Dressed in black, with a black headband around his forehead, he looked solid and strong and Savannah started toward him. In swift strides he crossed to her. "Damn him," he said, wrapping her in his embrace.

His strong arms around her were reassuring, and Savannah wanted to cling to him, but Adela was sobbing hysterically.

Savannah pushed away from him. "Adela," she said, returning to slip her arm around her sister's shoulders.

"What'll we do?" Adela cried.

"You two go—" Red Hawk was interrupted by a bang as the front door crashed open. A man carrying a rifle ran inside.

"Mrs. Platt? I heard a shot—"

Red Hawk spun around and hit the man, sending him staggering.

"Oh, no!" Adela screamed. "That's Rufus Nardin, our neighbor. Don't hurt him!" she cried.

As if he didn't hear her, Red Hawk was on Nardin, wresting the rifle from him. "Get out," he told Savannah. "Get her and get out."

"I shot him," he said to Nardin, waving the Colt in front of the man's face and putting himself between the man and Savannah.

"No!" Savannah cried.

"Savannah, take your sister and get out of here!" Red Hawk snapped. "Go!"

Savannah grabbed Adela's hand, and the two rushed out of the room.

Numb with shock, Savannah picked up their bags and her reticule and they hurried outside across the yard. They were going over the wall when Red Hawk caught up with them.

He went over swiftly and dropped to the ground. Savannah had tossed their bags over the wall and he fastened them to the saddles. Her wrist throbbed painfully, and she tried to avoid using it as she put an arm around Adela. Still terrified by what had happened, she was shaking almost as much as Adela.

"We have to hurry," Red Hawk said, moving to her side to put his arm around her waist.

"I killed him."

"Savannah, you were protecting yourself and your sister," Red Hawk said, tightening his arm around her. Adela moved away from them with a wary look at him. "That's self-defense. You did what you had to do, and it took courage."

He tilted her face up to his and looked at her. "Did he hurt you?"

"A little. I shot him."

"You were protecting yourself and your sister," Red Hawk repeated fiercely. "I'm sorry, we can't stand here until you calm down and get over your shock. We have to go. I tied the neighbor so he can get loose easily, so we'll only have a short head start. Can she ride?" He nodded at Adela, who continued to shake and cry.

"Adela, can you ride?"

"I can hold you," Red Hawk said to her, "and take you on my horse." Dropping his arm from Savannah, he stepped forward and scooped Adela up into his arms. Savannah saw her flinch as he reached for her.

"Sorry, Adela," Red Hawk said with such gentleness that Savannah was momentarily startled. Never had she heard him speak to her in such a tone. "Do you want to ride with me?"

"No!"

Savannah knew Adela was terrified of him. She could see her shaking. Her eye was swollen shut and her cheek was puffing up. Red Hawk lifted her gently into the saddle. "We'll have to ride fast. Can you do that?"

"Yes," she said. "Savannah, I'm sorry—" Her voice broke, and tears streamed down her cheeks.

"Don't cry." With tears streaming down her own cheeks, Savannah's stomach heaved and she turned to lose everything, feeling hot and clammy and sick over what had transpired.

"Are you all right?" Red Hawk asked again, slipping his arm around her waist and stroking her forehead.

Embarrassed over being sick in front of him, she merely nodded and turned to her horse.

"Wait." He grabbed a canteen and poured cold water on his bandanna. When he wiped her face and mouth, the cold water on her skin helped her churning insides. "Put this against your forehead or your nape," he said, giving her the handkerchief. He kept his arm around her waist. "Do you want to ride with me, Savannah? You're shaking badly."

"I'll be fine," she said, unable to stop crying and feeling as if she would be nauseated again. "I'm sorry—"

"Forget it. You think I haven't done that, too? And on

battlefields, I can't tell you the times I've seen strong men lose everything. Can you ride now?''

Red Hawk boosted Savannah up and then swung into his saddle and moved ahead. ''Try to keep up with me. We have to get out of town.''

He urged the horse forward at a swift trot. At the end of the alley, they turned and went two blocks to the north edge of town. ''Now, let's ride,'' he said.

He broke into a canter until they were a mile away, and then they ran at a full gallop. Savannah kept an eye on Adela, fearing she might faint, but she clung grimly to the horse and kept up the pace.

Leaving the road, they slowed and rode through woods into a stream. Feeling numb, Savannah rode beside Red Hawk, with Adela following. The horses splashed through the water.

''We're headed the wrong direction,'' Red Hawk said, reining his bay closer beside Savannah, ''but I want to lead them this way first. Now that our tracks are in the creek, we should lose them. When we get a little farther north, we'll turn west.''

Savannah merely nodded and he stretched out his long arm to take her chin in his fingers and turn her to look at him. ''Are you all right?''

''Yes,'' she replied woodenly, wondering if she would ever be all right again. Her stomach still churned and she rode numbly, trying to avoid thinking about the past hour.

Red Hawk patted her shoulder in a gesture of reassurance that surprised her and momentarily brought her out of her daze. Then she thought about what had happened and horror tore at her again and she felt alone in the world. She glanced at Red Hawk, who had turned to look over his shoulder at Adela.

Was this how he felt on the battlefield? This appalling shock and guilt? Or was a warrior immune to such feelings? He seemed calm and collected enough now.

He turned to Adela. ''Are you all right?''

Adela nodded.

''Then we'll go.''

It was another hour of hard riding before he finally motioned for them to stop. Savannah had no idea the direction they traveled, nor did she care. She had a nagging feeling they should go back and let her turn herself in. They were in thick woods, and she could hear an occasional rustle caused by something other than them or their horses. Her nerves were raw. She expected the sheriff and a posse to suddenly appear and order her arrest. It would be so much better to go back and tell the truth about what had happened.

Red Hawk lifted Adela down off her horse and then moved to Savannah's side to help her dismount. She held her hand away from her as he lifted her down and set her on her feet.

"What's wrong?"

"He tried to get the derringer from me and he hurt my wrist."

"You're still shaking," he said.

"I can't stop. It was dreadful!"

Red Hawk drew her to him gently and wrapped his arms around her. Remorse filled Savannah, and she yielded to tears. "I shot him, but if I hadn't—"

"Shh. You did what you had to. The man was a monster and you were protecting yourself and your sister."

"You said you did it," she said, pulling away and looking up at him. "You shouldn't take the blame."

He shrugged, wiping away her tears with his thumbs. "I won't let you take the blame. I'm going back to my people, so it won't matter. Lawmen won't find me. Don't ever tell anyone anything different. It's best this way. It will save you and Adela more heartache." He tilted her face up to look at her intently. She knew her cheek was puffy and bruised from Horace Platt's slap.

"That bastard."

Savannah tried to gain control of her emotions. "You've never even been introduced to Adela," she said. She took his hand, and they walked the few yards to where Adela sat huddled on the ground, her knees drawn up in front of her and her arms wrapped around them. "Adela, this is Captain Red Hawk. This is my sister, Adela."

"Thank you for rescuing us," Adela mumbled through swollen lips.

"Let me clean your cuts. They'll be less likely to become infected. I can put something on your cuts that might help," he added quietly. With huge eyes, she stared at him so long he thought she might be shocked beyond being able to function. Then, to his relief, she nodded.

Taking the bandanna from his head, he fetched his canteen. He knelt in front of Adela. "I'm going to clean up the cuts a little. I'll try to avoid hurting you."

Rage boiled in him that Horace Platt had treated her in such a manner. He knew she was terrified of him because of what another man had done to her.

Her hands were knotted in her lap so tightly that her knuckles were white. When he reached up to touch her face, she flinched.

"Adela, I swear I'll try to keep from hurting you," he said quietly.

She nodded and bit her lip. "Sorry."

"Don't apologize. You've been through hell."

He dabbed gently at her cuts, cleaning them and deciding that was all they needed. Time would mend her bruises. He turned to Savannah. "Let me see your wrist."

She held out her hand and he took her arm gently, moving her hand. "Nothing broken. If you'll put it in the cold creek water while we're here, it'll keep the swelling down."

She nodded and sat down at the edge of the water to put her hand in it.

"Will a posse come after us?" Adela asked.

Red Hawk shook his head. "I don't think they can track us. We've traveled a lot of our journey in creeks. You can stop worrying, Adela. If anyone should catch us—and they won't— I'm the one they want, not either one of you. There's no one for you to go back to," he added gently.

Savannah was amazed how gentle and kind he was with Adela. He spread a blanket for her and asked her if she wanted to eat now. She said she wasn't hungry, and Savannah suspected her jaw and face hurt too badly to eat. He uncapped a bottle of brandy and handed it to Adela, urging her to drink a little. She said she had never in her life tasted alcohol, and looked at Red Hawk as if waiting for a signal from him to drink.

In minutes, she was curled on the blanket, her eyes closed as she slept.

He came to sit down on the bank beside Savannah. "How's your wrist?"

"It isn't as painful with my hand in the water." She looked into his dark eyes. "I can't ever forget," she said, shuddering, every horrible moment of her struggle with Horace Platt replaying swiftly in her mind.

"No, you won't. Only the most vicious person could forget an experience like you've just had."

She covered her eyes, feeling foolish for yielding to emotion, yet unable to stop the flood of tears. He placed his arm around her.

"Savannah, just remember, he was evil incarnate and you were fighting for your life and for Adela."

"It seems so terrible and wrong."

"So is war. You fought for survival. What would he have done to you and your sister if he had taken the derringer from you and I hadn't been around?"

When she shivered, he tightened his arm around her shoulders. "You did what you had to do. There's no need to suffer guilt. It would have been hell if you hadn't. Look at your poor sister and then see how much guilt you feel."

"I suppose you're right." Savannah wiped her eyes with her fingers. He was pressed close against her side, his arm around her shoulders comforting.

"I worry that I allowed you to take the blame," she said. "If I had an excuse of self-defense, then you should have let me admit my guilt."

"No. I'm going where it won't matter. I won't be living by the white man's laws. The lawmen can find you, and they would bring you back for a trial that would be hard on both you and Adela. It's done, Savannah. Don't concern yourself."

She gave another shudder as the nightmare ran through her

mind again. He pulled her closer against his chest and stroked her head. "Stop worrying. You did the only thing you could do. You protected yourself. He was a monster. I told you, if you feel guilty, just look at Adela. The sight of her face makes me wish I had arrived sooner. I heard the screams in the yard and I'm certain the Nardins did, too."

Red Hawk stroked her hair, and she realized he was taking down her braids. She slid her arms around him, thankful for his comfort and strength in a moment when she desperately needed it. They had fought each other across Louisiana, but now she wanted his reassurance.

She was aware of his slender waist, the cottony smell of his shirt, his solid bulk. She was stunned that he had taken the blame of killing Horace Platt for her.

The enormity of what he had done was sinking in as the first shocks of the struggle and the shooting were wearing off. Red Hawk said it would never matter that he was taking the blame, but she wondered. He wasn't going to join his people until he had his nephew, and that procedure might take months. In the meantime, lawmen all across Texas could be notified by telegraph. Why had Red Hawk made such an enormous sacrifice for her?

She raised her face and looked at his firm square jaw. He had placed his life in jeopardy for her sake!

When she thought of the clashes of wills they had had, it astounded her that he had stepped forward to protect her. She couldn't imagine anyone else who would make such a sacrifice for her.

Tonight she had learned there was another side to him, a protective one. He was still unfastening her hair. Finally, she felt his fingers tug through it.

Don't admire him, an inner voice said. *His kisses are dazzling; he is exotic. He is a strong warrior who takes what he wants. Don't be awed by him. You are going home to Thomas. Your heart is pledged to another and to give your heart to this wild warrior would mean the disruption of your future, the breaking of all important promises, the destruction of honor.*

The voice battled with rising feelings of admiration and desire. She dropped her arms to move away from him. "Thank you again."

He caught her arm and tilted her face up to his, his dark eyes searching hers. "All right now?"

"As good as I can be," she whispered, amazed to see this gentle side to him.

"We'll rest a while. It's probably another hour and a half until dawn. I don't think they can pick up our trail. They may think I've put you on a stage home. Or they may realize exactly what we are doing and keep trying to find our trail, but with all the distance we traveled in streams, it will take them a long time. For now, go ahead and sleep. I'll keep watch."

"And when will you sleep?"

"I slept all day," he said easily. "Lie down, Savannah," he urged softly, his words like a silken caress.

She moved away from him and lay down, cushioning her head on her hand and falling asleep almost instantly.

Red Hawk checked the horses and moved around in a wide circumference near their campsite, making certain they were secure; then he returned. He found a tree stump and sat down to watch, glad he had slept all day. The night was cool and the sounds were usual night noises—the deep croak of a frog, the chirp of crickets, an occasional rustle of a night creature and later, in the distance, the forlorn cry of an owl. He looked at Savannah and his insides clenched with desire. She lay on her side, her hair falling over her shoulder.

He longed to go gather her into his arms and hold her and kiss her. If only he had been twenty minutes earlier to the Platt house! He condemned himself for all that had happened. If he had gone earlier than their prearranged time, he might have whisked them away before Platt returned. And if he had been there earlier, it never would have been Savannah who had to fight Platt.

His fists clenched, and he swore at himself for not getting there sooner. Never again in his life would he let someone he cared about run such risks.

Startled, he realized what had just run through his mind. *Someone he cared about.* How much did he really care about Savannah Ravenwood?

He looked at her and knew no woman had ever affected him as deeply as she had or stirred his desire as strongly. Yet he attributed his ravenous need for her to being away from women through these past war years. Yet the question haunted him. How much did he care for Savannah?

He swore impatiently and stood, moving around, becoming restless. It didn't matter if his whole heart was lost to her. She would never love him in return. So he should stop letting her stay in his thoughts every waking hour or ruin his sleep. He swore softly beneath his breath. He wanted her, and he could take her if he half tried. She never offered more than a few seconds' resistance before she responded wildly to his kisses.

Take her and be done with it! Bitterness coiled inside him, and he remembered his mother's cries when they had beaten him and then, later, seeing her soaked with blood, trying to shut out the sounds of men satisfying themselves with her body. He vowed he would never force himself on a woman, and he intended to keep that vow, yet he knew it would never be force with Savannah.

She is promised to another and that is enough. I will not take another warrior's woman.

He moved away from the sleeping women, walking silently into the trees to put more distance between them and himself, yet still be able to see Savannah and Adela and know they were safe.

When dawn finally crept over the horizon, he shook Savannah awake. Her lashes slowly raised and she looked up at him languidly.

"We ride," he said brusquely, and moved away from her. Just the sight of her relaxed, languorous, warm from sleep, and he wanted to gather her into his arms. He headed toward the horses, hearing Savannah trying to awaken Adela.

The two women talked softly. As Adela sat up and flinched from pain, holding her side, he swore at himself again for being too late to prevent what had happened. Adela's face was puffier today, black and blue from the beating, and he knew she was hurting. She moved slowly, standing with Savannah's aid. He started to go to her and help her, too, but he decided to let Savannah take care of her sister.

Adela started to walk, took one step and cried out, grasping Savannah. Red Hawk was at her side instantly. He steadied her as gently as he could, knowing he frightened her every time he moved too close to her.

"Your foot hurts?"

"I'll be all right in a minute, I'm sure."

"Let me look." He knelt to check her swollen ankle. It was black and blue.

"Can you move your foot at all?"

She bit her lip and twisted her foot carefully, then nodded. "Yes. It just hurts when I step on it."

"You should stay off your foot today. Will you let me carry you to the creek? Then Savannah can help you."

She nodded and when he picked her up, she flinched. "Sorry, Adela."

"My side hurts." She bit her lip again.

He was quiet. There was little he could do to alleviate her suffering. He wondered whether she had cracked ribs, and he knew only time would heal her. He set her down by the creek and moved away, hearing Savannah talk softly to her. He moved upstream out of their sight to wash.

It was late afternoon the next day when they reached Murfresburg, a small settlement on the Rosada River. Red Hawk's nerves were stretched taut after two nights and the past two days alone with Savannah and Adela. He wondered if Savannah had any idea what he felt or how much he wanted her.

They left Adela on the edge of town while they rode in for supplies. With her bruises and cuts, she would draw unwanted attention anywhere she went.

They learned it was market day, so Red Hawk went to the general store to get supplies while Savannah shopped for food. When he came out of the store, he looked around. The square was shaded by a few oaks. People milled in and out of the shops surrounding the square. To the east, vendors hawked their merchandise. He searched for Savannah in the crowd. He saw her crossing the wide, dusty street and stepping up on the boardwalk. Passing a one-story log building, she stopped, quietly staring at something. She glanced over her shoulder, and her gaze met his. He touched the brim of his hat with his finger to acknowledge her. She turned away and disappeared beneath an awning where a vendor was selling his merchandise.

Red Hawk made his purchases and strode across the street to find Savannah. As he approached the long low pine building where she had paused, he saw the iron bars over a small window to one side of the open door and realized it was the sheriff's office and the jail. Red Hawk stepped up on the boardwalk and walked past the open door. Glancing at the wall, he halted, a chill racing down his spine when he saw what had caught Savannah's attention.

CHAPTER THIRTEEN

Against the rough pine logs was nailed a series of posters, the white paper stark against the rough brown of the pine. It was the first poster on the right that held Red Hawk's attention.

WANTED DEAD OR ALIVE, the caption read, the thick black print bold enough that it was like a shout. *One thousand dollars reward for the capture of Quentin Red Hawk. Wanted for murder of Sergeant Millard Tothill and murder of Horace Platt.*

One thousand dollars! The amount was an enormous sum. The fresh white paper fluttered slightly as the breeze caught it. Red Hawk wanted to reach up and yank it off the wall, but people all around could easily see him.

Suddenly feeling as if every eye were on him, he walked past the poster to the end of the boardwalk. He stepped down and angled toward the vendors around the town square. Covered carts and open carts held a variety of vegetables and materials. Cooked food and the smells of broiling meat and wood smoke were enticing.

In the milling crowd, he searched for Savannah's auburn hair. He wanted to grab her and go, to get out of town as swiftly as he could. Common sense told him to take his time. If he did, he would draw less attention to himself. The poster hadn't held a picture or a description.

He spotted her buying apples. She stood in front of a cart piled with vegetables. She wore her blue poplin dress and the tiny blue hat. After days of travel, the dress was wrinkled and the hat slightly smashed, and he remembered how beautiful she had looked that first time he had seen her in the green silk dress and bonnet.

His gaze roamed over the vendors, the people shopping, the men standing around smoking their pipes or cigarillos. He felt as if too many eyes were on him, but he strolled to Savannah's side as if he had all the time he wanted.

Before he reached her, she glanced over her shoulder and met his gaze. His pulse jumped at the look she gave him, a faint smile tugging up the corners of her mouth as if she shared a wonderful secret with him. Someone jostled against her, and she dropped turnips she was holding. As the purple and white globes rolled in the dust at her feet, a slender, dark-haired man turned and knelt to pick them up.

"Let me get them, ma'am," he said, grabbing up the turnips and turning to smile broadly at her as he swept off a broad-brimmed black hat.

"Burford Cochran, at your service, ma'am."

"Thank you, Mr. Cochran. I'm Mrs. Meade and here's my husband."

In the most irrational manner, Red Hawk wanted to shove the man away from her. Surprised at himself, he slid his arm around her waist.

"Mr. Thomas Meade, sir," Red Hawk said, offering his hand and trying to control his temper. He knew the man had done nothing to warrant it except to try to please Savannah.

"Glad to make your acquaintance. Are you folks moving to our town?"

"No, sir," Red Hawk answered easily, holding Savannah close against his side. "We're on our way to Saint Louis."

"I see. Nice to have you here," the man said and tipped his hat before turning away, his blue eyes lingering on Savannah.

"Thank you, Mr. Meade," Savannah said impishly.

"You're dazzling the local townspeople."

She gave him another mischievous smile that made his pulse jump. "Surely you exaggerate, Mr. Meade. How nice it is to have a loving husband who is so attentive."

He knew she was teasing him, but her playfulness only made him want her all the more and he was at a loss for words, his throat closing up and desire burning in him.

"Now what would you like here?" she asked, glancing around her and waving her hand.

"You, Savannah," he answered quietly and her head jerked around, her gaze flying up to meet his. Her eyes were wide, a startled expression on her face, but then as she looked at him, he saw the transformation come.

As they stared at each other, he could feel the tension spark between them. He knew she was reacting to him as much as he was to her. His pulse roared in his ears and he forgot everyone milling around them. He couldn't resist reaching out and placing his hand on her hip.

"I don't think you should do that," she said breathlessly in a faint voice.

He knew she was right and in another minute they would be drawing attention to themselves. He dropped his arm and moved a step away from her, glancing back at her.

"Have you found everything you need, Mrs. Meade?" he said, injecting warmth into his voice and hoping most people thought they were husband and wife.

"I'm almost through with my purchases. They have apples and we can get some tamales to take with us. I want to get enough food that we won't have to stop until we get to San—"

"We can stop before Saint Louis," he drawled, interrupting her and knowing others were listening. He spoke in the thick southern drawl he had learned from soldiers he had known in Tennessee. He was taller than average and with his Indian heritage, he knew people noticed him. And every man in town would notice and remember Savannah. Even with the wrinkled blue dress, her flame-colored hair and her luminous green eyes would make any man stop and stare.

He moved away from her and picked up a potato. "Mrs. Meade," he said, speaking to Savannah, "have you bought any potatoes?"

"Not yet, Mr. Meade," she answered with amusement, falling in with his game so none of the local people would hear their real names. He and Savannah had decided they would use the name Meade before they ever rode into town, but now, after seeing the poster, it was even more important.

He took a basket of food from her and later, as they headed toward the general store, he leaned closer.

"Did you see the poster?"

"Yes," she replied, giving him a swift glance.

"Hopefully, no one here is paying much attention to—"

"Everyone is paying attention," Savannah protested. "We're strangers here. I've had several women introduce themselves and invite me to church Sunday and ask if we're moving here or if we're staying or visiting someone."

"Men aren't as questioning. Too many men are hiding their pasts. At least there was no drawing of me on the poster, but the sheriff who put it up saw it and it's a huge sum of money. Also, they'll remember us. I know you're receiving attention. Particularly male attention."

"That's not so!" she exclaimed, laughing lightly, and he looked at her, relishing the few moments when she laughed. Her smile and laughter warmed the day, a merry sound that made him want to hold her and try to cajole her into more laughter.

"Who was Sergeant Tothill?" she asked as they moved into the street and out of earshot of others.

"I didn't kill Tothill," Red Hawk announced, wondering whether she believed him or not. "There were five of us sent back to find medications. We were caught by a Federal patrol. The Union soldiers under Tothill's command were bringing us back to Vicksburg. Sergeant Tothill was a bloodthirsty bully. He mistreated his prisoners. We got a chance and took it, overpowering the Federals. After tying our captors and taking their horses, we decided to split up. I left the Federals alive, but as I rode away, I heard a shot fired. One of our men must have shot and killed Tothill. I'm wanted for the murder—maybe because to his men, I was the most likely one.''

''Why would you be?''

''Because Tothill hated Indians.''

''That's how you got the scars on your back,'' she guessed.

''Yes. I hated Tothill, but I didn't kill him.''

Savannah listened to him talk about his capture. He was wanted by the Union Army as much as she was, yet the farther they traveled from the war, the less likely it was anyone would recognize him.

Her arms as well as Red Hawk's were filled with their purchases, and now they would have enough to last them into San Antonio so they wouldn't have to risk riding into any more towns. Yet how many here would remember them and send someone searching for them?

Red Hawk was wanted for two murders, when they counted Horace Platt. He had explained the killing of the sergeant. She believed him, but it disturbed her to know there was a warrant for his arrest for something she had done. One thousand dollars was an enormous sum—more than any other reward she had ever known about. And it would mean bounty hunters as well as lawmen would be after him. They reached the horses that were hitched at a rail in front of the general store.

As Red Hawk took things from her hands to pack them on the horses, she watched him. She still wondered whether she should confess about Horace Platt and get that charge against Red Hawk dropped.

He met her gaze and his dark eyes searched hers while his fingers brushed against her hands. He took some of the supplies and set them on the ground, and then began to pack them carefully into their saddlebags. She was anxious to leave. She wanted to get away from all the people who were watching them. She felt on display, and she prayed no sheriff, or anyone else, stepped up and told Red Hawk that he was under arrest.

She reminded herself that people watched them because they were new in the town. Uneasy, because it was taking time to get their things loaded in the saddlebags, she tried to avoid looking around, but the impulse was too strong to resist. She turned her head and looked directly into the blue eyes of a man watching her.

He lounged against the door of the general store. He touched the brim of his hat as a greeting to her and she nodded, and then his blue eyes went to Red Hawk. Her gaze drifted down and she saw the glitter of the badge on his shirt. He was the sheriff.

Frightened, she was certain he knew their identity. Then she told herself that was ridiculous. There was no drawing of Red Hawk, only a poster with his name. And he had given another name to everyone he met today. A fictitious name. Yet there was a huge bounty on his head. She hadn't read all the small print on the poster. What else had it said about him?

She moved close to his side to help him as he packed a saddlebag. She handed him several folded yards of cotton material she had bought. "The sheriff is watching us."

"It doesn't matter, Savannah." Red Hawk moved leisurely and his hands were steady. Hers were damp from anxiety. If he were arrested now, she would have to step forward and confess and clear Red Hawk.

Her conscience nagged at her. She looked up at him as he worked. His head was bent over the saddlebag as he concentrated on what he was doing. His strong profile, the slightly curved nose, the firm jaw, reflected his strength. His thick lashes were dark above his prominent cheekbones. He cut a glance at her, and she gazed back steadily.

When he returned his attention to what he was doing, her thoughts still churned over the false charges. She was the one who had pulled the trigger. Red Hawk said he had not killed the Federal soldier, either, and she believed him. Yet feeling was strong in some towns against anyone with a drop of Indian blood, and Red Hawk clearly showed his heritage in his dark looks and black hair. The year before the war, she had seen a mob hang a man without a trial. She had run home, but she still couldn't forget that memory of the man protesting his innocence and no one listening.

She feared that if arrested, Red Hawk wouldn't get a fair trial—and with two charges against him, no one would wait to listen.

The constant watchfulness of the sheriff was making her increasingly nervous. In her peripheral vision she could see that he had moved closer and was leaning against a post at the edge of the boardwalk. The urge to look at him again was overwhelming, but she controlled the impulse.

Finally Red Hawk shifted out of her way and waved to her. "Mrs. Meade," he said politely. He helped her mount, handed the reins to her, and went to the bay to put his foot in the stirrup. He swung into the saddle as the sheriff came toward them. "Where you headed, Mister?"

"We're riding to Saint Louis, then maybe head on northwest to start a new life."

"Dangerous country for a man alone and his wife," he said, squinting his blue eyes as he watched Red Hawk.

"We'll keep to the traveled roads and at Saint Joseph, Missouri, my brother is joining us."

"Where've you come from?" the sheriff asked bluntly, a question not often put to people close to the frontier.

"N'awleans," Red Hawk replied with a drawl, and she guessed that any loyal Union sympathizer would not be particularly welcome in this part of Texas. While some counties had strong Union sympathy, most of the people were pro-Confederacy. In some areas of Texas, the feelings ran high.

"Good luck to you. Ma'am," the sheriff said, tipping his hat to her.

She smiled and nodded and followed Red Hawk as he turned the bay into the wide street. Her back was prickly, and she was certain the sheriff was still watching them.

Red Hawk turned at a corner and she caught up with him, looking at him quizzically again. "We're headed the wrong way to find Adela."

Sara Orwig

''I told them we were going to Saint Joseph, Missouri. That's northeast of here. We'll ride out of town to the north and then circle back to get Adela.''

Savannah saw the wisdom in this and wished she had thought of it herself. They passed small houses with gardens of neat rows of green corn, greens, feathery tops of carrots, and vines of pole beans. She wanted to urge the horse to a gallop, but instead, they moved at a slow walk past the houses, into the country. When they turned east and finally south, he still moved at a walk. Trees grew thick and tall on either side of the trail and the undergrowth was lush from recent rains. The morning was quiet, the only sounds their voices and the clop of the horses' hooves. She looked over her shoulder again, feeling any moment the sheriff might come riding after them.

''How can you be so calm?''

Red Hawk turned to give her a cool appraisal. ''You appear as calm as you did when you crossed the deck of that sternwheeler in Vicksburg,'' he drawled.

She raised her chin. ''Perhaps, but that was different. A woman who takes some bottles of medicine is different from someone with a huge bounty on his head. And two charges are even worse than one.''

''They can only hang you once,'' he drawled.

''Please, don't say that!'' His calmness was upsetting her. ''The bounty they have on you is excessive. Someone wants you caught badly.''

He shrugged. ''I imagine it's because most of the citizens of Nacogdoches thought Horace Platt was an upstanding citizen. They may think I have taken Adela against her will.''

''Surely not!'' Savannah exclaimed. It had never occurred to her that anyone would think such a thing.

''Look at both of you, battered and bruised and cut from Platt, but their neighbor Rufus Nardin didn't know that. For all he knew, I could have caused your pain and bruises—''

''Oh, great saints! They would hang you before even listening to your side of it. If they arrest you, I'll have to confess and tell the truth.''

His hand clamped around her wrist. "Savannah," he said firmly, in a quiet voice that was cold as ice, "don't you ever confess to that killing. Promise me now." His brown eyes held a determined glint that was becoming familiar to her.

"I can't promise you and let you hang for a deed done by me," she said, aware of his intense gaze on her and his hand still clamped on her wrist.

"Promise me!"

"I won't," she said, feeling the clash of wills that had happened constantly between them when they first met. "You mean well, but it isn't right."

"I won't hang for it. Now promise me."

"You can't say you won't hang!" she snapped, certain he would if he were caught. "No, I won't—"

He turned the bay, causing her horse to turn to avoid a collision. At the edge of the road, he dismounted and tethered his horse, took her reins and came back to stand beside her horse and look up at her. "Get down."

"I'm not going to argue with you. I—"

Reaching up, his hands closed on her waist and he pulled her out of the saddle. She slid off into his arms. "Just stop! I'm not going to argue with you, and you're not going to win this time."

His hand closed firmly on her waist, holding her. He looked into her eyes. "You're not to jeopardize yourself. Give me your promise you won't," he said with that quiet force that was like a steel saber sliding across the throat.

"I can't!" she cried, upset now with his insistence. "I can't promise I'll let you take the blame when you're innocent. I couldn't bear it if—" Suddenly she stopped, realizing what she had said as something flickered in the depths of his dark eyes and the intense look in their brown depths changed to smoldering desire.

Looking away, she burned as a hot flush crept into her cheeks. She twisted to break free of his grasp. "Release me." What had she revealed to him? Why had she said such a thing? He was no part of her life except in the most fleeting manner right now.

I couldn't bear it if—How could she have said that? And the unspoken words might as well be shouted—*something happened to you.* He had to know that was exactly what she was going to say.

Yet it would be wrong for him to stand trial, and she couldn't bear for any innocent man to suffer or be prosecuted for a crime she had committed. Why hadn't she given him that simple answer? She wouldn't want *anyone* to suffer over something she had done. Oh, why hadn't she just said that?

Yet she knew it was more than that. Much more. She turned her head away so she couldn't see him out of the corner of her eye. What was the matter with her? Why was he becoming so important?

"Damn you," she snapped suddenly. "Let them hang you and I will come watch!"

She turned away swiftly and rushed to her horse to mount up, but not before she saw the surprise and a flicker deep in his eyes.

He caught up with her, yanking her down, and she whirled, embarrassed, angry at his constantly telling her what she could or could not do. Her temper snapped and she doubled her fists to pummel his chest.

"Let go of me!" Embarrassed, furious with him and with herself for revealing too much about her feelings for him, she struggled with him.

"Savannah—" The word was coaxing, yet his arms were bands of steel around her, holding her tightly. He framed her face with his hands. "You couldn't bear *what?*"

"You let go of me," she snapped. His dark eyes probed her mind like fingers moving on her body.

His gaze dropped to her mouth and then he leaned down, silencing her as his mouth covered hers. Her protest was a muffled sound in her throat. She fought him wildly, knowing she was fighting herself and the wild surge of longing and excitement that blossomed in her. She felt as if she had dropped into space and were hurtling down, her stomach turning over, feeling dizzied, feeling too many emotions. Excitement, need, longing clashed in her.

Her protests were unintelligible; her struggles were weakening because she wanted his kisses and strong arms around her. Her lips parted and she was lost. His tongue went deep into her mouth, stroking hers, possessive and demanding.

She couldn't fight him or her own longing. She shivered and then he leaned over her. "Put your arms around me," he whispered before flicking his tongue over her ear.

She slid her arms around his neck and clung to him, reveling in the marvelous sensations streaking in her. This wild warrior was trembling as he held her, his desire all-consuming, his searing looks melting her before he ever touched her. And now his hands . . .

His hands were everywhere, tantalizing, stroking, building the fires that were burning her to cinders. He caressed her back, his hand sliding to her waist, over her hip, then down over her buttocks and back up to the neck of her dress. He caressed her as he kissed her and she responded, matching him move for move, her hands sliding over him, discovering the breadth of his shoulders, the length of his thighs.

She was faint from the sensations consuming her. Bright lights danced before her closed eyes; the only sound was the heavy pounding of her heart.

She could feel his arousal pressing against her. And then his fingers were warm, callused, caressing her nape lightly, sliding over her shoulders, the air cool on her skin as his hands slid down her arms and he pushed her bodice down. Her protest was a whimper that changed to a moan of pleasure when he bent and kissed her breast through the chemise. His breath was hot, bringing her to another level of awareness, making her tremble as much as he did.

He pushed away the chemise and cupped her breasts, his thumbs circling her nipples as he kissed her hard. She tugged his shirt from his pants and slipped her hands brazenly beneath it, curious, wanting to discover him.

He made a deep sound in his throat as her fingers skimmed over his bare skin. Then he leaned down to take her breast in his mouth and his tongue flicked over her nipple.

She cried out with pleasure, her fingers sliding out from beneath his shirt. One hand tangled in his hair; the other clung to his shoulder as if she were uncertain she had the strength in her legs to stand.

Pleasure was a roaring, white-hot need, stirring a longing deep within her that she had never known before.

She wanted this tall warrior, this man of the plains who was strong-willed and arrogant and would never love her beyond the way he was loving her now.

He wanted her body, but he would never want her heart. And she was promised to another. Another man . . . so far away.

Red Hawk leaned back and she opened her eyes to find him looking at her.

"You're beautiful," he whispered hoarsely.

His eyes made her reach for him, wanting his hands and mouth to work their magic.

His arm went around her waist and he yanked her to him tightly, wrapping both arms around her to crush her against his chest as he kissed her long and hard.

She clung to him, breathless, kissing him in return, her conscience a dim voice. He raised his head. "Promise me, Savannah."

It took seconds for the words to settle and become reality. Was this why he had kissed her so wildly? Did he know he could turn her to boneless, mindless mush and then demand and get whatever he wanted?

Twisting free, she moved away from him, pulling up the chemise swiftly as anger replaced the wild feelings surging in her. She clung to her anger, trying to ignore the clamorings of her heart and body, the yearnings that made her want to step right back into his arms and feel his hands on her body again.

She slipped her arms back into the sleeves of her dress and reached behind her to button the dress with trembling fingers.

The only reason he had kissed her senseless was to get his way, she told herself angrily. The kisses had meant nothing to him.

"I will not promise you any such thing!" she snapped and turned her back.

Again he caught her arm and spun her around, his scowl as stormy as a wind-driven rain. "Savannah, you said, *I couldn't bear it if*— What couldn't you bear?"

"I don't recall," she said swiftly.

"Savannah," he said, his voice seductive, coaxing. "What couldn't you bear?"

She raised her chin. "I couldn't bear for anyone to take the blame for something I had done," she snapped, her heart pounding with the lie. It was so close to the truth—and yet so far from the truth.

It sounded true, and she saw the flicker in his eyes again, a shuttered look coming to his features as he nodded and turned away. She couldn't ever tell him that she couldn't bear for him to suffer or be in prison or hang when he was innocent of the charges and she cared too much what happened to him.

Silently, he mounted. She mounted her horse, realizing it was the first time he hadn't helped her onto her horse since she had encountered him. He rode ahead, silent, probably angry with her, yet she knew it was best that way for both of them.

Her body tingled still from his touch and she wanted him more than ever. She would forget, she told herself. Soon, he would be a dim memory and then, when Thomas returned home, she would forget Red Hawk altogether.

She looked at his straight back. He was tall in the saddle, the width of his shoulders tapering down to slim hips. She rode behind him. Her gaze ran over him and she remembered what it felt like to be pressed against the solid length of him, to feel those hard thighs against her, to have his strong arms holding her, his rigid shaft pressing insistently against her.

Longing persisted, clamoring in her, and it took an effort to keep from reaching out and touching him now. Heated and perspiring from her erotic thoughts, she knew she had to get her thoughts off him.

It was an almost impossible task, but as she thought about the charges against him, her fears increased. She flicked the reins and caught up to ride on the trail beside him.

"We shouldn't have to go into another town until we reach San Antonio. You're not going to be safe there, either."

He shrugged. "San Antonio is large, with many people. I'll avoid the sheriff as much as possible."

"What will you do if you have to go to court to get custody of your nephew?"

Another shrug. "I'll do what I have to. I want legal custody of Matt because there is money involved that should be his. I just pray no one in San Antonio has paid close attention to those wanted posters and that by the time you and I arrive there, my poster will be covered by another one."

"I doubt if anyone who reads that you are wanted will forget it. The reward is the highest I've ever heard about."

His head swung around and a dark eyebrow arched. "Frightened to ride with me, Savannah?"

"No, I'm not! Why should I be afraid?"

"Because I could bring trouble down on you and Adela."

"You won't, I'm certain," she said and received a long, curious look from him.

They found Adela asleep, curled on a blanket. "She should stay awake when she's alone," Red Hawk said, dismounting. "I'll saddle her horse and you get her awake so we can go. We're still close to Murfresburg, and I'd just as soon put distance between us and the town in case the sheriff looks again at the wanted poster and thinks about the half-breed who was just in town. A thousand-dollar reward is worth making a mistake and holding someone until the marshal can come."

He dismounted and was thankful Adela was safe. If anyone had come upon her, she would have been helpless. As he saddled her horse, he looked over the animal at the two women. As little as he knew Adela, the two of them seemed as different as dust and water. Adela was shy, trusting, timid. Savannah was none of those qualities. He'd had to win her trust, and there was no shyness or timidity in her. His gaze rested on her and heat coiled in his groin while he remembered their kisses, her body half-bared to him, her eagerness and passion.

He swore softly. She would never leave her fiancé, never care about him other than in the same charitable manner she had toward others. She could never be his woman. She would never want to be. And he shouldn't want her except in the most basic, primitive way, because she was so many things he didn't like. She liked luxury. She had talked about her life before the war, and she loved that way of life. She held great store in her possessions, always carefully checking to see where they were.

He didn't want any part of the white man's way. He had lived that way for over half his life now, and he longed for the life he'd had before that, the life of a warrior, where material wealth was not important.

"How are you, Adela?" he asked gently, trying to always remember to be quiet and careful around her. She seemed terrified of him even after the time they had been together.

"I'm quite fine, thank you," she mumbled through swollen lips.

She was anything but fine, Red Hawk thought, looking at her bruises, the angry cuts that looked dreadful against her smooth pale skin.

They mounted up to ride, and he suspected it was agony for Adela, but he knew she was far too polite to complain—and far too grateful to be away from Platt forever.

That night when they camped on the plains, Red Hawk sat in the darkness, keeping watch, unable to keep from glancing every few minutes at Savannah, who had taken down her hair and fallen asleep instantly. How long would it take to get Matthew? How dangerous would it be for him in San Antonio? He would have no one to help him if he was arrested. Caleb was still fighting a war; there was no other family.

It was nearly dawn when Red Hawk turned to look at Savannah and found her cool green gaze on him. They studied each other in silence, and all he could think was that he wanted to kiss her and that he should walk away.

She sat up and stretched and his pulse jumped as her dress pulled tautly over her firm, high breasts. She looked at him as she stood.

"Lie down. I'll keep watch."

He nodded, stretching out, keeping his rifle in hand as he closed his eyes and dozed.

The next time he opened his eyes and looked around, the women were eating apples and talking softly. Savannah was brushing her hair and he lay still with narrowed eyes, watching her begin to braid it. He moved over beside her to drop down and sit cross-legged.

"Have a good sleep?" she asked.

"Yes. And both of you?" he asked, looking at Savannah. "Turn around," he said, taking a thick strand from her hand.

When she did as he instructed, he began to slowly braid her hair.

He glanced at Adela and saw her watching him with wide eyes. She looked away instantly the moment he glanced at her, yet she had looked perplexed. Maybe she had been puzzled about a man who would braid a woman's hair. He was certain Horace Platt would never have done such a thing.

Savannah was aware of the faint tugs on her scalp, of his fingers brushing her nape. Each little pull was a tug on her senses, a reminder of their moments alone. She was conscious of how close he sat behind her. When he finished the braid, Savannah took it from him and looped and fastened it around on her head.

He stood and took her hand to pull her to her feet. "Now I want to teach both of you how to use my pistol. Savannah, you've had a great deal of experience with this—"

"Oh, please! I never want to touch a pistol again."

"I want you both to know how. Something could happen to me, Savannah, and if it did, I'd want you to be able to handle a pistol. Something could happen to both of us, and Adela would need to know."

He persuaded them and reluctantly Savannah listened as he showed her his revolver. He stood between the two of them, explaining how to load and fire the Colt.

"Now, Savannah, we'll start with you. See that?" He pointed. A hundred yards from them stood a dead tree.

Red Hawk placed the pistol in her hands. The Colt was heavy and she loathed it, remembering Horace Platt and hating to ever pull a trigger again.

Red Hawk stepped behind her and put his arms around her, raising her arms. "Look down the barrel," he said softly into her ear. His warm breath tickled her ear and his arms encircled her. She was far more aware of him than the pistol or her target. Her first shot missed the tree entirely.

"I can't concentrate with you so close," she whispered, turning to look up at him.

His face was only inches from her, and desire blazed like firelight in his dark eyes. She could smell the leathery scent of him, and her pulse drummed rapidly. She turned around and pulled the trigger. The blast deafened her.

This time she hit the tree.

"Bravo!" he said. "I knew marksmanship would come to you. Fire again."

"You move away," she said.

"Why?" he asked, and for a moment she forgot Adela, forgot the pistol, forgot everything except him.

"You know why!" she insisted. "Move away from me."

He leaned down beside her ear, turning his head to whisper, "I wish we were alone."

"We're not!" she snapped, her pulse dancing. Yet conflicting emotions warred within her. She raised the pistol and he steadied her, his arms still around her and his body pressed lightly against hers. Even though it was for the benefit of hitting the target, all she could think about was him. She wanted to fling down the pistol and turn into his arms. Angry with him and with herself, she squeezed the trigger and saw a chip fly out of the tree trunk.

"Good!" he said.

She continued firing until there was only a click.

"You're out of ammunition," he said, taking the pistol from her and turning to Adela.

"I can't," she whispered, staring wide-eyed at the pistol as if he were holding a snake. "I can't," she repeated and shivered.

"Yes, you can, Adela," he said gently. "It's much simpler than many other things you do. It's not loaded right now." He held it out and squeezed the trigger and the click was audible. He turned the grip toward Adela. "Now take the pistol . . ."

Slowly she reached out and took it with shaking hands. "That's it," he encouraged. "Get the feel of it. Turn it over." He moved behind her and took her wrist in his hand and Savannah saw her flinch the instant he touched her.

"Adela," he said quietly, "I've promised I'll never deliberately hurt you. Just relax."

The honeyed coaxing in his voice made warmth curl inside Savannah. At the same time, she suffered a flash of annoyance because he never talked that way to her.

"Now hold it up and look down the barrel and squeeze the trigger."

Adela pulled the trigger and, again, there was only a click.

"Do it again," he said. After she had pulled the trigger on the empty weapon half a dozen times, he took it from her and carefully loaded it and handed it back to her.

"Keep it pointed away from yourself, away from us. Now take it and aim at the tree."

Savannah watched him as he carefully instructed her and stood behind Adela, helping her aim just as he had helped Savannah. Savannah knew Adela feared his touch or for him to stand close. It wasn't just Red Hawk. She would have been that way about any male. Yet his gentle manner with her seemed to be wearing away Adela's fear.

By the end of the hour, Red Hawk called a halt to the lesson, heaping praise on Adela and finally bringing a smile to her face.

* * *

Three days later they had stopped near a stream and Savannah and Adela set up camp. They were beneath a tall oak with blankets spread and the horses tethered nearby. A rabbit killed by Red Hawk was on a spit over an open fire and the roasting smell mingled with the wood smoke, making Savannah's mouth water. Potatoes were in a small skillet, and a jug of cider was cooling in the creek.

Red Hawk had gone to the creek to bathe. It had been four days since they had fled Nacogdoches. To Savannah's relief, Adela was finally beginning to mend. Her face was still black with bruises, but the swelling had gone down and she could straighten up and move about with more ease.

They had traveled across country, something Red Hawk seemed more at ease doing than following trails and roads.

Adela was curled up on the blanket, asleep. Savannah continued getting supper ready, seeing no need to waken her.

As she worked, she heard a muffled sound and the rustle of bushes nearby. She whirled around to peer in the direction of the noise, but saw nothing moving. Yet she was certain she had heard something.

Adela slept quietly and the flames crackled, a thin spiral of gray smoke rising in the air. Savannah's skin prickled and she glanced at the pistol Red Hawk had left with her.

Nothing moved. She could hear the whistle of a bird, the crackle of the fire. Still, she felt as if she were being watched and that something was wrong. She glanced over her shoulder. The woods were dense, but only a few yards into the trees ran the creek where Red Hawk had gone. He told her to fire the pistol if she needed him in an emergency.

She watched the bushes. When nothing happened as minutes passed, she let out her breath and returned to stirring a pot of boiling greens.

And then she heard a twig snap and another rustle.

CHAPTER FOURTEEN

She whirled around again and saw some leaves moving. It was twenty yards northeast from where she stood. As she grabbed the pistol, she shivered from fear.

"Adela!" she whispered. She hurried to kneel beside her sister. Keeping her eyes on the bushes, she shook Adela.

"What—"

"Adela," she whispered.

Adela's eyes grew round and she sat up swiftly. "What is it?"

"I don't know. I heard something," Savannah whispered.

"What sort of *something?*" Adela asked, now sounding terrified. Her blue eyes were filled with fear.

"I don't know," Savannah answered, moving close beside Adela. "One of us should watch the horses and our things. The other one should get Red Hawk. Whoever stays keeps the pistol. Which do you want to do?"

"I don't want to do either."

"Adela, I know I heard something. It could be a person or an animal, but I know there is something out there watching us."

"I'll go get Red Hawk."

Adela started to move away and then stepped back to Savannah's side. "You go. I don't want to leave here."

"Red Hawk showed you how to use this pistol. Just do what you did then."

"Please hurry! You know I can't fight anyone."

"Adela, if anyone comes out of those trees, you start firing. I'll hurry. And get down where you won't be a target."

"Savannah, don't go. Let's fire the pistol and see if the captain comes."

"I'll get him. If you see something, scream, shoot—whatever you have to do."

"Hurry!"

Savannah picked up her skirts and raced to the woods, glancing back at Adela, who was kneeling on the blanket, the pistol in her hands. Savannah plunged through the woods and when she heard splashing, she headed downstream.

She raced through the trees, her gaze searching the stream. As she pushed through brush, he was standing only yards away. He had just stepped out of the stream and held his black pants in front of him, ready to step into them.

Startled, Savannah halted and he held his pants closer in front of him as he stared at her.

He was decently covered, but she could see he was naked. His hipbones showed, and his long, muscular legs were only half hidden behind the pants. His smooth brown skin glistened with water, and drops rolled across his muscular chest. His hair was slicked back away from his face, leaving his features starkly revealed.

Her gaze raced over his broad chest and taut muscles and then down his long legs. Her mouth went dry at the sight of his lean, powerful body. He was virile, full of controlled energy. Then she realized how she was staring, yet she was still immobile, her mind a blank.

"What's happened?" he asked.

With a start she remembered the fright she'd had. "There's

someone or something in the bushes not far from us,'' she said. All fear was gone, replaced by another basic emotion.

"You want to turn your back, Savannah?'' he asked, as if there was a strong possibility she might not want to.

This startled her and she whirled around, embarrassment flooding her. "I heard something and woke up Adela. She has the pistol.''

"Damnation,'' he said. "Come on.'' He was already moving ahead of her, grabbing up his rifle and shirt and running silently through the woods. She tried to keep up with him, aware of how easily he moved. He carried his boots and she was amazed how he could run over the rough ground.

When they burst out of the woods and raced across an open field, he was already yards ahead of her and talking to Adela. He took the pistol and turned to hand it to Savannah as she reached them. Gasping for breath, she took the weapon.

"I'll go look. It must be an animal. If it had been a man, he would have attacked while Adela was alone.'' He yanked on his boots and picked up his rifle again.

Savannah nodded, watching him stride purposefully away and disappear into the trees. The danger had receded in her mind, replaced by embarrassment over her own reactions when she had seen him moments earlier. How could she have been such a dolt? She had stared at his body and acted as if she had lost her wits.

She wished she could lie down, pull some covers over her head, and not see him until the next day.

It was another half hour before he reappeared. Her pulse jumped at the sight of him, and she remembered how he had looked with his chest wet and bare, his hair slicked down on his head.

"It was coyotes and they ran, but they'll circle back. They can smell our supper cooking and it's drawing them.''

"Shouldn't we move on?'' Adela asked.

"No,'' he answered easily, moving to the spit to hunker down and turn the cooking rabbit. Smoke rose tantalizingly into the air, and the succulent smells made Savannah's mouth water. She looked at his long legs as he squatted in front of the fire, seemingly able to stay in the position indefinitely. She knew the strength in his arms, the ease with which he carried both her and Adela.

"This is about done," he said.

Adela moved close beside her. "Will we be safe when we sleep?"

"Yes," Savannah said, knowing Red Hawk would never allow anything like a coyote to harm them.

They passed out tin plates and divided the rabbit and potatoes and greens. While they ate, Red Hawk talked about his childhood, and in minutes he had them laughing. As Adela's laughter pealed merrily, Savannah glanced at her sister and wondered how long it had been since Adela had laughed as freely.

Her sister was beginning to relax around Red Hawk. Savannah knew Adela had been terrified of him that first night and the next couple of days, but she was finally beginning to accept him.

While Red Hawk tended the horses, Savannah and Adela cleaned their cooking utensils and finally, when the chores were done, they sat on their blankets around a dying campfire. Their voices were low and Red Hawk kept his rifle across his legs. He told Savannah to keep the pistol where she could get to it in a minute.

"The night frightens me," Adela said, her voice sounding sleepy. "Savannah has never been afraid."

"Of course I have," Savannah said quietly.

"No, you haven't. Remember when we slipped out one night when you were only nine years old?" She turned to Red Hawk. "We crossed the square. We were going to go look in the store window at the candy."

Red Hawk glanced at Savannah, and she wondered what was running through his mind. He reached out to pull the pins out of her hair and, while Adela talked, took down the thick braids.

"We reached the courthouse, and then Savannah saw someone coming out of the window at the silversmith's. We hid in the bushes and we saw—"

She paused and Savannah smiled. "You can go ahead and say his name, Adela. It was too long ago to matter."

"We saw Myron Featherstone climbing out of the silver-smith's shop and he carried a sack filled with something. We didn't know what to do. If we told Papa, he would be furious with us for sneaking out of the house. We went back home, but I didn't sleep much that night."

"So what did you do?" Red Hawk asked Savannah quietly. His fingers combed through her braids, and she wondered why he liked to wind his fingers in her hair.

"Savannah wrote a letter to Mr. Featherstone telling him that if he didn't put back what he had taken, she would go to the law," answered Adela. "I wouldn't have done anything."

He studied Savannah with a faint smile. "And I'm sure you would have gone to the law."

"I went the next morning and told Mrs. Rollins, our mother's best friend. She suggested the letter. She said I didn't have to sign it, but I did. And Mr. Featherstone put back what he had taken, because soon everyone in town knew that someone had broken into the silversmith's store."

Red Hawk chuckled. "Foiled by a nine-year-old child. I imagine he was quite unhappy with you, Savannah."

"After that, he always glared at me."

"Savannah was always the brave one. I wouldn't have slipped out at night, but she wanted me to go with her."

Savannah leaned across the blanket to get her brush and turned to look at Red Hawk.

His dark gaze rested on her. The fire still flickered, casting an orange glow over him, highlighting the flat planes of his face. When she straightened up, he took the brush from her hands and began to methodically brush her hair. It was a slow sensual grooming, and he continually lifted the heavy strands, his fingers caressing her nape and stirring longings she knew were better left dormant.

They talked far into the night. She was aware of the deep rumble of his voice, and she knew she could talk to him all through the night. They moved from one topic to another until Adela curled up on the blanket and fell asleep.

Red Hawk reached over to touch Savannah's nape, stroking her while they talked. Tingles radiated from each touch, reminders of moments in his arms, making her long to be there again. She was aware of him seated close beside her, his long legs stretched out, one hand playing over her nape and in her hair while he leaned against the trunk of a tree and kept his other hand on his rifle.

Every time the fire burned down, he placed more logs on it. The next time he rose to put another log on the fire, she watched him poke the embers. "Usually you put the fire out as soon as you can."

"I'm no longer worried about soldiers being after us. I don't think we have anyone tracking us, but the coyotes are out there and I want a fire. They won't attack, but I don't want them coming up close."

She shivered, unable to avoid thinking about animals watching them in the dark. She hoped he was right in his assumption that they weren't being tracked. How he could be so sure? "You can't know if someone is after us or not."

"No, and I don't intend to let down my guard, but I don't think there is anyone after us."

"Suppose you're wrong?"

He shrugged. "Don't borrow trouble, Savannah." Then he pulled her back into his arms. She started to protest, looked into his dark eyes, and closed her mouth. The dancing orange flames were reflected in the depths of his midnight eyes, compelling, spellbinding. Slowly, he bent his head, his mouth covering hers.

How easy it was to melt into his arms, to wind her arms around his neck, to return his kisses!

She clung to him, her heart drumming, telling herself to resist, yet raising her mouth to him at the same time. His mouth opened hers, his tongue touched hers.

Savannah moaned softly, feelings and emotions tugging at her while she kissed him. Each time was building more fires;

each time was coming closer to the loss of her control. Yet tomorrow they would reach San Antonio and in another day, she could be telling him good-bye forever.

At the thought of parting with him forever, her heart thudded and she wanted to protest. She would never again in her life see him.

She was going home to marry another man, yet it was in this tall, wild warrior's arms that she found excitement she had never known before. His Comanche passion stirred feelings in her and awakened longings that she hadn't known were possible.

She tightened her arms around him, knowing she was going to long for him over and over again for years to come.

Once again, she had to tell Red Hawk to stop. She moved away from him and he stood, picked up his rifle, and disappeared into the darkness.

She knew he was close at hand. She could feel his presence, his gaze on her. Covered by a blanket, she lay in the soft glow of the fire and thought about him. Sleep was lost to her as her body clamored for his caresses and kisses. Need was a throbbing ache that only he could assuage.

Would it, just once, be so wrong? Just once to be loved and love a man when passion was at its height, when it made her heart race and took her breath? She knew it would never be that way with Thomas. Yet she was pledged and she should put any other ideas firmly out of her mind. She was promised to another man. Would Thomas be faithful and true to her?

The question startled her. She had never considered it before. She had wild, erotic thoughts about Red Hawk, yet her mind closed down at the thought of intimacy with Thomas, who would be her lawful husband in another few years.

Years. When would the war be over? She sat up and looked at the ring of darkness that surrounded them, knowing Red Hawk was out there, probably watching her at the moment. So soon, too soon, he would have his nephew and go out of her life. The thought tore at her more than the thought of the long wait for Thomas to come home.

Am I in love with him? She ran her hand across her forehead. There was something wild and passionate and physical between them. Was it love? Was there trust and love and wanting to know each other forever? She did trust Red Hawk. She had trusted him with her life and Adela's and he had placed his own life at risk to protect her when he told Rufus Nardin that he was Horace Platt's killer.

She stared into space, memories swirling in her mind of moments with Red Hawk. *I love him. I can't love him,* she thought just as swiftly.

She got up and retrieved the cotton dress she was making. Gathering her sewing, she sat close to the firelight and began to work on the dress, knowing she wouldn't sleep for hours to come. She sewed and tried to sort out her feelings for Red Hawk. Was she already hopelessly in love with him?

Red Hawk reappeared over an hour later. He propped the rifle against a tree, removed his boots, and then yanked off his shirt. Muscles rippled in his chest and were highlighted by the glow of the fire. He sat down cross-legged to face her.

"Why aren't you asleep?"

She gave him a level stare. "I couldn't sleep. I keep thinking about everything that's happened, about arriving in San Antonio."

"At least your sister is safe now. He can't ever come after her, so you can go home to Mason."

Savannah nodded. "You still want to go back to your people?"

"More than ever," he said, and his answer hurt, even though she knew it was unreasonable on her part to want him to do anything else.

"You should sleep. But if you're not going to, I am, Savannah. Wake me when sleep overtakes you."

He stretched out only yards from her and she sighed in consternation as she watched him. His half-naked body, golden in the firelight, was a temptation and a reminder that took her attention from her sewing and destroyed any hint of sleep.

When she saw his chest rising and falling in a steady rhythm, she scooted close to him to look at him. In sleep he looked less commanding and severe. He looked handsome as well as tough, with his exotic features, his broad shoulders, slender hips, and long legs. She couldn't resist touching his hair. Her hand drifted to his shoulder, then down to his hip that was still covered in rough denim.

She let her hand roam over his hip, discovering the feel of him. She touched his thigh, and her own body heated and responded while Red Hawk was doing nothing except sleeping.

With a groan she stood and moved away, yet she had nowhere to go, stopped by a wall of darkness. Annoyed, she picked up her sewing and moved across the fire from him and sat down, trying to concentrate on the dress in her lap.

The next day, riding in from the northeast, they arrived in San Antonio. The streets were busy, filled with buggies and carts, with people on foot and on horseback.

Dazzled by the sights and sounds around them, Savannah experienced the rush of excitement she always did on entering the large town. She pointed out new shops and vendors to Adela, turning to Red Hawk to remark on the women's dresses and how the war wasn't as evident here.

Red Hawk saw the sparkle in her green eyes and he was aware of another wall rising between them. She was excited to be in a city. From her remarks, she loved the bustle, the crowd, the shops. Even if Thomas Sievert didn't exist, Savannah wasn't the woman for him. She would never accept his Comanche life. As a wall closed around his heart, he wondered again how much she had come to mean to him.

He rode close to her. "I'll get us rooms at the hotel. We could go to my house, but there are no servants and the place is probably covered in layers of dust."

"It would be safer for you to stay at your home. Adela and I can cook. What's a little dust after all the nights we've spent in the wild?" she argued, curious about his home. It was far easier to imagine him riding with the Comanche than in a home in San Antonio.

Her attention jumped to her surroundings. She loved large towns and cities—except ones like Vicksburg that were ravaged by war and deprivation. But Cairo and San Antonio were intact, life going on, the shortages and hardships not as noticeable. Excitement raced in her and she longed to get a new dress and shoes and bonnet. She would happily discard the blue poplin that she had worn until it was limp and wrinkled. It would never look the same as it had when she had first obtained it.

She glanced at Red Hawk and was surprised to catch him watching her. She smiled because she was happy for the first time in a long time. She was in San Antonio; she had Adela with her, safe and free from Horace Platt.

They reached the downtown and he halted. "Choose which you want, Savannah—my house or the hotel."

"Your house will be safer. We'll manage."

"It won't be as proper," he said.

She laughed, feeling giddy. "Adela is a chaperon, and what have I done these last weeks that has been proper?"

His brow arched and a dark gleam in his eyes sobered her as they stared at each other. She felt a silent challenge from him. She gave a toss of her head. "Your house."

He turned his horse, and she and Adela followed.

They rode into a residential area bordering downtown and he waved at a sprawling red brick mansion that made her stare in wonder.

"Here we are. You can see it hasn't been tended in years."

"This is your home?"

"Remember, my stepfather was a successful merchant here," Red Hawk answered.

She was astounded by the size and grandeur of the house. Beyond a wrought-iron fence, the yard was weed-filled and obviously neglected. Several shutters had broken and hung crazily from windows, and cobwebs and dust were abundant on what she could see of a wrap-around porch, but beneath the neglect was an elegant mansion that had to be one of San Antonio's finest.

"We're staying at the captain's house?" Adela asked softly.

"It'll be safer, Adela. He's wanted for Horace's murder."

"Oh, Savannah, if Papa had just realized what he was getting us into!"

"We can't worry about Papa now."

"Suppose Thomas hears about this?"

"Great saints! He won't hear a word about it. He is half a country away from us. Now stop worrying. We're going to the dressmaker's this afternoon and get new dresses!"

Adela smiled and nodded, but Savannah knew she still worried about Thomas.

They turned down a graveled drive, overgrown with tall weeds, and rode past the house to a hitching rail and a two-story brick carriage house.

"We can still go to the Menger, Savannah," Red Hawk said somberly. "The house will be filled with dust."

"This is safer for both of us," she replied, "and Adela and I can handle dust."

They dismounted and moved through the weeds to a back door. Red Hawk searched on a high window ledge and produced a rusty key. It opened the door and they entered a back hallway. He led them through a high-ceilinged kitchen with glass-fronted cabinets that still held dishes and glasses and assorted crystal. He pushed away the drapes, and sunlight spilled into the dusty room. Dust motes spun in the air, drifting in the beams of sunlight, while Red Hawk's boots scraped against the oak floor.

They followed him down the hall, past rooms with furniture covered by sheets and draperies drawn closed. As they climbed the wide, curving stairs that were carpeted in a deep green, Adela sneezed. Savannah looked at Red Hawk's broad back and then glanced downstairs at the wide hall, glimpsing into the spacious rooms that opened off it, and again marveled at his past.

At the top of the stairs, Red Hawk directed them across the hall to a bedroom. "You may each have your own room. Adela,

how is this?'' He crossed the room and flung open the drapes,
stirring more clouds of dust. When he opened the wide windows, fresh air spilled into the stuffy, musty house.

"This is fine," Adela said, sounding sincere and undisturbed
about the condition of the room. She moved to the four-poster
bed to touch it and Savannah could guess what was running
through Adela's mind. After the rough travel from Nacogdoches, the thought of a bed, dusty or not, seemed marvelous.

"Savannah, you will be in the next room and there's an
adjoining door,'' he said, opening the door. She and Adela
followed him into another bedroom with a rosewood bed and
carved rosewood chests. Savannah couldn't resist touching the
bed, too. "A real bed, at last!''

He threw open the drapes and windows, and fresh air spilled
into the room. She looked at him and was astonished to discover
this elegant home was his heritage as much as the wild, untamed
plains. Never once when he had talked about San Antonio had
she imagined anything like this house.

"There's a bathroom across the hall,'' he said, still leading
the way and moving into the large room to raise more windows.
"My father had this all plumbed so water can be pumped into
this room, but I'll have to see if everything is in working order.
I'm certain it'll be rusty at first.''

"You can get water in here without carrying it in?'' Savannah
asked.

"Yes. He even had something rigged up to heat it downstairs
so warm water would come into this tub, but that has probably
rusted away after all this time. At the end of the hall is my
bedroom.'' They moved back into the hall. "You can come
see where I am,'' he said easily, leading them to his room.

It held a mammoth bed with a carved rosewood headboard
and footboard. Marble-topped tables sat beside it. The chiffonnier was marble-topped and a rocking chair was dust covered. He opened windows while he talked. "I imagine the
buggy is still in the carriage house. I'll ride into town and see
if I can hire someone to drive it for both of you and hire
someone to clean this place—''

"Oh, no!" Adela exclaimed.

"There's no need," Savannah echoed Adela's protest. "We can take care of the house."

He shook his head. "I'll find someone."

"In the meantime, we'll start so we can get the kitchen in order," Savannah said, her mind running over what should be done for them to be able to get supper cooked tonight. "I'll give you a list of things to get when you're in town."

As they went downstairs to start work on the kitchen, Savannah took charge while Red Hawk left to go to town.

First he rode to the courthouse. The wanted poster was prominently displayed in the main hall of the tall building. He drew a deep breath, suddenly feeling as he had in Murfresburg—as if all eyes were on him and everyone knew he was a man with a price on his head. He prayed he would not have to go to court to get Matthew.

Feeling vulnerable and trying to spot any inordinate attention from strangers, Red Hawk headed to his attorney's office. He could almost feel his sister's dark eyes on him, and he vowed he would keep his promise to her and rescue her son just as she wanted.

Three hours later, laden with food and other things he thought they might need, Red Hawk returned home and strode into the kitchen.

Savannah's pulse jumped when she saw him coming, and she rushed to hold open the door. He placed sacks of cornmeal and beans and potatoes on the table. When he tossed aside his hat, she realized his hair was growing out again from the cut she had given him. It had a shaggy appearance around his face. When he stepped into the room, he seemed to dominate and fill it.

"When I was at my attorney's office, I sent a message to my sister's in-laws. I'm to see them early tomorrow afternoon. Tonight, I'll take you both to dinner. We'll take our chances on going out in public so you won't have to cook here."

"You brought food," Savannah said, looking at the potatoes

and cornmeal. "We can cook, and it will be far safer to stay here."

He paused, glancing over his shoulder at her with amusement in his dark eyes. "Very well, Savannah, but I offered."

"I know. This will be fine."

"You'll have help within the hour. My attorney is sending some of his help. I bought a cow so we'll have milk. Right now, I need to check the carriage house, the grounds, and the plumbing. We have a springhouse where we can keep things cool, and I'll look at it. I'll be outside if you want me," he said, and then he was gone, closing the door softly behind him.

Savannah turned to find Adela staring at her. "What is it, Adela?"

"Savannah, you look at him as if you—" Adela broke off and her face flushed.

"As if I what?" Savannah insisted.

"As if you love him. And he looks at you the same way."

"I don't love Captain Red Hawk!" Savannah denied vehemently. "I couldn't possibly. I'm betrothed to Thomas, and that's where my heart lies," she said, but the words had a hollow ring to them, and Adela's frown matched what Savannah felt in her heart. Was she being truthful with Adela? Truthful with herself?

"I hope you know what you feel."

They worked in silence a few minutes until Adela paused. "I'd like to see about a new dress and then, when I look more presentable, I want to see my friend Bertrice while I'm here." A big smile wreathed her face. "Won't she be surprised!"

"Yes, she will, Adela."

Adela touched her face. "I saw myself in a mirror in the bedroom. I look better now, but the bruises still show."

"They're almost gone. By the time you find a new dress or have one made, you should look your usual self."

Tears welled up in Adela's eyes, and she ran across the room and hugged Savannah.

"Thank you for saving me from him! He was a dreadful

man, and he was getting crueler all the time. I was certain he would eventually kill me. He broke my arm last winter—''

Savannah gave a cry and held Adela at arm's length. "You didn't write me about that."

"No. He read too many of my letters. I didn't want you to worry. Savannah, I'm so thankful you took me away from him. I couldn't have run away by myself." She ran her fingers across her brow. "I don't know what I'll do now."

"Don't worry, Adela. You can sew beautifully and you can tutor. We'll find something that we both can do."

"Thomas will come home from the war and marry you and you'll be with him."

"You know you're welcome to stay with us," Savannah said, thinking her marriage to Thomas seemed far in the future and less a reality than ever before. She and Adela discussed their plans as they worked.

Exactly as Red Hawk had declared, three women appeared to help with the cleaning. Relieved of their work, Savannah and Adela had a bath drawn. Afterward, they prepared to go see their dressmaker.

When Savannah was dressed, she went to search for Red Hawk to ask him to saddle the horses. She found him on the drive, stripped to the waist and swinging a scythe to cut the tall weeds. She stopped to watch him, suddenly forgetting everything else except his marvelous body. Muscles rippled across his back as he worked in an easy rhythm.

He glanced over his shoulder, saw her, and stopped. Once again, she had been caught staring blatantly at him. Her gaze flew up and met his look, and desire flared in the depths of his dark eyes.

"Adela and I are going to the dressmaker. Would you please saddle the horses for us?"

"Right away."

While he watched her, sweat beaded his forehead and his body and he swiped his face with the back of his hand.

"You look pretty," he said in a husky voice, and she met his gaze.

"Thank you," she replied. Their exchange was diminishing to breathless words, his voice husky, hers a mere whisper. She could see her wants mirrored in his eyes, yet now they were in town where others could see them and propriety became another barrier between them.

He left abruptly to saddle the horses and, shortly, she and Adela mounted to ride to town.

Red Hawk stood and watched them, his gaze resting on Savannah's back, sliding down over her hips. If he didn't have any difficulty with Celia's in-laws, he would be telling Savannah good-bye by this time tomorrow. The idea of parting tore at him. She had become part of his life.

He doubled his fists. He wanted her more than he had ever desired a woman, yet she wasn't meant to be his. He picked up the scythe to continue cutting weeds, swinging it, trying to work off his frustration over Savannah. He had already sent a letter to the Ashman house by his attorney's clerk, and received an answer back. Tomorrow he had a two o'clock appointment with Matthew's grandfather.

The next afternoon, as he rode to the Ashmans' house, he marveled at the changes in his life. They were back in his home in San Antonio where he had grown up. Like flowers in sunshine, Savannah and Adela were both blossoming. This morning, they had made another trip to the dressmaker. He had turned the hiring of a cook over to Savannah. She had interviewed several applicants and hired a tall woman named Matilda Thalheimer, whose references included a family Savannah knew. Matilda was to both cook and clean, but Red Hawk knew that Adela and Savannah would help her, too.

Staying under the same roof with Savannah was stretching every nerve to the breaking point. Red Hawk knew things would have to change swiftly, or he would not be able to resist taking her into his arms and into his bed.

As he rode along the wide street with tall, perfectly kept Victorian houses, he suspected that in the next hour his life might change again. If they handed Matthew over to him willingly, he would soon be on his way back to his people.

He touched his black coat, feeling the thick paper folded in the inside pocket. He had Celia's will with him. There were notarized copies with Celia's lawyer and a banker. Celia had not trusted her in-laws in the least.

He stopped at the hitching rail and dismounted, walking up the stone walk. The house where his nephew lived with his grandparents was an elegant frame Victorian surrounded by other Victorians and in the same neighborhood as Red Hawk's home. As Red Hawk climbed the steps, he wondered what he would find. Would Matthew be like Adela, cowed and beaten and mistreated? That was the impression he had from Celia, and he was braced for the worst. The house looked cheerful enough, not another castle of gloom like Horace Platt's home.

Red Hawk's boots scraping the wooden steps sounded loud. There was one blue jay noisily perched in the magnolia tree in the front yard. Red Hawk banged the iron knocker on the front door and removed his hat while he waited.

The door swung open and a uniformed maid looked up at him. For a second, her eyes widened in surprise. The look was gone almost as swiftly as it had come, and Red Hawk decided he had imagined a startled look on her face. But there was no mistaking her disapproval as she frowned at him. He suspected he was going to have a fight on his hands over Matthew.

"I'm Captain Red Hawk, Mrs. Ashman's brother. I've come to talk to Mr. Ashman."

"Just a minute, please." The tall, gaunt woman closed the door in his face. She was back in moments. "This way."

He followed her into a wide hallway with polished plank floors, ornate pictures hanging on the walls, and marble-topped tables decorated with delicate crystal vases. Pots of ferns lined the walls, and the smell of polish permeated the air.

They went into a library filled with leather-covered furniture and shelves of books. Behind a desk, Casper Ashman stood waiting. Red Hawk had met the Ashmans before his sister's wedding and had seen them occasionally since, but he had been away for years. Now Casper Ashman's thick brown hair was thinning and had grayed. As thick-chested as ever, with florid features and a gray-streaked beard, he merely nodded. If Red Hawk had not been watching closely, he wouldn't have seen that mere flicker of surprise in the man's blue eyes he thought he had caught in the maid's eyes. Then it was gone. He did not offer his hand to Red Hawk.

"Captain Red Hawk. It's been a long time," Ashman said.

"Yes, sir. It's good to be back in San Antonio."

"I know what brings you. Matthew and his money. Sit down, Quentin. Let's get this finished and over," he said, sitting behind his desk as if he were conducting an interview.

Red Hawk sat on one of the leather chairs and propped one foot on his knee. "There really was little need for Matthew's money to bring me back to San Antonio," he said softly. "That's incidental to the main issue. I have Celia's letter asking me to take guardianship of Matthew."

"So you say. But Hester and I have already become parents to him. We are his relatives as much as you, we have experience, and there are two of us. Matthew needs a woman's influence. He isn't a baby. I think you'll find that he won't want to live with you. As a matter of fact, wouldn't you like to meet Matthew?"

"Yes, I would," Red Hawk said, holding his patience. He had Celia's will giving him full rights to the money, but momentarily he was interested in meeting his nephew, who he still thought of as the laughing, adorable baby about whom Celia wrote so many letters.

As Casper Ashman rang a small bell to summon a servant, Red Hawk knew he was going to have a fight on his hands, yet he also knew he had the trump card with Celia's will. When the money was gone, he was certain from all Celia had written that the Ashmans would have no interest in raising their grandson. Red Hawk was tempted to pull out the will now, but he waited, biding his time until the exact moment his announcement would have the biggest effect.

The maid opened the door.

"Bring Master Matthew down, please."

Red Hawk felt prickly, his nerves on edge. Then the door opened and he looked around as a young boy came into the room. Shock surged in Red Hawk, momentarily stunning him.

CHAPTER FIFTEEN

A young boy, six years old, walked solemnly into the room. Like any well-dressed male child of his day, he was clad in black knee-pants, long black stockings, black shoes, and a frilly white shirt. At a distance, he would look like the son of a wealthy man. But as close as Red Hawk was, he looked like a Comanche child dressed in white man's clothing.

His hair was cut short, but it couldn't hide the Comanche heritage of prominent cheekbones, the hawk nose, the dark skin and midnight eyes. Even Red Hawk saw the incredible resemblance to himself. Matthew looked like his own son. The boy must have seen it, too, because for an instant, he looked startled. Then the moment was gone and a scowl replaced the surprise. Hatred blazed out of the child's dark eyes at Red Hawk, startling him and taking him aback.

"Yes, sir," the boy said, striding up to the desk to look at his grandfather.

"Sit down, Matthew. This man is your uncle, Captain Red Hawk. He wanted to meet you."

"How do you do?" he said with as much disdain as a six-year-old boy could muster.

"The last time I saw you, Matthew, you were a tiny baby."

The boy turned away and his nostrils flared, the hatred all too evident and puzzling to Red Hawk. Matthew sat in a large leather chair and smoothed the sleeves of his shirt. He drew himself up and looked away. Red Hawk glanced at Casper Ashman.

"Would it be possible for us to have a few moments alone?" Red Hawk asked.

"Yes, of course. I'll wait in the hall, Matthew," Ashman said, and Red Hawk couldn't miss the smug satisfaction in his faint smile. Something was amiss, but Red Hawk didn't know what it was. Ashman left the room and closed the door behind him. In the silence, a tall clock ticked loudly. Matthew sat scowling and looking tense.

"I have letters from your mother. Would you like to see them?"

"No." The boy looked at him, his anger blazing. "My mother was Indian. And you're Indian, too. I have her blood, but I hate it. I don't want her letters or anything about her. My father was an officer in the Army. He was a major."

Again, Red Hawk was taken aback momentarily. He wanted to reach over and shake the boy. He leaned forward. "Your mother loved you with all her being. And she would have given her life for you. She was a fine woman, and you have a fine heritage from her."

"No! She was trash—"

"That's enough," Red Hawk said quietly, but it was a cold voice that silenced the child instantly, and his face paled. He blinked in uncertainty while Red Hawk tried to keep control of his anger.

"Your mother wanted me to take you to live with me. I promised her I would," he said.

"No!" Matthew exclaimed, jumping out of the chair and backing away from Red Hawk. "I don't want any part of you or her or anything to do with her." His voice rose shrilly. "Grandpapa can give me everything I want. Do you have a house as nice as this?"

"No, I don't," Red Hawk replied patiently, aware his parents' home was as elegant as the Ashmans', but not wanting that to matter.

"Grandpapa has the best house in town and the most money of almost anyone in town. Do you have as much money as Grandpapa?" he asked.

"No, I don't," Red Hawk answered evenly, again suspecting the answer was misleading, "but if I answered yes, would that make you want to come with me?"

"No, because you're Indian." Hate filled his voice.

Angered, Red Hawk controlled his temper. "You aren't your mother's child," he said in a low voice.

"I don't want to be her child! I don't want to go with you anywhere! I hate you! And I'll hate you forever if you take me from Grandmother and Grandpapa!" Matthew ran from the room.

Stunned by the outburst, Red Hawk stood up and watched him run out of sight. *I tried, Celia.* Angry that the Ashmans had poisoned Matthew about his mother, he clenched his fists. He thought of Celia crying over her baby, and he was thankful she couldn't know how things had turned out.

Ashman strode back into the room, a smile on his face and so much satisfaction in the gleam in his eyes that rage enveloped Red Hawk. He clenched his fists more tightly and inhaled deeply to control his fury.

"I think you heard what Matthew wants."

"I heard what you've taught him to believe, but that's not what his mother wanted and he's not the child she raised."

"His mother is dead. Lawanda can show you to the door," Casper Ashman said dismissively.

"I can find the door." Red Hawk strode out, his emotions churning. The boy was a child, filled with hatred and prejudices adults had taught him. Even if Red Hawk managed to take him away from here, Matthew would never accept the Comanche way of life.

From the time he was taken to live with the white man, Red Hawk had encountered hatred because of his blood, but he hadn't expected to find it in his own nephew. Matthew's scorn and contempt stunned him and cut deeply. Before, he had always been able to keep a wall around himself, knowing that he didn't want to be friends with anyone who hated him for his Indian blood, but this was different. This child was part of Celia. Matthew had the blood of warriors and chiefs and Red Hawk had expected to love and care for him.

Instead, the boy hated him and his own heritage. Red Hawk's wall of indifference was no barrier here. He was angry, shocked, and hurt.

With his emotions in upheaval, Matthew's hate-filled words ringing in his ears, Red Hawk mounted up, rode back to town, and went to see his attorney. It was over two hours later when he left the office. He bought items he needed, then returned home.

Shrugging out of his black coat, he tossed it and his hat on a chair. When he couldn't find Savannah downstairs, he went upstairs, knocking on her open bedroom door. She turned to look at him and he forgot what he had intended to say to her.

Her hair was styled differently, parted in the center, caught up on either side of her head with silk ribbons, curls cascading down her back. She was wearing the blue cotton dress she had been sewing on since Nacogdoches. For a moment, he forgot his turmoil as he stared at her.

She was a vision of loveliness like that first day he had seen her, and he wanted to pull her into his arms.

"Savannah, you're a beautiful woman," he said hoarsely.

She smiled impishly at him. "Thank you," she said, looking pleased, her green eyes sparkling with mischievous delight, "but I know you didn't knock on the door to tell me that."

The past hour came back to him and he rubbed the back of his neck. "No, I didn't." He glanced around, unaware the room had changed since their arrival. "I want to talk. Where's Adela?"

"Adela is at the dressmaker's being fitted for new dresses and enjoying herself more than she has since Horace Platt married her," Savannah said. Red Hawk entered the room, moving around restlessly, finally stopping by a window.

"I'm glad someone is enjoying herself."

Savannah looked more closely at him and realized he was tense. A muscle worked in his jaw and his dark eyes were filled with anger.

"What happened this afternoon?"

As he related in detail his meeting with Matthew and Casper Ashman, he paced the room. Savannah listened with a growing horror over what had happened.

"They've turned him against his own mother," Red Hawk said bitterly. "He despises his heritage and would like nothing better than not to be part of it. He asked me if I had as much money as his grandfather or a house that was as fancy. This is a child—yet look what they've taught him!"

Red Hawk stared out the window and Savannah suspected he had forgotten her as he talked, sounding as if he were talking to himself.

"I'm guessing you have a house that is just as grand."

"Perhaps. But, damn, that shouldn't matter to him."

"Of course it shouldn't."

"I feel like I've failed Celia completely. Her letters had tearstains where she had cried over them. She desperately wanted Matthew away from them, and now I can see why— although they haven't acted as she expected them to act. She feared they would physically abuse him, as they abused Dalton. I don't think they've abused Matthew. Far from it. I suspect they've given him everything he wants."

"Now that they are grandparents, maybe they feel differently. Maybe it was just a conflict between Ashman senior and his son. Perhaps Matthew doesn't trigger the same feelings."

"Celia was adamant in her feelings about them, and from what she wrote me, their own son held the same attitude," Red Hawk said, turning to look at Savannah. He placed his hands on his hips. "I'm going to have to give him up," he said bitterly. His voice sounded agonized. "There's no use trying to take him from them or fighting them, because he would hate any kind of life I can give him. He hates me simply because I'm Indian. It's astounding when the same blood flows in his veins as flows in mine. Celia's child is going to grow up to be narrow-minded, hateful, and materialistic. Damn it, I hate that! I feel I've failed her completely.''

''You didn't fail her. You're not the one who taught him to hate.''

''I should have gotten here sooner. Before she died. I should have just left the damned war, but I couldn't.'' He rubbed the back of his neck and then focused on her. ''I can leave San Antonio tomorrow or whenever you and Adela like.''

Savannah's heart twisted. She didn't want to leave San Antonio. Nor did she want to tell Red Hawk good-bye.

''I'll always feel like I've failed Celia,'' he said again. ''I swore I could get Matthew, but he would never want to live with the Comanche.''

He rubbed his neck again and his dark eyes were stormy. ''I was in the middle of a war when I got Celia's letter. How could they turn him against her in only a little over a year?''

''He's very young and impressionable and that's a long time in his young life. He may not be as turned against her as you think.''

''I didn't mistake the hatred or his words.''

''They may shower him with things. He's only a small boy,'' Savannah said, knowing Red Hawk was hurting and wishing she could do something to alleviate his pain. He had protected her, helped her get Adela safely away from Nacogdoches. Now he was suffering, and she wanted to help him.

He moved restlessly from one window to the next, gazing out. She was sure he didn't see anything outside, but was still lost in thought about Matthew.

''Did you tell Mr. Ashman that you have Celia's will? That the money will not be theirs?''

''No, I didn't,'' Red Hawk said, sounding stricken. He turned to look at her and his dark eyes were filled with worry.

''Why?'' she asked, shocked by his answer.

''Matthew hates me, hates his heritage, hates the Indian way.

I'll give the money to them to raise him. They're good to him, obviously, and he is happy with them.''

"You shouldn't!'' Savannah said, coming to her feet. "You have to fight for him.''

"He doesn't like me or his heritage. And they're good to him. Why take the child from all he loves and holds dear?''

"He's too young to know what's important, and they've poisoned his mind. I don't think you should just give up.''

"I don't know,'' he said, staring out the window again as if lost in thought and barely aware of conversing with her. "Celia adored him. My sister was a good person. It's the first time in her life I've failed her. I promised, but it isn't a promise I can keep without taking him against his will and making everyone unhappy. Yet if he stays with them, he'll grow up to be a man like his grandfather—full of hate and prejudice and thinking money and material things are what matter the most.''

"He's a child! He must have loved his mother when he was smaller.''

"I'm sure he did. Celia's letters are filled with the love she had for him. She couldn't have felt that way about him if he was like he is now. If he had been filled with so much hatred then, she would have still loved him, but her joy in him wouldn't have shown in her writing like it did.''

"What about the grandmother? Is she like the grandfather?''

"Yes. Celia always said she was cold and harsh and interested only in herself and her house. I didn't see her.''

"If your nephew knew his mother for the first years of his life and loved her then, that love can't be completely gone from his memory.''

"You wouldn't think so, but to hear him talk today, it is. He's full of hatred.''

"Maybe, maybe not,'' Savannah replied, her mind working on how she could help.

"I have a letter that Celia sent me. It was from Dalton to Celia. In his letter, Dalton reminds her of his abuse and begs her to see to it that his parents never become Matthew's guardians. Their own son feared they would abuse his child as they had him. I wonder how he would feel if he could see Matthew now.''

''He would probably hate what they have done.''

Red Hawk stood staring out of the window, silent and steeped in his own thoughts. Savannah tried to think what he could do and how she could help. She didn't think he should give up on the boy.

''When we were just outside of Vicksburg, you asked me for my help to get Matthew. You said I was their kind of people—''

''Savannah, I didn't mean it as an insult. You're not selfish or cruel like they are. When I said that, I meant you're a southern lady with education and manners and social standing and they move in that world.''

''I know what you meant.'' She glanced around. ''It looks as if you were raised with all that yourself.''

''My mother married when I was eleven and we were moved into this life,'' he said, waving his hand dismissively with a casual glance at the room. ''By the time I was eighteen, both our parents were dead. Celia married at sixteen, and I was finishing at Baylor. Then Caleb and I left to fight in the war. We haven't been part of San Antonio society. The town was growing in the years before the war; it was in a state of change. I'm sure my parents knew the Ashmans and saw them, but there was little friendship between them. My stepfather has been dead a long time now, and this house has been sitting empty and forgotten. It belongs to me as the oldest, but I'm happy for Caleb to have it.''

''It's a beautiful home, and I don't know how you can bear to leave it,'' she said, running her hand over a mahogany window sill.

''This isn't the life for me. If I ever come back to the white man's ways, I'll buy land and move out of town. This is too confining,'' he said, looking around distractedly. He ran his fingers through his hair, and Savannah knew his mind was on the problem at hand.

"You said you would introduce me as your fiancée. With Adela along as a chaperon, it would be quite proper."

"Well, it won't be necessary now."

"Maybe it is."

He turned around to look at her, and for the first time since he had started talking, he seemed to really see her.

"Contact them again. Tell Mr. Ashman about Celia's will and that the money won't be theirs."

"I want Matthew to have his inheritance. I'd never take that from him."

"Of course not, but once they learn they can't spend his money, their attitude may change."

"They might not be as kind to him."

"Try to arrange for both of us to call on them," she said. "Introduce me as your fiancée and let me meet Matthew. We won't have the problems of race between us, and maybe I can reach him where you can't."

Red Hawk stared at her for so long she began to wonder if he had heard her. "Have you ever been around children?" he finally asked.

"Even though she's older than I am, I was like a mother to Adela. We had neighbors with small children who used to come to our house sometimes." She shrugged. "We can try. He's only a little boy and if he once loved his mother, that love can't be completely gone."

"I don't think it'll do any good."

"It won't do any harm."

Red Hawk wondered about her idea. He didn't think it would help, yet Savannah was warmhearted and young and she might strike a chord with Matthew. "It'll mean you stay in San Antonio longer and don't go home to Mason."

She smiled, one of those full-blown smiles that warmed him like hot sunshine. It was one of her smiles that made the nightmares of war recede a little farther in his memory.

"Adela is happier than she has been in years, and she has a friend here. I love this town. I want to move us both here. We were in Mason because of the fort and our father, but he's gone. I suspect Adela will agree with me that we should sell our house and move here. She will be very happy to stay longer, and so will I.''

He thought about his own dilemma. Each day he stayed in San Antonio, he was running chances he would be discovered and arrested and tried for two murders he did not commit. Savannah was still a woman wanted by the Union army. He wondered if she had discarded that from her mind.

If he were arrested, he knew few would listen to him. They would want to hang him. He didn't want Savannah drawn into it, either. How easy it would be to walk away and leave Matthew to the Ashmans.

Moving around the room restlessly, Red Hawk debated the matter. It was unlikely Savannah could really sway Matthew. That would take time, a lot of time, and Red Hawk didn't have time. Was it worth increasing his risks to try to win over a child who hated him?

Celia was gone and would never know. Matthew would have a good life. It looked as if they treated him well. Why try to take him away from what was making him happy? Why not go before he put himself at risk more than ever? Any attempt to win Matthew would probably be for nothing anyway.

Over the treetops and rooftops, Red Hawk could see the roof of the Ashman mansion. All he had to do was walk out. Matthew was evidently being given luxuries; Celia would never know that he hadn't kept his promises to her. He could go now and be safe and save himself trouble.

Yet he knew Celia would be heartbroken if she could have heard the exchange that had taken place between her brother and her son. The Ashmans were poisoning his mind.

The hatred in the boy was strong. By now it might run too deep to ever change. Red Hawk thought about his choices. Did he really want to risk his life for a child who hated his heritage, hated him, and had all kinds of luxuries and a good life where he was?

He thought of Celia and could see her dark eyes looking at him as she did when she counted on him. His anger vanished, replaced by pity and determination. This was not the way Matthew would have been if his mother had lived. Matthew should know what a fine woman she was.

Feeling pity for Matthew, Red Hawk realized Matthew might have been as mistreated as Adela and Dalton, only in a far different way.

"If it were the other way around," Savannah asked quietly, "what would you do? If Matthew had been your son and you had asked Celia to take him, what would you want her to do?"

He inhaled deeply and rubbed his brow with his fingers. "I'd want her to get him away from them. The hatred he feels is like a physical force, and it will sour him."

"Children see the world as good or bad without weighing all the in-between possibilities. I think you should try to win him over because he is Celia's child. He has to have her love instilled in him. They can't completely kill that in only a year. I'm guessing the hatred is very shallow."

Was Savannah right? Red Hawk knew he had to try because both of Matthew's parents wanted him to and he had promised Celia he would. He had never gone back on his word to his sister. He hated to run more risk of arrest. The thought of being a captive again terrified him, yet he owed this to Celia.

"You're right. But you'll have to be the one to reach him. All he can see when he looks at me is a detested Indian."

"That's only on the surface. He's a child," she said gently.

"Then we stay longer and try."

For the first time since he strode into the room, he gave his full attention to Savannah. She was again seated in the rocker, her blue skirt laying in soft folds over her long legs, her slender arms bare and resting on the arms of the chair. He became aware of being alone with her.

"I think you should tell me about Celia so if I get a chance to talk to Matthew about his mother, I will know about her."

"I'll give you the letter from his father so you'll know exactly what Dalton said about his parents."

Red Hawk crossed the room to Savannah to pull her to her feet and he gazed at her solemnly. "If you do this, they may tell their friends about meeting you. What if word gets back to Thomas?''

"Thomas is doctoring in Tennessee. I'll write him tonight and tell him about you and what I'm doing. He'll understand.''

"Then he's a hell of a lot more understanding than I would be.'' Red Hawk moved closer, sliding his arms around her waist.

"Thomas is very understanding. I can't imagine that he would not wholeheartedly agree with what I'm doing.''

"You're in my house, with my arms around you. No one else is around—''

She pushed against him. "He won't be agreeable about that.''

Red Hawk bent his head and kissed her, ending all conversation. Her heart thudded the moment his gaze dropped to her mouth. She knew what he intended, and she knew what she should do, yet she couldn't move away or stop him or even protest. More than ever, she wanted his kisses. All too soon she would tell him good-bye forever.

As her heart thudded and she responded, his arms tightened around her, pulling her close. She wrapped her arms around him, sliding them over his strong shoulders.

"Savannah? Savannah, are you home?''

Dimly, Savannah thought she heard her name called, yet their kiss continued.

"Savannah!''

She pushed against Red Hawk's chest. He raised his head and the look he gave her made her tremble.

"Adela's back.''

He nodded and she moved out of his arms and left the room without glancing back. Her heart was racing from his kisses and she left the room because she knew she had to, but she wanted to be back in his arms. She wanted his kisses, wanted them to never stop.

"Savannah?'' Adela had just come to the top of the stairs.

Adela's eyes widened. Too late, Savannah realized how she must look. It had to be evident he had been kissing her.

"Savannah!''

Savannah motioned to Adela's room and hurried inside. Adela followed, staring at her with wide eyes and evident shock.

"You're in love with him!"

Savannah slammed the door and wondered if he had heard Adela.

"Adela! I'm not, and he'll hear you. Shh, for heaven's sake!"

"He kissed you."

Adela's eyes were round, and she sounded deeply shocked. For a moment Savannah was annoyed along with her embarrassment, but then she took Adela's hand and led her to the bed and sat down. Adela's pink skirt billowed over Savannah's blue one. She smoothed it while she stared at Savannah.

"Yes, Red Hawk has kissed me, but, Adela, I'll marry Thomas."

"Then why did you let Red Hawk kiss you?"

Unable to answer, Savannah looked away. "I don't know. I just know that Thomas will come home and I will marry him because it's always been planned that way. And Red Hawk has never asked me to do anything any different from that. When he leaves here, he's going back to his people, the Comanche."

"Oh, Savannah! How can he? This is his home. He would leave all this to be with savages? They're the ones who killed Papa."

"I know, Adela, but Red Hawk isn't savage. No more than our father who was a soldier was a savage."

"This is the captain's home. I don't see how he can leave this."

"I don't either, but he's said that's what he wants to do," Savannah said, Adela's reaction mirroring her own. She looked at the elegant mahogany fireplace, the high ceilings and carved four-poster bed and wondered how he could turn his back on his comfortable, secure life, a life that could be peaceful and safe. Even more amazing, she was going to try to persuade his nephew to go with him.

"Savannah, I think you're in love with him. I really do," Adela said urgently, a frown creasing her forehead.

"I'm going to help him and then I'm going to tell him good-bye and wait for Thomas."

"You'll help Captain Red Hawk get his nephew?"

"Yes. He helped get us away from Nacogdoches; now I need to help him."

"I'm happy to stay here. Savannah, I saw Bertrice today and she invited me to come stay with her for a few days. She said you could come, too."

"I think I shall be far too busy, and Bertrice is your friend."

"You can't stay here alone with the captain!"

"Who will know besides you, Adela? I have traveled all across Louisiana and Texas alone with him."

"That's scandalous, and Thomas won't understand."

"He will never know, and it won't make any difference whether you're here or not."

"How can you marry Thomas if you love the captain?"

"I'm not in love, Adela. I can't be, because I will marry Thomas."

"Maybe you are in love with the captain and don't know it. I can't imagine choosing to kiss a man I didn't love." She blushed and studied Savannah.

"He's special," Savannah said, looking down at her hands and wondering just exactly what she did feel for him. Whatever it was, she wasn't ready to discuss it. "Let's go see about supper. We have lots of plans to make."

"I shan't stay with Bertrice. I know it would be scandalous, and Thomas wouldn't marry you if he got word of you staying alone in this house with the captain. Savannah, Papa used to say you were too independent. You should be careful about your reputation." Her hands flew to her face. "Listen to me! I shouldn't say one word after all both of you have done for me. He is the kindest man I've ever known."

"I shall tell him you said so," Savannah said, thinking she would never describe Red Hawk as the kindest man she knew. Yet he had been kind and gentle to Adela. "Right now, we need to see about supper."

Savannah had bought food, and she and Adela both cooked

from the first day they were in San Antonio. This night, Savannah had roasted beef with potatoes. She cooked ears of corn that she had purchased at the market.

As they sat at the long dining room table, Red Hawk watched her eat with relish and was amused. "Savannah, you and Adela are very good cooks, but I didn't bring you here to have you cook all the time. I asked my attorney to find us a cook and I expect to have my own regular cook and maid by this time tomorrow."

"We're perfectly capable of cooking," Savannah said.

"I have evidence of that," he said, motioning at his plate. "You said your father had a cook."

"Yes, he did," she answered. "Lots of them, but never very good ones."

"Hopefully, we'll have a good one."

"Adela, you and I need to go to the dressmaker's again tomorrow morning. We are going to need some dresses."

"Savannah," Red Hawk said with amusement, "what are you using for money?"

She turned wide green eyes on him. "Mason is close to San Antonio. Since we moved to Mason, we've shopped here in San Antonio, and the dressmaker knows us. She knows she'll get paid as soon as I get home to Mason. I receive Papa's pension."

She tapped her fingers on the table. "We should plan what we'll do about Matthew. I thought of perhaps inviting his grandparents to a dinner party. Adela will be here to talk to them, and maybe I can get Matthew off to myself to talk to him about his mother."

"They may refuse to come."

"I don't think they will. Have they ever seen your home?"

"Once long ago, when Celia was getting married, but not since."

"They'll come. In the meantime, I will call on them tomorrow. Don't you have friends here?"

"My friends are fighting in the war. There are friends of my parents still here," Red Hawk replied.

''Then we'll invite some of them. You supply me with a list.''

He sat back, watching her, amused and amazed at her taking charge of his household and the plans about Matthew. He didn't think she would succeed, because she hadn't seen how filled with hatred Matthew was, but he owed it to Celia to try. Yet how long would this plan of Savannah's take? How many days and nights would they be beneath the same roof? He was finding every encounter more searing, finding it more difficult to stop kissing her. He wanted her in his bed, Thomas Sievert or no Thomas Sievert.

While Savannah planned aloud, his thoughts drifted to captives who had been assimilated into the tribe. His mother had been one, but he had known nothing about that because he hadn't been born when she had been taken captive. But he knew captives, women and children. The women were taken by the men who wanted them, and he couldn't think of one he had known who hadn't grown to love her husband.

He stared at Savannah, imagining in his mind just carrying her off with him as he had done at Vicksburg.

The thought sent the temperature in the room soaring. To have her to himself, to know she was his completely—the idea sent erotic images spinning in his mind, images of her as she stood half-naked, stripped to the waist before him. He remembered the softness of her skin, the fullness of her breast in his hand, her eagerness and passion.

He shifted uncomfortably in his chair and knew he had to change his train of thought. He was aroused, wanting her. How could he live in the same house with her for days and keep his control?

Within seconds, his mind returned to the prospect of carrying her away. How long would she fight him? Would she fight him at all? He thought so. He suspected she wouldn't be fighting to go back to Thomas so much as fighting to get back to this life that she knew in San Antonio. She loved the town. Her eyes sparkled constantly now and she was filled with plans.

How she would hate being taken from all of this. That would never change.

Did he want to stay here—fight for Savannah's love and walk the white man's road? Yet he had no choice. He couldn't stay without facing trial for the two murder charges and he knew what that outcome would be. He wanted the Comanche life with all his being. The dream of returning to it had carried him through killing battles.

Later, when they sat in the front parlor, Savannah made more plans and his mind still brooded over the thought of just taking her and going. His gaze shifted to Adela. Adela—what about her? He suspected she couldn't fend for herself and had always relied on first her father and Savannah and then on Horace Platt. If he harmed Adela in any way, Savannah would despise him. And he couldn't take them both. Adela would be terrified.

He stared at Savannah, wanting to gather her into his arms, go out and get the horses and ride away. Why did he have to want a woman who liked comfort and material things?

Then Adela was saying good night and leaving to go upstairs to bed. Savannah left with her, both of them talking about dresses and food while he sat with his stormy thoughts until he left and rode to a saloon where he could try to forget green eyes and a soft body that tormented him.

Upstairs, in the quiet of the night, Savannah lay staring into the darkness and thinking about Red Hawk when she heard hoofbeats.

Curious, she slipped from the bed to the window. Moonlight shone on Red Hawk's broad shoulders and black hat. He rode the bay, sitting tall and straight, his Colt buckled on his hip. He headed down the drive and disappeared around the house. She rushed to the other side of the room and watched his dark silhouette.

Was he as unable to sleep as she was? The window was open and she could easily call to him. As if she had, he turned to look up at her windows. Startled, she stepped back, hating to have him catch her watching him. Then she decided that was foolishness. Why would it matter to him if he discovered her watching him ride away?

She watched until he rode into the street and headed toward town. The hoofbeats faded and the only sounds were the chirping of crickets. Fireflies winked in the darkness over the yard.

She stretched out in bed. She was hot, restless, wondering where he was going. This was the town he had grown up in. He knew people, might have old friends even though he thought most of them were away at war. Had he gone to a saloon? Or a sporting house? The last made her insides knot. Was she going to tell him good-bye soon and maybe never know real passion her whole life?

She sat up and mulled it over. Thomas never made her heart miss a beat or her blood heat and thicken or her insides turn to jelly.

Was she throwing away knowing the real depths of passion and the possibilities between a man and a woman?

She tried to remember kissing Thomas, but no memory would come. They had kissed lightly, chastely, and with as much enthusiasm as if she raised her own hand to her lips and planted a kiss on her fingers. Yet she was promised to him, and Red Hawk did not want a wife. He would never want a wife like her. Not one who belonged in town, in a house with a settled life of comfort and promise, a life of dinner parties and teas and shops.

His future was beyond the wild frontier, a future that could be filled with as much fighting as his past had been.

He wouldn't want her to be a part of that, and she wouldn't want to be. She couldn't imagine a life like that, so wild and primitive, and his people were the ones who had so brutally murdered her father.

Savages. That was all her father had ever called them. Wild, barbaric, savage, take what they wanted, yet she knew how gentle Red Hawk had been with Adela, how careful and patient and kind. Savannah ran her fingers across her knees, smoothing the thin cotton fabric. Red Hawk had put his life at risk to cover for her, taking the blame for Horace's murder.

Was she throwing away the one chance in her life to know ecstasy? Suppose life with Thomas was dull and tedious? It would never be the horrible marriage Adela had, but it might be disappointing.

She moaned softly and swung her feet to the floor, crossing the room to the window to look at the empty street and wishing she were a man so she could dress and ride to a saloon and play card games and be with people and get rid of the tormenting thoughts that drove sleep away.

Marriage to Thomas would be good. Thomas was a good man and a reliable man. She would feel differently when she was with him again. Had the war changed him?

She sighed and wondered what Red Hawk was doing. Did he hold some other woman now? The thought was tormenting and Savannah knew sleep was lost. She pulled the rocker to the window and sat down to rock in the breeze, mulling over her protests to Adela about being in love with him, yet knowing she didn't want to acknowledge what was happening. She was falling in love with him, hopelessly, impossibly, deeply in love.

The dinner party with fourteen guests was planned for Friday. On Sunday afternoon, they were invited to the Ashman's house. Thursday afternoon a storm blew in, with thunder booming in the sky and a sudden deluge that turned the streets to rivers of mud. The weather was no more stormy than Red Hawk's feelings.

He had spent too much time beneath the same roof with Savannah, and his nerves were worn ragged. While she seemed oblivious of the tension and the effort he made to control himself and keep from reaching for her, he was suffering like the damned.

He rode home in the rain, its cold drops pounding him, yet he barely noticed. He sat hunched over, his broad-brimmed hat protecting his face. His thoughts were storm winds, churning his emotions. He wanted Savannah, wanted to possess and know her, to have the memory—all he would ever have of her.

He had mentally listed more than a hundred times all the reasons to leave her alone. They were becoming empty arguments, tiny grains of sand flung at a rushing wave. He wanted to make love to her, to hold her in his arms all night long, to kiss her and not have her stop him or pull away.

He strode into the house, sweeping off his hat, drenched and tracking mud into the kitchen that smelled temptingly of succulent frying chicken and collard greens boiling on the stove. Savannah looked around at him.

"Great heavens! Look at you."

"It's pouring," he said, staring at her. She wore a new dress that was some kind of frilly material patterned in blues and greens that made her hair seem more red and her eyes more green. The tiny puffed sleeves left her slender arms bare and the neck had enough of a vee that his imagination stripped away the rest of the bodice.

"Where's Matilda?" he asked, looking for the new cook.

"When this rain started, I told her to go home while she could. Adela is staying at Bertrice's. They sent a servant over to tell me. They say the streets are mud and, judging from the looks of you, they are."

He pulled off his boots with only one thought pounding through him. Tonight, he had Savannah alone. All to himself. He tried to think of Thomas Sievert—but failed.

Red Hawk stripped off his wet shirt and hung it on the doorknob, where it dripped in small silvery puddles on the floor.

He should not take another man's woman while the man was away fighting a war. How many times he had told himself that, yet how little his heart was listening.

He was wet, he was muddy, and he was tired of waiting and doing what he knew he should do. He stood dripping in puddles on the floor while she bustled around him with her cooking. The kitchen was warm from baking, the windows steamed over, but nothing was as hot and steaming as Red Hawk felt. His emotions were tattered by longing.

Savannah was temptation and passion and he wanted her.

She wasn't wildly in love with Thomas Sievert. Red Hawk was certain that when they kissed, she forgot Sievert completely, but she was determined to hold to the old pledge made by her father.

She loved comfort and material things, another chasm between them. She had made it clear that she couldn't understand why he would consider returning to his father's people. She would never want the Comanche way of life, yet she teased and flirted and he knew she felt something when she was with him. From that first hour, there had been a crackling tension between them any time they were together.

She was bustling around the kitchen, talking about plans she had made, stirring pots of food. He removed his belt and placed it on a chair.

"It's cool with the storm, and I thought this would be a good time to cook chicken and peas. Are you—" She glanced at him, her gaze flicking down over his chest and then back up to meet his eyes. The words died in her throat.

CHAPTER SIXTEEN

His eyes had darkened to the blackness of midnight, but in their depths flames of desire burned. Surprised, she halted.

His look devoured her. The intensity in his demeanor and expression, even though he wasn't moving a muscle, startled her.

As if pulled against her will, her gaze drifted down across his broad bare chest, and she wanted to be in his arms. Why was it when she was with him, she seemed complete? Why was it when he was away, her thoughts were constantly on him?

He crossed the room.

Her pulse drummed as she watched him. In silence, he passed her to carefully put out the fires on the stove. His strong brown hands moved over the stove with deliberation, and the supper she was cooking went on delay. Her pulse drummed as loudly as the rain.

The air in the room seemed to grow thick and hot. With his broad shoulders, Red Hawk filled the empty spaces and made the room narrow.

In a flash, she wondered if the years stretching ahead of her would be empty and dull. When he rode out of her life, would he take with him the excitement, this breathtaking attraction that sizzled between them?

Rain beat against the windows and drummed on the house, a dull whisper next to the pounding of her heart as he turned to look at her.

"Supper won't burn."

She couldn't answer him. She didn't care about supper. She wanted him. Right or wrong, he was the only man who had ever touched her heart, the only man who had brought her to life as a woman.

He crossed to her, closing the space between them with deliberation. His intent was as plain in his eyes as if he had announced it. Now was the time to stop him, a dim voice warned, but she ignored the fading voice of reason.

Red Hawk's arm slipped around her waist, tightened, and drew her to him. His dark eyes were intense, and she lost herself, pulled into a darkness that held promises of pleasure.

His gaze lowered to her mouth, and she wanted his kisses, wanted him. With a moan, she tilted her head, her lashes coming down as he leaned forward. His mouth covered hers, his tongue plunging over hers. Her insides tightened and then seemed to let go like a free fall into a deep chasm.

His tongue stroked hers. She slipped her arms around him, feeling the solid hardness of him, the marvelous breadth of his powerful chest, the narrow width of his hips, his height that made her tilt her head back to kiss him, to look up at him.

In that moment, she knew what love was for a woman. *I love him,* she thought, all doubts vanquished. On one level she was aware of the depth of her feelings. On another, thought and logic were vanishing as his hands and mouth awakened her physically and brought her quivering to life.

It was right to be in his arms. This was the man who made her heart leap. He melted her with his kisses; he brought her to a trembling brink of need. They were of two different worlds, his wild and savage, a world where he took what he wanted. Hers was the old world of parlors and teas and polite customs.

Yet in his arms, it all burned away in the hot sun of passion. Her desire now was as raw and primitive as his.

He leaned over her, kissing her hard, and her blood pounded. His hungry kisses told her how badly he wanted her; her response had to reveal how much she wanted him. She wound her fingers in his thick, coarse hair, and her other hand ran across his shoulders.

His fingers tugged at the buttons of her dress. In minutes, he pushed it over her shoulders and down. With a rush of cool air, it fell in a heap around her ankles. He stepped back to look at her, and she trembled beneath his hot, possessive gaze.

Red Hawk tugged off her chemise, then knelt to remove her shoes. He leaned closer and kissed her through the thin cotton undergarments, planting kisses on her belly and causing dizzying sensations to streak in her. With her eyes closed, she clung to him, her breath coming in short gasps. She could not believe she was in his arms, letting him kiss her. At the same time, it seemed more right than anything else she had done.

Her fingers tugged at his clothes. She wanted to touch him, to look at him, to please him. At the same time, shyness enveloped her and battled desire. She ran her hands over his hips, down his hard thighs, and felt the rough denim of his pants beneath her palms. He placed his hands on her waist and stepped back.

Savannah trembled as his dark eyes roamed slowly over her. He cupped her breasts in his large hands and his thumbs encircled her nipples, sending wave after wave of exquisite torment pulsing in her.

Once again she reached out to tug at the buttons on his pants. He stepped back and unfastened them, watching her with that smoldering look that was as devastating as a caress.

As Red Hawk drank in her pale beauty, her cascade of fiery hair, her green eyes darkened with passion. Her lush breasts were high and soft enough to push his control closer to the edge. Touching her burned away his bones and his will.

He could no more resist her or stop caressing her now than he could stop breathing. For this night, she was his woman. It didn't matter what she thought about his future or his life or his past. It didn't matter about her own future. At this hour and this place, he could let his feelings and desire show.

He stood before her naked, aroused until he thought he would burst with his need for her. A red flush crept up her cheeks, yet she gazed at him openly and then trailed her fingers over his shaft. The touch almost shattered his control.

He shook. Remembering to be gentle with her, he turned her palm up and kissed her hand, trailing his tongue over her warm flesh. She gasped and stroked his chest, and he reached out to cup her breasts. They were buttery soft in his hands, making him shake again with a need that tore at him.

He wanted to shove her to the floor now and take her, to thrust into her warmth and lose himself, but she was virginal, innocent, and he knew for her sake he couldn't do as he pleased.

He leaned down to take her nipple in his mouth, sucking on the hard bud, hearing her moan of pleasure and feeling a tremor run through her. The more he aroused and excited her, the more it excited him. He wanted to pleasure her until she lost the last edge of holding back, until all blushes were gone and she was pushed beyond that brink of civilization into pure need and desire. He wanted her beneath him, crying out in passion.

He flicked his tongue over her nipple. At her moan, he picked her up to carry her to the next room. She had a fire built in the grate in the parlor, and he put her down on the braided rug, looking at her as he moved between her knees.

He trailed kisses over her stomach. His hands stroked her inner thighs, and then his fingers moved up, finding her softness, her feminine warmth, the bud of her desire. He watched her as he rubbed his hand over her again and again. As she moaned, he wondered if he could last.

Sweat popped out on his forehead, and he pushed her thighs wider, moving so his tongue could stroke and tease where his hand had been. She cried out in passion, her hands gripping him, her hips arched as her body finally rocked and spasmed in a release that was only a beginning.

He scooped her into his arms, kissing her hard and long. She returned it as wildly, and he knew he had pushed her beyond the brink. Her inhibitions were gone now, her hands tearing at him. And then she bent, sending him a slanted look as old as the first woman seductress. Her tongue flicked over his manhood and he gasped, winding his hands in her hair as she took him fully into her mouth.

His control slipped. Pushing her down, he moved between her pale legs, watching her as he lowered himself. While her long legs locked around him, pulling him closer, her hands ran over his back, tugging on his hips.

Savannah's heart pounded so loudly, she only dimly heard her own voice when she cried out. He was aroused, ready, his shaft thick and hard and his dark eyes glowing with need. He lowered himself and his shaft touched her. She gasped and arched against him. He didn't move, and the torment made her writhe and tug at his hips.

"Please," she whispered.

He thrust slowly, easing into her. Pain tore at her, yet at the same time, desire pulsed like devouring flames.

He moved slowly, and Savannah tightened her legs around him. As her hips thrust rhythmically against him, she cried out and clutched his shoulders.

Sweat poured off him and he tried to take as long as possible, moving slowly, rocking with her, wanting to build up the need in her until she was ready to burst, just as he was. His control began to shatter and he had to move, thrusting and withdrawing, plunging deep and moving with her.

She joined him, rocking together, her cries mingling with his, earth and reality disappearing.

"My woman," he cried. *"Ekahuutsu!"*

His hoarse cries were dim in Savannah's ears, her own pounding pulse drowning out her cries as well. They moved wildly together and rapture burst in her as she cried out in ecstasy.

She was lost in sensation, clinging to his broad shoulders. For now, this moment in time was theirs. He was in her arms; they were one.

She would take the moment, treasure it, hold it forever in memory and be thankful she had it.

Their dance of passion slowed, their breathing came in ragged gasps. Long strands of her hair were matted to her face from perspiration that dotted her skin.

While their pounding hearts slowed to normal, he showered kisses over her face and throat and murmured endearments. She stroked his back and marveled in his powerful body that was joined with hers. Awed by the power in his lovemaking and the ecstasy that had consumed her, she was complete.

"My love," she whispered softly, knowing he could not hear, knowing that she could never have much more of him than she had at this moment.

She ran her hands over his smooth back, down to his small waist, over firm buttocks and the backs of his muscled thighs.

His body was a marvel to her, so different from her own—hard and powerful and able to drive every thought from her mind.

He rolled on his side, taking her with him, their legs entwined, their bodies melded together while he looked at her with burning dark eyes, something unfathomable in their depths, yet pleasure wreathing his face in a smile.

Ekahuutsu," he said, stroking her head and lifting locks of her hair. "Beautiful."

He ran his fingers across her lips. "Soft, so soft. How I dreamed of this moment when I was on those damned battle-fields."

"So any woman would have—"

His finger pressed her lips to silence and his eyes focused on her fully, losing their faraway gaze. "No," he said flatly. "From the moment I saw you on that boat, I wanted you in my arms like this. And the more I knew you, the more I wanted you."

While her heart jumped with delight, she warned herself not to take his words seriously. They were being said in the glow of passion.

"You were insolent, bold, looking at me as if you were peeling away my dress."

He gave a deep chuckle. "That is exactly what I was doing. And I liked what I saw," he said, trailing his finger down her cheek to her shoulder, down over her breast while he watched her.

The moment his fingertip trailed over her breast and touched her nipple, she gasped and closed her eyes and tightened her arms around him. His manhood responded, still within her, coming to life again.

Startled, her eyes flew open and his dark expression took her breath. He leaned forward and kissed her hard, his arms tightening around her.

He rolled to his back and she was impaled, his shaft thick and hard within her. She sat astride him, her gaze locked with his and then his lowered, drifting down as he cupped her breast with one hand, the other hand going down between her thighs to stroke her.

She began to rock as his hips moved, the two of them moving in unison. The rhythm increased, the tension and need built swiftly, making her heart pound again and her pulse roar. She tilted her head; her eyes closed as she rode him furiously.

This time the white-hot pleasure seared and scalded and drove her to a frenzy, her hands gripping him as he moved and held her hips.

The climax burst within her. She screamed with pleasure as he cried out and his hot seed spilled in her. She came down over him, clinging to him as his strong arms wrapped around her and held her against his heart.

"My lovely," he whispered, stroking her head, his hoarse whisper ground out while he gasped for breath.

Finally she rolled beside him and he turned to hold her and stroke her.

Twice more they loved and fell sated, burnt to cinders, locked in each other's embrace.

"You are a greedy little wench, *Ekahuutsu,*" he said, pleasure thickening his voice.

"I'm not the only greedy one," she whispered back, biting his earlobe playfully. He turned his head quickly and his mouth covered hers as he kissed her long and hard. He held her close and when their kiss ended, he stared at her, smiling, stroking hair away from her face.

She sat up and stared at him solemnly. He gazed back as soberly, both aware they would say good-bye soon.

He took her hand in his and brushed his lips across her fingers while he watched her. Closing her eyes and tilting back her head, she relished his warm breath on her hand and his lips touching her fingers so lightly. The gesture was caring, and she wondered about the depth of his feelings. She knew she would never know, just as he would never know the extent of her feelings for him.

She wasn't certain she knew them herself. She opened her eyes to look at him, realizing they had spent nearly all their waking time together since that first encounter in Vicksburg weeks earlier. How much of her heart would he take away with him when he left?

It frightened her to think how much, and she closed her mind to any thoughts about the future. She would face that when she had to. Right now, he was here with her, his hip pressed against her knee, his fingers trailing over her languidly, stirring new fires like molten heat pouring through her veins.

Tonight he was here and tomorrow he would be here. Beyond that, she would not think. As soon as he got Matthew, he would be gone. Maybe sooner, if he gave up trying to get Matthew. Her gaze ran across Red Hawk's broad chest and flat stomach, down over him. He was aroused again and desired her and was ready for her.

A blush heated her face as she looked down at him. At the same time, it excited her to realize how he reacted to her. She wanted to touch him again, to feel his hands and body and mouth on her. She reached out tentatively, half shy, half brazen, to trail her fingers over his erect manhood.

He gasped and then she was on her back and he had rolled

over her and was kissing her again and once more she was lost in a tumbling spiral of sensation and ecstasy.

They loved through the night. He was insatiable, and she wanted him desperately each time, as if this night she were storing up memories for a lifetime. As she discovered his strong, lean body and touched his erect shaft, she knew she might not ever be in his arms intimately again.

Instinct told her that here was ecstasy she would never know with another man. Red Hawk's loving, his kisses were rapture.

For now, in the darkness of the night with rain beating against the house, they were safe, warm, shut away from tomorrow. Stroking her, he finally fell asleep in her arms only to waken in the night and stir her awake with delicious caresses and kisses.

Morning dawned, bright and clear, and with the rising of the sun, Savannah knew her interlude of bliss would end. She sat up, intending to slip away, but his arms wrapped around her and he pulled her down.

"I thought you were sleeping," she said, studying his dark features and amazed how much she cared about him.

"Morning is here," he said solemnly, and all the joy and rapture and completeness of the night slipped away like stars fading from the bright morning sky.

"Life has to return to what it was before," she said, knowing he wasn't in love with her, part of her determined she would not let him know how she felt.

"I did not intend to get you with child."

Cold reality intruded and her heart shattered. These were not the words she wanted to hear. "I should get up before Matilda arrives or Adela returns home," she said stiffly, hoping to hide her hurt.

He caught her and pulled her against him, kissing her hard. The faint stubble of his beard was rough against her cheek, but she barely noticed. Reason vanished while her heart pounded with eagerness. In minutes he was stroking and kissing her.

This time when their lovemaking ended, he kissed her and

then rose, striding across the room. She looked at the long, lean lines of his body, memorizing the sight of him.

He gathered his clothes. "I'll draw a bath and start breakfast. Take your time," he said from across the room, but she was hearing something else. *What we had is over. Today we go on with our lives. We go our separate ways,* were the words she heard in her heart, though her ears told her otherwise.

She merely nodded and got up, gathering her things.

An hour later, after he had eaten, he kissed her good-bye. "I'll be back later. Tonight is the big party. The Ashmans will come, and you'll meet them and Matthew."

She nodded, standing still, her heart racing while she ached to throw her arms around him and pull his head down for kisses. Instead, she stood quietly and watched him put on his hat and stride out the back door.

In a few minutes he rode into sight. He headed down the drive, but as he passed her he tipped his hat.

He might as well be riding away with her heart. "He'll be back," she told herself, mindless of the hot tears that fell over her cheeks and down on her hands that were knotted over her waist.

She was in love with him. Truly, deeply in love in a manner she never expected to be. This strong, wild warrior had captured her heart. He would carry it away with him when he left. He had made it clear someday he would go out of her life forever. They were from different worlds and wanted different lives.

Yet what paradise she found in his arms!

She wiped away her tears and squared her shoulders, knowing if she went back and relived the night, she would do exactly the same thing again. She touched her heart, feeling empty inside except for memories and longing that filled her.

Determined to erase all evidence of their lovemaking before Matilda arrived or Adela came home, Savannah headed for the kitchen. She had the party to get ready for. A supper party, a time to meet Matthew. Could she persuade the child about anything? she wondered.

* * *

After checking constantly on the cooking, Savannah drew a bath and finally left the kitchen to get ready for the party. She had hired Bessie Withers, an additional cook, someone Matilda knew. Red Hawk had hired Wesley Blanchard to serve as butler, a man he had known from his childhood and who had worked for friends of Red Hawk's parents.

Tingling excitement gripped Savannah over the party, the uncertainty of dealing with Matthew, and, most of all, over wearing the new dress she had cajoled the dressmaker into whipping up in time for the party. All she could think about was Red Hawk's reaction.

She and Adela helped each other dress. Here, Adela was adept, taking great care to get Savannah's hair exactly the way she wanted.

Adela had dressed first in her pale pink silk and Savannah wore her wrapper, her red hair falling over her shoulders while she began to loop and pin Adela's hair. "You look beautiful, like my sister should," Savannah said.

She looked in the mirror at Adela's reflection and was thankful that all evidence of Horace Platt's last brutality was gone. Adela's skin was pink, her cheeks flushed, and she was beginning to gain a little weight back. The pale pink dress made her look fragile, yet it set off her creamy skin, golden tresses, and blue eyes.

Finally, it was Adela's turn to do Savannah's hair. Savannah sat patiently while Adela combed and pinned.

At one point there was a knock at the door. "Savannah, I'm home," Red Hawk called. "I'll get ready for the party."

She heard his boots as he walked away down the hall. "Men!" She looked at the clock. "We have been washing and combing and dressing for two hours now and he will rush in, bathe, dress, shave, and be ready within minutes."

Adela smiled, but said nothing as she concentrated on what

she was doing. When she finished, Adela left while Savannah stepped into her shoes and picked up her list of the expected guests.

Downstairs, Red Hawk moved restlessly around the parlor and then went into the hall as Adela came down the stairs.

"How pretty you look," he said with sincerity when she reached the hall.

"Thank you." She smiled and blushed. "Savannah is almost ready. I'll see about supper."

He nodded and watched her walk away, her bearing regal in spite of her shyness. He heard a rustle and glanced up at the top of the stairs. His heart turned over when Savannah appeared.

She wore a new silk dress—where she had gotten it, he didn't know, but it was green like the first one she had been wearing.

His gaze drifted down over her, barely aware of the green taffeta, whisking away the dress in his imagination. His gaze flew back up to meet hers and his pulse jumped. He remembered moments from the previous night, not yet twenty-four hours ago. His mouth went dry and he wanted to storm up the stairs and pick her up and carry her back to bed with him.

Instead, he waited quietly. Her eyes widened, endless pools of deep green that changed, a languid look coming over her face. She slowed as she came within two steps of the bottom, leaving her on his eye level.

"You look beautiful," he said.

"Thank you," she whispered.

"Will you go back upstairs with me? Only for a minute?"

She inhaled and his gaze dropped. The neckline of the dress was cut low, clinging and revealing the curves of her breasts. Desire rocked him and he felt wound tight and hot.

"I can't. I have to see about supper. They'll be here any moment now."

He met her gaze again and couldn't resist leaning forward to brush her lips lightly with his own. Then he stepped out of her way and watched her pass, catching an enticing scent that was mysterious, sweet, different from the tea rose scent she usually wore.

She glanced over her shoulder at him. "Later."

A loud knock at the door broke into his reverie, and he turned to watch Wesley head toward the door.

CHAPTER SEVENTEEN

Hours later, Red Hawk stood across the parlor and watched Savannah move around the room, talking first to one person and then to another. He knew she intended to get Matthew off alone, but she was taking her time, spending a good part of the evening talking to the Ashmans.

Matthew sat stiffly on a deep green damask chair. He appeared bored, annoyed, and petulant. Red Hawk suspected the boy was suffering over having to attend the affair. He noticed the lingering looks Matthew directed toward the open doors to the porch and wondered if the boy longed to escape to the yard.

He sauntered over, pausing near Matthew, who looked up and then frowned. "Care to see the yard?"

The child hesitated as if torn between what he wanted and the image he wanted to project. His lips firmed, and he shook his head. "No, sir. Thank you."

"Your mother and your Uncle Caleb and I used to play out there. Your uncle and I built a tree house that's still there. Sometime when you want to see the yard, I'll show you the tree house."

Matthew shot him another look, but kept his lips tightly closed, yet his gaze slid past Red Hawk to the open door again.

"You won't rumple your nice black suit," Red Hawk said.

"I don't care about tree houses," Matthew replied stiffly.

"You might find you like them. When you climb up high in a tree, you can see all the town. You can see rooftops and over treetops and the streets," Red Hawk said quietly.

Matthew looked up at him. "No, sir," he repeated, but with less conviction.

Red Hawk smiled at him. "If you change your mind, I'll show the tree house to you." He walked away, leaving Matthew to think about it. He held his anger in check, wanting to step over to Casper Ashman and punch the man solidly for what he had done to Celia's child.

The Ashmans, on the other hand, looked pleased and both of them hovered over Savannah.

He watched her, wanting to whisk her away from everyone, back to bed, just the two of them shut away from the world. Last night he had been pushed beyond his endurance, finally throwing aside all the wisdom and considerations he had held to through his adult life. When he wrapped his arms around her last night, he thought he would satisfy himself with her. Instead, today and tonight, he burned with more longing for her than he ever had before. Now images and reality and discoveries taunted him.

His conscience suffered, but how easy it was to shove the guilt aside. Yet when he stopped to give it thought, he ran cold with the risks they had taken. If she was with child—and the possibility had not seemed to occur to her—it would spell disaster for her. That perfect Rebel lieutenant would not take her for his wife if she carried a half-breed's baby in her belly. Nor would she be accepted by the society that was openly welcoming her tonight.

She had been introduced as his fiancée. His parents' old family friends were here. His own close friends were all gone, caught up in the war.

His fiancée. It was as impossible as wishing he could pull

the sun down and have its hot fire light his house and life. For a moment he thought about the future. *How would she feel if I were staying here and starting a business?* The idea was so foreign to all he had wanted for years that he was momentarily startled. As he watched her, he knew it wouldn't matter. She was not the type of woman to marry a half-breed. She loved society and entertaining and a city life. She was in her element now, glowing, looking more beautiful than ever.

As if she could discern his thoughts, her green-eyed gaze shifted and met his. From across the room, he felt the fire jump between them, turning him hot and making his blood thicken.

Her dress turned her eyes more green, and the emerald material contrasted deeply with her fiery hair. She gave him a wicked little smile that made his breath catch. He swore softly to himself. He wanted to stride across the room, pick her up, and carry her off to make love to her. And she knew it. She looked like the consummate seductress—all woman, aware of her power, wanting him, taunting him. Her self-assurance was a challenge; her eagerness an invitation.

He swallowed the rest of his brandy and moved through the open doors to the porch to cool down. He didn't want one of the dainty cups of tea she had poured. He glanced over his shoulder. Her back was turned to him now. His gaze shifted and he looked at Matthew perched on the edge of the chair, staring into space, his hands knotted in his lap. The boy hated being in his house, and the few words Red Hawk had tried to exchange with him had been futile.

Red Hawk moved around the porch restlessly, certain this whole effort to win Matthew's acceptance was useless.

Red Hawk turned to look inside again and saw Savannah's slender figure in the cool shadows of the parlor. She was not his woman—could never be. He should leave her alone. More lovemaking could wreck her future and all she held dear.

He heard her laughter and drew a deep painful breath. How she loved entertaining and people and everything involved in the two!

He moved off the porch into the yard. Matthew was as lost

to him as Savannah. Red Hawk thought that the sooner he could pack and go, the better for everyone concerned.

Twenty minutes later, he returned to the house to join the guests. Matthew still sat on the chair, but now Savannah was perched near him on a small wooden rocker. The boy had lost his scowl and was talking to Savannah and listening to whatever she was telling him.

Adela stood talking to Hester Ashman and he thought that where Adela was concerned, things were going right. She already looked better and had gained some weight. Color was back in her face and she was a beautiful woman. Her dress was pale pink; it was some kind of delicate material that made her look fragile, yet lovely. Some of the men hovered around her, which Red Hawk knew made her nervous. Hester Ashman and another woman stood in the cluster of guests surrounding Adela, and she seemed to be enjoying herself.

He poured another brandy and became aware of someone at his elbow. "You didn't tell me about your fiancée," Casper Ashman said.

"It didn't seem relevant," Red Hawk answered.

"She's a very beautiful woman. You're a fortunate man."

"I think so," Red Hawk said, his gaze and his thoughts on Savannah.

"You didn't tell me her name or her connections."

Red Hawk pulled his thoughts from Savannah and focused on Casper Ashman, realizing the man was making friendly overtures and had had a complete change of manner from their last encounter.

"I didn't see that her connections had that much to do with whether I become Matthew's guardian or not," Red Hawk said, suddenly wondering what magic Savannah had worked on the man.

"Her father was Major Ravenwood."

"I'm aware of that, sir," Red Hawk remarked dryly. Casper Ashman's eyes narrowed a moment.

"He was close with Lincoln. She said I must see the letter of condolence President Lincoln sent to her upon her father's death. That's quite impressive. And she told me you are a captain in the Confederacy.''

"Yes, sir," Red Hawk replied, wondering whether Lincoln had actually sent condolences or Savannah had plied the Ashmans with deceit to impress them. Truth or lie, Casper Ashman was obviously impressed.

"She told me that in spite of your rank in the Confederacy, President Lincoln will be invited to your wedding.''

"I doubt the president will be interested in the wedding of a Confederate officer.''

"Perhaps your affiliation won't matter. You're no longer fighting.''

"Savannah is handling the wedding details, so I don't know anything about invitations.''

"President Lincoln visiting here would be a real coup.''

"I would never expect him to come as long as the war is on," Red Hawk said, wishing he and Savannah had planned more carefully. If Casper Ashman asked him a wedding date, he would be at a loss. He had no idea what Savannah had already told him.

"I think, with such a connection as you're making in your marriage, that it can be arranged for Matthew to visit you.''

"That's kind of you," Red Hawk said, amazed at how much change Savannah had wrought. Yet it was all built on lies and as fragile as a crystal vase thrust into a storm. "But I want more than visits from my nephew.''

Ashman swirled the drink he held in his hand. The amber bourbon caught the light and made Red Hawk think of the gold flecks he sometimes saw in Savannah's green eyes.

"Your fiancée said you are considering settling as soon as you marry and going into business here. She said you intended to buy the local ironworks, that you have a degree in engineering and you are interested in the railroads.''

Savannah had one hell of a busy mind, he thought, glancing at her. Why hadn't she told him all of this before he said something that revealed the falseness of her house of dreams?

With prickles of annoyance, he turned back to Casper, who watched him with narrowed eyes.

"I really hadn't intended her to tell anyone yet. I haven't fully made up my mind. That sort of business thing is best kept quiet until done," he said stiffly.

"True. But you're in love and your judgment with her is weakened. Not that I blame you," he said, looking at Savannah in a manner that made Red Hawk want to punch him more than ever. He wanted to step between Savannah and Casper Ashman so Ashman couldn't even look at her. Instead, he waited quietly.

"She's a very beautiful woman."

"Yes, she is," Red Hawk replied through clenched teeth. He told himself to stop being ridiculous. Savannah wasn't his woman, and he shouldn't burn with anger when another man looked at her.

"My lumber business is growing," Ashman said, finally pulling his attention back to Red Hawk. "If you build rails for the government and become involved in the railroad, you will need lumber and railroad ties."

"Yes, all that will be needed," Red Hawk said, suddenly seeing why Casper Ashman had become so friendly. "Sir, we need to talk. We can meet with my lawyer whenever you would like. There are things I want to go over with you."

"Why wait for a lawyer? Why don't we adjourn to your library now?" Casper Ashman asked, his blue eyes watching Red Hawk closely.

Red Hawk shrugged and glanced again at Savannah and Matthew. For Celia's sake, he had to try to get Matthew. Savannah had already softened the Ashmans.

"Fine," he said, motioning with his hand. The two men crossed the room and walked through the quiet hall to the library. Lamps already burned, as they did in every room in the house, since they were having a party. Before the first guest had arrived, Savannah had seen to it that the house blazed with lights.

Red Hawk closed the door and crossed the room to refill

Ashman's glass from a crystal decanter on a sideboard. He poured himself a small drink, closed the decanter, and picked up his glass, raising it. "To our futures."

Casper Ashman clinked his glass lightly against Red Hawk's. "Our futures."

Red Hawk moved around the desk and opened a drawer to withdraw a document which he tossed onto the center of the desk. "Celia sent this to me along with a letter. You might want to read it."

Ashman crossed the room, the coldness returning to his eyes. He picked up the letter and the document and Red Hawk waited, knowing from memory the letter from Celia that said she was enclosing her will. The will had been notarized, witnessed, and copies were with another lawyer and one banker in town.

Ashman dropped the letter and looked at the will that gave all rights to Matthew's inheritance to Red Hawk until Matthew came of age.

Ashman's face paled and a muscle worked in his jaw. As he clenched his fist, his knuckles were white. When he looked up, his eyes blazed, and Red Hawk tensed, ready for a fight.

Then Ashman tossed the will on the desk. "I could fight you."

"Yes, sir, you can, but there are several notarized copies and quite a few letters about what Celia and your son both wanted done with their son and his inheritance."

Ashman studied him. The man would be a formidable gambler. There was no expression in his face, yet Red Hawk was certain he was mulling which course to follow.

"You win, it seems. Only it may be a hollow victory. Matthew won't want to live with you, and he'll be a difficult child. And if I do decide to fight, he'll be on my side."

"Perhaps, but I made a promise to Celia."

Ashman shrugged. "I think I have few choices. Of course, I want my attorney, Fred Encino, to look at the will. I'd like his opinion on this."

"Yes, sir. I expected that. You saw the list of men who have copies."

Casper Ashman nodded, tossed back his drink, then turned on his heel and left the room.

When Red Hawk returned to the parlor, his gaze sought Savannah. He caught sight of her just as she stood. Matthew slid off the chair and the two of them went out the door onto the porch.

Savannah walked down into the yard with Matthew. "This is a very grand house, isn't it?"

"Yes, ma'am, it is."

"Look at the night sky. Your uncle Quent has legends he knows from his boyhood when he lived out beneath the stars. You should get him to tell you about them, and about how he hunted buffalo and fought in battles."

"He said he has a tree house here."

"I didn't know that." Savannah steered Matthew to one of the benches on the porch. The iron bench sat in the light that spilled through open doors from the dining room. There were no people in the dining room to disturb them. She sat down. "Come sit, Matthew. I have some letters to show you."

She pulled out several letters that were folded and tucked into one of her puffed sleeves. Carefully unfolding one, she turned to read to him.

> *My dear Miss Ravenwood,*
> *I deeply regret to hear about the loss of your father. I send my condolences and prayers. He was a fine officer, a gentleman, a trusted citizen who gave his life for his country in the act of duty. I had the opportunity to meet him on several occasions and I will hold his memory deep in my regard.*
> *May God be with you in this time of your sad loss.*
> *Sincerely,*
> *Abraham Lincoln*
> *President*

"President Lincoln wrote that to you?" Matthew asked, curiosity in his voice.

When she handed him the letter, he shook his head. "I can't read yet."

"Ah, then I should like to tutor you. You'd like to read, wouldn't you?"

"Yes, ma'am."

He took the letter from her and ran his finger over it. "Grandpapa talks about President Lincoln."

"Here's another letter to your Uncle Quent." She smoothed the paper and began to read:

Do you remember the hot summer nights and how we would ride for hours? I want Matthew to know those times, yet I fear he never will. I had two brothers, and Matthew doesn't. What fun we had, Quent! What a carefree time. I want you to know Matthew and Matthew to know you—

"That's from my Indian mother."

"It's from your mother who loved you very much. Listen."

You should see Matthew now. He can pull himself up and take two or three steps all by himself. I know he has to be the most beautiful and the smartest baby in the whole world. He laughs most of the time.

Today I had only turned away no more than two minutes, I'm certain, when I heard him yell. He had climbed over the front fence. I don't know how he managed to scale that tall iron fence, but he did. I screamed and he jumped down on the other side and landed in a puddle. He thought it was great fun, but I shook for the next hour. He could have fallen on one of the sharp points at the top of the fence. That fence has iron spikes, and it terrifies me to think that he got up over the top.

Dalton—or you or Caleb—would probably share his male humor and pride at having accomplished such a feat, but I shall not let him out of my sight for even one minute after this.

*I screamed and went running through the gate and he
was stomping in the puddle, covered with mud, laughing
and having a wonderful time!*

Savannah paused to look at Matthew, who was listening
attentively. "Do you remember climbing the fence?"

"No, but I remember Mama talking about it," he said. "It's
a big fence."

"Here's the rest of the letter:"

*All I have to do to get a smile is look at him. Can you
tell that I love him beyond measure? I know, bachelor
that you are, you aren't interested in all this about an
adorable baby—who, by the way, looks exactly like you.
Even his father says that, and Dalton doesn't seem to
mind. He says he looks a little like his mother, too. I
don't think so. I can't wait for you to come home and
see him. He grows incredibly fast and I suspect will be
as tall as you when he is grown.*

*I will close now. I miss you. Take care of yourself.
Dalton and you and Caleb are in my prayers constantly.
I want you all to come home and see how adorable
Matthew is. And how smart. And how sweet.*

Your loving sister

"Do you remember your father?"

"Yes, ma'am. He'd let me ride in front of him on his horse."

"Want to walk out in the yard?"

Matthew hopped up and lost his reserve, bounding down the
steps and hopping on one foot while he waited for her to catch
up. Hope kindled in Savannah. Matthew's frosty manner had
vanished and he was becoming friendly, his cold reserve gone.

They walked through the yard and she found a frog. She
called to Matthew, who came on the run and started to pick it
up. He snatched back his hand and bit his lip.

"It won't hurt you."

"Grandmother said I shouldn't touch frogs or bugs or nasty

creatures. They'll mess my hands and my good clothes and they might bite.''

"Grandmother might not mind if you held a frog for a little while, as long as you don't take it back into the house," Savannah said, bending down to scoop up the frog. She had never held a frog in her life and didn't want to now, but she could feel barriers between herself and Matthew crumbling. She wasn't going to let squeamishness or a small frog stand in her way of becoming friends with him.

"See, he doesn't hurt," she said calmly, wanting to scream and toss the cold, slimy creature as far as possible. "I promise you, he won't bite, and you can wash your hands afterward.''

To her relief, Matthew reached up and took the frog from her. "Blinking stars, he's big! I'd like to keep him.''

"You know your grandmother would never allow that. Set him free and let him jump.''

Matthew set the frog back on the ground, and it hopped away furiously.

"Let's wash our hands, Matthew," Savannah said, leading him to the fountain of sparkling water tumbling over rocks. They both let the cold water splash over their hands as it ran down to the lily pool. Savannah was enormously relieved to wash the frog off her hands. She shivered in the darkness and was thankful Matthew couldn't see her reaction.

"I wondered if you two had abandoned the party," said a deep voice. Red Hawk stood nearby, watching them.

"We found a frog.''

"And I found a snake," he said, holding up a tiny, writhing snake.

"Mercy!" Savannah exclaimed. Matthew gave a cry of glee and ran to look.

"I'm returning to the party and you two males can look at the snake," she said, gathering her skirts and clutching the letters. She left swiftly, her back prickling. She half expected Matthew to run join her and refuse to stay with Red Hawk.

At the edge of the garden she looked back over her shoulder. Man and boy were kneeling in the grass looking at something—

the snake, most likely. "I told you he's only a child," she said softly, feeling a rush of satisfaction. Red Hawk could reach his nephew. Matthew was a little boy and his prejudice was only a thin veneer developed in the past year since his mother's death.

It took only some conversation, letters, a frog, and a snake to make him forget his disdain for his mother's side of the family.

Savannah stepped into the parlor, looked at the guests and spotted Hester Ashman. She crossed the room to join her, glancing out one of the open windows across the porch and the darkness beyond, wondering how Red Hawk was faring with Matthew.

Red Hawk scaled the oak, going from limb to limb, ignoring the small boards nailed to the trunk that he and Caleb had used as children. Matthew was already in the tree house and Red Hawk moved up beside him, startled by how small it seemed now he was a man. Through the years he had carried his childhood memories, it seemed larger, far more grand, and the commanding view of the city he and Caleb had had was now partially obscured by limbs grown longer and many more leaves. Yet Matthew seemed enchanted.

"I can see the cathedral! I can see our rooftop!"

Red Hawk was thankful for the bright moonlight that bathed the city. Otherwise, Matthew would have been able to see little at night.

"You can see far more in the daytime than at night," Red Hawk said, letting his long legs dangle down to rest his booted feet on a lower branch.

"Savannah said you know legends about the stars and about animals."

"I know some." Red Hawk settled back against the trunk. "It is said that thunder was caused by a great bird that flew south when winter came. Then in summer, it followed the sun north, bringing heat and rain. The great bird was called the

Thunderbird. The flashing of the Thunderbird's eyes made lightning and the flapping of its great wings produced thunder,'' Red Hawk said, spreading his arms wide.

In minutes Matthew was listening, sitting as still as the tree itself, his dark eyes large and his expression enthralled. All of Red Hawk's anger at the child's prejudice and arrogance fell away. Savannah had been right. He was only a little boy, and the Ashmans' influence was shallow. Red Hawk knew Matthew's dislike wouldn't disappear this night, but both he and Savannah had made great cracks in the wall of hostility he had first encountered in Matthew.

He talked quietly, weaving tales and taking himself back to a time when he was young and sat around a campfire and listened to his elders relate legends, passing along a culture that went far back in time and had never been put down on paper.

"Red Hawk?"

He recognized Savannah's lilting voice and leaned forward to look below. "Yes?" He saw her standing in the shadows of the tree.

"Some of the guests are leaving and I suspect the Ashmans may start searching for Matthew before long."

"We're coming down. I'll go first," he told Matthew, wanting to make certain he would be there to catch his nephew if he slipped.

Aware she should return to the party, yet unable to resist being with Red Hawk, Savannah waited. She watched him climb down easily. He had shed his coat and his white shirt was bright in the darkness. Her heartbeat quickened as she looked at his long legs and broad shoulders. How handsome he looked tonight in his fine white linen shirt and black suit! If only he were staying—if only he deeply loved her—too many *if onlys*. He dropped the last few feet to the ground, lithely landing on his feet, then reached up to swing Matthew to the ground.

"Time to go in," he said. He turned to pick up his coat, pulling it on. Savannah moved close to straighten his tie and he watched her intently. She was aware of Matthew standing beside her, waiting for them to go with him.

When she turned, Red Hawk draped his arm across her shoulders as they headed back to the house. On the porch, she reached out to catch Matthew lightly by the arm. "Wait a minute, Matthew. Let's straighten you up a little." She brushed more leaves and grass off his coat.

"I'll go ahead," Red Hawk said, leaving them and striding back into the parlor.

She straightened the child's collar, brushed leaves from his hair. "Now you look quite presentable. No one will know you've been to the top of one of the trees."

He grinned and then turned to run, suddenly stopping and walking sedately back into the parlor, and she suspected he'd remembered training from his grandparents about running in the house.

She followed, spotting Red Hawk immediately. He stood with a group of men, engaged in conversation. Matthew was perched on the wing chair once again, but the bored, annoyed look was gone from his face.

The Ashmans were the last to go. As they walked to the door, Savannah, Adela, and Red Hawk followed.

"I will contact you as soon as I've talked with my attorney," Casper Ashman said coolly, his friendliness of earlier in the evening gone.

"We'll see you at our house tomorrow afternoon." Hester smiled at Savannah and Adela. "It was a lovely party."

Red Hawk listened politely, aware of Matthew standing silently beside his grandmother.

"I had a nice time," he said perfunctorily, but the hatefulness was gone from his tone, and Red Hawk knew his relationship with Matthew had changed.

"You come back, Matthew," he said easily. "Perhaps I could pick you up Monday afternoon."

"Can he go with us when his Uncle Quent buys a new horse?" Savannah asked, smiling at Casper Ashman. "Would that be allowed?"

"It should be great fun," Adela added, smiling also, and he wondered how anyone could resist two such ensnaring smiles.

Casper Ashman couldn't and agreed readily, receiving a killing look from his wife that he ignored, but Hester Ashman didn't yet know about Celia's will.

A time was set to pick up Matthew. Fascinated by how easily Savannah got what she wanted from them, Red Hawk told the Ashmans good night. Even Adela seemed more at ease during the party and dealing with guests, and he suspected the two women had grown up entertaining their parents' and then their father's friends.

He longed to put his arm around Savannah's waist, but the Ashmans seemed stiff and proper, and he wanted them to think as highly as possible of Savannah. Whatever he did, he knew he could never win their high regard.

As Red Hawk stood beside Savannah while the Ashmans climbed into their carriage and drove away, Adela went back into the house. The maids and Wesley Blanchard were working inside. Red Hawk suspected Adela had gone to oversee what they were doing. While the clop of the horses' hooves and the creaking of the carriage wheels faded, he looked down at Savannah. He could see her green eyes in the glow spilling from the open doors and windows of the house.

"I want to be alone with you tonight like we were last night," he said in a husky voice. As memories assailed him and he stroked her nape, he was aroused, wanting her.

"We can't," she whispered. "Adela's here. The servants—"

He slid his arm around her waist and pulled her to him. To hell with the world. He leaned down to kiss her hard and long.

They were both gasping and shuddering when she pulled away again. "You have to stop. We aren't alone now. Last night was a special moment, but a moment we both yielded to when we shouldn't have. I have a fiancé, and you have your own life." She wriggled out of his arms and walked inside.

Standing quietly, Red Hawk waited for his body to cool down. He glanced at the clear night sky with its myriad of winking stars. Thanks to Savannah, he knew he would get

Matthew. It was only a matter of time. Because of the will and because of Savannah's influence, Casper Ashman's attitude had changed. And even if the Ashmans went home and decided to fight him, Red Hawk now was assured that he could win Matthew over.

He looked at the house. He wanted Savannah. How much? He hadn't stopped to think about it before, accepting that they would part and he would join his father's people, while she would go home to Mason and her Rebel lieutenant.

Red Hawk moved restlessly, his body hot with desire that burned like a wild grass fire. The only way he could ever win Savannah's heart and hand away from her lieutenant fiancé would be to settle in San Antonio, to live a life that he had watched his stepfather live, a life that made him feel confined and as if he were missing what was important and lasting.

Wanting Savannah, he moved restlessly, tormented by memories of this time last night. Tonight sleep was impossible. He turned and strode toward the back of the lot where the horses were kept and shortly had saddled the bay. He mounted up. As he passed the house, he saw Savannah at the window. He knew she could see him, if only as a dark silhouette. He touched the brim of his hat as a salute to her.

The night was cool; the dinner had been a triumph over the Ashmans and over Matthew's hostility. Red Hawk should be feeling jubilation instead of turmoil. War had made him realize how valuable and fragile life was, which was why he wanted to return to his roots, to know again the frontier, the untamed and wild land, a true freedom. Now green eyes and red hair and a strong, beautiful woman had ensnared him and changed his wants and longing and plans.

How long would it take him to forget her? She had been a storm in his life since the moment he reached out of the alley and snatched her from her pursuers.

The street was quiet, his horse's hooves dull thuds on the hard-packed ground as he rode toward the lights along the square. As he neared the saloons, he could hear fiddles and a piano and shouts. He passed an adobe cantina, its interior a dark haze of smoke and dim lights and guitar music.

At the Golden Bear Saloon, he dismounted, tethering his horse at the hitching rail and moving inside, aware every time he got in a crowd that he was a wanted man and only blocks away was a poster offering a huge reward for his capture.

While a fiddler played diligently, Red Hawk's gaze went over the crowd, looking for a badge, any sign of the Union officer he had accosted out of Vicksburg, anyone who paid particular attention to him. A tall woman, one of the saloon dancers, with flashing brown eyes and a cascade of fiery red hair, smiled at him and moved away from watching a table of gamblers.

For an instant her red hair made him think of Savannah and his insides knotted. He watched the woman saunter toward him, a beautiful woman in a tight, red-and-black-lace dress that was cut high to reveal her legs and high-top boots. Her full breasts and long legs were luscious, but she held no appeal for him. There was only one woman he wanted. Savannah.

He stood rooted to the spot as the woman threaded her way through the crowd. A haze of smoke hung like a rain cloud over the room, and Red Hawk couldn't move as he realized how deep his feelings ran for Savannah. She was the *only* woman he wanted.

"Savannah," he whispered her name. He glanced over his shoulder beyond the open door, not seeing the horses at the hitching rail or the saloon across the street, but lost in thought about the woman at his house and in his heart. What was he willing to sacrifice for her?

CHAPTER EIGHTEEN

Dressed in a white linen shirt and his black trousers, Red Hawk kept his appointment Monday afternoon with Casper Ashman, who brought Matthew with him when they came to call. Savannah immediately took charge of Matthew while Red Hawk ushered Casper into the library and closed the door.

"Have a seat," Red Hawk said easily.

Looking stern and imposing, Ashman sat in a leather chair. Red Hawk took the one facing him. He remembered from before that Ashman gave nothing away by his expression.

"My attorney talked with yours. The will is legal, quite binding, and quite clear. My son and my daughter-in-law both wanted you to take charge of Matthew. The money all goes to you. Actually, it goes to you whether you have Matthew or not. And I have been told that I must restore the amounts I moved from her account to my account."

"It was Matthew's," Red Hawk replied, feeling a surge of elation. There would be no court battle.

"I can have the money in his account this afternoon."

"I don't intend to take him forever from grandparents who

love him and have treated him well. You'll want him to visit—''

"Actually, once Dalton was grown, after years of freedom, we've found ourselves tied down by Matthew. At this point, I don't think we need to plan visits. There'll be time later for that. Hester wants to travel a bit now that the boy won't be a care.''

Relieved even more, Red Hawk nodded. He was not surprised, suspecting the Ashmans had cared far more about Matthew's large inheritance than about him.

"Hester and I think it would be in the best interests of all concerned if you take him as soon as possible.''

"Does Matthew know anything about this?'' Red Hawk asked.

"No. You should tell him. Perhaps we can make the exchange this afternoon. I told Hester to have the maid pack up his things.''

"This afternoon is sudden,'' Red Hawk said, his pulse jumping. He had won Matthew from the Ashmans without a battle, and the results would be immediate. Now if he could only win over Matthew. "Suppose he doesn't want to come live with me?'' Red Hawk asked quietly, wanting to know if his judgments were correct or if Casper Ashman was hiding his hurt over losing Matthew.

"You're very persuasive. Without the money, it is impossible for us to take him.''

"Oh, come now,'' Red Hawk said. "You have enough to raise six more boys and be comfortable.''

Ashman gave him a frosty smile that held no sincerity. "That is not how I wish to spend my hard-earned money. No, you wanted him. You have the money, you have the boy. Your sister and my son made up their minds. I brought Matthew to leave him with you.''

"I think I'd better talk to Matthew right away.''

"He'll cooperate. He has no choice.''

Red Hawk's anger flared and died. Ashman was handling things poorly, yet Red Hawk would have Matthew.

"We'll send the rest of his things over," Ashman said, rising and striding to the door.

"You're not even saying good-bye to him?" Red Hawk asked. "Don't you think—"

"We've given him our time and attention for nothing," Ashman said coldly. "You wanted him, so he's yours." He strode out and Red Hawk clenched his fists. They had won the child's love. In their callous abandonment, Matthew would be hurt and would feel abandoned.

Squaring his shoulders, Red Hawk strode into the hall. Casper Ashman was already heading down the front walk.

"Matthew, let's put your things in one of the upstairs rooms and then we'll get Savannah and go look at horses," Red Hawk said easily, certain the child did not have an inkling of what had transpired.

"I'm only staying until Grandpapa comes back to get me."

Red Hawk took a deep breath and shook his head, kneeling to get on Matthew's level. "Matthew, your grandparents decided that you should be with me—"

"No!" he yelled. "No!"

He jumped up and raced out the front door. Red Hawk sprinted after him.

Casper Ashman had just climbed into his buggy. He and his driver watched as Matthew raced to the buggy and climbed inside, flinging himself on his grandfather.

"Grandpapa, I want to go with you. Don't leave me here!"

Red Hawk was only yards behind Matthew and met Casper's cold gaze before the older man looked down at the boy.

"Get out of my carriage, Matthew. Your grandmother and I are leaving on a trip, and we're not taking you. Your mother and your father wanted you to live with your uncle, so that's what you'll do."

"No, please!"

Red Hawk clenched his fists. Why couldn't Casper give the child a hug and be kinder?

"Matthew, do as you're told," Casper snapped, his voice becoming stern. The child cried.

"Did his grandmother tell him good-bye?" Red Hawk asked.

"Matthew, get out of my carriage at once!" Ashman ordered.

"Please take me with you!" he cried, clinging to Casper's knees.

"Get out!" Ashman raised his hand, and Red Hawk's arm shot out. As he caught Casper Ashman's wrist, the two men glared at each other.

"Don't touch him," Red Hawk said quietly.

Matthew had seen the blow coming, and his face paled. Releasing Ashman, Red Hawk held his hand out toward Matthew. The boy clamped his mouth closed and wiped his eyes. He refused Red Hawk's hand, but he released his grandfather and climbed out of the carriage.

Savannah stood only yards away, her eyes filled with curiosity.

"They've moved Matthew here," Red Hawk told her, moving away from the carriage and watching Matthew.

She rushed forward to kneel and talk quietly to Matthew. He let her take his hand, and the two of them headed back to the house. With a glance over her shoulder at Red Hawk, she held open the front door and she and Matthew disappeared inside. Red Hawk turned to watch the Ashmans' buggy as it disappeared down the street.

"You were right about him, Celia," he said quietly, knowing he would have a task now to win Matthew's trust and love.

Striding toward the house, he paused and studied it, suspecting it might be better to leave Savannah and Matthew alone for a time. He was certain that Savannah could cope with Matthew.

Red Hawk turned and headed back to get his horse. In minutes he rode away, making mental lists of things he wanted to do now that he had a child in his care. He marveled at his life. Only a month ago, he had been alone, fighting a war. Now he had two women and a child in his charge, a new cook, a house to oversee, and three horses in his care. What had happened to his solitary life? He suspected it was gone forever.

* * *

Inside the house, Matthew sobbed in Savannah's arms. She sang to him and stroked his head until he quieted.

Savannah heard a horse on the drive and guessed that Red Hawk might be leaving Matthew to her, which was just as well. She fought back anger at the Ashmans, knowing her fury wouldn't help Matthew. "Let's go sit in the backyard," she said, and he nodded.

"They don't want me," Matthew said stonily, and her heart twisted. She couldn't deny his statement, and she hurt to see him so pained.

"Matthew, people are complicated. They've been good to you, and now they want you to be with your uncle."

"I hate him and I don't want to be with him."

Sitting down in a chair in the hallway, she pulled him to her to hug him. "Give me a hug," she said gently, and he put his arms around her stiffly without moving close to her. She hugged him, holding him and stroking his head. Suddenly he burst into tears again and this time as she tightened her arms around him, he let her pull him close and hold him while he cried.

She sat quietly, letting him wear himself out and vent his emotions. When he quieted, she leaned back and wiped his wet cheeks with her fingers. Tears glistened on his long black eyelashes, and she thought again how the resemblance he bore to Red Hawk was amazing. His nose was red, and he looked like a very unhappy little boy.

"Let's get something cold to drink."

He nodded, and together they went to the pump and drank cold water. She pulled her handkerchief from her sleeve, dampened it, and wiped his face. "You know, there are lots of things stored in the attic of this house. Why don't we go see if your mother or your uncles left any toys up there?"

Without a change in his expression, Matthew nodded his head, so they returned to the house and climbed the stairs to the dusty attic. She moved to a stack of boxes and pulled out her handkerchief to wipe dust off one so she could sit down.

She pulled a box to her and opened it. "Let's see what's in here."

Matthew stood quietly by her side, but when she opened the box, he stepped closer to look inside.

They went through crates and boxes of clothes until she opened a crate of metal windup toys. In minutes, Matthew was crawling on the dusty attic floor, his voice high with eagerness as he played. She was thankful that Red Hawk's mother had saved their childish things.

The attic was hot, dusty, and dim because it had few windows, but Savannah settled to stay and let Matthew play. He shed his shoes and coat and finally his shirt. Black locks of hair fell in his face. She had rolled her own sleeves as high as possible and unbuttoned her blue dress as much as she dared. Her hair hung down her back in one thick braid and she continually wiped her damp forehead and nape.

"Matilda told me where to find the two of you," Red Hawk said, stepping into the attic and placing his hands on his hips. He stood in the center of the room, where the slanting roof was high enough for him to straighten up.

"Look at this," Matthew said, winding up a small train that ran in a circle on a narrow track.

"I haven't seen those things in years. I can't believe Mama kept them."

At one time, Savannah would have been unable to imagine him as a boy playing with the toys spread before her, but now all she had to do was look at Matthew, and she knew how Red Hawk had been.

"It's hot as a smithy's shop in midsummer up here," Red Hawk drawled. "Let's take all these downstairs. Matthew, pack them carefully in the crate, and I'll carry them down. Tomorrow you can come look again for more toys if you want. I think you may find some more."

While Matthew scrambled to do what Red Hawk said, Red Hawk turned to Savannah. He winked and smiled at her and she was pleased, knowing that he was relieved and happy to see Matthew enjoying himself. She knew there would be more bad moments, but hopefully, the good would begin to replace the bad.

When they climbed downstairs, they waited while Red Hawk easily carried down the crate.

"Matthew, I'll show you which room will be yours, and we'll put the toys in there."

Matthew's face was a brief reflection of his emotions as he frowned and then nodded. Guessing they might have passed another hurdle, Savannah breathed a sigh of relief.

"I'm hot, covered with dust, and I'm shutting myself in the bathroom to have a bath," she announced. Red Hawk's gaze swung to her, and the desire that flared in his dark eyes took her breath and made her forget Matthew and everything except Red Hawk.

While she was caught in his gaze, both of them stood immobile, staring at each other, invisible fire singeing the air between them.

"Uncle Quentin?" Matthew said tentatively.

Red Hawk turned away. "Down here," he said, walking away with Matthew. Her heart raced, and she remembered being in Red Hawk's arms.

Red Hawk swore to himself. He wanted Savannah more than he had before. The thought of her bathing made desire a raging fire in him. Glancing down at Matthew, he knew this was a time he needed to concentrate on the child.

They entered Caleb's old room. "This is your Uncle Caleb's room, but he's away fighting in the war." Red Hawk set the box on the floor. He sat on a chair and put his hands on his knees. "Matthew, you're here with me now. I know this is hard for you, but this is the way it has to be."

Matthew frowned and chewed his lip. "Yes, sir," he said quietly, but tears filled his dark eyes. "Why don't they want me?"

Red Hawk took a deep breath and thought about his answer. "I think right now they feel you should be with me, as your mother wanted. Also, they want to travel. They want to take a trip."

Nodding, Matthew swiped at his eyes. "They won't let me go home, will they?"

"For now your home will be here," Red Hawk said quietly. "That's why I got something for you that will be yours to keep if you want, and maybe since you have it, you won't feel so alone."

To Red Hawk's relief, curiosity replaced the hurt in Matthew's expression. He cocked his head to one side and looked around the room as if searching for his present.

"It's downstairs. Let's go look. Want to?"

The boy nodded solemnly, and together they went down to the back porch. Red Hawk pushed open the door. "There in the box in the corner."

Matthew looked at him and then walked to the box.

"Oh! This is mine?" he exclaimed, his voice filling with surprise and eagerness.

"If you want him."

"A pup! I can have a pup?"

"Yes, you can."

Matthew already had the retriever pup in his arms. "He's mine!" he exclaimed again, laughing delightedly. "I want to show Miss Ravenwood."

"Go ahead."

Matthew was gone in a flash. Red Hawk suspected he forgot the training the Ashmans had given him about running in the house, because he raced through the kitchen.

"You got him a dog," Matilda said. "That's a happy little boy now. I don't suppose this dog will stay outside?"

"Sorry, Matilda, but he's too important to put outdoors."

She nodded and sighed and went back to stirring batter.

Red Hawk heard yelling upstairs and quickened his step. He took the stairs two at a time and could hear Matthew yelling to Savannah.

"Come out here and see what I've got, Miss Ravenwood! Come see!"

"I'm bathing, Matthew."

"Just look out the door! Hurry!" The wiggling puppy was

tired of being carried and Matthew set him on the floor, plopping down in delight beside him. The child was covered with dust and dirt smudges. His thick black hair was in disarray and his pants were rumpled, but he looked happier than Red Hawk had ever seen him look and a quiet joy filled him.

"Come here, Miss Ravenwood! Please look!"

The door opened a fraction and Savannah thrust her head out. "Matthew, just call me Aunt Savannah. It'll be easier."

She held her towel wrapped around her, but her shoulders were bare, and Red Hawk was ensnared again. He wanted to join her, shut and lock the door, and have her all to himself for hours.

"A dog!" She looked at Red Hawk in surprise, then saw the way he was looking at her. "I guess you know what you're doing." She closed the door.

"Can I keep him in my room?" Matthew asked, his eyes shining.

"Yes. I'll put his box in there. Matthew, if you keep him, I want you to take responsibility for feeding him."

"Yes, sir! Thank you for him," he added shyly. Then he began to play with the pup.

"Let's take him outside for a while," Red Hawk suggested and picked up the puppy to carry him downstairs again.

An hour later, as he sprawled on the lawn with Matthew and the new puppy, he knew no matter how much trouble the dog was, he would be worth it. Matthew's reserve and hurt had vanished. He played with the pup and his voice was filled with eagerness and joy.

After supper, Adela and Savannah had to see the dog, and then all the adults sat on the porch while Matthew played with his new pet.

When Red Hawk got Matthew upstairs, the box with the puppy was beside the boy's bed. Red Hawk suspected as soon as he left the room, the pup would be in bed with Matthew.

Red Hawk moved restlessly through the house. Savannah and Adela sat with their sewing in the parlor, and he joined them for the next hour, sitting close beside Savannah and touching her occasionally. Finally she and Adela went upstairs to bed and he moved restlessly outside, getting his horse and mounting to ride to town.

Unable to sleep, Savannah sat up at the open window. She lifted her hair off her neck. The night was hot and still and she longed to be in Red Hawk's strong arms. *Only four nights ago.* Ecstasy and torment. She wanted to be in his arms again, wanted more of his loving, wanted to hold him close. At the same time, she knew they shouldn't cross that line again.

She had known passion and rapture. Would a lifetime of marriage make her love Thomas the way she loved Red Hawk right now? But she was pledged to Thomas and she would keep her vow. She belonged with Thomas, not with a wild warrior like Red Hawk.

Nor did he want her. No vow, no promises had ever crossed his lips. He was going back to his plains, to his wild life. She could never be a part of that.

Hot tears filled her eyes and spilled over her hands, and she yielded to the despair that swamped her, cradling her face in her hands to cry.

Finally she wiped her eyes and moved to the washstand to pour cold water from the pitcher into the large bowl. She dipped a cloth into the water, wrung it out, and wiped her face.

The house was stifling. Savannah picked up her white cotton wrapper, pulled it on, and tied the blue silk sash around her waist. She went downstairs, tiptoeing quietly, thinking about Matthew and his large dark eyes. The boy was so thrilled with the dog that he seemed to settle into the household without difficulty, and she suspected that while the Ashmans may have given him a great many things, they showered very little love on him.

Where was Red Hawk now—with a woman? The thought was a painful stab in her heart, and she hoped he was merely gambling or entertaining himself some other way.

She stepped outside. The night air was cooler than being in the upstairs of the house. She moved across the yard toward the tree house, looking up at it and wondering what it would have been like to be a boy and have such a wonderful thing as a haven built up in a tree.

Curious, Savannah reached up and grasped a rough board. She put her bare foot on one and stepped up.

It was too tempting to resist. She climbed another step and another, until she was scrambling up the tree and feeling as if she were breaking some sacred law. Her father never would have allowed her to climb a tree. A slight breeze fluttered her nightgown around her bare legs. The wrapper was a nuisance, catching on branches, and she paused to shrug it off. She leaned out and tossed it, watching it float down until it snagged on a branch, dangling above the ground.

Climbing higher, she moved slowly to be sure of her footing, careful not to scratch herself on branches until she reached the platform of rough boards, where she pulled herself up. She stood carefully and looked out, her breath catching at the twinkling lights she could see on the nearest square, moonlight spilling over the tall roof of the cathedral and, beyond the town, moonlight sparkling on the ribbon of the Olmos River and bathing the open land in splashes of white.

She didn't know how long she stood enjoying the spectacular view. Through the leaves she could view the yard and house. When she heard the clop of hooves, she peered through the darkness. The noise grew louder and she waited, hoping Red Hawk was returning home. She was hidden in her lofty lair. Across the yard, he rode into view below. Through the leaves, she watched him ride around the carriage house and disappear from her view.

Waiting to catch another glimpse of him going into the house, she stood where she was, but when time passed, she decided she had missed him and she sat down to lean against the rough trunk of the tree and dangle her legs in the air. She pulled the nightgown above her knees, relishing the tree loft and the cool night air.

She heard a rustle.

"Savannah?"

Startled, she sat up so suddenly, she almost lost her perch. She yelped and caught a branch. "Red Hawk?"

His head appeared and his hand closed warmly on her knee. At his touch, heat flashed in her like lightning streaking the sky.

"Ready to come down?" he asked.

"No," she said, recklessness and the magic of night seizing her, all her resolutions crumbling like ashes hammered on an anvil. "I've never been in the top of a tree before. And I've never been kissed in the top of a tree," she added breathlessly, looking at him, yet unable to fathom anything in his eyes.

He climbed up swiftly and pulled her to him. "We'll change that right now," he stated in a husky voice. "You'll be kissed when you're standing high above San Antonio. All the rest of your life, you can remember the night you were kissed in the top of a tree."

He pulled her close. A branch scraped her shoulder; leaves brushed her cheek and neck, but she barely noticed. It was foolhardy of both of them. They could fall. Even more reckless, she was risking her heart again, binding it to him with invisible chains forged by a passion she suspected she would never again experience.

She was aware only of Red Hawk, the warmth of his body, his strong arms, the smell of whiskey on his breath. He leaned down and his mouth covered hers in a hard, hot kiss that she returned, standing on tiptoe and sliding her arms around his neck to cling to him. His hands slid down beneath her arms, trailing over her breasts. She moaned softly, moving her hips against him.

Red Hawk bent over her, kissing her, while his blood thickened with desire. He raised his head and glanced around him at the tiny space. Branches hampered their movements. He started to take her hand and climb down, but then he thought of the wildness in her voice when she said she had never been kissed in a tree. It had been a sultry challenge, an invitation he couldn't ignore.

He unfastened his collar and tossed it away. Unbuttoning

his shirt, he yanked it off and let it fall. She watched him, her eyes huge. As he stripped away his clothing, she trailed her fingertips over his shoulder then across his chest. He groaned, wanting her with a ravenous need.

Tugging off a boot, he threw it to the ground, then pulled off the other.

"Red Hawk," she whispered.

He straightened and reached out, pulling her thin cotton nightgown over her head and tossing it away. He was aroused, wanting her more than ever. He shed his trousers, stepping out of them, kicking them away as he stepped close to kiss her. He caressed her breasts, cupping them in his hands, running his thumbs in slow circles over her nipples. He bent down, taking her nipple in his mouth.

While he kissed her hungrily, his hands stroked her. Savannah thought she would melt. He picked her up, lifting her and settling her on him.

Impaled on him, she moaned with pleasure. Need burst within her. She clung to him, her legs locked tightly around him, her fingers wound in his hair. With his legs braced apart, his muscles tight, he rocked them.

Clinging to him, Savannah moaned softly while sensations dazzled her.

"Savannah!" He ground out her name. While his hips moved rhythmically, she clung to him, transported higher than the treetops, feeling as if he had flung them beyond the stars.

The moving was frantic, an urgency and need. Was he as desperate as she? Thoughts spun away as she held him tightly, moving with him until rapture burst in her. His hoarse voice cried her name, and he pumped into her, spilling his hot seed. Their breathing was ragged as they drifted back to reality, to awareness of their precarious perch, the dark night surrounding them, the faint breeze that cooled their sweat-covered skin.

She slid her legs down and he lowered her to lean against him while he held her and stroked her head.

"We could have fallen and killed ourselves," he said quietly.

She smiled and trailed her fingers down his cheek and over

his jaw. Her smile vanished as he looked at her. He was trailing his hands over her, his gaze drifting down. He stepped back to look at her, holding her with his hands on her waist.

"My gown is somewhere down below. We should go. We weren't going to do this again for so many reasons," she said quietly, her mind jumping to the most important thing of all.

"We'll say good-bye soon," he whispered, kissing her ear. "I'll go down first." He climbed down, picked her gown off a tree limb, and tossed it up to her.

Savannah slithered into it and turned to climb down, looking around her at the crudely built platform and knowing tonight she had gained a memory that would be with her the rest of her life.

Red Hawk yanked on his trousers and looked up to watch her descend. She wore only the thin nightgown that billowed out. Her bare legs were long, and he remembered them locked around him. As she neared the ground, he reached up and closed his hands on her tiny waist to lift her down and embrace her.

She came eagerly, winding her arms around his neck, and he kissed her, wanting her again just as strongly as before. He wove his fingers in her thick hair and tilted back her head. "Woman, I can't get enough of you."

Savannah's heart pounded. She wanted him as intensely. She knew each kiss, each caress was a bond, and with each consummation she gave him her heart and soul.

He growled deep in his throat and kissed her hard, making her heart thud. She was wanted, loved, desired in a way she had never been. In turn, she desired him. Instead of satisfaction, each encounter stirred new needs. She was surprised by her own reactions, awakened to physical desire and far deeper longings of the heart.

"Come here, Savannah," he said, leading her away from the tree, beyond it, completely out of sight of the house. Knowing she should go back, she tugged on his hand, shaking her head when he looked at her.

"Savannah," he coaxed, pulling on her hand. His voice was

seductive, irresistible. He pulled her gown over her head and spread it on the ground, and then took her into his arms.

"You've already broken vows, so another time isn't going to change anything," he said as he bent to kiss her.

"I haven't ever said any vows of any sort. My father made the pledge—"

"You haven't told the lieutenant you love him?"

"No," she said, knowing what she was admitting. She was going into an arranged marriage that she had willingly accepted as a small child and grown up expecting. And it was no different for Thomas. Yet what did it matter to Red Hawk? There had been no vows of love, no commitment from him, no asking her to change her plans.

"Then you don't love him at all," Red Hawk said with satisfaction in his voice. Before she could answer, his mouth covered hers. Forgetting conversation, she clung to him and was lost again in another dizzying spiral that carried her into ecstasy.

He stroked and kissed and caressed her, pulling her down on her discarded gown. He spread her legs and moved between them while she stroked his powerful thighs and trailed her fingers over his shaft.

He came down over her, thrusting slowly into her warmth and softness, and she locked her legs around him. They were again one. Savannah held his strong body in her arms.

Rapture burst with her release and, at the same time, he shuddered. They clung to each other until he shifted and rolled on his side and turned her to face him.

He swept her hair away from her face. "You're a wonderful woman, Savannah," he said, trailing his fingertips across her cheek.

She turned her head to kiss his hand. Those were not the words she wanted to hear from him. She didn't want him to let her go, yet she knew she had to go back to her life as she had always known it and Red Hawk had to go on with his own.

"We should go inside before we're missed." she said. "This

is Matthew's first night and he has the puppy. He might not sleep. He might look for us."

"In a moment," came Red Hawk's deep reply. "For a few more minutes let me hold you and enjoy the night and my woman in my arms."

"I'm not your woman," she said stiffly, the words both thrilling and hurting at the same time.

"You're my woman right now," he said, a fierce note in his husky voice. She twisted to look at him. He lay on his back, holding her in his arms.

"I'm going inside," she said, standing.

He rose and handed her gown to her, which she slipped over her head swiftly. "I have to find my wrapper."

He strode back to the oak and she followed, noticing he moved casually, at ease even though he was nude.

When she caught up with him, he held out her wrapper. He had pulled on his trousers and held his clothing in his hand.

"The puppy was good. It made Matthew very happy."

"How did you know we had toys in our attic?"

"I didn't. It was a guess. Even if we hadn't found any, it took his mind off things to go up there and look through boxes."

"You're good with children, Savannah. You'll be a good mother."

She couldn't answer because she knew he would not be the father of her children and she didn't want to think about a future without him.

They walked in silence to the house. Inside, Red Hawk closed and locked the door and they climbed the steps together. At the top of the stairs, when she turned for her room, he caught her wrist.

"Would you come to my room?" he whispered.

She shook her head. She had to say no to him. He wasn't going to be part of her life and too easily she had succumbed to him. She had let him seduce her, then fallen swiftly into his arms again and again. She could be carrying his child. If she was, her life would be torn apart. Yet she had no more been able to resist him than she could stop breathing.

"I'm going to my room," she whispered and turned to rush inside her bedroom and close the door without looking back. Yet she tingled, and she wanted him to stop her. He had let her go. Soon he would let her go forever. Tears stung her eyelids, yet there was no other solution. Wiping her eyes, she shrugged away regrets and hurt. She had known true passion. If their union was not meant to be forever, at least she had known that.

She thought about tonight, and her mouth turned up in a smile as she remembered him appearing in the top of the tree. Her smile vanished while her body heated with scalding memories of his lovemaking. As long as she lived, she would have those memories, and memories could make the heart sing. If she had to live the rest of her life in Mason, where Thomas would practice, she would remember this night of passion and wildness, clinging to Red Hawk high above the city, caught up in a passion that soared far higher; held, kissed, and caressed by a strong, virile warrior who trembled with his need for her. He had never declared words of love, but when he looked at her, his eyes offered his heart.

Red Hawk moved restlessly around the room he had grown up in. The large bedroom that belonged to his parents was down the hall and stood empty. As he often had as a boy, he felt confined in this room. He used to climb out into the oak that stood beside the house. He yanked off his shirt and wiped his brow with it. It was balled in his fist and as he wiped his face, he caught the scent of tea roses. His heart clenched at the mere fragrance of Savannah. He wanted her as desperately as a man could want a woman. He held the shirt against his nose, inhaling the scent again, closing his eyes and remembering.

"Damnation," he swore, throwing down the shirt. He had to get over her—or stay and fight for her. Which did he want to do?

He paced the room restlessly and then left, going downstairs and prowling through the house, letting memories pour through him. This was where he had lived his most impressionable years, not the early years of his life with the Comanche. His Indian life was a dim memory, brightened by time into a shining bauble.

Could he settle here, start a business? If it meant having Savannah's love, could he give up the other?

He moved through the house, recalling the times he had been hemmed in and confined by the house and the town. But if he joined the Comanche, would he find he had been wrong? Life with them would mean hardship and more battles. When the war was over, the U.S. Army would turn its attention west, as it had before the war interrupted the expansion of the western frontier.

He stood in the library at the open window and looked outside, feeling caged in the house. He turned to stare at the darkened room. Business, city life—if he would accept that life and fight for Savannah's love, she might marry him. Would he give up the other life for her? If he didn't give it up for her, would he regret it forever?

He ran his hand over the woodwork and touched the cool windowpane. He had to go back, had to join the Comanche. There was still something unsettled in him. Even if he gave up that life, he couldn't settle here in a city. It would have to be on a ranch, where he could work outside and deal with the elements. Right now, with two murder charges hanging over him, he had few choices.

If he returned to his people, would Savannah go with him? He suspected he knew his answer now, but he would ask her. She had denied being his woman, but she was, if only for now. He had been the first man she had given herself to, and he was certain she had not done so lightly. He wanted her. Clenching his fist, he placed it against his heart and grimaced. He ached for her. He *loved* her.

He wanted her as his woman, wanted her forever. He had never told her, had never fully acknowledged it himself before this night. He knew her answer if he asked her to go with him, yet he had to ask. He had to give her the choice.

Walking into the hall, he gazed into the darkness at the head of the stairs. She was up there, asleep. He could wake her, ask her right now.

He rubbed the back of his neck, knowing this was not the time. He had yet to tell her he loved her. But how could he have told her before when he just realized it himself? Now that he acknowledged the depth of his feelings for her, he began to think about tomorrow and beyond. He wanted her as part of his life forever. He needed her. He was complete with her.

Tomorrow he would tell her. He would ask her to share his life. Could he win her over? Could he convince her to give up San Antonio and the life she loved so much?

As he climbed the stairs, his heart leaped at the thought of a future with Savannah. Drawing closer to her bedroom door, he stared at it. Longing tore at him. He wanted to storm inside, tell her he loved her—and ask her to be his wife.

CHAPTER NINETEEN

Red Hawk stood outside her door in the silent, darkened hallway, the hot, cloying air wrapping around him while doubts assailed him. Savannah would never leave this life. He saw it in the sparkle in her eyes and the eagerness in her voice each day as she talked about parties and shops and fiestas. She loved this house; she loved the city. To give it up to live on a horse, to constantly move, to sleep in a tipi—he couldn't imagine her doing so willingly. Once again the fleeting idea crossed his mind to simply take her with him, but he knew that would never be the way to win her heart.

He clenched his fists and went back downstairs, sleep lost, striding outside to walk into the darkness, feeling a need to move and think about what he should do.

Debating with himself all through the next few days and watching the barriers around Matthew crumble as the child became more responsive daily, Red Hawk was torn between the futility of asking Savannah to marry him and the necessity of trying to convince her to do so.

He couldn't think about a future without her. At the same

time he knew her first question would be whether he would give up his Comanche life.

He began that day to withdraw money from his account and buy land northwest of San Antonio. As he signed the papers, he looked at the legal description set in front of him, and he wondered whether he would ever live on the land or not. Before he could, the murder charges would have to be settled. The untended land was as close to civilization and city life as he ever wanted to be. He couldn't go back to living in San Antonio. He was a man of the earth and he needed to be outside. If it couldn't be with the Comanche, it would have to be on his own land as a rancher.

One night, as he paced his room restlessly, a cry startled him. He dashed to Matthew's room. Thrashing about in bed, the child cried out again, and Red Hawk picked him up. "Matthew!"

Matthew's dark eyes opened, rolling wildly as he gasped and stiffened.

"Matthew, it's Uncle Quentin."

Matthew blinked and his eyes focused and grew round. "I didn't mean to wake you, sir."

"You didn't wake me. What's wrong?"

"Nothing."

Red Hawk sensed something amiss. Matthew had obviously been dreaming, but why wouldn't he say so? "Did you have a bad dream?"

"No, sir. I'll go back to sleep."

"You cried out like you had a bad dream," Red Hawk said, brushing straight locks of hair off Matthew's forehead.

"You're not mad at me, are you?"

"Mad at you? Why would I be?"

"For waking you."

"That's no reason to get angry, and I wasn't asleep anyway." Red Hawk studied the child, who looked worried. "Did your grandfather get angry if you disturbed his sleep?"

"Yes, sir. He didn't want me to wake him."

"You can wake me anytime you want," Red Hawk said

quietly, tightening his arms around Matthew. "I don't ever mind."

Holding Matthew, Red Hawk stroked the boy's head. "What did you dream?" he asked quietly.

There was a moment's silence. "I dreamed a bear was after me," Matthew answered with hesitation. "He was chasing me, and I couldn't run fast enough."

"There are no bears in San Antonio to chase you. I promise you. The only bears I've ever seen were small and ran from me, even though I wasn't a lot bigger than you are."

"You saw bears?"

"Yes, when I lived with the Comanche." Red Hawk looked down at the child in his arms. "We were farther north and west of here—far, far from here. We traveled most of the year, except in the winter. Then we camped through the cold months. When I was a small child, the scariest animals were the buffalo, even though they're good animals for our people."

"I haven't ever seen buffalo."

"I'll show them to you. They're big animals with shaggy, woolly hair around their heads and hundreds run together in a herd, their hooves sounding like thunder. The ground shakes as if a big steam locomotive were chugging past. When I was older, I hunted them. When we went after a herd, we rode in close, the horse right there with all the charging buffalo. You draw your arrow and try to shoot for the heart."

"Can I learn to shoot an arrow?"

"Yes. We'll get wood and make you a bow tomorrow, and then I'll teach you how to make arrows."

"When you shot a buffalo, then what happened?"

As Red Hawk answered, Matthew calmed. Telling him about his days with the Comanche, Red Hawk lifted him into his bed and sat beside him in the dark.

"If I would take you, would you want to go live with the Comanche?"

"Yes! Aunt Savannah and Aunt Adela would go, too, wouldn't they?"

"I don't know. I don't think Aunt Adela will want to."

"I think she will," he said with childish confidence. "Tell me about when you saw the bears."

Red Hawk talked quietly until Matthew's eyes closed and his breathing became regular, then leaned down and brushed his nephew's cheek with a kiss. "Good night, Little Brave. Your mother can be at peace now."

He tiptoed from the room and stood gazing at Savannah's closed bedroom door. "No, Matthew, my lady won't come with us," he said softly in the darkness. He turned for the stairs and went outside to saddle his horse again to ride to town, hoping to distract himself with a card game in a saloon.

As the days passed, Savannah watched Red Hawk steadily win Matthew's regard. She knew, with time, the child would think of him as his father. Already, Matthew had a quiver and bow and arrows. Red Hawk had made targets for him and Matthew practiced several hours each day. She knew from morning rides with Matthew that even though he was only six, he was an excellent horseman and had been riding with his mother since he was a baby. He talked about living with the Comanche, and she knew Red Hawk was laying the groundwork for the move. Matthew already seemed eager.

Since they no longer needed to entertain the Ashmans, their social life had ended and she was disappointed, yet she was with Red Hawk daily and she was beginning to enjoy Matthew. Every morning she tutored him for an hour. He was still young, and she kept the lessons simple, but he was beginning to learn his letters and to write them.

Savannah's nerves were stretched thin from constantly living in the same house with Red Hawk. Yet with Adela and Matthew and Matilda in the house and Wesley working outside, she and Red Hawk were rarely alone, and then for only a few minutes at a time. There had been no more trysts or lovemaking, just as she had asked, but her heart and her body couldn't follow the logic of her mind. To see him constantly, to brush against him or have him touch her as he handed her a book or pulled out a chair, was building her desire for him to a scalding heat.

How many times during supper or sitting in the parlor reading to Matthew had she looked up to find Red Hawk's brooding gaze on her and desire burning in his eyes? Too many times to count. Each time her pulse had jumped and she lost awareness of everything else around her.

Thursday morning, as she planned their supper and stood before the well-stocked pantry, she glanced out the window and watched Red Hawk stride across the yard.

"Savannah, you should write Thomas and tell him about Red Hawk."

Her gaze flew back to Adela, who was seated on a stool with a bowl in her lap for shelling peas. "There's nothing to tell," Savannah replied, watching Adela's slender fingers move adeptly as she snapped the long pods. "Soon we'll be back in Mason and all this will be forgotten."

"You're in love with him," Adela said quietly. She smoothed her hands over the apron that protected her blue calico dress.

"No, I'm not," Savannah snapped.

Adela's big blue eyes focused intently on her, and Adela's brows arched.

Savannah had never lied to Adela. She ran her fingers across her forehead. "Adela, I don't know. I may love him, but it's hopeless. He's going back to his people and he hasn't asked me to go—"

"Would you go with him if he asked?"

"No! I can't imagine such a life. I belong here."

"Maybe he would give up the Comanche for you," Adela said quietly. "He has a wonderful home here."

"No, he won't. When we crossed Louisiana, he spent hours at night telling me about his early life and how much he wanted to get back to it. And he thinks it will be splendid for Matthew."

Adela shivered. "I think it's dreadful."

"I agree. I promised to marry Thomas, and that's exactly what I shall do."

"There's nothing worse than a loveless union. Don't marry

Thomas if you don't love him. You'll regret it all the rest of your life.''

"Thomas and I are well-suited. We grew up doing the same things, having families who were friends, sharing the same types of things. We will understand and appreciate each other and, hopefully, grow to love each other.''

Adela's blue eyes clouded. "Do you really feel you'll love Thomas?''

"Of course," Savannah answered. "At least, I hope I will. Adela, what I feel for Red Hawk is hopeless. Absolutely hopeless.''

"You're so in love with him. And he with you. When you two are together in a room, it's like the rest of the world doesn't exist.''

"It isn't!" Savannah replied, blushing, amazed how much Adela had noticed. Savannah shook her head, her thick braid falling over her shoulder down her back. Twisting free one more button at the neck of her pink and green cotton dress, she pushed the collar open and fanned herself with her hand. "I don't think he's so in love with me.''

"Then you're blind. I quite feel the air will burst into flames when you two are in the room.''

"We need to get the things ready for supper." Embarrassed, Savannah tried to concentrate on picking out what she wanted for the evening meal. She blushed hotly from Adela's remarks. Had they been so incredibly obvious?

"You can change the subject, but I'm not mistaken about you two.''

Savannah didn't answer and tried to remember what she had come out to the pantry to search for. Finally she remembered she wanted cornmeal, but she couldn't recall why. She stared at the staples stored on the pantry shelves, but she saw only Red Hawk's dark image.

You're so in love with him. And he with you. It's like the rest of the world doesn't exist when you two are together in a room.

Was it really that way? Savannah wondered. Without question, it was for her. The thought of marriage to Thomas had become something ghostly, far in the distance, bearing little reality. Reality was wanting Red Hawk's arms around her. Yet with every day that Matthew adjusted more fully and drew closer to Red Hawk, she knew farewells were coming.

Also, Red Hawk still ran incredible risks by staying in town when there was a reward for his capture. Each time he had driven them to town, she had seen him scan the crowd, and she knew he was searching for someone who might be after him. He never left home without his Colt strapped on his hip.

She loved him and wanted to be with him. Yet there had never been words of love from him. Even if he had said them to her, it would do nothing to bind their futures together.

She picked up a canister of cornmeal and carried it back to the kitchen, where Matilda was browning a thick cut of beef.

When she had hired Matilda, Savannah had explained that the job was only temporary. The woman had merely shrugged. "I will find another job when I leave this one. There is always work."

Now Savannah knew more about Matilda and wondered about her stoic acceptance of whatever life presented. Through bits and pieces, she had learned that Matilda had come to the States from Germany only four years earlier. On the way, her husband and two sons had died of cholera. She had arrived in Texas unable to speak the language and completely alone except for friends she had made of fellow passengers on board ship.

Matilda had told Savannah how she had traveled with a family from the ship to San Antonio where she had settled because there were other German immigrants. Twenty-nine, tall and thin, she kept her blond hair in a braid looped and pinned on her head and worked diligently and silently most of the time. Savannah couldn't remember seeing her laugh even one time. Yet she was a steady and competent worker, and Savannah wanted to hire her to cook and clean when she and Adela returned to Mason. She had talked to Matilda twice about it and had gotten an acceptance.

For a time after Matthew came to live with them, Savannah

worried constantly that Red Hawk would announce he was closing his house and they would go. But as the days passed and August came, he busied himself with business and Matthew. She began to stop worrying about the day they would leave.

Late on a Wednesday morning, after finishing tutoring Matthew and seeing him off with Red Hawk, Savannah hummed as she dressed in a new green dimity and placed a small bonnet on her head. Her hair was parted in the center and caught up in a net, and emerald earbobs from her father dangled in her ears. She and Adela were going to shop for material, go to the dressmaker's, and then stop to see Bertrice, Adela's friend.

Picking up her reticule and parasol, Savannah went downstairs. She had asked Wesley to hitch her horse to the buggy, and she was ready for an afternoon in town.

Adela stood waiting quietly at the back door, talking to Matilda about supper. Savannah experienced a surge of satisfaction when she looked at her tall sister, whose beauty had returned. With her hair fashionably curled and pinned on her head, Adela would turn heads in her pale blue dress and bonnet. Pink had returned to her cheeks and she had gained weight. Once again, she looked breathtakingly beautiful. Savannah knew that nightmares still plagued Adela and that she was terrified of most males, but that terror was slowly disappearing, due in part to Red Hawk's patience and kindness.

"I'm ready," Savannah said. "We'll be back late in the afternoon," she told Matilda. The carriage waited at the end of the walk and Wesley sat patiently, ready to drive them to town. Adela climbed in first and then Savannah, and they began to move slowly down the drive.

It was cool and still, the air fresh and not yet muggy with the heat of the day. Turning into the drive and approaching them on horseback was Red Hawk. At the sight of him, Savannah's pulse jumped. Red Hawk was dressed in his blue denim pants and a blue chambray shirt with sleeves rolled high. He had a red bandanna tied around his forehead, and his hair had grown long since that haircut she had given him. Now the ends curled on his broad shoulders.

He had left early, as he did most every morning. Matthew rode in front of him, and Red Hawk reined in before he reached them and swung the child to the ground. Scampering toward the back of the house, Matthew waved at Adela and Savannah as he raced past them.

When Red Hawk rode up beside them, Wesley slowed and halted the buggy. Nodding to Wesley, Red Hawk stopped near Savannah.

"I almost missed you," he said. "Morning, Adela."

"Good morning, Captain."

"Savannah, I want some time with you."

"Adela and I have appointments and Bertrice expects us for lunch. Later this afternoon—"

"I need to talk to you before then."

Curious, but seeing no way to change their plans at this point and not wanting to disappoint Adela, Savannah shook her head. "I simply can't right now."

"Go ahead, Savannah," Adela said softly, looking concerned. "I'll explain to Bertrice."

"I'll be home this afternoon."

"I know you will," he remarked dryly. "Sorry, Adela. You go on with your plans. Savannah is coming with me." He leaned down and lifted Savannah out of the buggy and swung her up in front of him. "Go ahead, Wesley," he ordered calmly, ignoring Savannah's cry of indignation.

"You can't do this," Savannah snapped, annoyed with him now for his high-handed manner. Wesley flicked the reins and the buggy moved away. "You'll scare the wits out of Adela."

"No, I won't," he said. "She knows I won't hurt her or you, and you can miss one day at the dressmaker's and one day of visiting friends. I want you to come with me," he said, turning the horse and riding across the yard to reach the road long before the buggy did.

Savannah's temper snapped. "I can't ride this way with you. It's indecent and unladylike!"

A corner of his mouth lifted in a grin. "If my memory serves me well, you've spent hours riding this way with me and I don't recall such protests.''

"We weren't in town then, and I wasn't dressed in one of my best new dresses.''

"And you look pretty enough to eat,'' he said in a husky voice that demolished her anger.

"Thank you,'' she said, smoothing her dress and trying to adjust herself in the saddle. With the movement of her hips, she felt his arousal and stopped instantly.

"You've done that before, too, and you know exactly what effect you produce,'' he said softly in her ear.

She glared up at him.

His grin flashed. "Ah, Savannah. Once again, I'm glad you don't hold a revolver in your hands.''

"You're a scoundrel. Now what's so all-fired important that you yanked me away from Adela? I'm certain you did frighten her. You know how she feels about men, and when one gets domineering and arrogant, as you just were—''

He turned her head and his mouth covered hers. Her words died in her throat. She returned his kiss while her insides clutched and then heated. Her breasts tensed, nerves tingling, all of her body attuned to his touch, all the longings of the past weeks pouring through her.

She wrapped an arm around his neck. When she returned his kiss, he growled deep in his throat. He was aroused, his shaft hard against her bottom.

When his hand touched her throat, she remembered they were on a public road. She pulled away, opening her eyes, dazed and trembling with need. She looked around her and realized he was headed away from town and now they were in an area of smaller single-story houses on the edge of San Antonio.

"The world will see us, and it's scandalous!''

"Only to anyone who knew you before the war and knows you are pledged to that lieutenant. Otherwise, for all they know, I'm your husband.''

"No husband would be acting in such a manner.''

"I would be if you were my wife."

His words thrilled her and she gazed up at him. "Where are we going?"

"I have something I want to show you."

"Is this where you go every day?"

"No. I've been taking care of business that's been neglected while Caleb and I were away. Taking care of Matthew's funds, too. I put the house in Caleb's name."

"You're certain you won't come back to it?" Savannah asked, startled and feeling a stab of pain to hear he had relinquished his house. It seemed as final a step as he could take.

"No, I won't."

She turned to stare ahead. "Does Caleb want to come back?"

"Yes. He was content here. He's studied architecture and is anxious to come home and get started in business. After the war, there may be a need for architects."

They had ridden away from San Antonio. Red Hawk left the road, cutting across a field, and she gave up trying to guess where he was taking her.

"Matthew is doing well with his letters. He's very young, and few children his age read yet."

"He's a smart little boy, just as Celia always said. I know she read to him a lot and tried to teach him."

"He's taken to you completely. I'm certain before long he will think of you as his father."

"I'll think of him as my son. Already it seems that way. I don't think the Ashmans gave him any love."

They talked as they rode, but she was aware of him and curious what he was taking her to see. Why had he been so insistent that she go with him?

Red Hawk held her tightly against him. Today, in her green dress and new bonnet, she looked as beautiful as that first day he had seen her on the *General Thibodeaux* and smelled as enticing, too. He was going to ask her to marry him today. Once he had decided to ask her, it was all he could think about. Right now he wanted to stop and pull her down on the ground and love her until she accepted his proposal.

He had all his business wound up, land purchased, the house in Caleb's name, and repairs made to the place. Matthew was ready and willing to go with him. Now, Red Hawk knew, all he had to do was pack and go. But he wanted Savannah to go with him. He didn't want to think about life without her, and he was going to fight to keep her. He knew the battle was not with a distant fiancé whom she didn't really love, but the dispute would be with Savannah's love of city life and her own independence.

They topped a rise and he gazed over the land spread before him along the banks of the meandering Medina River, a silver ribbon across the green lush grass covering the earth. The smells of summer, the hot earth, and the scent of wildflowers filled the air. He reined in and swung his leg across the horse, dropping to earth.

He moved close to the horse and put his hand on Savannah's waist. "Look at all that, Savannah."

"At what?" she asked, glancing around and then looking at him with a puzzled expression.

"All the land," he replied, knowing she would never understand. Yet whether she understood his feelings or not, he loved her and it was time to make his feelings known to her.

"Come down here, Savannah," he said quietly.

Savannah stared at him. Her first reaction was habit—an obstinate refusal because of his cavalier command. But before she could move, she realized he was going to tell her he was leaving. He had brought her up here to show her that over those hills were the Comanche. A chill turned her icy. *He's leaving me now.* Her hands shook, and everything inside her hurt. *He's leaving. He's going forever and taking Matthew. God, give me strength to say good-bye . . .*

"Get down," he ordered again and reached up to pull her off the horse, setting her on her feet.

"You're leaving," she said, wanting to throw her arms around him and cling to him and kiss him. Feeling tears well up, she fought for control of her emotions.

"Do you care?"

"Of course I care! I don't want you to go."

He placed his hands on her shoulders and turned her around, standing behind her and leaning down. "Look at the land, Savannah."

Puzzled, she looked at the rolling green hills covered with wildflowers and trees, the silver glint of sunshine on the winding river. "I see it. It's just empty land."

"It's mine. I've bought it."

Savannah's heart missed a beat and she whirled around to look up at him. "You're staying!" she exclaimed, joy bubbling in her.

Red Hawk shook his head. Again, she couldn't follow what he was telling her. She glanced over her shoulder and waved her hand. "You said this is all yours, yet you don't intend to live on it?"

"Not now. I've got it for the future if I want to come back. I wanted you to know that."

Her joy vanished as swiftly as it had come. Her first guess had been right. He was going to tell her good-bye.

He turned her to face him again and his dark eyes held her. Her heart thudded, and she wanted to touch his mouth and keep him from saying that he was leaving. When his gaze lowered to her mouth, she couldn't breathe. Standing on tiptoe, she pulled his head down to her.

"Go on, damn you," she whispered. "Go on to your wild people and your wild life, but you'll remember me on long winter nights and hot summer evenings." She placed her lips on his, her tongue going into his mouth.

Hurt and anger burned, and she poured all her stormy emotions into her kisses. She had given him her heart and now, in the most cavalier manner, he would take it, like his people took scalps, and ride away victorious.

His arms crushed her against his chest and held her so tightly she could barely breathe. His tongue played over hers and went deep into her mouth.

Even as he stood in her arms and kissed her passionately, Savannah knew in spirit he was already on his way back to his people. He had made his decisions, cut his ties to the white man's world. He had brought her out here to sever the bonds they had forged in rapturous passion. Hurt, loss, and fury battled within her. *How can he turn his back on all we found together?*

She ran her hands over his back and down over his buttocks, then to his thick shaft that was hard, ready, confined by the tight denims. Her fingers fumbled with the buttons, and she shoved down his clothes, kneeling to take him in her hands and in her mouth. His hands fisted in her hair. With a groan, he caught her up and framed her face with his hands. "I don't want to leave you. Go with me, Savannah. Go with me back to a life that's good—"

"No!" she cried, hurting, wanting him to stay with her, loving him too much. "It's savage and wild—"

"You're just as savage and wild, Savannah," he said. His eyes darkened and the look he gave her made her heart pound. His hands roamed over her and he ripped buttons loose and peeled away her clothing as if storm winds had caught it. He bent to take her breast in his mouth. His breath was hot on her nipple and then his tongue stroked and circled it while his hands cupped her breasts.

They were at each other in a fury of passion. She suspected he wanted to win her to his way as much as she wanted to bind him to hers. He pushed her to the ground and his hands trailed over her while he kissed her breasts. His fingers moved between her thighs and he raised his head, his dark eyes burning. "This is good between us. As good as it could possibly be for a man and a woman. Do you want to give this up, Savannah? Do you?"

She could hear him talking, hear the words, the insistence in his voice over her roaring pulse, but his hands were causing her to move wildly beneath his touch and the magical strokes and caresses took all her words. She could only cling to him and seek release as he drove her relentlessly.

"I want you, Savannah. You're part of me now. You're my woman."

Dimly she heard him, but his hands wrought their magic and

words were impossible. She clung to him, carried to a brink and then over, release shuddering in her as he moved above her.

Sunlight spilled over him, highlighting taut muscles beneath his bronze skin while the wind whipped his long black hair. He was virile, handsome, his dark shaft thick and ready for her. His brown eyes devoured her, and she wanted him more than ever as she wrapped her legs around him. He came down to take her, hard and fast. They moved together, urgency tearing at them.

"I love you, Savannah."

The words carried her along with their savage, desperate lovemaking. Her cries floated away on the wind while her hips drove against him as hard and fast as he thrust into her. He turned his head to kiss her, to take her as completely as he could.

Lights danced before her eyes and her pulse raged, drowning out all else. She was spinning away in sensation, bound to him, one with him for these precious moments. And then release burst in her while he shuddered and she began a descent into reality.

As she gasped for breath and relished his weight and body on hers, his words danced in her mind. *I love you, Savannah.*

She was certain that's what she had heard him cry out. *He loves me!* Her heart was ready to burst with joy, but as swiftly as joy came, she remembered before when he had told her about his land and she thought he intended to stay. He was going. He owned land, he said he loved her, yet he was leaving her.

She held him, thinking about all the words he had said to her. *I want you, Savannah. You're part of me now. You're my woman.*

Each thrill was crushed by the knowledge that none of it mattered. He would still go back to his people. This wild warrior could not be held in civilization any more than the brave eagle would easily settle into captivity. Beyond all loves, the deepest love he held was for his land and his people.

And hers lay elsewhere. She could never live with the Comanche. She couldn't even begin to think what that life would be like. Whatever it was, it held no future for her.

Her arms and legs locked around him. She knew when she let him go, he would keep going. Hot tears stung her eyes and she fought her emotions. She would not cry.

I want you, Savannah. You're part of me now. You're my woman. I love you.

Had he really said those words to her? She knew he had, and they ran through her mind over and over.

You're my woman. I love you. She had waited to hear him say words of love, to ask her to be part of his life forever. Now that he had, she couldn't accept.

He kissed her temple and raised up, propping himself on his elbows to look down at her. "I need you," he said simply, and her heart turned over.

"Come with me, Savannah. Be my woman, my wife, my heart."

"I can't," she whispered, feeling as if she were losing everything important. Her tears fell unheeded. "I've promised to marry Thomas."

"You don't love him. You never have loved him. Nor does he love you."

"Even so, we've made a pledge."

"You made a pledge or your father made a pledge?"

"Our fathers, but we're bound by it. And even if Thomas changed his mind, would it matter? You're going back to your people, aren't you?"

"Yes. That's a part of my being. I belong with them, and that life was taken from me when I was young. I've spent every year since then wanting it back."

They stared at each other, and in the depths of his dark eyes was tenderness, along with a look she had never seen before. She knew it was love. He leaned down to kiss her slowly, a deep, lingering kiss that made her feel wanted and cherished and broke her heart.

He came down to roll on his side and hold her, still kissing her, and she didn't want to let go of him. When she did, it would be forever.

Finally, he raised his head and brushed hair away from her face. "Think on it, Savannah. Don't tell me no tonight. I want you with me the rest of my life."

"Then stay in San Antonio!" she cried. "I can't live the kind of life you want with the Comanche. It's wild and dangerous, and you've told me time and again that you expect it to become more dangerous."

His gaze shifted beyond her and she knew he was as lost to her as a wild creature that could not be tamed. Wind blew locks of his black hair across his cheek and the image of him against the backdrop of a cerulean sky was indelibly etched in her mind.

"I belong there, and you might find you would grow to love it, too. You survived the trek through the wilds to get here and you didn't seem to suffer any from it." He stroked her cheek and leaned down to kiss her for a long time. When he finally raised his head, he gazed into her eyes. "I love you," he said.

"I've waited to hear you say those words. I have said the same to you in my heart many times."

His eyes darkened to midnight as she tightened her arms around his neck and pulled his head down to kiss him. Red Hawk embraced her, holding her against his lean, bare body. He was aroused again. In spite of their kisses, their declarations of love, nothing was solved. They were at an impasse. She held him tightly and loved him desperately again.

As if he felt the same way, his lovemaking was intense, his hands everywhere until she forgot their differences and knew only they were together and he was driving her beyond reason.

As she writhed beneath his touch and kissed and caressed him in turn, he moved between her thighs. His fingers stroked her legs as she parted them and he leaned down to kiss her and trail kisses where his fingers had been.

Her hips arched and she wound her fingers in his hair, gasping, her eyes closed tightly while she reached for him. "Look at me, Savannah,'' he ordered, and her eyes focused on him. His eyes blazed with desire as he knelt poised above her.

"I love you. No man will ever love you like I do." He ground out the words, and her heart thudded as the thrill of them burned within her.

"And I love you," she answered solemnly, as if she were taking vows. She might as well have pledged her heart to him. He would have it forever.

He shifted, lowering himself, his shaft entering her, filling her, and Savannah moved with him, words forgotten. She was lost in desire, pushing back the inevitable a few more minutes.

She cried out, clutching him as she arched against him, another climax wracking her. He shuddered and called her name as he spilled his seed in her.

They gasped for breath, slowing, their bodies drenched and locked together. When their heartbeats had returned to normal, he stood and pulled her up, swinging her easily into his arms.

"My clothes—"

"You won't need them," he said, carrying her down a slope in long easy strides until they reached a creek that branched from the wide river. He waded in while she screeched and clung to him as the cold water closed over their heated bodies. In minutes, she was splashing with him, and then in only a few more minutes, they were locked in each other's arms, passion heating to flames once again.

Shadows were slanting from the west when they rode home. His arm was tightly around her and she rested her hand on his thigh as she sat half-turned in the saddle in front of him. *The last time, the last time* kept running through her mind.

The words had all been spoken and a future together was impossible. She knew the real hurt would come later when he rode away. Now, pressed close against him after an afternoon of loving, she hurt, but she knew it was nothing like she would hurt when he was gone.

They turned down his street. Two blocks from the house, she saw Wesley seated in the buggy at the end of the street. He saw them and urged the horses forward.

"Something must have happened for Wesley to be waiting."
She chilled, frightened. "I look a sight," she said, aware of
her wrinkled dress with a button or two missing. "What could
have happened?"

Red Hawk urged the bay to a trot to meet Wesley. "What's
happened?" he asked. "Is Matthew all right?"

"Yes, sir, he is. Mrs. Platt sent me to meet you. There's
company, and she thought Miss Ravenwood would want to
ride up in the buggy."

"Oh, mercy, I wonder if Clovis Poindexter came to call and
brought her mother!" Savannah exclaimed, relieved to know
everyone was all right and understanding Adela's sending Wesley out to intercept her and warn her about company. "Clovis's
mother is particular and such a gossip."

"Stop fussing, Savannah. You ride up with Wesley and I'll
come in later. No one will think anything about it."

"I look as if—" She bit off her words, seeing temptation
dance in his dark eyes as he gave her a look that made her
pulse skip.

When Red Hawk swung her down into the buggy, his hand
lingered on her waist. He straightened and watched while Wesley turned the buggy and headed back toward the house.

She tried to smooth her dress. If Mrs. Poindexter was there,
Savannah could never explain her wrinkled dress or missing
buttons. Her mind raced for some excuse. Looking down at
her bonnet in her hands, she dropped it on the floor of the
buggy to retrieve it later. She pulled a ribbon from her bonnet
and tied her hair behind her head while she rejected first one
excuse and then another. Maybe she could slip in the back and
get to her room and change quickly.

"Take me to the back, Wesley."

"Yes'm."

At the back door he stopped. She stepped out of the buggy
and rushed across the porch to reach for the back door. Before
she could grasp the handle, it swung open. She looked up into
Thomas Sievert's blue eyes.

CHAPTER TWENTY

Stunned, Savannah stared at him. She was light-headed, shocked.

"Savannah," he said, the word soft, his voice incredibly weary. He leaned down to brush her cheek with a kiss.

She couldn't think or move. Adela came forward. "Savannah, isn't this a surprise! I've been talking to Thomas. He's home from the war."

"I see he is," Savannah said, guilt washing over her at how she had spent the afternoon while Thomas had been waiting for her. "You're home." She tried to get her mind to function. They were standing here talking in Red Hawk's house. Had Adela explained that to him? If so, what had she told him?

He waved his arm slightly, and then she realized it was in a sling and he held a cane in the other hand.

"You're hurt!"

"Yes. I was hit in the hand. Not a direct hit, thank heavens."

"How dreadful!"

"I expect to recover fully, but right now, without use of my right hand and being unable to stand long periods of time, I was of no use to them as a doctor or a soldier, so they sent me home. I don't expect to go back,'' he said sadly.

"We're glad you're home,'' Savannah said. She looked at Adela. "Where's Matthew?''

"He's gone next door with Billy Latham to play.''

"Good afternoon,'' came Red Hawk's deep voice.

Savannah turned and saw him come through the door from the hallway. He crossed the room to Thomas. For once in her life, she couldn't say a word, but could only stare at the two men.

"Thomas, I want you to meet Captain Red Hawk, whom I told you about,'' Adela said warmly. "Captain, this is Lieutenant Thomas Sievert.''

Thomas propped his cane against his leg and extended his left hand to shake hands with Red Hawk. "Adela has told me how you came to their rescue when Mr. Platt attacked Adela. It was kind of you to escort them to San Antonio.''

"I was glad to do it. Why don't we sit on the porch in back? It's probably cooler there than anywhere else. I'll get drinks. I know Savannah and Adela prefer cider.''

"Bourbon and branch water will do fine,'' Thomas said. "Go ahead, Savannah. I'll come out with the captain.''

She couldn't glance at Red Hawk. Memories of only an hour ago assailed her. She turned with Adela, and as soon as they were away from the men, she leaned close. "Thank heaven you sent Wesley. I want to run upstairs and change my dress. He hasn't even asked where I was.''

"I told him you were helping a neighbor move some things to her attic. He would expect you to look rumpled and hot after that.''

Surprised at Adela's careful story, Savannah gave her sister's hand a grateful squeeze. "Thank you.''

"I wouldn't change, Savannah. That might draw more attention to you.''

Savannah glanced over her shoulder. "What on earth could they talk about?''

Adela shrugged. "Captain Red Hawk will manage Thomas.

And Thomas is"—she paused and thought. "He's nice," she finished.

"Yes, Thomas is very nice." Savannah had not been fair to him. Or faithful. She thought about Red Hawk's marriage proposal. She could never go back on her promise to Thomas. Even if there was no love between them, she would hold to it.

They stepped onto the back porch and Savannah sat on one of the tall wooden chairs while Adela sat in a rocker and gently rocked. "Thomas came shortly after you left. I've talked to him all afternoon. He wanted to look at the yard. He said it's been so long since he had been in a house and in a yard. I feel sorry for him, Savannah. He sounds as if he's had a dreadful time of it."

"I'm sure he has," she said, thinking about the two men in the house together. Yet no matter what was transpiring, she couldn't imagine Thomas becoming angry, and she knew he would never suspect the true situation.

The men joined them, Red Hawk holding the door for Thomas, who hobbled outside with the use of the cane. Savannah was amazed how gaunt he was.

The two men were a contrast—one blond, the other dark. Thomas was as tall as Red Hawk. Red Hawk's features were far more rugged, his appearance carrying that aura of wildness of which Thomas bore none, looking far more the gentleman. Now Thomas appeared frail and weary, yet he said he was on the mend.

"What was happening when you left the fighting?" Red Hawk asked as they sat down.

"I don't know how it can go on," Thomas said quietly, his voice filled with sadness and he had a faraway look in his eyes that she'd seen in Red Hawk's eyes too often. "In May, Joe Johnston fought General Sherman at Resaca. Johnston's men were outnumbered two to one. They fought at Adairsville, Kingston, and Cassville, and then Sherman launched an assault on Kennesaw Mountain. Johnston's men had to fall back to Atlanta, and Johnston has been replaced by General Hood."

"The Federals have reached Atlanta?"

"Just before I left, Hood attacked at Peachtree Creek and lost almost three thousand men."

"Damnation," Red Hawk said quietly, and both men looked at each other. Savannah suspected they were lost in war memories and had forgotten her and Adela.

"Hood attacked again and lost thousands. I've heard seven or eight thousand men."

"Seven thousand!"

"I don't know what happened after that. They sent me home, and I was heartily ready to come. I don't see how the South can hold out through another winter. They'll have to send more troops to battle Sherman."

"It's worse than when I left."

"I appreciate your accompanying Savannah and Adela," Thomas said again, glancing at both women.

"This is no time for women to be traveling alone. It's bad along the Texas border and in Louisiana. It was dreadful coming home. Where there has been fighting, the land is ravished, homes burned, all crops gone. Thank heavens Texas has been largely spared, even though we're suffering shortages and high prices."

Savannah listened as the two men discussed the war. Her shock wore away and she began to plan. They would have to leave now for Mason. How could they all stay under the same roof for more than tonight? She glanced at the two men as they sipped their drinks and compared war notes, and she realized they were truly interested in what each had to say. Thomas wanted to know where Red Hawk had fought and listened until Savannah stood.

"You two discuss the war. I want to freshen for dinner and I'm certain Adela will, too."

Both men came to their feet. "Please don't get up," Savannah said to Thomas, but he smiled and continued to rise.

"I'm not feeble, Savannah. I'm recovering now."

She smiled in turn, aware of Red Hawk's gaze on her. She glanced at him and her pulse jumped, even though his expression was impassive and gave away nothing he was feeling.

Adela joined her as they turned to leave the room. Behind her, the men resumed their talk about war.

"They're friends, Savannah," Adela said. "But then, who wouldn't be friends with either one of them? They're both gentlemen."

"Red Hawk?" Savannah asked, never thinking of him and the world gentleman as one and the same.

"Yes. Red Hawk truly is a gentleman."

"I suppose he has been, Adela. He has been to you."

"He has to you, too, Savannah."

While they climbed the stairs, Savannah glanced down at the empty hallway. "Should I send Wesley for Matthew yet?"

"No. I talked to Patricia Latham and she said she would send Matthew home."

"Adela, he asked me to marry him."

Adela's eyes grew round. "Captain Red Hawk? Are you going to?"

Savannah glanced downstairs at the empty hallway again and motioned Adela into her bedroom and closed the door. "No, I'm not," she said, squaring her shoulders.

"You're sure? You love him, Savannah."

"I know I do," she said, turning her back to Adela, afraid she would burst into tears at any moment.

"Don't marry Thomas if you don't love him. You'll both suffer."

"How can I break my promise to him?"

Before Adela could answer, Savannah continued, "Red Hawk's going back to his people. He wants me to go with him and he won't consider anything else."

"Oh, no! You can't do that," Adela cried.

"I don't intend to."

"Of course you can't do that. Savannah, that life would be horrible! How can he give this up?"

"He already has given it up. He's put this house in his brother's name. He's been taking care of all his business here to set things up so he can go, but I can't go with him, Adela.

Even if I weren't pledged to Thomas, I can't live a Comanche life with Red Hawk.''

When Adela hugged Savannah, Savannah lost control. Tears spilled from her eyes. She hugged her sister in return and cried. ''I do love him,'' she whispered.

''I'm sorry, Savannah. So sorry. How dreadful it must be, but I can't but think you're better off to let him go his Indian way.''

They stood quietly until Savannah moved away, drying her eyes and trying to control her emotions. She opened her armoire and looked for something to wear. ''We should dress for dinner, Adela.''

''We'll be going home to Mason soon, won't we?''

''Yes. With Thomas here, we don't have to wait for Red Hawk and Matthew to go along.''

Adela turned and left the room, closing the door. Savannah sat on the rocker, thinking about the past hour and Thomas's arrival. Upon seeing him, she had experienced nothing but shock. No joy, nothing. Would she ever grow to love him? She thought of their childhood and the years growing up. They had been so alike and their families had been alike. Surely that would meld them into two compatible people who would eventually come to love each other.

Unbidden, images assailed her of the afternoon in Red Hawk's arms, of his naked body, virile and strong, of his hands on her skin. She tingled, ached, wanting him again and blushing with the remembrance of what they had done together. Aside from their wild passion, she thought of the moments he had helped her, his strength, his wisdom, his saying that he killed Horace Platt to protect her. He was the man she loved. She loved him and she always would.

She stood impatiently. She would have to turn her back on all she had done and known with Red Hawk, all except memories that she would treasure like the most precious jewels.

She dressed in a white dimity embroidered with red roses with green leaves and tied by a green sash. Adela helped her put up her hair and she wore her green earbobs.

She fixed Adela's hair partly in curls, the rest cascading down the back of her head. "You look so pretty," Savannah said, looking at Adela's yellow cotton dress. It made her look golden with her blond hair and rosy cheeks.

Together they went downstairs to find the men. The moment she walked into the room, her gaze flew to Red Hawk's.

He looked at her in a thorough assessment that made her feel as if he had just whisked away every garment she wore. Her gaze moved to Thomas, who stood smiling, looking from her to Adela.

"How beautiful you both look," he said quietly. "I know I'm dreaming."

"It takes a while to realize this is real and you're not going to wake on a battlefield," Red Hawk said quietly.

"We will try to drop all discussion of war over dinner," Thomas promised.

Matthew came into the room and was introduced to Thomas. He sat quietly on a chair, his gaze traveling outside. Savannah knew he longed to be playing, yet the Ashmans had instilled polite manners in him and he remained quietly seated. She sat next to him. At one point, she asked him about the afternoon and listened while he told her about Billy Latham's wooden soldiers and the sand fort they had built.

"And we practiced with my bow and arrows. I can hit the center of the target almost every time now," he said proudly.

"You like shooting your bow and arrow?"

"Yes, and Uncle Quent promised to take me hunting soon. I can really shoot something and bring it home to eat."

She glanced across the room at Red Hawk. He was engaged in a discussion with Adela and Thomas, but his gaze slid to meet hers. For a moment, they stared at each other and her pulse quickened. She wanted to throw herself into his arms, yet all she could do was partake of friendly conversation with the others, listen to the tall clock tick, knowing that with every tick she moved closer to the moment she would tell Red Hawk good-bye.

When they went to dinner, she rose and walked into the

dining room beside Matthew. Thomas came along with Adela and Red Hawk followed. Since Thomas could not pull out chairs, Red Hawk seated Adela and Savannah, and his hands lingered on her shoulders before he moved away. She glanced at Thomas, who was turned away, talking to Adela.

They ate without any mention of war. Red Hawk told Thomas about his horses, and they discussed the future. Thomas asked about how San Antonio had changed during the war years. Savannah had little interest in the conversation and left it up to Adela, who seemed relaxed with both Thomas and Red Hawk and conversed as easily as she did with Savannah in their moments alone.

After dinner, they all moved to the back porch, where they watched Matthew give a display of his skill with the bow and arrow. They sat in a row on rockers—Thomas, Adela, Savannah, and Red Hawk. Savannah was aware she wasn't seated beside Thomas, yet it seemed far more natural to be beside Red Hawk. She knew if Thomas weren't present, Red Hawk would casually touch her or put his arm across her shoulders, but he had become quite circumspect and hadn't touched her or brushed against her since he had seated her at dinner. The lack of his touch did nothing to diminish her longing for him. Instead, it fueled her needs until she was intensely aware of him only a few feet from her.

The night was cool and, as darkness set in, a breeze sprang up, carrying the scent of roses. Matthew lolled on the porch swing while the adults talked and Savannah let conversation swirl around her.

"I think we shouldn't impose on Captain Red Hawk's hospitality," Thomas said. "Savannah, I can accompany you and Adela back to Mason. If you can get packed, we can leave tomorrow or the day after."

"You're not imposing," Red Hawk said casually, before Savannah could answer. "I will leave soon, too. We might as well all travel together. It would be safer. There aren't as many soldiers now to guard the frontier, and incidents have occurred often. You'll be safer if I accompany you."

"Very well," Thomas said. "It's kind of you to take us all in as your guests."

"I'm enjoying the company. We can go look at horses in the morning."

"Fine," Thomas said. He glanced at Savannah. "I need to get a horse. Thank heavens, we're far removed from the war and I have some funds left to do such things. I pity those poor fellows returning home across the South. They've lost everything and have nothing to start over with."

Conversation once again returned to war and Savannah sat quietly, her thoughts seething. *He's leaving.* As Red Hawk answered something Thomas had asked, she looked at him, studying his profile. He was only a few feet away, yet he might as well have been halfway around the world. She clamped her lips together and fought back tears. She couldn't cry now, not in front of him and the others.

Finally she stood and said she would retire. Adela stood at once, and so did the men. Before she turned to go, Savannah looked at Red Hawk. Everything in her screamed to be with him, yet all she could do was quietly say good night and leave.

The moment she was in her room, she flung herself on her bed to cry. "I love him," she whispered. "I love him and I will always love him." Later, she fell asleep across the bed, still in her dress. Her dreams were troubled and stormy.

The next morning, she was in the kitchen when Matthew burst into the room with the pup at his heels. "Aunt Savannah! Aunt Savannah! Aunt Adela! Matilda! Come quick!"

Terrified something had happened, Savannah rinsed her hands and dried them. "What is it?" she asked, rushing across the kitchen.

Matthew was already running ahead of her, bounding down the porch steps and racing for the gate, the pup running behind him. Adela came dashing behind Savannah.

Red Hawk stood at the gate with a small pinto pony. Thomas sat on a wooden chair under the shade of a tree. Seeing that everyone was all right, Savannah slowed. She walked up to the men, glancing from one to the other and to Matthew, who was jumping up and down with excitement.

"Look, Aunt Savannah! Look what Uncle Quentin brought me!"

"First a dog and now a pony," Matilda muttered, returning to the house.

When Matthew pointed to the pony, Savannah sighed as she halted. "Mercy! Matthew, I thought something dreadful had happened. That's a fine pony."

"Look at him. His name is Marvel. Isn't he the best horse you've ever seen?"

Red Hawk grinned, and Thomas looked happy. Adela stopped by Thomas, who rose to his feet to talk to her. Savannah moved closer to the pony to pat its nose as she looked at Red Hawk. "It's a marvelous horse," she said. "And how nice of Uncle Quent."

"He should have his own horse, and this pony will be the right size for him," Red Hawk said, yet his dark eyes conveyed other messages that made her forget everyone else.

"I think he's extra special," Matthew said proudly, patting the pony's nose.

"He's very extra special," she said, looking only at Red Hawk and thinking of him.

Matthew rode his new pony around the drive for all of them to see. Savannah and Adela clapped and he beamed. Red Hawk moved closer to Savannah. "I have you to thank for this. I was ready to give up and go on without him."

"He's a little child, and they only had him a year. Their influence couldn't be as strong as that of his mother. I simply got him to talk to you. You've done the rest yourself."

As she talked, she turned to look at him. This time they stood only inches apart. She smoothed her hair, knowing it was unruly, with locks springing loose from her braid. She had on her apron and her dress was wrinkled already from the heat in the kitchen.

Yet all she could see in Red Hawk's dark eyes was approval

and desire. Fires danced in the brown depths of his gaze. "How soon will we go to Mason?" she asked.

"Thomas is anxious to go. Now that Matthew has his horse, I have done the last thing I wanted to do in San Antonio except for closing the house. I understand Matilda and Wesley will go with us to Mason when we go."

"Yes. I'm hiring both of them."

"Ah, Savannah, you'll fill my dreams," he whispered. Then he strode past her to help Matthew.

She glanced over her shoulder to see if Thomas had heard, but he and Adela were deep in discussion, both laughing over something. It warmed Savannah's heart to see Adela laugh and to see her relax around these two men, both of whom were good for her. Savannah turned back to watch Red Hawk with Matthew, knowing now they would leave San Antonio.

Later that afternoon in the shade of an oak in the pen behind the carriage house, as Matthew watched, Red Hawk groomed the horses. While he brushed down the bay, Thomas appeared, sitting carefully on a bale of hay. The bay and the pinto were tethered to a fencepost and stood quietly flicking their tails to keep flies away.

"You have a fine pony, Matthew," Thomas said.

"Yes, sir. I think so," the child answered proudly. He perched on the top log of the fence and watched Red Hawk.

"This morning I went to town," Thomas said. "The war news worsens. Sherman has extended his lines around Atlanta and is destroying the rails into the city."

"Damn." Red Hawk paused in the grooming. "It'll mean Atlanta will fall to him. I pray that my brother is still safe and out of the intense fighting."

"I didn't hear about Louisiana."

The men were silent, and Red Hawk returned to his grooming.

"I want to thank you for your hospitality," Thomas said. "I feel terrible being unable to help and do my share."

"You can't help your wounds."

"I expect to heal completely. Perhaps I'll have a slight limp, but I hope not. My hand should heal, and that's what's important. But when I heal, I'm not going back. The South's cause is lost. I can't imagine why you fought for it.''

"I wasn't so much for the South as against the army that took me and my family from my people.''

"Matthew!'' Adela called from the back of the house. Matthew scrambled from the fence.

"She said I could lick the bowl when she iced the cake!'' he exclaimed and bounded out of sight, calling to Adela.

With a smile, Thomas rose and moved closer to Red Hawk. "I don't want to stand in the way,'' he said.

Red Hawk paused to look at him. "How's that?'' he asked carefully. He realized that Thomas's sallow skin was gaining a little more color. The breeze tugged at locks of his thick blond hair, and Red Hawk supposed that women found the man quite attractive. His blue eyes were clear, thickly fringed, his features symmetrical. He was almost as tall as Red Hawk, with broad shoulders and a quiet, self-assured manner. And Red Hawk found him likable when he had expected to detest him. They shared a common hatred of war and a mutual suffering from it.

"I've seen you look at Savannah and Savannah look at you,'' Thomas answered quietly. "She's honorable and will hold to the promise we gave as children, but I would never keep her from finding her real love.''

"Savannah makes her own choices. She will have no part of my way of life. I have spent every day of my life since I was ripped from the Comanche wanting to go back to them. It's something I have to do, just as a man sometimes has to go to war.''

"Adela told me the truth about Horace Platt,'' Thomas said. "It was Savannah who shot him, not you. She did so to protect Adela.'' He looked away and a muscle worked in his jaw. When he faced Red Hawk again, anger burned in his eyes "I can't tell you how I regret not being here for both of them.''

"I should have gotten there sooner. If I had, it would have been different.''

"It's done, and thank goodness the monster is gone. But if you ever need help, I'll be glad to do what I can."

"Thank you," Red Hawk said, nodding at Thomas and deeply touched by his offer, guilt stabbing him over his love for Savannah.

"If you weren't joining the Comanche, I would say we should go to the authorities and let Savannah confess. She would never be held accountable after the way he treated Adela."

"Juries can surprise you," Red Hawk stated. "It won't matter. I'll be beyond the reach of the law."

"You're not beyond it yet, so take care." Thomas turned away. "I'll go see about that cake Adela is baking."

"Thomas," Red Hawk said, and Thomas turned back.

"Perhaps you shouldn't let Savannah keep you from finding *your* real love," he said quietly.

Thomas had a faint smile. "I'm bound by honor just as much as Savannah. The war hasn't killed that." He turned to walk toward the house, limping and leaning on his cane.

Red Hawk swore softly, thinking what a tangle they were caught in because of his driving need to return to the Comanche and Savannah's deep love for the kind of life she had always known. He liked Thomas and respected him and realized he was a very intelligent man. When Savannah married Thomas, both were intelligent and likable enough that they would probably make the marriage work. Yet he had seen the looks that Thomas gave Adela. It was Adela who Thomas watched and sat beside and talked to when he had a chance, not Savannah.

Red Hawk suspected Savannah had no idea how Thomas felt.

Two mornings later, they were packed and ready to travel. As Adela hurried down the steps, her arms laden with boxes, Thomas turned from the buggy to help her. Before he reached her, she missed the bottom step and plunged forward, giving a cry as she landed on the walk.

Savannah was already in the buggy, arranging their things,

when she saw Adela fall. Red Hawk turned to run to Adela, but Thomas was there first, dropping his cane and going down on his knees to see about her. Both men helped her to her feet, and she gave another cry of pain. Savannah climbed down and hurried across the yard.

"I'm all right," Adela said. "I've hurt my foot."

"Maybe you should take my cane," Thomas offered.

"No—"

Red Hawk lifted her in his arms, carried her to the buggy, and set her in the seat. All of them crowded around.

"Wesley is driving," Red Hawk stated. "Matilda can ride beside him. Thomas, you and Adela ride in the buggy along with Matthew. Savannah and I will ride our horses and tie the other horses to the rear of the buggy."

"Fine," Thomas said, climbing into the buggy with great care. Savannah watched him move like an aged man and lower himself slowly beside Adela.

"Matthew, careful now," Red Hawk cautioned and watched as the child climbed eagerly into the buggy and settled between Adela and Thomas. The pup scrambled in and jumped into his lap.

Matilda already sat beside Wesley and clutched a bag that held her belongings. Red Hawk motioned to them. "Go ahead. I'll lock up and Savannah and I will catch up with you."

The buggy moved off and he turned back to the house. Savannah followed him inside and closed the door, hearing his boot heels scrape the floor in the otherwise silent, empty house, aware this might be the last time she would be alone with him.

Casper Ashman pushed back his chair in the sheriff's office. "You have my report on the theft. I'll put dogs in my lumberyard after this and hire a guard."

"I'll do what I can, Mr. Ashman," Sheriff Gray said, standing and holding the report he had written on the theft of a truckload of Ashman's lumber during the night. "This is wartime and lumber is scarce and costly. We've had several reports of theft of supplies lately. I'll get my deputy to patrol your place the next few nights.''

''I hope they come back,'' Casper snapped. ''I'll be ready the next time.''

''I'll let you know if I catch the thief.''

''I wish you had said when instead of if,'' Casper replied. He turned away, straightening the brim on his hat, and left the office, striding down the hall of the courthouse. He glanced at posters on the wall and headed toward the door. Hot sunshine spilled over the grounds outside.

Something caught his eye, and he turned back to look closer. He walked to the wanted posters along the wall and his pulse jumped as he recognized a familiar name. He stopped to read, not caring that he was reading aloud.

''Wanted for murder. Dead or alive. Reward.'' He laughed and read the poster again. Captain Quentin Red Hawk had two murder charges against him, and all this time he had been living openly in town. Casper's smile faded, but triumph made his heart race. If only he'd known.

He strode back toward the sheriff's office. With two murder charges, the man was as good as dead. With Red Hawk out of the way, Matthew had no relatives except the uncle away fighting in the war. Celia and Dalton had not stipulated in their will that Matthew was to go to Caleb. No, a court would give Casper and Hester the child and the money. This time he would see that it was done in court and binding and all that money would be theirs.

He paused, turned, and went back to the poster. ''Wanted— Dead or Alive.'' He smiled with satisfaction. He could deliver Quentin Red Hawk and collect the reward. The poster was a death sentence.

Casper Ashman strode swiftly from the courthouse and headed for his carriage. He needed to go home to get his gun.

CHAPTER TWENTY-ONE

Savannah trailed after Red Hawk, finding him in the parlor. She watched as he closed the shutters, blocking out the bright rays of sunshine that spilled through the long windows until the room was dusky. Sheets covered the furniture as they had when she and Red Hawk had first arrived. She wished it had all been different, that he had wanted to stay, that she could marry him.

He strode toward her in the shadowed room and her heart thudded. She wanted him to wrap his arms around her and kiss her.

He paused only a few feet away. "Ready to go?"

She couldn't answer him. He frowned and inhaled. "Your answer is still no, isn't it?" he said harshly.

"I love you," she whispered.

Fire danced in the depth of his brown eyes, and they stared silently at each other while she felt as if her heart were being ripped from her.

"Damn," he whispered and closed the distance between them, his arms wrapping around her.

Instantly, she raised her face to his, flinging her arms around his neck to hold him as tightly as possible. His mouth came down over hers and she met him eagerly, kissing him as passionately as he kissed her.

His tongue played over hers and went deep, fueling desire into a blaze. Her heart beat wildly and she wanted to pull off his shirt, to run her hands over him, to have the barrier of clothes torn away, to be in his arms and give herself to him again, one more time, just once more. Yet she knew it couldn't be. Others waited for them, and they had to go.

Reluctantly, oblivious to her hot tears, she pushed away. "They'll be watching for us."

His face was a thundercloud and a muscle worked in his jaw as he stepped back. She couldn't stand there with him another second without going back into his embrace. She turned and fled out the back door, rushing to her horse.

She mounted up and waited in the shade of one of the oaks and watched Red Hawk step outside, turn and lock the door and place the key on a window ledge. With a stormy countenance, he strode across the yard in long steps. Wearing his denim pants and a black shirt, a red bandanna tied around his head, he looked ready to join his people.

She adjusted the skirt of her green cotton dress, the dress he had given her so long ago. Flicking the reins to her gray horse, she turned down the drive. He mounted the bay and in seconds was beside her. They rode away from the house, straight down his street for three blocks before they turned a corner. As they turned, she glanced back and saw someone riding up Red Hawk's drive. When she glanced at Red Hawk, starting to tell him, the words died. His face was like granite—hard, unyielding, forbidding.

If someone was going to the house, it no longer mattered. Red Hawk was leaving that life behind with every step of their horses. He had wound up all his important business, so a caller now couldn't matter. Knowing she had hurt him, yet hurting herself, she glanced surreptitiously at him again.

In another twenty minutes, they caught up with the others and rode in front of the buggy. Occasionally when she glanced back at them, Adela and Thomas were deep in conversation. Matthew played with his puppy and ignored the adults.

Savannah was sorry Adela had hurt her foot, yet she couldn't keep from relishing the trip beside Red Hawk. Otherwise, she would have been in the buggy with Thomas and Adela would be riding alongside Red Hawk, as they had originally planned.

"Matthew couldn't wait to get started this morning," Savannah said.

"How swiftly he's changed. Now he can't wait to join the Comanche and see what that life is like."

"Suppose he doesn't like it?"

Red Hawk glanced at her and a corner of his mouth lifted in a faint smile. "He'll like it, Savannah. I was his age when I lived with them and I can tell you he'll like that life very much."

"I hope it's not dangerous for him," she said, glancing back at the boy and knowing she was going to miss him terribly. Yesterday morning, as she had been going over his letters with him, he had suddenly dropped his book and come close to her to hug her. She had lifted him onto her lap and held him.

"Come with us, Aunt Savannah. Come with Uncle Quent and me."

"I'd like to," she said, "but I can't do that. I'll marry Lieutenant Sievert and have a life here. You and Uncle Quent can come back and see me."

"We'll be far, far away. Uncle Quent said we'll go far from San Antonio and we won't come back here for a long, long time. Come with us, please. I want you to come."

"I can't, Matthew, but I'd like to."

He hugged her tightly. "I'll miss you."

"And I'll miss you, Matthew." She held him and stroked his head, feeling a knot in her throat. She would miss him badly, she realized. This child, who had been a part of her life for such a short time, had wound his way into her heart.

That night when she had read to him and kissed him good night, she stroked his forehead and whispered, "I love you."

"I love you, too," he said, sitting up and winding his thin

arms around her neck to hug her. She closed her eyes and held him. Soon she was going to lose them both, the only two males in her life whom she truly loved.

He lay down and closed his eyes and she sat quietly, singing an old lullaby to him. In minutes he was asleep, and she watched him, thinking about telling him and Red Hawk good-bye. She wiped tears away and tiptoed from the room to find Red Hawk waiting in the hall.

"Is he asleep?" he asked, then frowned as he approached her. He wiped a tear from her cheek.

"Tears, Savannah?" he asked quietly.

"I'll lose you both soon."

Red Hawk's eyes narrowed and he stared at her intently. "You don't have to," he said quietly.

She nodded and looked down, wishing he hadn't caught her with tears in her eyes. "Matthew's asleep."

"I meant to get home before he fell asleep. He likes you to read to him at night, though. I think you remind him of Celia. You're bringing back memories of her."

"That would be nice," Savannah said, finally looking up and once again in control of her emotions.

"This morning when we were out riding, he asked me to tell him about his mother. That's the first time he's freely talked about her."

They stood staring at each other while silence stretched between them. "Thomas and Adela are downstairs," she said quietly.

Red Hawk glanced over his shoulder toward the stairs and then took her wrist. "Come here."

She knew she shouldn't, but she followed as he stepped into his darkened room. He turned to her.

"I should go—"

"Shh, Savannah. You're here because this is what you want." His voice sounded raw. He stepped close, his arm going around her.

She put her hands up against his chest. "Thomas—"

"I don't give a damn about Thomas. There's no burning

love between you and him. Those tears in your eyes weren't for Thomas. You're not hurting him. Has he even kissed you since he arrived?'' Without waiting for an answer, Red Hawk bent his head and his mouth covered hers.

While her insides heated and desire blazed to life, Savannah wrapped her arms around him and returned his kiss. She had no idea how long they stood kissing in his darkened room, but as his hands began to roam over her, she pushed him away.

''We can't do this,'' she said, wriggling out of his arms.

''You don't love him and he doesn't love you. I do love you.''

''If Thomas didn't exist, I couldn't go with you.'' She saw the same devastation in his eyes as was in her heart. She turned and rushed out of the room, heading downstairs, trying to smooth her clothes and her hair back into place.

Savannah shook away the memory. There were too many memories that, while precious, also tore at her heart. She glanced again over her shoulder at the buggy to see Matthew with his head down, looking at something in his lap while Adela and Thomas talked. Matilda clutched her bag in her lap. While she had said little except to Savannah, Savannah knew she was terrified of an Indian attack between San Antonio and Mason. Since her arrival in San Antonio, she had never left the city and it was as close to the frontier as she wanted to be. Savannah had tried to convince her they would be safe because Red Hawk would be able to keep peace for them.

Wesley seemed happy simply to stay employed, and Savannah suspected he enjoyed Matilda's company whether Matilda noticed him or not.

The sun bore down hotly and the steady clop of hooves and creak of the buggy wheels were the only sounds. Savannah's gaze swung to Red Hawk, who rode beside her, sitting straight and tall. As if he became aware of her gaze on him, he glanced around and then turned his horse closer to hers.

''Will you move back to San Antonio?'' Red Hawk asked, riding close and reaching over to catch a stray lock of her hair and tuck it behind her ear.

"I don't know. With Thomas home, things have changed. I expected to have to take care of Adela and myself, but now he's here . . ." Her voice trailed away, and again Red Hawk gazed at her with brooding, stormy eyes.

"And you'll marry and live in Mason with him. Will you take Adela to live with you?"

"Oh, I'm certain we will. Adela is no trouble, and they get along quite well. Thomas has a gentle nature, and Adela is as at ease around him as she is around you."

"Do I assume from that that you think I, too, have a gentle nature?"

"Hardly," she answered. "As gentle as that knife you carry. Yet you have been gentle with Adela and I appreciate all the kindness you have shown her."

"You mean I haven't been kind to you?"

She shot him a look and blushed, knowing he was teasing her, yet half annoyed with him. "Kindness isn't the first quality I think of with you."

"Is that right? What's the first quality?"

"Arrogance!" she snapped, and he chuckled.

"I'm hurt."

"No, you're not. You're enjoying yourself."

"Yes, I am," he said, suddenly solemn and studying her. "We can have a wonderful time, Savannah. Life together might make up for the parties and dresses in San Antonio."

She gazed back at him, thinking about what he was promising. "And what happens when you're attacked by the U.S. Army? You're not talking about living one place versus another, but a way of life that is threatened daily. How safe will you be when you ride in attacks against the Army? If something happens to you, what will become of Matthew?"

"I've set everything up for Caleb to take care of him if something happens to me. There's danger in our way of life—I can't deny that."

"Don't go!" she cried and grasped his wrist, feeling the thick bone. Instantly, she yanked away her hand and turned away, knowing it was useless to ask him. She only made herself hurt when she thought about the possibilities.

They rode in silence for a time until Savannah looked at him. "We'll never see each other again, will we?" she asked.

He shook his head. "Not for years. Maybe someday I'll come back and settle on that land I bought, and maybe we'll pass each other on the street in San Antonio. By then, Savannah, you won't remember or care," he added softly.

"Of course I will! I'll always remember." She looked at him. "And I care far too much. I couldn't possibly hurt like I do if I didn't care."

His jaw clamped shut, and he wheeled his horse around and rode back to talk to those in the buggy. He took Matthew on his horse in front of him, and Savannah knew she wouldn't have any kind of a personal conversation with him as long as he carried Matthew.

They rode into a small German settlement, Fredericksburg, where they got rooms at a hotel, Savannah and Adela sharing a room, Matthew in with Red Hawk, while Thomas had a room to himself. They ate in the hotel dining room and went to their rooms to get an early start.

Savannah and Adela sat in bed in their white cotton nightgowns, the windows open wide while they talked in the darkness. "Adela, Thomas hasn't said one word about our union. Until he does, you and I will have to plan on what we'll do now that Papa is gone. If Thomas were still away at war, I would want to sell our house and move to San Antonio, but with Thomas home and his family in Mason, he will probably want to live there."

"He does," Adela replied. "He told me that he will start his practice when he gets home."

"Father's house is owned by the military. They'll let us live there, but it isn't our house."

A light tap interrupted Savannah's conversation and she frowned. She scooted out of bed and yanked up her wrapper, slipping into it and lighting a lamp.

"Savannah, be careful," Adela whispered.

"No one will hurt us. Red Hawk is in the next room on one side and Thomas is in the next room on the other."

There were two more taps on the door. Savannah leaned close to it. "Who is it?"

"Red Hawk."

She unlocked and swung open the door to face Red Hawk, who was dressed all in black and wore a black bandanna around his forehead. He stepped into the room and closed the door behind him. In the dim light of the one lamp, shadows were large, and with all his dark clothing, he looked dangerous. "Thomas has been at one of the saloons. The sheriff received a telegram that I'm wanted for murder, and men are talking about the reward.

"I'm riding out now. Thomas will escort you two and Matthew from Fredericksburg and then I'll join you. If you ladies don't mind, I'll go out through your window in case they are watching mine or are in the lobby," he said, crossing the room and swinging his long legs over the sill.

Savanna rushed to the window to catch his arm. He stood outside on the ground and she leaned out. "Will we see you again?"

"Yes," he replied. He reached up, sliding his hand behind her head to pull her closer and brush a kiss across her lips. Then he was gone, vanishing into the dark night. Had that brief moment been their final good-bye?

She heard another rap on the door. Adela had already slipped into her wrapper and was standing near the door. She went to open it, limping, but able to put some weight on her swollen foot. Thomas entered the room and closed the door, leaning on his cane. His white shirt was open at the throat.

"Matthew is getting dressed. I think we should go. We can sleep somewhere along the way. After supper tonight, I couldn't sleep and went to a saloon where I heard men talking. They got word by telegraph from the sheriff in San Antonio that Quentin is a wanted man. If we wait until morning, we may have many questions and then someone may follow us from here. I think there is at least one bounty hunter on Red Hawk's trail.''

His words frightened Savannah and she prayed Red Hawk was already safely riding away from town.

''We can be ready in a few minutes,'' Adela said.

Thomas nodded, his gaze sweeping over her. ''How's your foot?'' he asked. ''Should you be on it?''

''It's much better,'' she said, holding her foot out and wiggling it slightly. ''It still hurts to walk, but not as badly.''

Thomas knelt to take her foot in his hand and look at it.

With her thoughts on Red Hawk, Savannah turned away to get her bag and commence packing.

''Be careful,'' Thomas said to Adela. ''You may use my cane anytime you'd like.''

''Oh, no! Of course not, but thank you.''

''I can manage without it.''

As Savannah glanced at them, Thomas touched his shirt. ''I'll change my clothing. Wear something dark that isn't as easily visible in the night.'' He reached out to squeeze Adela's shoulder. ''Don't worry unduly, Adela. They're after Red Hawk, not us.''

She nodded and followed him to the door. He touched her cheek again. ''I'll come back shortly, or you can knock on my door when you're ready. I'll see about Matthew.'' Thomas left and closed the door behind him.

The minute he was gone, Savannah threw off her wrapper and gown and began to dress. Her hands shook and she prayed that Red Hawk was all right and had escaped unscathed.

When they were ready, Thomas and Matthew appeared. ''We'll go out through the window. We've paid our bill with the hotel, so they have their money and won't care. He stepped outside, then helped Matthew, Savannah, and Adela out. They hurried across the yard to the stable, where Wesley and a stable hand worked by the dim light of a lantern to get the horses hitched to the buggy and another horse saddled.

Soon they rode quietly out. Adela, Thomas, and Matthew

crowded into the buggy again. Wesley and Matilda were up front and Savannah was on horseback.

Savannah peered again into the darkness, watching for any sign of Red Hawk. Gradually the lights of Fredericksburg disappeared behind them and she was relieved that they had escaped town, but she knew that now Red Hawk wouldn't be able to come into Mason with them. She expected to see him again for only as long as it took him to get Matthew. Hoping Thomas noticed nothing and praying she could say good-bye without becoming emotional, she was numb.

When they had left San Antonio and she had seen someone turning into Red Hawk's drive—had that been related to what was happening to them now?

Red Hawk sat on a slight rise and saw the small party silhouetted against the night sky when they topped a hill. He hurt because he was going to have to tell Savannah good-bye tonight. They would be with everyone else; there would be no way to have her to himself.

He was thankful to escape Fredericksburg, and he owed a debt to Thomas now. He thought about Thomas. Only Savannah was blind to what was happening right beneath her nose, and it was as obvious as he and Savannah had been obvious in their feelings for each other. Red Hawk was certain Thomas had never so much as kissed Adela, yet he couldn't take his gaze from her when she was in the same room with him. And now, even though Adela's foot was far better, Red Hawk knew that the lone figure on horseback was Savannah.

Once more, he thought about simply carrying her off. He wouldn't hurt Thomas, who was in love with Adela and yet being true to his sense of honor. Red Hawk hoped the man came to his senses before he ended up in a loveless marriage to Savannah, with Adela around constantly to torment him.

Bare-chested now, Red Hawk sat with catlike stillness, thinking about simply carrying Savannah away with him as he had done in Vicksburg. If she hated the life he took her into, their future together would be miserable. And he knew if she truly hated it, she would run away the first chance she got. Yet how tempted he was to try to take her for a year. If she hated it, then he would return her to her old way of life.

He had explained to Matthew that he had false charges against him and he didn't want to stand trial. In the manner of a trusting child, Matthew seemed to accept what he was told. Red Hawk prayed that the boy believed him.

He urged his horse forward, wishing he could hold back the night, wanting Savannah alone, in his arms one last time.

Savannah heard a jingle and looked to her left to see Red Hawk loom up out of the shadows. Her pulse jumped and she wanted to reach out and touch him.

"We're safely away from there," she said as he turned to ride beside her. In the dark of the night, he reached over and gave her hand a squeeze. She caught his hand and held it. "I thought you would stay with us in Mason for a time."

"I can't now," he replied.

"I know. Thank goodness Thomas heard them talking about you."

"Thomas knows everything," Red Hawk said. "He knows I took the blame for you killing Horace Platt, that you did it in self-defense."

"How does he know all that? He hasn't said anything to me."

"Adela told him."

"Mercy! Well, I'm glad. I feel I should tell the world and have that charge dropped against you."

"Don't do it, Savannah. It won't matter."

"It will matter if you want to return to civilization."

"It won't be significant," he repeated firmly, and she knew he wasn't ever coming back. She ran her fingers over his large knuckles and wanted to raise his hand to her cheek and kiss his fingers.

"Just a minute, and I'll come back." Red Hawk withdrew his hand and rode back to the buggy. She twisted in the saddle and saw him ride beside Thomas. Adela was slumped against Thomas, his arm around her, and Savannah guessed Adela was asleep. Matthew wasn't in sight. He was probably sprawled asleep on their laps.

The two men talked, Red Hawk leaning down. Finally, he rode back to catch up with her. He reached over to tug on her reins and her horse halted as his stopped. Surprised, Savannah looked up at him. ''Are we stopping here?''

''No, both Thomas and Wesley said they can keep going. Matilda is terrified that Indians will appear out of the night and scalp her, so she neither wants to stay nor does she want to go on. Anyway, they're riding ahead. I told Thomas I wanted to talk to you alone for a few minutes and that we would catch up with them.''

''Thomas didn't object?''

''No, he didn't, Savannah. How can that surprise you?''

She had already shoved Thomas from her mind. Her heart raced. She would be alone with Red Hawk. This was good-bye. She didn't want him to go. He was part of her heart, part of her soul now, and she would be losing that part of herself. She drew herself up and turned away, unable to speak as emotions buffeted her. The buggy passed them, wheels squeaking, harness occasionally jingling.

They sat in silence, watching the buggy move out of sight. Then Red Hawk turned his horse. ''Over this way, Savannah. We'll catch up with them easily enough. I know where the road goes.''

She turned her horse to follow him and he dropped back to ride beside her. They moved through the darkness without talking until they finally came to a lone oak. Red Hawk reined in and swung his leg over the horse's withers and dropped to the ground. He tethered his horse and moved to hers to take the reins from her and tie them. Then he reached up, his hands closing on her waist.

He looked up at her. ''Come here, Savannah, so we can say good-bye.''

CHAPTER
TWENTY-TWO

As she dismounted, her mouth went dry. He took her in his arms. She was lost from that moment, wanting him, wanting to hold him forever, forgetting everything else. He was in her arms now, with her now, loving her now.

Tomorrow didn't exist. She would have the rest of her life to go without Red Hawk, but this night he was hers and she was his.

Red Hawk leaned over her, molding her body to his, cupping her buttocks with his hand to pull her more tightly against him while his other arm held her close. His kiss was passionate and deep and Savannah was eager, her heartbeat mingling with his and as wild as his own. He had intended to spread a blanket, but now he didn't want to wait. He wanted her, to take her and know she was his woman, truly, completely, to try one more time to make her realize what she was throwing away.

"I want you," he said, grinding out the words. Savannah's heart thudded as she was thrilled to what he was saying. His hands were at the buttons at the back of the neck of her dress while hers were at the buttons of his tight denims. He wore no shirt, and she trailed her hands over his smooth, bare chest and then down to his tight denims, feeling his manhood thrust against the thick material. She tugged at the buttons as he pushed her dress away. It caught on her shoulder and he couldn't get it off. He growled deep in his throat and ripped it. She heard the material tear and gasped, peeling it away herself because this was the dress that he had given her and she would treasure it always.

He flung off his boots and shed the last of his clothing. Her hands kept drifting over him, but when she tried to touch his hard shaft, he caught her wrists and stopped her.

"Not yet, Savannah," he said, his voice hoarse.

He yanked away her chemise and underdrawers, peeling away her stockings and then bending to take her breast in his mouth while his hands stroked her. His tongue drew circles over her nipple and she gasped, clinging to him with one hand wound in his thick hair, the other hand holding to him with her arm around him.

She gasped when pleasure streaked in her. Her hips moved and she wanted him desperately. Her fingers ran through his hair while her other hand stroked his broad, smooth back, sliding down to the narrow small of his back and then over his firm buttocks. She wanted to touch, to kiss, to love, to store up memories that would have to last a lifetime. He went down on his knees, his hands stroking the inside of her thighs. Then he pulled her down.

She sprawled across their jumble of clothing while he moved between her legs and bent his head. He watched her as his tongue stroked her. She gasped and arched. Her legs spread wide for him while his tongue worked more magic than his hands and she tensed and moved wildly, clinging to him, lost in sensation, forgetting the circumstances, forgetting everything else.

"You're my woman," he said roughly. His hand replaced his mouth, taking her over a brink to release that simply made her want more of him. She ached and was on fire and ripped with need.

"I want you," she said intensely. "Now," she said, pulling on his hips.

He lowered himself slowly, the velvet tip hot and smooth, sliding into her, filling her and withdrawing partially, driving her wild again. Her pulse pounded, shutting out all sounds in its roaring, while fiery lights danced behind her closed eyes and sensation made her writhe and tug at him with need.

"Now, Savannah, now, you're mine," he whispered in her ear. Then he kissed her while they moved together and she stroked his back and down over his buttocks.

Red Hawk was drenched in sweat as he struggled for control, wanting to keep loving her, slowly, heatedly, prolonging the ecstasy. She thrashed wildly beneath him, her legs wrapped tightly around him.

He could feel his iron control going and knew it would end. And then he was moving with her, as lost as she was.

"Savannah, love!" His cry was torn away on the night wind.

Her cries were loud in his ears, yet he didn't care. Release burst in him as he thrust into her warmth. He spilled his seed into her and almost hoped there was a child, because then she would go with him. But by the time she knew there was one, he would be far, far away.

She screamed with ecstasy, feeling release and still moving with him. How long before they began to slow, she couldn't guess. Their breathing was ragged, their bodies soaked in sweat, yet she clung tightly to him, wanting to hold him longer, wanting it never to end.

He rolled over and raised on his elbow to look at her, stroking her face, showering kisses on her, murmuring words to her in his exotic language that she couldn't understand. *"Ekahuutsu,"* he whispered, lifting locks of her hair and rubbing them across his cheeks. "Ahh, Savannah, how I dream of you."

"I love you," she whispered.

"If only you loved me above all else," he replied, his dark eyes like knives cutting to her soul.

"I do love you above all else, but I can't live the kind of life you're going to live. I shall cry for you, miss you, want you when I return to Mason, but I can't do anything else. I will wed Thomas and I will live in Mason and I will love you always.''

"Then don't wed Thomas. Don't go into a loveless union.''

She couldn't answer and didn't want to think about her future or Thomas or anything beyond Red Hawk and this moment. She stroked his jaw, running her hands over him, relishing being able to touch and explore his marvelous body that was so hard where hers was soft, that was all flat planes where hers was curves.

He sighed and wrapped her into his arms. "I want to hold you all night, but we need to catch up with the others.''

They kissed, long, deep, and heartbreakingly. Then Red Hawk stood and pulled her to her feet. She began to dress, wondering if she could put herself back together enough to be presentable when they reached Mason.

She tried to pull together the seam over the shoulder where the dress had been ripped. Red Hawk rummaged in his saddle-bag and returned to stride to her, carrying something in his hand. Moonlight glinted on silver and Red Hawk held out his hand.

"This was my mother's. I want it to be yours,'' he said.

She picked it up, moving her hand so moonbeams fell directly on the bright silver chain with silver feathers dangling from it.

"It's beautiful!''

Red Hawk stepped behind her to put it around her neck and fasten it.

She touched it and then turned to him. "Thank you,'' she whispered, struggling against tears. "I love you and I always will. You know how I'll treasure this. It's the only part of you I'll have.'' She gazed at him, momentarily at a loss. "I have nothing to give you in return.''

"Yes, you do.'' He unloosened the scabbard at his waist and removed a large knife. Moonlight glinted on the blade. With deliberation, Red Hawk reached out and took a handful of her hair. He paused and looked at her.

"Go ahead."

He cut her hair and then coiled the locks in his hand. He untied the bandanna around his forehead and placed the ring of her hair carefully in the center of the square. Then he folded the cloth over the locks of hair and put it in a saddlebag.

"Come here. I'll help you mount."

"I want to ride with you part of the way."

He swung up on his horse and leaned down, picking her up easily and settling her in front of him. He grabbed up the reins of her horse and turned to head northwest.

She settled against him, feeling his warmth through her dress, resting her hand on his arm that was wrapped tightly around her waist.

She laid her head back against his chest, and he rested his chin on her head while they rode in silence.

Gray dawn came in the east, growing lighter steadily. She straightened up and saw the buggy in the distance ahead of them. Beyond the buggy, she could see trees and houses and knew they approached a town.

"Do you want to ride your horse now? We'll catch up with them soon."

"Yes," she answered, twisting around to look up at him. He lowered his head and kissed her and she held him, kissing him in return.

He lifted her to her horse and she settled carefully in the saddle, taking the reins from Red Hawk, her fingers lingering on his when she touched him.

"When we reach them, I'll take Matthew and go."

She nodded, unable to speak. He turned and they rode, catching up with the buggy. Only the men were awake. Matilda lay with her head in Wesley's lap and Thomas held Adela while Matthew sprawled over them.

Red Hawk rode up to talk to Wesley, who halted the buggy so Red Hawk could free the pinto pony and a pack horse that carried his and Matthew's belongings. He picked up the sleeping child and carried him easily in his arms, mounting up with him and holding Matthew in front of him. Matthew stirred and came awake, as did Adela and Matilda. The women sat up, both looking embarrassed.

Savannah paid no heed to what all of them were saying. *He's going; he's going . . .* The only thought running through her mind was *he's going.* She watched as Red Hawk transferred a swiftly awakening Matthew to the pinto pony. Wesley picked up the pup and handed him to Matthew. Then Red Hawk shook hands with Thomas and leaned over to kiss Adela's cheek. He said farewell to Wesley and Matilda and turned to look at her.

"Good-bye, *Ekahuutsu,"* he said. She rode forward to hug and kiss Matthew, and then she turned.

"Good-bye," she whispered, unable to see clearly for tears.

He turned away to head directly west and Matthew rode with him. Matthew turned once to wave, but Red Hawk didn't look back.

Wesley started the buggy and she fell behind, letting her tears flow and watching the tall man on the bay horse and the child on the pinto pony until they were mere dots against the western horizon. Never in her life had she hurt as deeply.

Two weeks later she was no happier. She and Adela were back in their father's house. Thomas had returned to his family home and was starting a medical practice in a small office in a building above his father's bank. Every evening, Thomas came to call.

When they were invited to the Sieverts', both Savannah and Adela were invited. Savannah moved through each day feeling only half alive. Her heart had gone with Red Hawk, and she missed him more fiercely each day. She missed her morning tutoring of Matthew and reading to the child at night, hearing him run across the porch, his peals of merry laughter.

Thomas had never mentioned their wedding, and she had no interest in bringing it up, disturbed more all the time at the thought of going into a loveless marriage. It had seemed so reasonable when she was a child and a young girl, but now it loomed bleak and unpromising and wrong.

She stood at the window one Thursday morning, unaware of tears streaming down her face until Adela cried out.

"Savannah!" She rushed to Savannah's side. "What's wrong? It's Red Hawk causing you to cry, isn't it? You miss him."

Savannah covered her face with her hands. "Adela, I made a mistake. All the things I thought were so important aren't important at all."

Adela put her arms around Savannah and held her lightly while she cried. "Maybe you should go to him."

"Where?" Savannah cried, raising her tear-streaked face. "He's gone and he told me he wouldn't be back this way. He said there was no way for us to cross paths for years."

Adela frowned and glanced out the window, staring at their small yard shaded by an oak. "You didn't want his way of life."

"Now I don't want my life without him. I thought living here was so important. It's empty and meaningless, but I can't do anything about it. He's gone—it's as if he walked off this earth when he said good-bye."

She moved away and wiped her eyes. "Sorry. I'm going to wash my face."

She went to her room to wash her face, the cold water feeling good against her hot skin. She glanced in the mirror at her red eyes and nose and wondered how many tears she would shed over him. If she could find him, she would get on her horse and go right now. The realization startled her. What a costly mistake she had made.

She clamped her jaw closed and squared her shoulders. She needed to help Adela with more housework, and all the Sieverts were coming for supper tonight.

Savannah worked diligently, trying to drive away hurt and worry about Red Hawk with cooking and cleaning. That night she dressed in her white dimity and remembered when she had put it on wanting to see Red Hawk's reaction.

She found Adela in the kitchen supervising Matilda and Wesley, who worked over dinner. Adela wore her yellow dress and her hair was fastened high on both sides of her head and fell in curls over her nape. Her sister had never looked prettier. Adela glowed with happiness, and Savannah was overjoyed that at least one thing had turned out well. She moved across the room to help.

"Adela, you've worked all day. I can take over here until our guests come."

"I don't mind," Adela said, then looked more intently at Savannah and turned to leave. "Thanks, Savannah."

The Sieverts arrived promptly and Savannah stood at the door with Adela and greeted the elder Sieverts and Thomas's three sisters: Mavis Jane, Annabelle, and Lucinda Lou. His brothers were all away fighting. While Wesley took care of the Sieverts' carriage and Thomas's horse, Thomas came inside. His gaze rested on Adela and then Savannah.

"How beautiful you both look," he said. Smiling, he moved between them to take Adela's arm as well as Savannah's to go to the parlor.

The house filled with the chatter of females and Thomas and his father. All through the supper, served by Wesley and Matilda, Savannah barely heard the conversation, but tried to pay attention and smile when she should.

After supper, they sat in the parlor and talked about what had happened in Mason while Adela and Savannah had been away.

Savannah was aware Thomas was dressed in a black coat and pants and a soft white linen shirt. A year ago, she would have thought him quite dashing and handsome and she would have been flattered and pleased with every little attention he gave her. Now she barely noticed him, even though she tried politely to follow his conversation.

When his family finally said good-bye, Savannah walked to the door with them.

"Savannah, it was a lovely evening," Mrs. Sievert said,

placing her arm around Savannah's waist. "Our Thomas will have a wonderful wife, and I know both of you will have many happy years."

"Yes, ma'am."

"Savannah, are you still mourning the loss of your father?"

"Maybe a little," she said, hoping Mrs. Sievert would accept that as an excuse for her lack of liveliness.

Mrs. Sievert hugged her waist. "I understand, my dear. Just think of our family now as your family."

"Thank you," she answered politely.

"Come see us tomorrow, Savannah," Lucinda Lou said, smiling broadly. "And bring Adela."

"I'll do that."

"Thank you for the supper," Lucinda Lou added.

"I'm glad you could come."

While Savannah stood on the small front porch, one by one each of the Sieverts except Thomas thanked her for the evening and told her good-bye as they piled in the family carriage. Thomas had come by horse and now he stayed behind and was still in the house talking to Adela.

Savannah waited on the porch as the Sieverts drove away. She waved to them, moving listlessly into the yard, and stood in the darkness, thinking that Red Hawk and Matthew were under the same twinkling stars.

"Do you miss me as I miss you?" she whispered into the night, touching the silver feather necklace she wore. "I made a mistake. There's nothing here without you. You and Matthew are everything to me. The rest is unimportant, but I didn't know that until too late."

There were no answers, only the chirp of crickets and the deep croak of a frog. She stood waiting, pretending that Red Hawk was looking right now at the same stars.

She drifted around the side of the house and finally went in through the kitchen. Matilda and Wesley had cleaned up the kitchen and both had gone to rooms they had rented in a boardinghouse in town.

Savannah moved quietly through the empty kitchen and went down the hall, stepping into the parlor.

Across the room, Thomas stood holding both of Adela's hands. He was just brushing a kiss across her lips.

Savannah went stone still with shock.

CHAPTER
TWENTY-THREE

"Savannah! Oh, Savannah," Adela cried, sounding stricken. Her face turned deep red.

Thomas was far more calm. "Adela, if you'll leave us alone for a time, I need to talk to Savannah."

"Savannah, I'm sorry," Adela said, then glanced at Thomas, who smiled reassuringly at her. She turned and hurried from the room, closing the door behind her.

Savannah's shock began to wear away as images floated in her mind—Adela asleep in Thomas's arms in the buggy on the ride here, Adela and Thomas talking while Savannah and Matthew and Red Hawk fixed a tree swing for Matthew, Adela and Thomas's laughter floating up from the porch on a summer evening.

"I've been blind!" she exclaimed.

"Yes, you have," Thomas said gently, "but I knew someday you'd see. You were blinded by your own concerns. But, Savannah, I made a promise to you long ago," he said solemnly. "I will keep that promise."

"No!" She realized that Adela and Thomas were probably deeply in love for them to risk even a chaste kiss in the parlor.

"No! You both deserve happiness. It would be evil to hold you to that promise made by our fathers."

Thomas crossed the room to place his hands on her shoulders and shake his head. "You're not thinking this through. You always act—sometimes rashly, sometimes impulsively, sometimes wisely—but you act while Adela and I are lost to indecision and meditation about the consequences in matters such as this. Think, Savannah, before you lightly toss away that pledge. You might not marry. You might not have someone to care for you, although you'll always be welcome in any home of mine or my parents.

"Do you love her, Thomas?"

He gazed steadily at Savannah. "Yes, I do."

She reached up to take his hands. "Dear Thomas, who would be so kind to keep your promise to marry someone you don't love. You're free. I absolve you completely. I love my sister and I'm fond of you. This is truly wonderful! Adela has been through a hell she didn't deserve and she has earned some happiness in life."

"You deserve that chance at happiness, too. If I could find him for you, Savannah, I would. I know you miss him dreadfully."

"Yes, I do. I made the wrong choice. Now don't you and Adela make the wrong one."

He smiled and kissed her forehead lightly.

"I think I should let you propose to the woman you love," Savannah said.

He wrapped his arms around her to hug her lightly. "Dear Savannah. We'll be good in-laws. I adore Adela. Thank you. I would do anything in my power to make you happy."

"Let me get Adela," Savannah said, moving away from him. A weight lifted from her heart, and she realized she hadn't wanted to go through with the marriage. Now she was doubly happy, because she was glad to see Adela and Thomas happy.

She opened the door to the hall and stepped into the hallway. Adela turned around, a frown creasing her brow. She hurried to Savannah.

"Savannah, I'm sorry."

"Don't be. Now go see Thomas. He wants to talk to you. And, Adela—I'm so happy for both of you."

Adela's gaze flew from Savannah to the parlor. She rushed inside the parlor and closed the door. Savannah went out through the kitchen into the night and sat in one of the wooden chairs placed on the lawn.

It was quiet and cool and she could think. Why hadn't she noticed them? Because of her preoccupation with Red Hawk and Matthew. She lifted her chin and wondered about her future.

"Savannah!" It was half an hour later when she heard Adela's cheerful call.

"Out here," she replied. "I'm in the yard."

Adela and Thomas came outside. Adela's face was wreathed in a smile and she glowed with happiness. "Savannah, Thomas has asked me to be his wife!"

"How wonderful!" She stood to hug Adela, then turned to him. "You wasted no time."

"No, Savannah. I was going to talk to you about this tonight anyway. I'm home from the war and I know how important and fragile life is. I don't want to waste it. We'd like to marry within the month."

"A month!" She smiled as Adela looked concerned. "I think it would be grand. I'll help get things ready."

"I'll have to break the news to Mother and Father, although my family loves both of you," Thomas said.

Savannah hugged him lightly. "Congratulations, my brother-in-law-to-be. I'm happy for both of you."

Thomas left and returned with a bottle of brandy and glasses. "We'll have a sip of brandy to celebrate the occasion. There's no champagne to be had, so brandy it will have to be."

The moment Savannah took a sip, she was transported back to that afternoon when Red Hawk got her tipsy with brandy. She could barely swallow the fiery liquid and didn't hear what was being said. She wanted to be with him again, to have another chance, to change her answer to him.

She moved numbly through the next hour, trying to share their joy, yet thinking more than ever about Red Hawk.

Finally, she knew she could politely leave. From the looks Adela and Thomas were giving each other, they were ready to be alone.

"I must say good night. I'm happy for you both."

"Good night, Savannah," Thomas said.

Savannah went into the kitchen and started down the hall.

"Savannah."

She turned to find Thomas standing in the hall doorway. He came forward. "I'll try to find him for you if you'd like. I can contact soldiers and ask if they have contact with any of the tribes or any Comanche."

"Thank you. I don't think it'll do any good."

"I'll try."

"Thank you, Thomas. I truly am happy for both of you."

"I know you are. You've been very good to Adela."

She turned and went upstairs, closed her door and threw herself across her bed to cry, pulling a pillow over her head to muffle the sounds.

By the time Adela came upstairs and knocked on her door, thrusting her head into the room, Savannah had changed and was seated near an open window.

"Savannah?"

"Come in. I'm happy for you, Adela, and sorry I was so blind. I should have noticed long before I did."

"Red Hawk knew."

"He did? Why didn't he tell me? Or you tell me?"

"You were so concerned with Red Hawk and, at first, Thomas and I didn't mean for this to happen."

"I can understand that," Savannah said dryly. "Oh, Adela, I made such a mistake. I would go with him now without thinking about it."

"Even with the danger and the hardships?"

"Yes. If he can live with those things, then I can, too. This life is empty. I didn't realize how empty."

"Perhaps Thomas can find him for you."

Savannah shook her head. "I don't think so, and I don't want him to put himself at risk to try."

"He won't do that. But he can ask questions."

Savannah touched her stomach. "How I wish that I carried his baby. Then I would have part of him to claim as mine."

"Savannah, you can't wish that! It would bring ruin on you and the baby."

Savannah smiled at Adela. "Enough about my problems. Let's talk about your plans with Thomas."

"You have to help me plan my wedding. It should be very simple. I'm sorry if all this hurts you."

"Nonsense! It never hurts me, Adela, for you to be happy. Let's plan this simple, small wedding."

September passed. Adela was married on the first Saturday morning in October. She looked radiant, and Savannah momentarily was whisked out of her heartache, happy to see her sister so overjoyed.

Thomas had discarded his cane and exercised his hand daily to get back full use of it. He was busy practicing medicine and had opened his own small office in a front room of the new house where he and Adela would live.

Their simple wedding had grown until most of Mason crowded into the Ravenwood house. Savannah wore her deep blue silk dress and Adela wore a pale blue taffeta. Thomas looked more handsome than ever, and they were so in love it hurt to look at either of them. Happy for Adela and Thomas, yet hurting badly, Savannah stood beside her sister and listened to her take her vows. Thomas kissed her and they were husband and wife.

After the ceremony, a party was held at the house. Later, Thomas and Adela left for a brief trip to Austin. Each day, Savannah thought more earnestly about moving to San Antonio. Adela no longer needed her and she thought she could find a degree of happiness in the city, where she would be far busier than in Mason. She was tutoring children, thinking about what she could do when she moved. She still missed Red Hawk more than ever.

By the end of October, she moved into her new small house in San Antonio. While it was in a different section of town from Red Hawk's, it suited Savannah just fine.

Adela and Thomas and Lucinda Lou helped her move. As she stood in her new living room, she turned to find Adela studying her. "Savannah, I worry about you here. You're so thin, too thin. You won't know as many people—"

"I'll be all right, Adela, and I promise to come see you often. And you and Thomas can come see me often."

Thomas came into the house. He had been talking to a neighbor, and his expression was grim.

"What's wrong?" Adela asked at once, stepping to his side.

He took her hand and looked down at her. "I just learned Atlanta fell to Sherman. This damned war—" He broke off. "Sorry, ladies. Savannah, I'll bring your trunk inside. Where do you want it?"

"If you'll place it in my bedroom," she said, leading the way.

Spending two days with her, they helped her arrange furniture and get settled. Matilda and Wesley now worked for Thomas and Adela, but they had come along and helped with the move.

Finally Savannah was alone. She had brought the mahogany furniture from her father's house, the four-poster bed she had had as a girl.

The house was silent, yet she knew she would become accustomed to it. Tears started and she longed for Red Hawk. She was resigned that she would never stop loving him, and she wondered if anything would bring him back to San Antonio.

One Saturday on a warm mid-November day, she encountered Casper Ashman on Commerce Street. While traffic and people moved around them, he tipped his hat and his brows arched. "So you didn't go with him and marry him after all."

"No, I didn't."

"Very wise choice. Are you living in his house?"

"No, I have my own house and I tutor children."

Ashman's gaze swept boldly over her, taking in her blue cotton dress and bonnet. "You live alone, Savannah?"

His question chilled her. "Yes, except for servants. My brother-in-law and sister visit on weekends."

"I see," Ashman said without interest. "If I had just known a day earlier Quentin was a wanted man, I would have Matthew now."

"You turned Red Hawk in to the sheriff?"

"Yes. And someday they'll catch him and hang him and Matthew will be mine again."

"I don't think they'll ever catch him. He's back with his people."

"Savages. But they'll be eliminated when this war ends. Nice to see you, Savannah. Perhaps I'll call sometime soon."

"You can leave your card with the butler," she said, wondering if she would have a problem with Casper Ashman. She dismissed the meeting, certain he would never get Matthew in his clutches again.

When she reached home, she unlocked the door and carried her packages inside. As she returned to close the front door, she saw Thomas ride into the yard. Dressed in his black suit, he was on horseback, so Adela wasn't with him. His horse was lathered and Savannah knew instantly that something was wrong.

Her first thought was Adela, and Savannah ran outside to meet him as he dismounted.

"Thomas, what is it? What's happened?"

He motioned toward the house. "Shall we go inside, Savannah?"

She turned icy, terrified of what news he had brought. One look at his expression and she knew it was terrible. He came into the front hall and closed the door, leaning against it. "I came right away. And I'll go from here to Fort Worth."

"Fort Worth?" She couldn't follow what he was telling her. Fort Worth had nothing to do with Adela.

"Is Adela all right?"

"Adela is fine. It's Red Hawk. The army captured him. He's been arrested and is to be tried in Fort Worth on the murder charges."

when she saw Adela fall. Red Hawk turned to

CHAPTER
TWENTY-FOUR

"How? When did this happen?" Savannah cried.

"I don't know the details. We just heard that he was caught by the army. A patrol attacked a group of Indians, and he was with them. He was caught because he stayed behind to fight while others escaped. He'll be tried in a civilian court."

"When?" she asked, terrified he had already been tried and sentenced. She couldn't breathe and the room spun while she waited for Thomas to answer.

"The trial is scheduled in two weeks. They've contacted Adela to be a witness. I'm sure they'll contact you within a day or two, but I wanted you to know as soon as possible. I'll go right now to Fort Worth—"

Relief poured over her and all her anxiety changed to joy. She would see him. She knew now where to find him. "I'm going with you."

"You can't do that!" Thomas looked stunned. "You can't travel with me."

"You can bring Adela if you want to make things look right, but I'm going. Don't leave without me. I'll pack," she said, racing to the bedroom, leaving him sputtering. He followed her and stood in the doorway, looking awkward while she flew around the room, flinging clothes on her bed.

"Savannah, stop and think. You're reacting with your heart and not your head. You can't travel across country, and it would wear poor Adela to pieces. She wasn't meant to travel like I'll have to. Neither are you."

"Of course she can travel like that," Savannah said, impatiently rummaging through a drawer, "and so can I. We did it with him."

"What are you talking about?"

"Red Hawk took me all across Louisiana with him and then Adela and I traveled across country on horseback with him to get from Nacogdoches to San Antonio."

She realized there was silence and glanced at Thomas to see him staring at her round-eyed. "I'm sorry if I shocked you, but Adela did nothing that wasn't circumspect and she's really stronger than you think. Now I'm going to Fort Worth, with or without you and Adela."

"Ahh, Savannah, I should have known what you'd do," he said, sounding resigned. "Slow down. You don't have to pack in the next five minutes. Let me have a glass of water and something to eat."

I'm sorry, Thomas," she said, at once contrite. "Help yourself in the kitchen—" She realized that he probably was helpless in a kitchen. With his family of females, she was certain someone had waited on him all his life. She hurried past him. "Come here and I'll fix you a supper. I'll pack while you eat."

Looking amused, he trailed after her. To her surprise, he was more help than she'd expected. In a short time, she was back in her room, her heart pounding with eagerness because she would see Red Hawk.

She could burst with joy, trying to think about what she would want with her. She went to her chiffonnier and looked in the back of a top drawer, withdrawing the extra pistol that her father had always kept locked in his desk drawer. It was a Colt, and she had boxes of ammunition. She knew Adela had never given it a thought, and Savannah had quietly packed it with her things when she had moved to San Antonio. She placed it in the bottom of her bag. Then she studied her room and began to pack what she wanted to keep, feeling that she would never return to this house.

She changed to the blue poplin and looked around the room, finally closing a bag and going to find Thomas.

He was stretched on the davenport asleep and she sat down, knowing he probably needed to rest, wondering if he had ridden straight through without stopping, yet certain he wouldn't push his horse that hard.

She thought about what she should do before she left, and went outside to feed and water Thomas's horse. Then she went next door to tell Maribelle Thompkins, her neighbor, that she was leaving town. She left word with Maribelle to tell her students that she was gone. She returned home and closed up the house and went to get something to eat so she wouldn't have to eat again soon. She brewed a pot of coffee because she suspected when Thomas awakened, he would need it.

When she finished eating, she packed bundles of food they could easily carry, knowing they would ride first to Mason and then on to Fort Worth, so she would only need something for them to eat between here and Mason. She looked at the knives in the drawer and took one to place in the bottom of her packed bag.

Next she went outside and saddled her horse, all the while humming a tune. She would see Red Hawk! The thought of the trial was a cloud, but she intended to tell the truth about Horace Platt. That would eliminate one charge instantly. He had to be set free. Now that she had found him again, the thought of losing him once more was impossible. She couldn't bear to consider the possibility that that might happen.

She returned to the house and looked at Thomas, who was still sprawled asleep. She wanted to wake him and go, but she knew he needed his rest, so she continued closing the house and then sat down to wait.

To her relief, he woke in another hour. He sat up and rubbed his forehead and glanced across the room at her.

"Savannah, sorry. I was exhausted. I've switched horses and ridden straight here from Mason."

"And we should return the same way so we can get on to Fort Worth."

He shook his head. "I should have known you would want to tear right up there to see him."

"Yes, I do."

"We'll be in time for the trial, but you mustn't get your hopes too high. He's in a bad situation."

"I intend to tell the truth about Mr. Platt."

Thomas frowned. "Frankly, I doubt if anyone will believe you."

"They have to. Adela will tell them."

"Adela is your sister. If they don't believe you, they won't believe her, but they will believe that neighbor who rushed in and saw Quentin standing with a pistol in his hand."

"They have to believe me because it's the truth."

Shrugging, Thomas stood. "I want to take time for coffee."

"I've already brewed a pot because I thought you'd like some before starting out again."

He smiled. "Good. Let's go get my coffee so we can get you to Fort Worth."

They closed up her house and rode to Fredericksburg. The entire time, Savannah was barely aware of her surroundings. Excitement and eagerness to get to Fort Worth hummed in her.

As they rode along the main street, Thomas turned to her. "We can get rooms at the hotel—"

"Can we keep riding? I can keep up."

"It might be dangerous at night."

"I'll take the chance."

He rubbed his forehead and finally nodded. "Very well. We'll keep going. I had my rest. When you want to stop, tell me."

She nodded, thankful they would continue traveling. "I'll sleep when we get to your house, just as you did today at mine."

It was afternoon the next day when they reached the small frame house he shared with Adela.

Savannah dismounted with aching muscles. Adela rushed outside to hug her and in minutes Savannah was in bed in their guest room while Adela sat on the side of the bed.

"Savannah, I knew you would want to go see Red Hawk. After Thomas left, I thought about it and guessed you would return with him."

"Will you come with us?"

"Of course. I'm already packed and ready to go."

"Adela. I've found him."

Adela's blue eyes were clouded with worry. "Thomas said you shouldn't get your hopes too high. Two murder charges is bad, and his being an Indian won't help his case."

Anger flashed in Savannah, and she knotted her fingers in the coverlet. "He'll get off, Adela. He has to go free."

"Thomas will do anything he can."

Nothing could diminish Savannah's joy that she had found Red Hawk. In minutes she was asleep.

The following morning they left for Fort Worth.

The trip seemed interminable to Savannah, and she knew she was pushing Thomas and Adela, who would have taken more time had she not been with them. Four days later they rode into Fort Worth, a town of saloons and hastily constructed buildings. Savannah barely saw any of it. Her excitement was at fever pitch, and it was all she could do to politely ride to a hotel with Adela and Thomas instead of tearing down the street to the jail.

She changed to her dimity dress and bonnet. On the trip, she had spent spare moments sewing pockets into her petticoats. In them, she placed the knife and the Colt and ammunition, knowing that Thomas would never aid her, nor would he approve of her slipping weapons to Red Hawk.

She paced the room impatiently until Thomas appeared to escort her to the jail. He looked solemn. "Savannah, when I was at the livery stable, they were talking about a hanging. I hope I haven't brought you here to have your heart broken worse than ever."

"They can't hang him without a trial," she snapped, yet she chilled with fear because she knew too well that they *could* hang him without waiting for a trial. "I shall help him escape."

"Savannah, you can't!" Thomas's face clouded. "I won't let you do that and I won't be involved in it, nor will I let Adela become involved in it. I'll tie you in this room before I'll let that happen."

She saw the steel beneath all Thomas's gentleness and she realized that he meant every word. She rubbed her upper arms. "Of course. You're right, Thomas, but I won't survive if they hang him."

Thomas crossed the room to place his hands on her shoulders. "Yes, you will survive, Savannah. You are a survivor. I won't let you break the law to help him, but I'll help any other way I can. If you're ready, I'll accompany you to the jail."

She nodded and picked up her reticule. "If only Papa were still alive—"

"Savannah, if your Papa were still alive, he wouldn't let you near that jail," Thomas replied harshly.

"I suppose you're right," she said, remembering how her father hated Indians. "Let's go."

Thomas took her arm and they left the hotel. As they approached the low, flat building that housed the jail and the sheriff's office, she saw a barred window overlooking the street. The interior was in shadows. She wondered whether Red Hawk was looking out and could see her. She tingled with anticipation, her pulse racing.

She barely heard anything said to the young blond deputy, who stood and took down a ring of keys. They followed him into another room, past one empty cell to another cell.

Red Hawk stood waiting. He was far darker skinned than when she had told him farewell. His shaggy hair was longer. He wore buckskins and moccasins, and a headband was tied around his head. His eyes lit up as his gaze swept over her. It took all her control to keep from crying out with joy and running to throw herself against the bars.

Red Hawk stared at her, wondering if she were real or his imagination. There was Thomas, looking solemn beside her. Were they married now? It hurt to think about their union, which he knew was absurd. He had left her so she could marry Thomas, and that's no doubt what she had done.

His gaze swept over her while his pulse raced. She wore a dress sprigged with green leaves and a matching bonnet with green silk ribbons that brought out the green of her eyes. He caught a sweet rose scent from where he stood. He wanted to rip the bars right out of the walls and take her into his arms. *She's married. Her husband is there beside her.*

He clenched his fists to keep from reaching through the bars for her. How beautiful she looked! Her eyes sparkled and her cheeks were rosy. She looked like she hadn't a care in the world. His gaze raked over her again. She was too thin and he wondered how her life had been.

He didn't want her in Fort Worth because he didn't expect a good outcome for his trial. He had known if he were caught, it would go harshly for him. The first chance, he would tell Thomas to get her out of town when the trial started—if a trial started. He had seen the small angry mob that gathered outside the jail at night. He didn't want Savannah to become the object of any of that hatred, yet another swift glance at her and he knew she would never become the object of hatred of any male.

His gaze met her green eyes that sparkled with joy, and pain stabbed him for what might have been and could never be. And then she was only a few feet away, iron bars between them.

"May she go inside to talk with the prisoner?" Thomas asked.

"It's not—"

Savannah turned to the deputy and flashed a big smile, touching his arm lightly. "Please, let me talk with him inside. I would be so indebted to you," she said breathlessly, gazing into the deputy's wide blue eyes.

"Yes, ma'am," he said, staring at her for a long moment. "Yes, ma'am." He unlocked the cell and watched Savannah as she swept into the cell. She turned to flash him another brilliant smile.

"I do thank you," she said in a sultry voice. "I'll call when I'm ready to go."

Red Hawk would have been amused at her devastating effect on the deputy except she was causing an even greater one on him. Dimly, he thought it generous of Thomas to be so free about what she did, but that was a flickering notion, lost swiftly as he watched Savannah and clenched his hands so he wouldn't reach for her.

"Yes, ma'am," the deputy said, still staring and looking as if mesmerized by Savannah. He blinked, glanced around as they all stared at him, and he turned away. Reaching through the bars, Thomas shook hands with Red Hawk.

"I'll see you at the hotel, Savannah."

Red Hawk nodded to Thomas, but all he was aware of was that Savannah only a foot away, her tea rose scent tormenting him.

Red Hawk's gaze swung to Savannah and then, Thomas or no Thomas, Red Hawk put his arms around her. She clung to him, kissing his face wildly until his mouth covered hers and he bent over her, kissing her passionately.

Red Hawk's joy over having her in his arms was tempered by what he knew his future to be. He had little hope, and he intended to make certain that Thomas kept Savannah from coming forth to say that she killed Horace Platt. After wanting to be alone with him in his cell, it wouldn't matter as much. Word would get out that there were strong feelings between Red Hawk and Savannah and no one would believe her if she confessed. They would simply think she was trying to save a man who was important to her.

He tasted salty tears as he kissed her and he couldn't stop kissing her. He wanted to possess her, but he knew he could never do that in the cell. Finally he raised his head to look at her.

"You're beautiful, Savannah—"

"I want to marry you."

Red Hawk stilled, thinking he had heard wrong, but she was looking up at him with wide green eyes, and she looked earnest and as if she were waiting for an answer. He frowned. "Won't that be difficult? Aren't you and Thomas married?"

Her mouth formed a surprised O for about two heartbeats and then he received a radiant smile.

"Thomas married Adela," he guessed, remembering and feeling one weight fall away. "Oh, Savannah," he swept her into his arms again.

"Yes. I guess I was the last to realize because I had been so wrapped up in my own feelings about you and Matthew. They were married in October, and both of them are so happy. How is Matthew?"

"He's fine. Growing. You'd be surprised to see him. And he loves that life just as I knew he would."

"Do you love it like you thought you would?"

Red Hawk stroked her face. "Yes, love. I belong there, and so does Matthew."

"I want to marry you."

His pulse jumped until logic told him that she was doing this because she, too, guessed what the outcome of his incarceration would be. She wanted to give him this satisfaction before he was hanged.

"Ahh, Savannah. I think we've pushed luck enough for one lifetime."

"No, don't say that! I want to marry you. I made a dreadful mistake. I want to be with you and Matthew. It's been terrible without you. I don't want anything if you're not there with me to share it. I miss you both."

Red Hawk realized what she was telling him and a great sadness swept over him. "Ahh, my beautiful, fiery darling, we're too late—"

"No!" She gasped and covered his mouth with her fingers. He flicked out his tongue to touch and kiss them.

"I want to marry you either here in this cell—"

Another wave of sadness washed over him as he shook his head. "No. I won't have you tie your life with mine like that. When they find me guilty, they will attach a stigma to you. No, Savannah."

"Stop saying no," she hissed, her chin set with determination. "I'll get you out of here. Thomas refuses to help—"

Red Hawk thought he was hearing things again, but then he saw the determination in Savannah's eyes and he had to laugh, although sadness still filled him. "My determined, strong-willed darling, you'll do no such thing. You couldn't if you tried."

"Didn't you escape from those Federals?"

"Yes, I did, but it was different. I don't want you at risk ever again."

"Life is a risk. It was a risk when you went back to the Comanche." She glanced over her shoulder. "I don't want to wait for a trial or for anything. I want to be with you, to be your wife. I made the worst mistake of my life."

He framed her face and searched her eyes, looking into green depths that gazed back honestly. She meant what she said. "You really can give up San Antonio and Mason and parties and dresses—"

"They're nothing without you and Matthew!"

"My life is dangerous, Savannah. I won't deny that."

"I want to be with both of you."

For an instant he forgot his circumstances, lost in what she was saying to him. He leaned down to kiss her with heartbreak, with sadness for what might have been. When he raised his head, he whispered, "I love you with all my heart."

"What's important is now. I want to get you out of here."

He shook his head. "I won't let you. I'm telling Thomas to take you home."

"Listen to me," she said. "You've escaped before and you helped me escape. We can do this. I'll have horses tonight and I can bring some brandy laced with laudanum. This deputy will let me in. I want you and I love you."

Afraid to breathe, Savannah gazed up at him, waiting for his answer as he studied her. She knew she was finally getting through to him. He glanced beyond her at the door to the sheriff's office. "That deputy won't be on duty until tomorrow night again."

"Then I'll come several times so they all become accustomed to seeing me. I brought a knife and one of my father's revolvers. Thomas doesn't know this."

Suddenly Red Hawk grinned and kissed her hard and swiftly. "I should have known you would do this. If I escape and they ever catch me again, I'll be a dead man."

"They won't catch you again."

He grinned and shook his head. "Ahh, Savannah, how I've missed you! Let me find the weapons," he said, his eyes twinkling as his hand slipped beneath the neck of her dress and caressed her breasts. She drew a deep breath and all laughter died out of his expression, to be replaced by a hunger that made her tremble. Watching her, he reached beneath her skirt, stroking her legs. Then he found the pockets with the Colt and the knife. He turned to slip them beneath the blanket on his bed.

"Come before midnight. Later would be far more suspect. Have the horses behind the jail and wear something you can ride in, something dark. Do you have fast horses?"

"Yes."

"Savannah, there are some Comanche in town. They have been watching, waiting to see what happens. They, too, will try to free me. They are dressed like white men and one is called Running Horse. He comes to see me every evening at dusk. I'll tell him and perhaps he can help."

"Thomas would stop me if he knew."

"And he should. I should stop you, but you're irresistible and I want you for my wife."

He gazed into her eyes and saw desire flash. His body tightened. He drew her to him to kiss her long and lingeringly, and then he released her.

She ran her fingers over his face, tears of joy springing to her eyes. "I thought I'd lost you," she whispered. Her gaze fell to a cord around his neck. In the middle it was laced with red strands and she realized what she was looking at. She picked it up and ran her fingers over the red locks braided into the rawhide.

"Yes, it's your hair. I wanted part of you with me all the time, and that's all I had of you."

She threw herself into his arms again to kiss him, her tears flowing freely now as she clung to him.

Savannah was with him an hour before she finally called to the deputy. He unlocked the door and she swept out, flashing him another of her smiles. "I do thank you for being so generous. You have the most exciting job."

"Oh, not really, ma'am."

"It's Miss Ravenwood, Savannah Ravenwood. How did you get into this line of work? Are you one of those darling gunfighters I hear about?"

"Oh, no, ma'am! I hope not," he said, walking to the office with her. She stood talking to him, looking around the office. "Is this your desk?"

"Well, it's the sheriff's desk, but we all use it."

"I've heard this is a wild town. That it's not safe for a lady to be out alone after dark. My brother-in-law feels strongly about that."

"No, ma'am. You should have someone with you."

She looked out the front window. "Am I safe returning to my hotel now all by myself?"

"Well, ma'am," he glanced around and looked at the clock. "In another twenty minutes, my replacement will be here and I could walk you back to your hotel."

"Oh, would you do that?" she gushed. "I would be so delighted and feel so safe with that big gun you wear on your hip." She moved close to him. "I just am so intrigued with men of the law. You seem so strong and forceful."

"Yes, ma'am," he said, his voice dropping a notch as he looked down at her.

"I'll bet the ladies follow you around. Is there a special lady in your life?"

"No, ma'am. Not right now."

"Please, just call me Savannah. I feel like we've known each other a while. Sometimes you just feel that with people."

Red Hawk stood at the bars of his cell and caught snatches of the conversation between Savannah and the deputy. He shook his head and turned back to get the Colt, relishing the heavy weight of the gun and saying a prayer of thanks that Savannah had come back into his life.

That night he stood by the window of his small cell. He had talked to Running Horse, and several Comanche were ready and would help. They had fast horses not far from town where he and Savannah could change.

Red Hawk considered his plans. If he tried to escape and failed, he would be hanged. If he succeeded in escaping, he would be wanted the rest of his life. If he ever wanted to go back to the white man's way and ranching, he would have to sell the Texas land and settle farther west. He dismissed that concern. He was happy with his people and he thought Savannah would be, too. Matthew fit into Comanche life as if he had been born into it.

The following night as Red Hawk stood by the window, the air was still and cool with a bit of chill. Across the street, banjo and guitar music spilled from the saloons. It was midweek and quieter on the streets, better for him. On the weekend, there were two deputies on duty and they were busy with drunken brawls.

He wondered how Savannah would escape from Thomas and Adela. A twinge of conscience struck Red Hawk for letting her take such risks and become involved in his escape, but then he thought about holding her in his arms and having her tell him she wanted to marry him. He had no other course to follow.

He watched a carriage loom into view and his pulse jumped. The driver moved through the crowd on the street, his passenger dimly visible in the light from the saloons. Red Hawk saw the large plumed hat and recognized that it was a solitary woman passenger. They passed out of view. In minutes, he heard voices and recognized Savannah's as she talked with the deputy.

He touched the Colt in the back of his pants beneath the black shirt he wore. Running Horse had brought him the shirt today. The knife was strapped to his leg.

Red Hawk moved to the door of the cell to wait. Now it was up to Savannah.

CHAPTER TWENTY-FIVE

Savannah perched on the sheriff's desk while the deputy stood close by. "I just couldn't stand it in that dreadful old hotel. There is nothing to do and I've been cooped up there since we came to town, so I slipped down here." She looked around and leaned forward. "Look what I brought." She opened her reticule and produced a bottle of brandy.

"Lawrence, let's have a little drink. Then won't you please let me take a little drink to your prisoner?"

"That's against rules, ma'am," he said, eyeing the brandy and looking at Savannah. To her satisfaction, he could barely pull his gaze from her. She wore her best green silk and had pulled it low in front, low enough to reveal the curve of her breasts. She wore the silver feather necklace Red Hawk had given her and she had splashed in rosewater.

"Do you have glasses? Just a tiny drink, Lawrence. I am so tired of sitting and doing nothing and being good!"

He inhaled, and she could see the mental debate he was having with himself. "Very well," he said. "Just a little."

He fetched two glasses and moved close to her while she uncorked the bottle and poured the amber liquid. He reached out to take the glass, his fingers stroking hers and lingering. She looked up at him and smiled. He stood close and she uncrossed her legs, her knee touching his thigh. His eyes darkened and he raised the glass of brandy.

"To exciting men," she said and clinked her glass against his, taking a sip while he gulped his down and wiped his mouth with the back of his hand.

"Tell me the most dangerous thing you've ever done," she said. Her pulse raced and she prayed no one started a fight in a saloon or anything to take the deputy away from the jail for the next hour. So many things had to work together.

In minutes, she poured him another drink.

"Savannah, I can't," he said, moving even closer.

"Just one more. Brandy makes me feel good," she said, pouring her glass full and raising it. "To dashing lawmen."

"To beautiful women," he said, watching her as he threw down the next brandy.

After the third brandy, sweat beaded his brow and he put his hand on her waist. "Savannah, I believe you're getting me soundly smashed."

"But we're having such a good time," she said slyly.

He leaned down to kiss her and she let him, feeling nothing, but letting him kiss her because it moved her inches closer to getting Red Hawk out.

He raised his head and his breathing was ragged, his eyes dark with desire. "That hotel—which room are you in?"

"On the west corner on the ground floor. The windows are so wide open," she said in a sultry voice. Her pulse raced, and she prayed she could succeed in getting Red Hawk free.

Lawrence tilted the brandy bottle and took a drink, then carefully corked it up. She slid off the desk, moving sensuously. "I want to see the prisoner now. I have to do that before I go back to the hotel."

Deputy Lawrence lifted down the ring of keys and she followed him to the cell. Red Hawk stood to one side of the door and Lawrence unlocked it and pushed it open. She had dropped back, far from the deputy.

Red Hawk raised the pistol, pointing it directly at the deputy's heart. "Don't move and put your hands high."

Startled, Lawrence looked surprised, then stricken. Then a flush of anger spread over his features as he glared at Savannah.

Red Hawk moved swiftly, taking Lawrence's gun. "Turn around and put your hands behind your back."

In minutes, Red Hawk had him tied with strips cut from his blanket. He placed a gag over his mouth.

"I'm sorry, Lawrence," Savannah said, "but I had to do this."

"Shut up, Savannah," Red Hawk commanded, not wanting her involved any deeper than she was.

He locked the tied deputy in the cell and then grabbed Savannah's arm. "Let's go."

They went out the back where the horses were. As Red Hawk mounted up, she yanked off the green dress, tossing it aside.

"What the hell?"

"You told me to wear dark clothes. I'll be seen easier in that green dress and I can't ride as well in it," she said as she pulled on black pants and wiggled into a black shirt she had folded on the ground. "I won't need it anymore where I'm going," she added.

"Ahh, Savannah, I can't wait."

As soon as she mounted her horse, Red Hawk led the way. Cutting across the field behind the jail, they took a deserted road from town. In minutes, they broke into a gallop and her heart soared. He was free and she was going to marry him and be with him and with Matthew for the rest of her life.

Five miles from town, they met Running Horse and changed horses. As she dismounted, Red Hawk lifted her down into his arms. The other men turned to ride ahead, leaving the two of them alone.

"You did it, Savannah. I'm a free man because of you." Red Hawk kissed her hard and then raised his head. "I want to love you all the rest of the night, but we can't take that chance. Let's ride."

As they mounted, he glanced at her. "Where did you get the two horses?"

"One was mine and the other was Adela's. She and Thomas will forgive me, I'm sure."

Red Hawk grinned and mounted up to lead the way. They joined the others and rode hard for another hour before they slowed.

When the sun rose, she could tell they were riding straight west. They rode all day, stopping that night to camp and riding again before dawn the next day. As far as the eye could see, they were on a flat plain covered in dry, high grass that had yellowed with the coming of winter and the first frost.

It seemed she had ridden hours on the endless, windblown land and she turned her horse closer to Red Hawk. "How much longer before we find your people?"

"You'll see," he said. Only a quarter of an hour later, as she gazed ahead, suddenly the land split and there was a great chasm. Amazed to find such a thing where the land had looked as flat as if it extended unbroken forever, she reined in at the edge of the canyon when Red Hawk did. While the wind whistled in the otherwise unbroken silence, she looked below. The red walls of the canyon were dotted with stunted trees bending north in the prevailing south wind. Down in the floor of the canyon were rows of tipis, smoke rising from fires inside and outside. People moved around, horses grazed, and she saw a whole community spread before her, acre upon acre of tipis.

"Ready, Savannah?" Red Hawk asked.

She nodded. "I want to see Matthew."

They began their careful descent.

Wearing a white buckskin-fringed dress with wildflowers in her hair that cascaded over her back and shoulders, Savannah stood beside her tall husband while they spoke their vows. Dressed in deerskin like Red Hawk, Matthew stood beside his uncle. While Savannah had been carefully taught the words to say, she was learning a little Comanche, discovering this was the common language for the Indians of the plains.

Each day she learned more about her new way of life. Following tribal tradition, she moved in with a family who seemed to adopt her, but now it was their wedding day, and Red Hawk's tipi was ready for her.

When the ceremony was over, the celebration began, going into the night around a blazing bonfire.

"Now you're really my aunt and you'll be my mother, too," Matthew said, hugging her.

"Yes, but we'll always remember your true mother."

"Since Savannah's with us, you can continue learning your letters and continue with your English," Red Hawk said, standing behind Matthew. He looked over the boy's head at Savannah. "I want him to be able to move in the white man's world, because I'm certain he'll return to it someday."

"I'm staying here," Matthew said firmly. Savannah and Red Hawk both smiled. She gave Matthew another hug, amazed at how he had grown since she last had seen him. His skin had darkened and his Comanche heritage showed strongly in his features.

For the next few nights he would stay with his friends so she and Red Hawk would have their tent to themselves. She turned as White Lark and Race the Wind, two of her new friends, came to talk to her.

Then, as drums beat and dancers chanted, Red Hawk took her hand and led her away from the crowd. He raised the flap of his tipi and she entered, looking at her things, a small fire burning in the center and smoke curling up to escape at the top. Red Hawk closed the flap and secured it, turning to cross to her. He took her in his arms and looked down at her.

"I thought this day would never happen, yet here you are, just as I had dreamed—in my arms."

"I knew so soon after you left that I had made the worst mistake of my life. Thomas offered to try to find you, but I knew that was hopeless and, at the time, he was in no condition to search for you."

"And there are no regrets now that you've lived with us?"

"No regrets. My heart is filled with joy."

His dark eyes held her and then his gaze lowered to her mouth and he leaned down to kiss her, wrapping his arms around her. He kissed her long and slowly, letting go all the deep yearning that had built up in him.

Raising his head, he framed her face with his hands. "My wife, my heart. For our lifetime I'll show you how strong and deep my love is for you."

Watching her, he yanked off his deerskin shirt and flung it aside. Then he took her in his arms again.

Savannah wrapped her arms around his neck, feeling his strong, broad shoulders, her heart bursting with happiness. She knew she was where she belonged, in her brave warrior's arms. This was what was important. This was where she wanted to be for the rest of her life.

Savannah stood on tiptoe to return his kiss, relishing his strong arms around her, knowing she was home.

Put a Little Romance in Your Life With
Janelle Taylor

Put a Little Romance in Your Life With
Fern Michaels

__Dear Emily	0-8217-5676-1	$6.99US/$8.50CAN
__Sara's Song	0-8217-5856-X	$6.99US/$8.50CAN
__Wish List	0-8217-5228-6	$6.99US/$7.99CAN
__Vegas Rich	0-8217-5594-3	$6.99US/$8.50CAN
__Vegas Heat	0-8217-5758-X	$6.99US/$8.50CAN
__Vegas Sunrise	1-55817-5983-3	$6.99US/$8.50CAN
__Whitefire	0-8217-5638-9	$6.99US/$8.50CAN
